At the Captain's Table

Also by Gervase Phinn

THE TOP OF THE DALE SERIES
The School at the Top of the Dale
Tales Out of School
A Class Act

THE LITTLE VILLAGE SCHOOL SERIES
The Little Village School
Trouble at the Little Village School
The School Inspector Calls!
A Lesson in Love

THE DALES SERIES
The Other Side of the Dale
Over Hill and Dale
Head Over Heels in the Dales
Up and Down in the Dales
The Heart of the Dales
A Wayne in a Manger
Twinkle, Twinkle, Little Stars
A Load of Old Tripe
The Virgin Mary's Got Nits
Out of the Woods but not Over the Hill

POETRY
It Takes One to Know One
The Day Our Teacher Went Batty
Family Phantoms
Don't Tell the Teacher

Gervase Phinn

At the Captain's Table

HODDER &
STOUGHTON

First published in Great Britain in 2022 by Hodder & Stoughton
An Hachette UK company

1

Copyright © Gervase Phinn 2022

A CIP catalogue record for this title is available from the British Library

Hardback ISBN 9781529389159
eBook ISBN 9781529389166

Typeset in Plantin by Manipal Technologies Limited

Printed and bound in Great Britain by Clays Ltd, Elcograf S.p.A.

Hodder & Stoughton policy is to use papers that are natural, renewable and re-
cyclable products and made from wood grown in sustainable forests. The logging
and manufacturing processes are expected to conform to the environmental
regulations of the country of origin.

Hodder & Stoughton Ltd
Carmelite House
50 Victoria Embankment
London EC4Y 0DZ

www.hodder.co.uk

At the Captain's Table

I

'Did you need to bring all these bloody cases?'

The speaker was a broad individual with an exceptionally thick neck, fleshy nose, and small darting eyes. A bald patch showed through the stringy colourless hair. With a sallow, sweating face he pushed a metal trolley laden down with luggage. His companion, a small woman with severely bleached hair with signs of black at the roots and a nose as sharp as a pen nib, walked ahead at a brisk pace. Her face seemed set in a permanent frown.

'Oh Albert, do stop complaining, for goodness' sake!' she snapped without turning around.

'We're going away for two weeks not on a bloody world cruise,' he shouted after her. 'And slow down, I can't keep up with you.'

The woman stopped, turned, and looked daggers. 'Albert, will you stop swearing!' she hissed in that censorious way to which he had become accustomed. 'I don't know what the other passengers on the ship will make of you using such language.'

'I couldn't give a monkey's what other passengers on the ship make of me, Maureen,' he answered.

She gave an extravagant sigh and walked on, this time at a slower pace.

'I mean, what have you brought with you, the bloody kitchen sink?'

She turned to face him again and stopped. The trolley came to an abrupt halt. 'I can't wear the same outfit every day,' she informed him. 'Mrs Mickleby, who came on this cruise last year, said there are three formal evenings and a themed night when the ladies have to wear evening dresses.'

'And I have to put on that monkey suit,' Albert grumbled. He waited for her to respond, as was her wont. She didn't.

'Then there's the Captain's reception,' Maureen carried on, 'and Mrs Mickleby said we will probably want to eat out on some occasions and visit some exclusive places. I can't very well sit in a restaurant in Seville or Mallorca wearing old clothes or walking around the Vatican in jeans.'

'Sitting in a restaurant in Seville or Mallorca,' scoffed Albert. 'You can forget about that. This cruise has cost me an arm and a leg as it is. I'm not shelling out any more money. All the food is included anyway.'

'And it's not just dresses,' the woman continued, ignoring the comment. 'There's my shoes and accessories.' She walked on. 'It's different for men. They can wear the same suit, and they don't need the same amount of clothes. I told you all this back home. I think your memory must be going. It's either that or you just don't listen. Now do stop going on about the cases. It's not as if you're carrying them. Mrs Mickleby said they will be taken up to the cabin. It's all done for us. All you have to do is push the trolley and you are making such a song and dance about it. I hope I'm not going to have to put up with your complaining for the next fortnight, I get enough of that at home.'

Albert sneered. 'Well, that's the pot calling the kettle black, if ever I heard it. You've done nothing but complain since we set off.'

'Just be careful with that trolley,' directed his wife, not minded to respond. 'I don't want my cases falling off.'

'And what's with this big bloody umbrella? I don't see anybody else taking one of these.'

'It's a parasol, not an umbrella,' she told him. 'Mrs Mickleby has lent it to me. She said it gets extremely hot where we are going. I don't want to get sunburn. And while we are on about it, you need to make sure you put some cream on your bald patch before you go out. You might remember the year before last when we were in Mablethorpe, and you stayed too long in the sun and your head came out in those unsightly blisters and you spent most of the holiday scratching your scalp. I never heard the last of it. It was an embarrassment going out in public with you.'

'Give me strength,' he muttered.

There had existed between the couple a mutual hostility for as long as either of them could remember. Trivial slights and differences of opinion soon escalated into major grievances. Surprisingly, despite this antagonism and constant bickering, the marriage possessed staying power and they had been together for twenty-five argumentative years. Albert had taken some persuading to come on the cruise. His idea of a restful holiday was not being confined on a ship with hundreds of strangers, braving rough seas, stuck in his cabin with sea sickness and no Yorkshire bitter. However, his wife's unremitting nagging had finally worn him down. For ten years the couple had spent a fortnight in a caravan on a campsite in Mablethorpe, but last year, when it rained incessantly, Maureen vowed this was the very last time. Her neighbour, Mrs Mickleby, had waxed lyrical about the holiday she had spent on a luxury liner. Since coming back from the cruise on the *Empress of the Ocean*, she had not stopped for breath, telling Maureen about the wonderful two weeks at sea: the comfortable cabin, excellent service, fantastic food, first-class entertainment, nice people, and interesting places to visit.

'All right! All right!' Albert had finally surrendered. 'Anything for a quiet life.' As he had said it, he doubted that there would be any peace and quiet for the next fortnight. At least in the caravan in Mablethorpe he could disappear most nights to the social club while Maureen played bingo. On the ship there would be little chance of eluding his wife's incessant badgering.

At the cruise terminal, as he parked the trolley, Maureen asked, 'Did you check the labels on the luggage?'

'Yes.'

'I don't want them delivered to the wrong cabin.'

'They won't be.'

'Have you got the passports?'

'Yes.'

'The boarding passes?'

He sighed theatrically. 'Yes.'

'The itinerary?'

'Yes,' he muttered.

'The joining instructions?'

'Look Maureen, I'm not a complete idiot. Of course, I've got all the bloody bumf.'

'Well, you had better check you have them handy to make sure. I know how forgetful you can be. Mrs Mickleby told me when she came on this cruise last year there was a couple at the check-in holding all the queue up looking for their travel documents. People got very impatient and bad-tempered.'

'*I'm* getting impatient and bad-tempered,' muttered her husband.

Before his wife could respond, a porter arrived smiling widely.

'Is this your luggage, sir?' he asked cheerfully.

'Yes,' replied Albert, 'all four suitcases and the holdall and the travel bag and the large, multicoloured umbrella.' Then he added sarcastically, 'My wife prides herself on travelling light.'

Maureen scowled.

The porter chuckled.

'Well, just leave everything here, sir,' he said. 'I'll unload it. Your cases will be put aboard and placed outside your cabin.'

'What did I say,' stated Maureen smugly.

In the first-class passenger lounge sat a slim, middle-aged woman of elegant bearing with a small delicate nose and expensively tinted hair scraped off her face and curled in wreaths on her head. Sadly, her personality was far from attractive. Mrs Frances De la Mare could be by turns rude and deferential depending on the status and position of the person to whom she was talking. In her late forties, she was materially better off than she had ever been in her life but emotionally she was beset by loneliness and melancholy. Her life had become drab and predictable.

It had been five years' ago, just after her husband died, that she had last been on a cruise ship. At Southampton she had boarded the *Alexandra* ('the very latest in world class liners, elegance personified, stylish in design and sophisticated in atmosphere' – so the glossy brochure had assured her) and spent two rather cold, but not entirely unpleasant weeks visiting the Norwegian fjords. Giles, her late husband, had invested prudently in stocks and bonds and left her very well provided for and, a month after the funeral, she had bought a new wardrobe of clothes (with accessories) and booked a state room to 'discover the delights of spectacular Norway'. Of course, it had not been all plain sailing, for Mrs De la Mare always found something not to her liking. As she had explained to her one and long-suffering friend, Marcia, on her return, she had refused to lower her standards; only the best was good enough. The

highlight of the cruise for her had not been the wonders of
the spectacular fjords or the delights of Copenhagen and
Oslo, it was when the Captain had invited her to dine at his
table with other privileged passengers. 'Such a charming
man,' she had told Marcia, 'with impeccable table manners
and most diverting conversation. We had so much in common.' A photograph of her posing with the ship's master
on the steps of the atrium at the first formal evening, had
pride of place on her mantelpiece.

It was Marcia who had persuaded (or rather pressured)
Mrs De la Mare to come on this cruise.

'Of course, Michael and I would love you to come with
us again to the Algarve for the summer, Frances,' she had
lied. The holiday Mrs De la Mare had spent the previous
year with her friend and family, had been an ordeal. Marcia's
husband had said there was no possibility, none whatso-
ever, of having 'that dreadful woman' spoiling his holiday
again. Frances had remained silent, so Marcia persevered.
'It's likely to be a scorcher in Portugal this summer and you
know how unbearable you found the heat when you came
with us last year and then there were the mosquitoes which
you said were so irritating. A cruise would suit you down to
the ground. You'll be the life and soul of the party, the talk
of the Captain's table.' She knew, of course, that the likelihood of her friend being the life and soul of the party, was
more than fanciful. Since her husband's death, when she had
reinvented herself as the *grande dame* with an inflated idea
of her own importance, her friend had become even more
disagreeable – short-tempered, fault-finding, and argumentative. Marcia had decided that their friendship, such as it
was, would lapse.

Unenthusiastically, Mrs De la Mare had booked the cruise,
but she knew as soon as she saw some of her fellow passengers, it had been a mistake from the start. She noted, with a

sinking heart and a scornful expression, the throng of people in the reception lounge at the cruise terminal: elderly couples, some in wheelchairs or with mobility aids, overweight women in tight jeans, tattooed men in shorts and trainers and noisy children. She noted with distaste that the young woman at the reception desk wore a little silver stud inserted in the side of her nose. She predicted that this cruise would not be to her liking at all. Even the sultry heat and the irritating mosquitoes of the Algarve, she thought, would have been an improvement on this.

In the general reception area at the cruise terminal sat two elderly ladies. One was a small stout woman with hair the colour of brown boot polish and a heavily powdered face. She sported a long rope of artificial pearls and matching earrings. Her companion was an equally corpulent woman with the same substantial bosom and wide hips. She had elaborately coiffured silver hair and thin lips, red with too-bright lipstick, and fingered the large cameo brooch at her collared neck.

'Did you see that, Miriam?' the first woman asked her companion, staring at Mrs De la Mare.

'Did I see what, dear?' asked her sister. She looked up from the magazine she was reading.

'That woman who has just disappeared into the first-class lounge. She had dyed hair piled up on her head and a face that would curdle milk.'

'No, Edna, I didn't see her.'

'Very hoity-toity. I've seen her type before. You would think she owned the ship the way she paraded down the room with her nose stuck up in the air as if there was a bad smell, going to a reserved desk and getting prefermental treatment, while the rest of us had to queue up.'

'Preferential,' prompted her sister sotto voce.

Edna had bottomless curiosity and an extensive repertoire of facial expressions. She was also a persistent user
of memorable malapropisms and amazingly inventive non
sequiturs.

'What?' asked her sister.

'She didn't need to queue up,' explained Miriam. 'She's in
first class, that's why she's got *preferential*' (she emphasised
the word) 'treatment.'

'I know she's in first class. I've just said so!' snapped her
sister. 'Anyway, I don't suppose we'll be seeing much of her
on the cruise, and I shan't lose any sleep over that. "All fur
coat and no knickers", as our sainted mother would say.'

Edna was a woman possessed of a bluntness, a thick skin,
and a sharp comic talent for description, someone who injected
her opinions forcefully. She had a devouring interest in other
people and was not unforthcoming in sharing her opinions
about them, usually to her sister who listened, for most of the
time, with consummate patience. The smallest details of other
people were the topics for comment, their appearance, behaviour, relationships all came up for speculation or dismissal.
Edna now turned her attention to an elderly couple with a
small boy, who were sitting by the window.

'That's all we need,' she complained.

'What now?'

'I didn't know we would have children on board. What is
a boy of his age doing on a cruise to the historical sites of
the Mediterranean? He should be at Disney World or some
such place. I hope he behaves himself. I can't be doing with
badly behaved children running around the deck like head-
less chickens, shouting and screaming and molopolising the
swimming pool.'

'And when was the last time you were in a swimming pool?'
she was asked.

'That's beside the point. Children these days don't know how to behave themselves. There's no discipline at home or in schools.'

Miriam shook her head and smiled. Her sister's experience of raising children was hardly comprehensive. She looked at the boy.

He was a serious, self-absorbed young man of about eleven or twelve, unaware that he had two observers; his nose was buried in a book. He was an oddly old-fashioned looking child with startling, grass-green eyes and an eye-catching crop of red hair cut in the short-back-and-sides style and with a neat parting. He had a meditative, intelligent face peppered with a constellation of freckles. He looked as if he had walked out of the 1950s. The boy wore short grey trousers held up by an elastic belt with a silver metal snake clasp, a dark blue jumper, white shirt and tie, knee-length grey stockings and sensible sandals. It was not the sort of outfit one would expect to see a youngster wearing on a cruise ship bound for the Mediterranean.

'He looks a well-behaved little boy to me,' remarked Miriam. 'He doesn't look the sort to go shouting and screaming around the deck.'

'Yes, well looks can be perceptive,' pronounced Edna. 'Never judge a book by what's on the cover.'

Miriam returned to reading her magazine. Her sister continued to scan the passengers. A couple heading for the first-class lounge caught her interest. The man was a tall, bald individual with a rugged face the colour of an overripe russet apple and hands the size of spades. He wore a loud suit and a flamboyant tie and was accompanied by a plump, round-faced little woman with the huge liquid brown eyes of a cow and thick springy hair. They were chattering excitedly.

'Well, will you look at that,' said Edna suddenly.

'What?'

'There's a very odd-looking couple just gone into the first-class lounge.'

'And?'

'They don't look like first-class passengers to me.'

'Yes, well, as you've just said, looks can be *deceptive*,' said Miriam. 'Never judge a book by the cover. It takes all sorts.'

'You can say that again,' agreed her sister, studying another passenger who was dressed in a ridiculously garish Hawaiian shirt festooned with brightly coloured exotic flowers and birds and wearing cut-off, knee-length denim shorts. He wore socks and sandals. 'Just look at the state of him.' The man, who was endeavouring to engage a smartly dressed woman in conversation, was a tall, bony individual of poor posture with a curiously flat face, a little lump of a nose and crinkled hair cropped close as a doormat. His shoulders hunched and his long thin neck stretched forward. He reminded Edna of a tortoise.

'Travelling alone, are you?' the man asked the smartly dressed woman, speaking in a high nasal tone of voice.

'Yes,' she replied looking around, clearly made uncomfortable by the man's unwanted attentions.

'Snap! I'm travelling solo too,' he said.

'Really?'

The man rubbed his neck and leaned closer as if he were being overheard. 'I'm a seasoned cruiser myself. I've been on this ship more times than you've had hot dinners. I know it like the back of my hand.' The woman glanced at her watch. 'Do you cruise much yourself, then?'

'No, not a great deal.' She looked around again, desperate to get away.

'Cruising for me is a way of life . . .' the man began.

'Would you excuse me,' interrupted the woman and, not wishing to hear any more, promptly walked away.

'She's given him his marching orders,' remarked Edna as she watched the woman move off.

'Who?'

'The well-turned-out woman who the odd-looking man in the silly coloured shirt and half-mast shorts was trying to get off with. Course there's always some man on a cruise ship sniffing around single women who look as if they've got a bit of cash. We shall have to keep our wits about us, Miriam.'

'I don't think we need to worry in that direction,' replied her sister, turning a page in her magazine.

The Reverend Christopher Hinderwell and his wife Esmé stood in the queue before the reception desk waiting to check in. The clergyman had a long oval face and a crop of grey hair neatly brushed back. With a long-pointed nose and heavy hooded eyes, he resembled a melancholy bird. His companion was a handsome woman with bright blue eyes and light sandy hair tied back to reveal a finely structured face. Behind them was a rotund, bearded little individual with a thick head of woolly chestnut coloured hair. With him, in a dramatically cut red dress and high-heeled sandals, was an attractive young woman. She was resting her hand in his arm.

Mr Hinderwell turned to the couple and smiled.

'I don't think we should be too long now,' he said. 'They appear very efficient and well-organised.'

'Have you cruised before?' asked the little man.

'No, no, this is our first. We've been saving up for it for quite some while. My wife and I are very excited. I have always dreamed of visiting Rome, the Vatican and the churches, and Esmé to see the Roman remains.'

'I imagine I won't have much time to go ashore,' replied the little man.

'Oh, why is that?' he was asked.

'I need to spend a deal of time practising each day. I am the concert pianist on the cruise. Getting away from everything for a couple of weeks gives me the opportunity of tackling a few new and difficult pieces.'

The young woman patted his hand and looked at him affectionately. 'I'm sure I can persuade you to leave the piano for a couple of hours when we are in Rome,' she said.

'Maybe,' he said reaching over to kiss her cheek.

'Did you see that, Miriam?' said Edna who was watching like a hungry cat.

'Did I see what, dear?' asked her sister. She gave up on the magazine and put it on the seat beside her.

'That couple queuing up in front of the reception desk.'

'I wasn't looking.'

'Well, take a look.'

'Do you know, Edna, you could make a career out of noticing things, which is something of a miracle since you're always complaining about your bad eyesight.'

'I'm just interested in people that's all,' responded Edna sounding peeved. 'There's nothing wrong with that. Anyway, as regards the couple queuing up in front of the reception desk that I was telling you about, I wonder what an attractive young woman like that is doing with that little old man?'

Miriam looked at the couple in question. 'She might be his carer,' she said.

'I've just seen him kiss her. That's not the action of a carer.'

Miriam picked up her magazine. Edna continued to scrutinise her fellow passengers and pass comment, until the person on the public address system invited those who were in first class or who were with young children or who were disabled to board the ship first. Despite her bad hip, about which she frequently complained, Edna grabbed her walking frame and pushed her way to the front of the line. 'Come along, Miriam, don't dawdle,' she shouted. 'Make a move.'

Her long-suffering sister rolled her eyes and wondered if going on this cruise was such a good idea.

The passengers, in whom Edna had taken such a searching interest, now boarded the *Empress of the Ocean,* each with varying expectations of the journey to come. They were unaware that the experience during the two weeks of cruising around the Mediterranean would in some ways change their lives.

2

'We should have opted for an outside cabin,' said Maureen, looking around the confined space in which they would be spending the next two weeks. 'There's no window and it's far too small. I feel hemmed in. You couldn't swing a cat in here.'

'You picked it,' said her husband unhelpfully.

'I imagined it would be bigger. It looked bigger in the brochure.'

'We're not going to be spending all the cruise stuck in the cabin, are we?'

'Mrs Mickleby suggested we should get an outside cabin with a balcony, but it was you being tight-fisted as usual and not wanting to splash out on something larger. I should have listened to her. It's too cramped in here.'

'There would be more room if it wasn't for all your bloody cases,' moaned Albert. 'There's nowhere to put them. They won't go under the bed or in the cupboards.'

'Please don't go on about the cases again,' she said irritably. 'You sound like a gramophone record and will you please stop swearing. The times I tell you. Using language like that people will think you're common. Mrs Mickleby said there are a lot of sophisticated people on this cruise so try and watch your manners and if you are asked what you do for a living don't tell them you're a plumber.'

'Well, I am a plumber,' he told her.

'I know you're a plumber, but say you're a water and heating engineer, it sounds better, and you are not wearing that vulgar T-shirt with "I'm a Plumber and I do it Under the Sink". I can't imagine we'll get an invite to sit on the Captain's table with you wearing that.'

'Who says we're going to sit on the Captain's table?'

'Mrs Mickleby said sometimes certain selected passengers are invited to sit on the Captain's table.'

'What, eat with the crew?'

'I thought there'd be more cupboard space than this,' said Maureen, ignoring the comment. 'There'll be no room for *your* clothes. You will have to leave your things in your case.'

'They'll get all creased.'

'You can iron them before you put them on. There's a laundrette on the ship.'

'I can iron them!'

'Well, they are your clothes and I'm not spending my holiday slaving over an ironing board.'

'This holiday is turning into a disaster from the start,' said Albert under his breath. 'We should have gone to Mablethorpe in the caravan.'

'Why don't you get out from under my feet and go and explore while I unpack and while you're about it, see if you can get some more coat hangers.'

'Stuff the coat hangers,' he said as he stomped out of the cabin.

Albert took the lift to the Jolly Sailor Tavern on Deck 13. Most of the other passengers were checking in, coming aboard, unpacking, or were queuing outside the Galleon Buffet for lunch, so he had the place virtually to himself. There were two elderly ladies sitting by the window chattering non-stop, a small boy of about twelve reading a book and a couple at a corner table. Albert sat at the end of the long shiny wooden bar and rested his elbows on the top. 'Peace at last,' he said, giving a satisfying sigh.

'What can I get you, sir?' asked a genial barman, smiling widely to display a set of very white even teeth.

'A beer please. Make it a pint.'

'Have you any preference, sir?'

'I don't suppose you have Yorkshire bitter?'

'I'm afraid not, sir.'

'Well, any will do. I'm not fussy.'

He had just taken his first mouthful of the drink when a man in a lurid coloured shirt and cut-off, knee-length denim shorts sidled up to the bar and perched himself on a stool next to him. There were circles of sweat under his armpits. The passenger smiled and scratched his neck. His uneven teeth were the colour of putty.

'Travelling alone, are you?' asked the man speaking as if there were a peg on the end of his nose.

'No, I'm with the wife,' Albert told him. 'She's unpacking.' He returned to his beer.

'I'm travelling solo.'

'You're what?'

The man scratched his thin, red mottled neck again and leaned closer as if he were being overheard. 'I'm by myself.'

Lucky for him, thought Albert, contemplating his own circumstances – two weeks closeted with Maureen in the broom cupboard of the inside cabin.

'As I said, I'm travelling solo,' restated the man.

'Yes, I heard you.'

'My name's Neville, by the way.'

'I'm Albert.' He smiled grimly.

'So, what do you do for a living then, Albert?'

'I'm a plumber.'

'That's interesting.'

'Not really.'

'I have my own business. Property. That's where all the money is these days, in bricks and mortar. I mean the banks don't pay any interest, do they?' Albert refrained from answering and drank his beer. 'So, are you a seasoned cruiser then, Albert?' asked the man.

'Am I what?'

'Have you cruised before?'

'No, it's the first time.'

'Oh, I've been on over twenty. If there is anything you need to know about cruising, just ask me. I've been all over the world. Of course, I still have a few places on my bucket list.'

'On your what?'

'Places I want to visit. I've booked for the Suez Canal later this year.'

Albert offered no reply. He breathed out long and slow. So much for the peace and quiet, he thought.

'I always come on this ship,' continued the man cheerfully. 'I've been on the others, but the *Empress of the Ocean* is my favourite. It's like a home from home. Everyone knows me: the cabin stewards, the waiters, Bimla on reception, Martin, the Entertainment Manager, Becky up at the Ocean Spa, Leon in the gym, the Restaurant Manager, Executive Chef, and most of the officers. The Captain's new to the ship. I've not got to meet him yet but, no doubt, I will before the cruise ends. I'm hoping to get an invitation to sit at the Captain's table one evening.'

Albert took a gulp of his beer and glanced pointedly at his wristwatch. He didn't wish to encourage any more mindless chatter from the wearisome individual. His face was short on expression.

'So, what do you think of it so far?' asked the man. He smiled clammily.

'Think of what?'

'The cruise.'

'We've only just got on the boat.'

'Actually, it's a ship or, if you prefer, a liner, designed for high-speed transoceanic travel,' the man informed him self-importantly. 'It's not a boat. A boat is a much smaller craft; an ocean liner is a ship, unless it happens to be a submarine and then it *is* called a boat. People often make the mistake of confusing a ship and a boat.' He reached the end of his monologue.

'You don't say.' Albert stifled a yawn.

Neville was one of those aggravating people who are excessively fond of their own voice; endlessly and pedantically knowledgeable. He was a man who has seen and done everything and took delight in telling a captive audience. There always seemed to be one such character on a cruise ship. It was Albert's misfortune that the first passenger he met was Neville.

'What cabin are you in?' he was asked.

'I'm on E Deck near the front,' Albert told him, deliberately vague. The last thing he wanted was for this bloke to come knocking on his cabin door.

'The forward.'

'The what?'

The man scratched his neck again. His Adam's apple jerked in his throat. 'The front of a ship is known as the forward, or if you prefer, the bow. The back of the ship is called the aft, or if you prefer, the stern. Two of the other most common nautical terms are port (left of the bow) and starboard (right of the bow).'

'Really,' Albert said, not as a question but as a way of making him shut up. He took another mouthful of his drink.

'I always choose an aft balcony cabin on A Deck because you can get an uninterrupted ocean view over the wake of the ship. The wake, by the way, is the backwash caused by the vessel as it travels over the sea. Aft cabins tend to be bigger than the standard cabins and quieter because they are far away from the bustle and activity on the decks below.'

'You are quite the expert,' remarked Albert. He glanced at his wristwatch again.

Neville couldn't tell if he was being ironic or trying to flatter. It did not deter him, however, from trying to engage Albert in conversation and he carried on.

'There's nothing much you can tell me about cruise ships,' he said. Albert gave a non-committal grunt. 'You see, cruising for me isn't a holiday.'

'What is it then?'

'It's a mindset,' said Neville. He rotated his head several times as if he had a stiff neck.

Albert puffed out his cheeks.

'It's a way of life.'

'So, which is it?'

'Pardon?'

'Is it a mindset or is it a way of life?'

Neville gave a small laugh. 'Well, it's both really.'

They were quiet for a time.

'So, are you a good sailor, Albert?' he asked.

'Am I what?' Albert blew out his cheeks again.

'Do you get seasick?'

'Not that I know of.'

'If you do, you should avoid aft cabins. They experience vibrations from the engine or anchor which can add to the feeling of motion. Of course, it does not affect me because I'm never seasick. I've sailed on some rough seas in my time and never felt queasy. On one cruise, when we were crossing the Bay of Biscay in terrible stormy weather, I was one of the few passengers in the restaurant. When it gets really rough, I like to walk on the deck. I find it exhilarating with the sea heaving and pitching, a bracing wind and a salty spray in your face, the ship tossing up and down beneath your feet.'

Albert was not the sort of person who disliked many people, but he had acquired a strong distaste for this boastful and mind-numbing individual who had invaded his peace and quiet. He had listened so far magnanimously, but with increasing impatience, he was conscious of the urge at that moment to strike the man over the head with a crowbar. Enough was enough.

'Of course, if you are super sensitive to the rolling of the ocean,' Neville rattled on, 'you best have a cabin in the middle of the ship.'

'Amidships,' Albert butted in.

'I beg your pardon?'

'Isn't amidships the nautical term for the middle of the ship?'

'Oh, yes,' said the man, sounding rather deflated. He gave a slack-jawed frown. His self-confidence had visibly waned.

Albert drained his glass in one great gulp and then wiped his mouth on the back of his hand. 'Well, I shall have to make a move.'

'Yes, I've got things to do,' said the man, desperate for another audience. He climbed off the bar stool. 'TTYL.'

'What?'

'Talk to you later.'

Not if I can help it, thought Albert.

The Reverend Christopher and Mrs Hinderwell, the elderly couple sitting at the corner table, were watching the small boy with startling, grass-green eyes and the crop of red hair that Edna had commented upon earlier. The child was reading with a serious expression.

'It's good to see a young person so engrossed in his reading, isn't it, Esmé?' remarked the cleric, looking at the boy in a kindly, avuncular way.

'It is indeed,' agreed his wife. 'When I was teaching at St Hilda's, it was a real source of regret that so many children, particularly the boys, didn't pick up a book. Of course, there are so many distractions for the young these days.'

'It's a fair old tome the lad is reading,' observed her husband. 'It's obviously got his interest. He hasn't looked up for the last half hour. I should have thought that he would be exploring the ship like the other children rather than sitting up here reading.'

As if sensing he was the topic of the couple's curiosity, the young reader looked up passively from his book and glanced over at them.

'I'm sorry we were staring,' apologised Mrs Hinderwell to the boy, her good-natured face beaming. 'It's just that my husband and I are most impressed to see such an avid reader in one so young.' The boy looked at her with a faintly puzzled expression. 'Most young men of your age, I guess, would sooner be playing video games or running about the deck or in the swimming pool than reading a book.'

'Those sorts of activities don't interest me,' he told her in a serious tone of voice. He appeared surprised by the compliment.

'Might I ask what you are reading?' she enquired.

'*Great Expectations*,' replied the boy.

'Ah, Charles Dickens.'

'Have you read it?' she was asked.

'Indeed, I have. I am a great fan of Dickens.'

'So am I,' replied the boy eagerly. His green eyes became bright. 'I have read some of his other novels. My favourite is *David Copperfield*.'

'I believe it was that particular book the author considered his favourite too,' said the woman. 'Tell me, what is it about Dickens you like?'

The boy placed a bookmark between the pages, closed the book and looked reflective for a moment. 'He's a great story-teller,' he replied. 'His plots are full of incident, mystery and suspense, the characters are spellbinding, and his descriptions are superb.'

Mrs Hinderwell laughed. 'Well said, young man. I couldn't have put it better myself.' The boy's thoughtful and insightful reply hinted at a sharp intelligence.

'Yes indeed,' acquiesced her husband, smiling with benign pleasure. 'Is it not a hard book to read for someone of your age?'

'I must admit it is quite difficult in places,' said the boy. 'It has some out-of-date expressions and there is a lot of dialect but that makes it more interesting. I have a notebook and if I come across a word I don't know the meaning of, I jot it down and look it up in the dictionary later.' He reached into his pocket and produced a small black notebook. 'These are the words I have come across recently – "scatological", "habitude", "stertorous", "costive", and "lubricious".'

Esmé and her husband exchanged a meaningful glance. Most children his age would have been shy, nervous, and reticent talking to strangers, but this young man was perfectly at ease, a child clearly comfortable with his own company and with adults. His eyes had an ageless quality, a gravitas that belied his youth.

'It's a good way of learning new words,' said Esmé, regarding the boy with a knowing smile. She had taught for many years, firstly in a large inner-city primary school, then at the schools on the army bases where her husband had been stationed as the chaplain and until her retirement from St Hilda's Preparatory School. She recognised in Oliver one of those gifted children whom she could predict would succeed in life and, no doubt, become a high court judge, an eminent ambassador, a prominent politician or a distinguished academic; someone rather serious and intense and with a self-confidence and a sharp intelligence.

'Could I ask what *you* are reading?' the boy said, interrupting her reverie.

Mrs Hinderwell picked up her book. 'It's a work of fiction by Elodie King. She is a fine writer of historical novels and is one of the speakers on the cruise. I am so looking forward to hearing her speak. You may be interested in going along to hear her.'

'I intend to,' replied the boy. 'I am interested in history.'

'When I have finished reading her book, I can lend it to you if you like,' Esmé told him.

'That's kind of you,' said the boy. 'I may read it when I have finished the Dickens, but I have quite a bit to go. It's four hundred and forty-four pages long. I do enjoy fiction, but my preference is for historical non-fiction.'

She was amused by the boy's quaintly outdated manner.

'What about you?' the boy asked the man. 'May I ask if you are reading something at the moment?'

'I am indeed, but I don't imagine it is the sort of book in which you would be interested,' he replied.

'But I'm interested to know what it is,' persisted the boy.

'I hardly think it will appeal to you,' he said.

'Do tell him, Christopher,' prompted his wife.

Her husband smiled. 'Very well. It's called *The Philosophy of Religion and Religious Ethics, a Theological Perspective* by the Reverend Dr Iain Spottiswood.'

'My husband is an Anglican priest,' explained the woman.

'I see,' said the boy. 'Well, you are correct; the book is not really my cup of tea.'

'Nor mine either, my dear,' said the woman chuckling.

When the boy had returned to his reading, Mr Hinderwell leaned over to his wife.

'I wonder what he will make of the words "scatological" and "lubricious" when he looks them up in his dictionary,' he whispered. 'I can't imagine a child of his age will have much call to use those words in his schoolwork.'

Edna, sitting by the window with her sister, had caught the tail end of the conversation.

'Did you hear that, Miriam?' she asked.

'Did I hear what, dear?'

'What the man was saying to the little boy.'

'No, Edna, I didn't hear him.'

'He's a vicar.'

'Who is?'

'The man who was talking to the carroty-haired little boy with the sticky-out ears.'

Her companion glanced over at the elderly man. 'He does look rather ecclesiastical. I thought when I first saw him that he has an odour of sanctity about him.'

'Yes, he looks very parsononical,' agreed Edna, sniffing, and pursing her lips.

'I mean, you can't imagine him in a T-shirt and shorts and flip-flops,' reflected Miriam. 'I wonder what he's doing on a cruise.'

'I don't suppose there's much for him to do at home,' remarked her sister. 'I mean, I guess he's got plenty of time on his hands. It's not a harduous job being a vicar, paid money for saying a few services one day a week, doing the odd marriage and funeral and the occasional baptism, getting up in the pulpit and pontifificating and telling people what to do.'

'So, what was he saying?' asked Miriam.

'He was telling the funny looking boy with the red hair and the jug ears that he's into philosophy and ethics and something called biological perceptives. I hope he is not one of the speakers. I've not come on holiday to sit through a talk about that sort of thing. I remember on the last cruise, the one to the Baltic, when you tripped going down the gangplank and had to be hauled back on the ship, we sat through the lecture from the strange little man with the twitch who bored us all to tears with his talk on "The Fascination of Fjords". It certainly didn't fascinate me. I recall saying to you at the time, how dreary he was and if they threw him after you, you wouldn't turn around to see what the clatter was. He could send a glass eye to sleep. And, as I said to you, once you've seen one fjord, you've seen the lot.'

'I wasn't *hauled* onto the ship,' her sister answered, piqued. 'You make me sound like a sack of coal, and I wouldn't have slipped on the gangplank if you had been more careful with your blessed walking frame.'

'Don't let us go through all that again.'

'You brought it up.'

Edna did not respond to this but proceeded to comment on the clergyman. 'Well, I'll say this, if the vicar is one of the speakers, we'll give his lectures a miss. I don't imagine his talks will be a barrel of laughs. "DAD", that'll be him.'

Edna had developed a shorthand for the people she observed in case she should be overheard. 'DAD' was 'as dry as ditch water', 'MDL' was "mutton dressed as lamb', 'SU' was 'stuck up', 'BB' was bad breath' and 'AAAC' was 'avoid at all costs' Her compendium of largely critical comments on others was endless.

'I'll have a look at the week's itinerary and see if he's on,' said Miriam rootling in her bag. She produced the cruise newsletter and began scanning the paper.

'Is he?'

'Give me a chance.' Her sister ran a finger down the page. 'No, he's not on. There's an author, Elodie King, who writes historical fiction; Hubert Carlin-How, the port lecturer; Lorenzo Barritino, an Italian tenor and Stanley Mulgrave, the concert pianist.'

'They sound promising, although I do wish the pianists would play more popular music rather than plinky-plonky classical stuff with all the twiddly bits and I hope the singer gives opera tunes a miss. I'm thankful there's no ballet dancers like those on the last cruise, hopping about the stage like frogs that had been trodden on. What else is on the programme?' she asked.

'At seven in the morning there's "Limber Up with Leon, a challenging workout not for the faint-hearted, with the ship's personal trainer". At eight there's "Walking into Fitness, a leisurely morning stroll around the promenade deck", then later Pilates, whatever that is, with Bambi. At ten there's "Mixed Yoga, a class which helps you stretch, meditate, and relax".'

'I've not come on this cruise to get up with the cock and start doing all those physical jerks, not with my bad hip,' Edna informed her sister, 'so I shall give that little lot a miss. What else is on?'

'On Wednesday at eleven there's, "Healthy Bodies, a workshop to improve your suppleness and mobility",' Miriam continued, 'and at twelve there's "Step into Fitness, a fun, upbeat dance routine with Bruce and Babs, the dance tutors, a lively activity to help you shed those unwanted pounds". After lunch there's line dancing with Peter and Katya or "On Your Bike, a cycling class to develop your cardiac capacity". On Thursday morning there's "Cleansing Your Body, a detox session to reduce cholesterol and lower blood pressure", and during the cruise there's plenty of other activities including interactive bowling, a shuffleboard competition, quoits, what-ever they are, archery, darts, table tennis, golf and then—'

'Let me stop you there, Miriam,' said Edna, holding up a hand. 'Do I look as if I'd be interested in any of that, what with my medical conditions? I'm not likely to do challenging workshops, upbeat dance routines, riding a bicycle and line dancing with a bad hip, bunions and fallen arches, am I?'

'Well, you did ask what was on the programme,' her sister told her peevishly. 'I was just telling you.' She sometimes thought that her sister gained too much joy from her suffering.

'Is there anything on there that might *possibly* be suitable for me?'

'There's the "Burning Fat to Lose Weight" workshop on Friday which is after lunch and later a seminar, "Arthritis Pain Solutions, using ancient Chinese acupuncture techniques to alleviate needless discomfort", then before afternoon tea a "Puffy Eyes" seminar with Becky in the Ocean Spa, followed by an informative session on "Relieving Aches and Pains, how to overcome back trouble, sore shoulders, painful legs and foot problems". I should think these might be of some interest to you.'

There was an upward roll of Edna's eyes. She looked point-edly at Miriam.

'It sounds like a doctor's waiting room. I'd sooner listen to the vicar and his biological perceptives,' she announced.

Miriam read on. 'There's the "Travelling-Alone Get-Together" where solo travellers can meet up with other like-minded passengers".'

'I'm not travelling alone,' replied Edna. 'I'm with you.'

'I know that,' replied Miriam, her voice shrill with exasper-ation. 'You asked me what else was on, I'm just telling you.'

'We'll give that lot a miss,' her sister informed her.

'What about "A Knit and a Natter, an informal get-together for those would-be knitters"?'

'I haven't come on a cruise to sit knitting,' replied Edna, 'I can do that at home.'

'What about the craft workshop? That might be interesting.'

Her sister blew out her cheeks in frustration.

'Not to me,' answered Edna, sniffing and pursing her lips again. 'Anyway, we had better make a move, before they close the "all-you-can-eat" buffet. Pass me my walking frame, will you.'

3

Later, when Mrs De la Mare and the other first-class passengers dined in the Diamond Grill restaurant, reserved for the wealthy and more exclusive passengers, and Albert headed back to his cabin, the sisters sat in the crowded Galleon Buffet for lunch with not an unoccupied table in sight. Seeing Edna shuffling stiffly in the restaurant earlier that lunchtime, huffing and puffing (a technique she had perfected to gain maximum sympathy) a couple had very kindly given up their seats for the two women. Neville scanning the crowd for his next victim spied the two elderly women he had seen earlier in the Jolly Sailor Tavern. Rubbing his hands together and with a cheerful grin on his flat face, he went and stood before them.

'Good morning, ladies,' he said jauntily, talking through his nose. Miriam looked up and stared at him with a narrow inquisitive gaze. Her sister gave him a pitying glance but refrained from comment. 'Busy in here, isn't it? Not a free table. May I park myself?' He sat down without awaiting a reply. He began his rehearsed patter. 'So have you two ladies been cruising before?'

'Yes,' said Miriam, gazing over his shoulder at the buffet bar and eyeing the food. 'This is our second.'

'I've been on over twenty cruises myself,' he started, 'always on this ship and for me—'

'Could I just stop you there,' Edna told him. 'I wonder if you would be so kind as to get me and my sister a cup of tea and something to eat?'

'Pardon?'

She patted her walking frame. 'As you will no doubt have noticed, I'm physically disabled,' Edna told him. She adopted her martyred face. 'I can't manage a tray. I also experience a lot of pain standing and there is a long queue. My sister has arthritis.'

It was the first Miriam knew.

'Well . . . I—' began Neville, swallowing feebly.

'Put two teabags in my cup,' Edna instructed in a brisk, no-nonsense manner. 'I like it strong enough to stand a spoon up in it. Not that you would.'

'What?'

'Stand a spoon up in it.'

'I was about to—'

'That's how Nelson lost his eye.'

'What?' He scratched his neck.

'That's what our mother, God rest her soul, used to say if either of us left a spoon sticking up in the cup.' Miriam chuckled at the memory. 'My sister likes the decaffeinated tea – with just the one teabag mind – and semi-skilled milk. And while you are there, could you get us a selection of sandwiches, not the salmon, a couple of sausage rolls and a cake or two. We won't want anything hot.'

'I was just going—' Neville began again but was cut off.

'I'd like a scone with some jam,' continued Edna regardless, 'and my sister is partial to a square of Battenberg.'

'I was just going—' Neville attempted again.

Edna cut him off again. 'If you're quick you can get in the queue before that lot who are coming into the restaurant.'

'The thing is . . . ' he said, making a further attempt to speak, but his words petered out and he abandoned trying and just stared at her vacantly.

'You'll have to be quick,' she told him. The tone of voice and the firmness on her face brooked no argument. He shook his head slowly and surrendered and, like an obedient school-boy, with grudging acceptance, he joined the queue at the buffet bar.

'Strange-looking man,' remarked Edna. 'I've seen better looking faces eating hay. He could do with paying a visit to the Ocean Spa and getting his teeth whitened. Mr Ellerby, who owned the shop I used to manage, had very white even teeth. They sparkled when he smiled.'

'Edna,' said Miriam, rolling her eyes, 'Mr Ellerby's teeth were false.'

'Yes, I know that, but they were very even and white. That young man could do with getting his teeth seen to and going up to the gym to limber up with Leon and do something about his poor posture. He looks as if he's carrying a sack of bricks on his back.' She shuffled her heavy hips and bay window of a bust. 'Of course, some folks just don't take care of their bodies.'

Miriam didn't say anything.

Sometime later Neville delivered the plates of sandwiches and cakes and the two cups of tea (which Edna examined).

'Milk,' she said.

'Pardon?'

'The milk. You've forgotten the milk.'

Neville departed obediently and returned a moment later with the milk. Then, making a mental note never to speak to this couple again, he effected a quick exit. They were not his sort of audience.

While the sisters tucked into their lunch, Albert made his way back to his cabin. He came across a cabin stewardess in the corridor.

'Is it possible for me to have a few more coat hangers, please?' he asked the young woman.

'Yes, of course, sir,' she replied, before disappearing into a storeroom and reappearing with a clutch of hangers.

'Will this be enough, sir?'

Probably not, he thought. 'Thank you,' he said. 'You've been extremely helpful.'

'Have a nice day,' said the stewardess.

Chance would be a fine thing, Albert said to himself, thinking of the reception he would receive on returning to the cabin.

Maureen was waiting impatiently. Her arms were folded over her chest and her face wore a disgruntled expression.

'What's up now?' he asked.

'Where have you been?' she asked tetchily, sounding like an angry teacher remonstrating with a pupil who was late for class.

'Where have I been?' he repeated. 'I've been doing what I was told to do and get out from under your feet.'

'You've taken your time. What kept you?'

Albert threw the coat hangers on the bed. 'I've been searching for these,' he replied.

'Well, you needn't have bothered. Ernesto got me some.'

'Who the hell's Ernesto?'

'Our cabin steward. He's a very nice young man and he's taken the cases and put them in a storeroom out of the way so you can stop complaining about them now.'

'He's put them in a storeroom?' asked Albert.

'There is no need to repeat everything I say!' she snapped. 'You sound like an echo.'

'So are my clothes still in my case?'

'No, they're not. Ernesto's put them on the top shelf with the life jackets.'

'So, every time, I want a shirt or a pair of underpants, I've got to climb up there, shift the life jackets and rummage through all my things. That's bloody marvellous.'

'Oh, do stop moaning, Albert, for goodness' sake,' answered his wife. 'Now come along, we want to get to the "all-you-can-eat" buffet for lunch before it closes. Mrs Mickleby said it is advisable to get there as soon as we got onboard before the rush and when there's plenty of choice, but you put paid to that after taking your time wandering around the ship.'

Albert opened his mouth to speak but thought better of it. He looked at the menacing, pinched face and pictured his wife with one of the wretched coat hangers wrapped around her neck.

Mrs De la Mare had wasted no time in getting to her state-room as soon as she boarded the *Empress of the Ocean* unlike Mrs Sandra Smith, a first-time cruiser, who gazed around in amazement at the beauty of the interior of the ship. She had never seen anything so luxurious in her life. As her husband, Frank, might have remarked at seeing her open-mouthed and staring, her eyes were 'like chapel hat pegs'. She took in the spacious atrium with its tropical plants and sparkling fountain, the golden sculpture of two mermaids flanking the imposing figure of Neptune holding a trident, the huge vases of fresh flowers, the glass encased elevators, the sweeping staircase with the thick crimson carpet and gold banisters, a huge, gilded Chippendale-style mirror which caught the light from an enormous crystal chandelier. There were highly polished antique cabinets, deep armchairs and sofas, heavy, plum-coloured curtains, occasional tables with magazines – all of which conveyed a comfortable opulence. She had stared around in wonder.

A young steward in smart white uniform approached her, smiling.

'It's wonderful,' Mrs Smith said, her voice scarcely raised above a murmur. 'I've never seen anything like it.'

'It is rather magnificent,' he agreed, looking around.

The *Empress of the Ocean* was indeed magnificent and the finest ocean liner in the fleet. It possessed eight luxurious lounges, a range of bars, a casino, a cinema, an art gallery, a fully equipped gymnasium and a well-stocked library with adjacent games' room, wood-panelled reading room and computer suite. The Excelsior Theatre had a vast stage with comfortable plush red seating for five hundred passengers. On the top deck was the Ocean Spa which boasted a whirlpool, thermal suites, a massage parlour, hydrotherapy pool, hairdresser, and a beauty salon. One of the great attractions of a cruise was of course the food. The ship offered a variety of dining experiences: the Sunset restaurant, the Galleon Buffet, the Neptune Grill, a steak and seafood restaurant, the Rumbling Tum Patisserie, Café Antionette, L'Epicureo Italian restaurant and for authentic Indian cuisine A Taste of Bombay.

Each evening passengers receive a newsletter outlining the many events that would be taking place over the course of the following day: sports activities, quizzes, bingo, art and handicraft classes, a passengers' choir, ballroom and line dancing sessions, lectures, classical recitals, and then in the evening stage shows and comedy performances.

'I'm not really sure where to go,' Mrs Smith said to the steward. 'It's all so big. I'm on A Deck, cabin twenty-seven.'

'If madam would care to follow me,' he told her, 'I will escort you.'

At her cabin Sandra reached into her handbag and took out a purse.

'No, no, madam,' the steward told her, holding up his hand, 'that will not be necessary. Enjoy the cruise.'

'Oh, I shall,' Sandra replied. 'I shall.'

Mrs De la Mare's passenger accommodation, the Bermuda Suite, was one of the four most luxurious and expensive staterooms on the ship. Those fortunate to occupy this superior cabin are assigned a butler, there to respond to every request: to unpack the cases, make reservations in the restaurant, book the tours, make appointments at the Ocean Spa and hairdresser, deal with the laundry, serve the drinks and stock the bar. They enjoy a spacious area with a huge crescent-shaped desk, a small library of hardback books, flat-screen television, sofas, easy chairs, a king-size bed, double balcony, bathroom with premier toiletries and a sunken bath with full-size whirlpool. Displayed on the walls are colourful watercolour prints of exotic places. Canapés and fresh flowers are provided each day and breakfast is served in the suite. A small and exclusive restaurant, the Diamond Grill, and a private lounge and sun deck are reserved for such esteemed (and, of course, prosperous) VIP travellers.

The sole occupant of this penthouse sat up stiffly on a heavily cushioned balcony chair, watching the bustling dock prior to the ship's departure like an actor surveying the audience. Her face was clear-skinned and defined and not yet revealing the signs of age, but it was an expressionless face. It was as if she had become accustomed to hiding her feelings. Her pale eyes were hidden behind fashionable tortoiseshell sunglasses.

Frances De la Mare (née Goldsborough) had grown up in a red-brick semi on a sprawling council estate. Her mother was a good-looking Irish woman with a cheerful nature and a warm heart but a woman firmly under her husband's thumb. As she grew, Frances watched her mother gradually being broken by a sour, unpredictable, and cruel father whose foul moods cast a blight on the household. Few could understand why such a gentle, vulnerable, and self-effacing woman as Kathleen Riley had married the dour older man with a fierce temper who had little time for either his wife or his daughter. Frances never knew the sort of father who would hug and tease and tickle her, read her stories, take her swimming, push her on a swing, ask about her schoolwork, a father who had a kind word of encouragement. He seemed to be perpetually ill-tempered and belittling. She would know by the tightening of his jaw and the narrowing of his eyes when there would be a flash of temper. He expected obedience from his wife and daughter in everything he ordered, believing that he always knew best. There were no saving moments of laughter when he was in the house.

When she was fourteen, she had come home from school one afternoon to find her mother sitting at the kitchen table staring into space. Her tired eyes were rimmed round with red. She had been asked to sit down.

'Is something the matter?' she had asked.

'Sort of,' her mother had answered. There had been a pained expression on her face.

'What is it?'

'I'm not well, Frances. I've seen the doctor and there's something wrong inside.' She had touched her stomach.

'Will you be all right?' There had been a tremble in her voice.

Her mother had given a tired smile. 'I don't know, but I want to tell you something. You must have wondered why I stayed all these years with your father.' Her daughter had nodded. 'It was because I had no money and there was nowhere for us to go. I thought about leaving many times.' She had reached for her daughter's hand. 'Now listen to me, Frances, if anything happens to me, and God willing nothing will, I want you to be strong. You need to leave this house as soon as you can and get on with your life. You will do well for yourself. I'm sure of that but don't let any man control your life as your father has controlled mine. Promise me that.'

The following weeks had been a dreadful time. Frances's mother had fallen ill with cancer. An operation had held out a faint hope, but the illness had returned with a vengeance.

Mrs Goldsborough had accepted the inevitable with stoicism. Propped up on her pillow, her skin puffed up under her hollow eyes and her hair plastered to her pale face, she had squeezed her daughter's hand. Her eyes had had a fierce brightness.

'I'm so proud of you,' she had said. 'You have everything going for you. You're good-looking, clever, quick-witted and nobody's fool. If you are respectful of others, always look neat and tidy and clean and don't fall head-over-heels for some man, you will be a success in whatever you do. Remember what I said, Frances. When I am gone you need to leave this house and get on with your life. Promise me that.'

Frances had fallen into her mother's arms.

In her mind's eye Frances had pictured the woman she would become: calm, capable, cool-headed. She now stood on the balcony of the plush ocean liner in a melancholy mood, thinking about her mother's words that she should get on with her life. She gave a wry smile. 'And what a life it has been,' she said aloud. Despite her success, and she had indeed succeeded against the odds, and enjoyed the privileged lifestyle of the affluent, her life had been empty and unfulfilled, and the future looked just as bleak. Her miserable childhood and treatment by her father had left its mark. Of course, with her looks and her poise she had attracted many admirers, but she was suspicious of the men who invited her out and found it hard to maintain any relationship with other women. She knew that she appeared cold and unfeeling and came across as arrogant but that is how she was, she couldn't change.

There was a soft-knock at the cabin door.

'Come in,' she called.

The butler, immaculately attired in morning dress entered and joined her on the balcony, his hands by his side. He was a striking-looking man about her age, with deep-set, long-lashed brown eyes and a thick head of black hair.

'Good afternoon, madam,' he said with polished courtesy. 'I shall be your butler for the duration of the cruise. My name is Dominic. If there is anything you require you only need to ask. I am available at all times.'

'Thank you,' she said. 'Could you see if my cases have arrived yet, please?'

'Yes, madam, they are outside. Shall I bring them in?'

'Yes, if you would.'

As soon as the butler had carried her cases into the cabin, hung up her dresses and coats and put away her shoes, he was instructed to bring her a light lunch and then contact the maître d'hôtel and, for dinner that evening, reserve a table in the Diamond Grill for one with an ocean view. The butler reminded her that there would be a safety muster at four o'clock prior to the ship's departure, a requirement for all passengers. She disregarded this and remained in her stateroom, ignoring the Captain's request, broadcast to every cabin, for passengers to attend the obligatory safety-at-sea measures and lifeboat drill. She was not inclined to join the other passengers crowding together at a muster station wearing their life jackets and having to listen to the endless instructions about not throwing things overboard, what to do in case of a fire and the action needed if someone should fall into the sea. She recalled the experience on the last cruise, of how irksome it had been, not least trying to get into the wretched orange life jacket with all the dangling straps and fastenings.

'Stuck in the lift for fifteen minutes,' complained Miriam. Her sister remained uncommonly silent. 'You're a liability with the walking frame. If I get hold of it, I'll throw the blasted thing overboard. Crammed in the lift for fifteen minutes like sardines in a tin with I don't know how many passengers and with a man smelling of beer breathing down my neck and an armpit in my face, some hysterical woman with a fear of enclosed spaces and a bawling child who needed the lavatory. What a start to the cruise this is.'

On their way back from the safety drill, a strap dangling from Edna's life jacket which was hanging from her walking frame, had got caught in the closing doors of the lift that immediately creaked, shuddered, and came to a grinding stop. The angry passengers (including the woman with claustrophobia and the incontinent child) had to wait in the hot and packed space until an engineer arrived and managed to rescue them.

Edna spoke at last. 'They should have shorter straps on the life jackets, then it wouldn't have got caught,' she ventured, 'and as for the woman who was afraid of small spaces, she should have used the stairs.'

'In a wheelchair?' asked Miriam.

'It beats me why the man with that squawking child of his didn't take him to the toilet before they got in the lift,' carried on her sister blithely. 'Some people have no consideration.'

Miriam shook her head, looked heavenwards, and groaned quietly.

Until her retirement the previous year, when the problems with her hip had got worse, Edna had worked as an assistant in a shop (although she styled herself manageress) that sold medical supplies. She had spent the days waiting for the infrequent customer, sitting contentedly in a comfortable deluxe leather dual motor recliner chair surrounded by wheelchairs, surgical corsets, incontinence pads, crutches, trusses, walking frames, orthopaedic appliances, corrective underwear, hearing-aids, elasticated stockings, walking sticks and mobility scooters. Should anyone on the cruise ask her what she used to do for a living she would tell them she had been the manageress of a department store which sold specialist goods, situated in the centre of a thriving town. Mr Ellerby, the small, doughy-faced part-owner of the shop, devoted little of his energies to the business and spent most of his time on the golf course or 'with the other woman'. He called in infrequently, just to deal with the paperwork and check on the takings. He left Edna, who he found dependable and unflappable, to run things, which suited her. She enjoyed the work, which was steady and unchallenging. Like her sister she was spirited, good-humoured and talkative and enjoyed chatting away with customers and hearing all the gossip.

Miriam worked behind the counter of the station buffet. Should anyone on the cruise ask her what she used to do for a living she would tell them she had been a senior sales executive for British Rail. Some of the customers who had arrived at her counter were rude and annoying, but they did not intimidate Miriam. On one occasion when she had been tidying the magazines and newspapers on the rack, an impatient passenger had rapped on the counter.

'Are you serving?' he had demanded.

Miriam had stared at the man for a moment without moving. 'Would you like a little hammer,' she had asked, 'and then you can bang a bit louder?'

'I wish to speak to the person in charge,' he had ordered. His face had turned an angry red.

'You're speaking to her,' Miriam had said, placing her hands on her hips. 'What do you want?'

Neither of the sisters had married and they lived with each other in the semi-detached house that had once belonged to their parents: a small unprepossessing building with a sagging tiled roof, crazy-paving path, and a bright red door with a brass knocker in the shape of a grinning pixie. The garden had a wishing well and an assortment of brightly painted gnomes, birdbath, a small lawn and carefully tended flowerbeds. The interior of the house, unchanged since their parents' demise, was cheerful and homely and decorated in a style several decades out of date. It suited them very well. They had agreed that when they retired, they would go on a cruise – one which

offered lots of luxury and plenty of sunshine. The previous
year they had been on a short voyage to the Baltic and so
enjoyed it, they had booked another straight away on the
same ship. And now, here they were, making their way to the
Galleon Buffet for afternoon tea.

'And after all the carry-on in the lift, we'll be lucky to get
a cup of tea,' complained Edna, as if the incident were her
sister's fault.

4

The Galleon Buffet was crowded and thick with chatter, the rattle of plates and the clatter of cutlery. Arranged on the counters were all manner of sandwiches, sausage rolls, savoury pies, quiches, flans, Danish pastries, currant scones with clotted cream and strawberry rose jam, meringues, and fairy cakes, blocks of fruit cake, lemon curd tartlets and shortbread cookies and large wedges of sponge cake with redcurrant jam and vanilla buttercream. The counters groaned under the weight of such a banquet.

Edna, stood by the door in full view, surveying the crowded room, in a blatant bid for sympathy. Her face was a mask of practised tragedy. A kindly couple surrendered their seats.

'Can you see that, Miriam?' said Edna crossly, plonking herself down and parking her walking frame.

'Can I see what, dear?' asked her sister distractedly.

'Those two teenagers on that table by the window, acting the fool and leaving a mess. It's what I said earlier about young people these days. They don't know how to behave. They shouldn't be on cruises.' She pointed to two gangly boys of about thirteen or fourteen years of age. One boy, a pimply faced youth with an unruly thatch of mousy brown hair, was leaning back in his chair and laughing loudly. His companion had spiky black hair and a thin, pale complexion. The table was covered in the remains of their meal. 'If it wasn't for my bad hip, I'd go over and give them a piece of my mind.'

'Best not to get involved,' remarked her sister calmly.

'They want putting off the ship, behaving like layabouts,' Edna told her. 'I shall certainly mention it to the Captain when he decides to show his face.'

'Yes, you do that,' said Miriam. 'Now what do you want to eat?'

Edna confronted the pimply faced youth on his way out of the restaurant. She pushed forward her walking frame to impede his passage.

'I want a word with you,' she said sharply.

'What?' he asked in a surly tone of voice.

'You want to behave yourself,' she told him.

'I haven't done anything,' he retorted, pouting.

'Go and clear up the mess you've left.'

'What mess?'

'The mess you've left on your table. It needs clearing up.'

'Waiters do that.'

'Stop answering back and go and do it,' ordered Edna.

'Get a life, grandma,' the youth replied, and pushing the walking frame out of his way, he walked off with his friend in tow.

'You see what I mean,' Edna told her sister. 'A pair of louts.'

The pimply faced boy caught sight of Oliver sitting by himself with a book on his lap and strutted over.

'What yer reading, Ginger Nut?' he asked.

'I doubt that you would be interested,' replied Oliver looking up at the boy before returning to his book.

'Has anyone told you, you look like a carrot?'

'No,' Oliver told him, his eyes fixed on the page.

'I think ginger-headed people are gross,' persisted pimply face.

Oliver looked up and stared at the boy. 'I suppose one might say that about people with an unfortunate complexion,' he replied.

'What?' The boy bristled like an angry cat.

'Do go away,' said Oliver. 'You are very tiresome.'

'You're asking for a punch in the mouth, freak.'

'Come on, Lewis,' said the other boy. 'Leave it.'

'I'll see you later,' threatened pimply face, poking Oliver's shoulder.

'Not if I can help it,' muttered Oliver, turning a page.

Albert and Maureen weaved themselves through the throng and began helping themselves to the spread.

'You know, if you'd lost some weight before we came on holiday,' said Maureen, giving her husband the benefit of her advice, 'you would have been able to get into the life jacket. It was embarrassing watching you struggling to get into it and trying to fasten the straps. Just look at your plate.'

'Look, Maureen,' he replied. 'I hope you are not going to keep harping on about me losing weight. I've not come on this cruise with all this food, to go on a bloody diet.'

'We'll sit over there by the window,' she said.

Albert followed her, grumbling to himself. Maureen approached an ancient and extravagantly smart couple who were sitting by the window.

'Do you mind hawfully if we join you?' Maureen asked in an affected accent.

'Not at all,' replied the woman with a warm smile, 'we will enjoy your company.'

Albert placed his plate before him. It was piled high with all manner of food. He noticed that the two aged passengers sitting opposite had little on their plates: a couple of precisely cut finger sandwiches each and two thin slices of fruit cake. Maureen was more interested in the ring on the woman's finger – a large square-cut emerald set in a circle of diamonds. She glanced at the ring on her own finger: a remarkably small, solitaire diamond chip.

'That's a beautiful ring,' she commented.

'A present from my husband,' the woman replied. She reached over, stroked the man's wrinkled cheek, and kissed him lightly. 'He spoils me.'

'You deserve to be spoiled, sweetheart,' he said and kissed her back.

The aged couple ate their sandwiches, after which the woman cut the fruit cake into thin little strips and posted them daintily into her mouth.

'He gave me the ring for my birthday,' she said.

Maureen looked at Albert and glowered. 'I got a box of chocolates,' she grumbled, 'a *small* box of chocolates.'

'For my birthday,' said the man extending his arm to show a shirt cuff with a large gold cufflink. 'Pat bought me a pair of Tiffany gold cufflinks.'

'I got a pair of socks,' spluttered Albert, his mouth spitting out bits of puff pastry.

The elderly woman reached over and took her husband's hand in hers and stroked it gently. 'We've splashed out on this holiday and have a lovely cabin on the top deck with a balcony.'

'Oh, really,' said Maureen, throwing an accusatory glance in her husband's direction.

'We are so taken with the cruise so far,' continued the woman. 'We've not even set sail yet but we so like the ship we are hoping to stay on for another three weeks. We popped into the cruise office, and they said that if a cabin becomes available on the next cruise to the Caribbean, we'll be the first on the list, didn't they, darling?'

'Yes, sweetheart.'

'That's nice,' said Maureen unenthusiastically. The constant handholding, stroking, kissing, and eye-gazing of the aged couple was making her feel uncomfortable.

'Well, as I said to Pat,' the man declared, smiling at his wife, 'there are no pockets in shrouds. Life is for living. We might as well spend the money while we have the chance. After all, you can't take it with you and you're a long time dead.'

'I wish Albert would take a leaf out of your book,' said Maureen. 'Fat chance of him spending his money. He's from Yorkshire, you see, and you know how they hang on to their cash. "Tighter than a miser's fist" as my mother used to say. "Shake a bridle over a Yorkshireman's grave and he'll rise up and steal your horse." I'm from Oldham myself, "home of the tubular bandage".'

'A Lancashire lass,' said the man chuckling. 'So, it's a mixed marriage?'

'You could say that,' conceded Maureen glancing at Albert who was tackling a Cornish pasty. 'My friend, Mrs Mickle-by, who came on this cruise last year and recommended it, advised we get an outside cabin with a balcony like yours, but Albert wouldn't have it. It took me all my time to persuade him to come on the cruise.'

Her husband, who had made short work of the food on his plate now spoke.

'I'll have you know, Maureen,' he said, 'that Yorkshire people are known for their generosity. We are not mean, we're just thrifty and like value for money.'

Well, thought the aged man, glancing at Albert's empty plate, *he has certainly had his money's worth that afternoon.*

'The other thing about Yorkshire people,' stated Maureen, wanting to have the last word, 'is that they're never wrong. You know what they say, "You can always tell a Yorkshireman, but you can't tell him much".'

'I take a dim view of this, a very dim view.'

The speaker, a tall square-shouldered man with abundant dark hair greying at the temples, was of elegant bearing. He was dressed immaculately in a dark blue blazer with shiny gold buttons, grey flannel trousers with creases like knife edges, a bright crisp white shirt, college tie and highly polished black shoes. He was not in the best of moods. His grey pebble-like eyes glared behind rimless spectacles, which rested on the bridge of his long, narrow nose.

Martin, the Entertainment Manager, listened patiently. The tall and quietly self-assured young man with slicked back black hair, high cheekbones, and large dark eyes attracted many an admiring glance from women passengers. There were no admiring glances that afternoon from the man who was complaining.

'Well, I'm afraid there is nothing I can do, Mr Carlin-How,' he explained shrugging. 'I don't make the rules.'

'That's as may be,' responded the Port Lecturer irritably, 'but it seems to me to be quite unacceptable. I noticed on the ship's manifest that the other lecturer, the author, Dr King, has been assigned a passenger cabin with a balcony, on A Deck. Perhaps you might explain why he has been allotted such superior accommodation and I have been condemned to a cubical at the very bowels of the vessel next to the engines.'

'Actually, Dr King is a woman,' he was informed.

'Whatever,' the Port Lecturer snorted. 'My accommodation is like the Black Hole of Calcutta down there.'

'Hardly that,' said the Entertainment Manager. 'My cabin is not dissimilar, and I guess you will not be spending a deal of time in there.'

'No window, no television, no tea-making facilities, a thin carpet and it's like a sauna,' the Port Lecturer resumed his tirade. 'It is beyond my comprehension why this Dr King has been given such a comfortable passenger cabin, with a balcony I might add, and I have been consigned to such a cramped and distasteful berth. And as for the bed on which I am supposed to sleep—'

The Entertainment Manager smiled the patient, detached smile he reserved for difficult passengers and interrupted the diatribe.

'Dr King is designated SGE and you PL, that is why,' he said evenly.

'What?'

'She is termed a Special Guest Entertainer and you are a Guest Lecturer.'

'What is the difference?'

'A passenger cabin for one thing.'

The Guest Lecturer scowled.

'You see, she has been given a higher status than you,' explained Martin, 'if I may put it like that. She has a celebrity status which you have not.'

'Celebrity status!' exclaimed the Port Lecturer. 'I've never heard of the woman.'

'Well, many people have and quite a number on the cruise have mentioned how they are looking forward to her lectures.'

'You don't say.'

'Dr King is a bestselling, widely published author who has appeared on radio and television and she is a professor at Oxford.'

Mr Carlin-How scowled again.

'This is discrimination!' he snapped.

'You may think so,' answered the Entertainment Manager calmly, 'and I do have some sympathy with what you feel but, as I have said, I do not make the rules.'

'Is there not another cabin available?'

'Unfortunately not. The ship is full. If there were, I should be more than happy to make it available to you but—'

'I must say that I think this inequity is intolerable. Had I known I would receive this shabby treatment and be confined to such a small cabin, I should not have countenanced agreeing to lecture on this cruise. After all, I am not getting paid for it.'

'Yes, that's true, but you do get to visit some outstanding places, have all the meals included, enjoy the evening enter- tainment and you can make use of the ship's many facilities—'

'Except a passenger cabin,' added the Port Lecturer.

Faced with a dissatisfied passenger Martin always remained unruffled. He was invariably bland and unfailingly courteous. In his line of work he was well-versed in dealing with disgruntled people on a day-to-day basis, mostly passengers who complained about the most trivial things and had the most ridiculous requests. One woman grumbled about the movement of the ship and asked him to speak to the Captain and see if he could prevent it from rolling from side to side and going up and down. He was tempted to tell her that the ship was moving up and down because there were several honeymoon couples on board, but he resisted. Another grouchy traveller, a self-confessed light sleeper, demanded he stop the person in the next cabin from snoring and he also complained about the sound of the sea outside his window, which kept him awake most of the night. A first-time cruiser, who had booked an outside cabin, asked if she could have some extra blankets in case it got too cold on deck. One stressed passenger asked if he could do something about the dreadful screeching of the seagulls. When faced with such individuals, Martin would remain perfectly calm, nod sympathetically and tell them he would deal with the complaint or see to the request as a matter of urgency. He had learned from experience that if one nodded and smiled, it gave the appearance of listening. Over the course of a typical day, he smiled so much it was a wonder the effort didn't have a wearing effect on his cheek muscles.

'The fact is, Mr Carlin-How,' he said now, 'we receive many requests from people wishing to lecture on our cruises. We are never short of speakers keen to join the ship. Since you feel so upset about the situation, I advise you to take up your grievance with head office on your return.'

'I shall most certainly do as you say.'

'Of course, if you feel so strongly about it, you are at liberty to disembark at our first port of call in Cádiz. We do have a member of our Entertainment Team who could, at a pinch, take over your lectures.'

'Leave the ship,' echoed the Port Lecturer. He had lowered his voice. 'Well, I wouldn't want to leave the ship.' The wind had been taken out of his sails.

'Of course, if you do decide to leave the ship, you would have to cover the cost of returning to the United Kingdom and in doing so, you would be in breach of your contract.'

'I can see I am getting nowhere arguing the toss,' replied Mr Carlin-How, 'but as you suggest, I shall most definitely be expressing my dissatisfaction to head office on my return home.' He turned to leave.

'Oh, before you go,' said the Entertainment Manager, 'may I offer you a word of advice?'

'Which is?' he asked crossly.

'I gather that this is the first occasion you have lectured on a cruise ship.'

'Yes, and it will be the last unless my working conditions are improved.'

'You are to give eight lectures on the sea days in the after-noons and—'

'Yes, I am well aware of that,' he interjected impatiently. 'I *have* seen my programme.'

'Well, I suggest you keep the lights on in the theatre during your talks. You see, most of the passengers, some of whom are getting well on in life, will have had a substantial meal at lunchtime and should you have a dark theatre they are prone to fall asleep.'

'I have never had anyone fall asleep in my lectures at the college where I teach,' stated Mr Carlin-How, sounding affronted.

'Nevertheless—'

'I need to have the lights off,' stated the Port Lecturer. 'This is in order for my audience to get the full appreciation of the many photographic slides showing the places we are to visit, scenes which I present on the screen.'

'Very well, just as you wish,' said the Entertainment Manager, not wanting to detain the man further. 'I will leave it up to you. Now, if there is nothing else.'

When Mr Carlin-How's parents died he secured a position at a London college. He sold the rambling old house in Dorset which he had inherited, for a goodly amount, and bought a spacious ground-floor flat in Acton, which he kept immaculately clean and tidy. He furnished it with much of his parents' furniture: deep-cushioned sofas and chairs, velvet cushions, an inlaid Georgian corner cupboard, a richly patterned Indian carpet which covered most of a polished oak floor and pale green drapes at the windows, all of which took a great deal of effort to keep clean and dust-free. A collection of photographs in polished silver frames was arranged precisely on an antique oak dresser. On a wall three insipid watercolours had been exactly positioned. A longcase clock with a gleaming brass face ticked reassuringly in a corner.

Mr Carlin-How was a man of punctilious habits, a stickler for order. His watchword was that there is a place for everything, and everything should be in its proper place. His colleagues at the college where he worked as a senior lecturer in the history faculty, often joked about his obsession with neatness. His room was free of clutter; the filing cabinets contained folders carefully classified, the shelves had rows of books all symmetrically organised according to size, the contents of the cupboards were meticulously ordered, and his desk was a model of tidiness.

In his appearance he was equally fastidiously neat, always immaculately dressed for work, usually in a smart grey suit, pristine white shirt and college tie, black shoes highly polished and hair short and neatly parted.

He had had a brief relationship with a teacher whom he had met at a historical society meeting, and she had moved into his flat, but after two weeks she had tired of his preoccupation with domestic order and left. She couldn't bear that everything had to be so clean, tidy, and organised, that everything had to be continually washed and scrubbed, dusted and polished. Crockery had to be scoured of stains, plates had to be stacked in a certain way in the dishwasher, towels needed constant realignment, tins and packets had to be arranged in the cupboards in a particular order, newspapers had to be folded carefully and cutlery had to be carefully polished and placed in the drawer in a uniform fashion like soldiers on the parade ground. The table had to be set out for breakfast the evening before. There were even different coloured plastic bags for the rubbish.

'You need to get a life, Hubert,' the teacher had informed him after packing her bags. She had wearied of the fanatical precision of everything in the apartment. 'Everything here is so . . . so clinical, uncluttered, controlled. It's a nightmare living with you. You have a profound OCD problem and need to get some help.'

Now on his way back to his small inside cabin, resentment rising in his chest, he caught sight of 'Miss Celebrity' herself, a tall striking looking woman who was striding down the deck smiling at the passengers. Hubert bit his lip. Well, he most certainly would not be attending *her* lectures and should he meet her he would act coolly. His deep sense of indignation increased when he surveyed again the berth where he would be spending the next fortnight.

'Cabined, cribbed and confined,' he said out loud, recalling some quotation or other. Shakespeare perhaps. He had taken no time in organising the small space in the way he liked it.

His steward, arriving at the cabin to clean the day following the ship's departure, discovered there was nothing he needed to do. Everything was scrupulously clean and tidy. The bathroom had a surgical spotlessness, the bed was made up neatly and the cups and glasses had been washed up and put away after use. He had commented to a colleague later that he wished all the occupants of the cabins were as neat and tidy. Then, he mimicked the passenger's voice. 'I do so like things to be shipshape and Bristol fashion.'

5

The first morning at sea, the butler,' arrived at the Bermuda Suite with breakfast.

'Good morning, madam,' he said, wheeling a trolley into the cabin.

Mrs De la Mare was attired in an ivory silk dressing gown.

'Good morning,' she replied.

'It's a beautiful day, madam. The sky is clear and the sea is calm.'

He set out the breakfast table with a white damask table-cloth and napkin and a place setting of sparkling silver cutlery and fine ivory bone china and then placed an envelope against the slim crystal vase containing a single white rose. Her name was printed on the front.

'Will there be anything else, madam?' he asked.

'No, thank you, Dominic,' she replied. Noticing the envelope, a pleasing smile broke on Mrs De la Mare's lips. This was the desired invitation to dine at the Captain's table she thought. Things are looking up. Her face dropped, however, when she read the contents:

As you were unable to attend the pre-departure safety drill yesterday, the Chief Safety Office invites you to attend a safety briefing and drill at twelve noon in the Games' Room, a small area adjacent to the library. This is to comply with international maritime directives that all newly boarded passengers and crew attend a mandatory safety drill.

'This is to ask me to attend some safety drill?' she told the butler, holding up the letter. 'Do I really have to go?'

'Yes, madam,' he told her. 'Failure to go will mean you may be asked to leave the ship.'

'How did they know I wasn't present at this drill?'

'A register of those attending is kept. Your absence will have been noted.'

'Ridiculous,' she said, throwing down the letter.

'It's for your own safety, madam.'

'Ridiculous,' she repeated. 'I can well recall what was said when I was last on a cruise. It's only common sense.'

'You will need to go, madam.'

She gave a faint sigh. 'Well, I suppose I must comply.'

'I'll get your life jacket,' he said.

Following the safety briefing, an ill-tempered Mrs De la Mare returned to her stateroom, ordered a light lunch to be served there, after which she made her way to the executive sun deck. It was clear to all who saw the striking-looking woman in the expensive sunglasses ascending the stairs, that here was someone of wealth and position. Everything about her exuded money: the tailored navy linen trousers, the stylish cream top, the delicate daytime pearls, the flawless make-up, the designer handbag. She found a recliner, tilted her sunglasses slightly on the bridge of her nose and settled herself against the cushions. With a small wearisome sigh, she closed her eyes momentarily.

'Hello.'

Mrs De la Mare opened her eyes, removed her sunglasses, and placed them carefully on the table beside her. She looked up to see the cheery face of a woman staring down at her.

'Good afternoon,' she replied, her voice deliberately cold and superior. The last thing she wanted was for the woman to disturb her.

'May I join you?' asked the passenger, not waiting for a reply and sitting on the adjacent lounger. Mrs De la Mare's companion was a small, spry, elderly woman with large, inquisitive blue eyes and thick wavy white hair. The object of her scrutiny was wearing a brightly coloured cotton smock – shapeless and timeless.

Mrs De la Mare gave a condescending little smile and narrowed her eyes like a cat. 'I think,' she said, 'that you are perhaps in the wrong area of the ship.'

'Oh, am I?'

'This is the executive sun deck reserved for first-class passengers only,' she was told. 'One has to have a gold cruise card to use this amenity.'

The woman rootled in a capacious handbag. 'Like this?' she asked, holding up a gold cruise card.

Mrs De la Mare raised a plucked eyebrow. Her face was as hard as a diamond. 'Yes, like that,' she acknowledged.

'I saw you sitting here all by yourself,' burbled the woman brightly and stretching out on the lounger, 'and I thought you might like a bit of company.'

'How kind of you,' replied Mrs De la Mare, her face as inexpressive as a blank wall. There was a quiet sarcasm in the tone of her reply.

'You looked such a lonely soul,' said the woman.

'I beg your pardon?' Mrs De la Mare drew a deep exasperating breath, which was quite lost on her companion.

'Sitting here all on your own.'

'As a matter of fact, I enjoy my own company,' she was informed tartly.

'You're travelling by yourself then?'

'Yes.'

'I didn't see you at lunchtime in the Diamond Grill,' said the woman cheerfully.

'I dined in my cabin.'

'I like to get to know people myself and mealtimes are nice opportunities to do that.'

Mrs De la Mare remained resolutely silent. Her unwilling-ness to respond did not deter her fellow passenger.

'Do you think the sea will get rough?'

'I doubt it.'

'If truth be told, I'm a terrible sailor. I only have to look at a wave and I go green at the gills. I get seasick gutting fish.' She laughed at her own witticism. 'I remember when me and my husband went on the cross-channel ferry. Up and down was the sea like a fiddler's elbow. I thought I would die. I was inside, heaving and splashing in the ladies' lavatory and the sea was outside heaving and splashing like there was no tomorrow and Frank was in the café with a French bap and a glass of red wine. He never got seasick. Mind you, he spent most of his working life at sea and his father was a sailor. It probably runs in the family.'

'Well, I don't get seasick,' Mrs De la Mare informed her, replacing her sunglasses, and wishing the woman would depart and leave her alone.

'My son, Eddie, doesn't,' the woman told her. 'He has a real liking for the sea; he takes after his father and his grandfather. It's in his blood. He is a sailor too. Frank loved the ocean; he was an engineer in the Merchant Navy, but he wasn't keen on coming on a cruise. He's passed on now. Had a stroke tying up his boots. Eddie asked if I wanted him to see if he could arrange to scatter his father's ashes at sea.'

'From what I was informed at the safety drill,' Mrs De la Mare told her, 'nothing must be thrown overboard. I assume that this incudes ashes.'

'Oh, I don't think so. Well, anyway, I said I didn't want that. I wasn't keen on Frank ending up floating in the North Sea on the currents of time. I wanted a grave on dry land that I could visit.' She paused for a moment and inhaled deeply, then stretched further back on the lounger and felt the warmth of the sun on her face. She sighed with contentment. 'This is the life.'

Mrs De la Mare did not deign to answer.

'Is it your first?' she was asked.

'My first?'

'Cruise? Is this your first cruise?'

'No, I have cruised before,' she told her. 'Several times, actually.'

'You'll be something of an old hand then?'

Mrs De la Mare arched her finely pencilled eyebrows to their fullest extent. She did not condescend to reply. She did not like to be referred to as 'an old hand'.

'It's *my* first cruise,' explained the woman, 'and oh, how I've enjoyed it so far. I cannot put into words the thrill and excitement of the first sight of this beautiful gleaming white cruise ship in the berth and the breathtaking foyer. Everything is so spotlessly clean, and everybody is so friendly and helpful, aren't they? Nothing is too much trouble for them. And the food, it's out of this world and there's so much to choose from, all beautifully presented and served by polite and smiling waiters. And my cabin! Well, it's luxurious – lovely bathroom, television, tea-making facilities, balcony. It's got the lot. My cabin stewardess, Madelena, cannot do enough. I have never been so pampered in all my life. To tell the truth, I wasn't all that keen on coming on this cruise. It was my Eddie who persuaded me. My son loves the ocean. Always has done, ever since he was a little boy, when he sailed his toy boat on the boating lake in Clifton Park. Never wanted to do anything else but go to sea like his father. "You're going on a cruise, Mother," he says. He just would not take no for an answer. He got some sort of deal for me.'

Mrs De la Mare smiled and felt a tinge of triumph. *Yes*, she thought as much – *the woman was on some kind of special offer.*

'He's been on and on at me since my husband died two years' ago to come on a cruise, but I was a bit nervous,' proceeded the woman. 'As I said, I'm not the best sailor in the world and coming by myself was a bit of a worry, I don't mind saying. Frank and me went everywhere together. It's strange going places without him. But everything has been simply perfect. Are you travelling alone?'

'Yes, I am,' replied Mrs De la Mare without any elaboration.

'There's lots of us travelling by ourselves and Peter and Katya, the Entertainment Officers – lovely young people aren't they – they've organised this "Travelling-Alone Get-Together" every morning where you can meet and get to know other people who are on the cruise by themselves. I'm looking forward to going. You ought to come along. You'd like it.'

'I think not,' observed Mrs De la Mare, imagining the nightmare of the little get-together.

'There's so much to do on the ship, isn't there?' continued the woman. 'Ballroom dancing, line dancing, art classes, flower arranging, whist drives, bingo, quizzes, the casino, concerts and lectures, trips ashore, films, aerobics.'

'I *have* seen the itinerary,' Mrs De la Mare told her stiffly.

'I'm going to have my hair done tomorrow,' the woman told her. 'I'm pushing out the boat. Are you tempted?'

'No, I am not,' replied Mrs De la Mare, rewarding her companion with an icy look. 'I couldn't trust anyone with my hair, except, of course, my own hairdresser back home.'

'When I went up to the Ocean Spa to book my hair appointment with Becky,' rattled on the woman, 'there were people having all sorts done: hot stone massages, seaweed wraps, manicures, pedicures and facial treatments. Talk about a facial treatment, I must have added a few more laughter lines listening to Becky. She is such a character. I don't think I've ever chuckled as much hearing about some of the passengers she had to deal with on her last cruise. One woman asked her what time the ten o'clock – what do you call it – the ship that takes people ashore?'

'The tender,' Mrs De la Mare informed her.

'Oh, yes. Well, this passenger asked her what time the ten o'clock tender was leaving. "Ten o' clock," Becky told her. Don't some people ask some silly questions?'

And don't some people never stop talking, thought Mrs De la Mare.

'One passenger asked Becky,' continued the woman, 'what end of the pier will the tender be leaving from? "The one in the water," Becky told her. Then there was a woman who wanted to know how much coal the ship used on a voyage and the man who asked if there was a bus service in Venice. It's on islands, you know, is Venice.'

'Yes, I am aware of that,' said Mrs De la Mare. 'I have been to Venice – several times actually.'

'Becky said you get all sorts on the cruise ships,' she said, untroubled by the edge in the other woman's voice.

Well, that is something we can agree upon, thought Mrs De la Mare, uncrossing her elegant ankles, and making ready to escape.

'This cruise is going to be the holiday of a lifetime,' sighed the woman.

'I'm afraid I cannot share your enthusiasm,' Mrs De la Mare declared, getting to her feet. 'This being your first cruise, I am sure you are finding it most enjoyable. Now, if you will excuse me, I think it's time for my afternoon siesta.'

'It's been nice meeting you,' said the woman. 'I thought I might try my hand at line dancing this afternoon. My name's Sandra Smith by the way. I'm sure we'll be bumping into each other again.'

Not if I can help it, Mrs De la Mare said to her herself as she departed.

One person as horrified at the thought of line dancing as Mrs de la Mare, was Katya, a member of the Entertainment Team. Marshalling a group of largely elderly passengers through a series of dance steps filled her with dread. With Peter, she had been dragooned into running the line dancing sessions. When Martin approached Bruce and Babs, the Dance Tutors, to ask if they might consider adding line dancing to their repertoire, it was as if he had suggested something indecent.

'We are traditional, professional, classical ballroom dancers,' Babs had told him snootily, 'and not in the business of teaching mindless steps to a bunch of geriatric would-be cowboys.'

'Line dancing,' scoffed Bruce dismissively, brushing back a strand of his thinning hair like a male model catching sight of himself in a mirror. 'The very thought.'

Martin then approached two members of the Entertainment Team. Katya had begged to be assigned other duties for she knew from bitter experience how fraught these line dancing sessions could be. Inevitably there would be the experienced dancers who knew all the steps, who liked to demonstrate their indubitable skill on the dance floor, got impatient with those who couldn't keep up and were most forthcoming with comments, suggestions, and criticisms. Then there would be the raw beginners with two left feet, poor coordination, faulty memories, with their constant requests to Peter and Katya to slow down and go over the steps again. And there was sure to be sprained ankles.

Peter, a small, pale young man, didn't share his colleague's reservations and happily agreed to run the sessions.

'It will be fun,' he told Katya.

'About as much fun as an ulcerated tooth,' she replied.

For the line dancing class, Peter had dressed appropriately in too-tight denim jeans, a brown and yellow checked shirt, a spotted kerchief around his neck and a bright blue, wide-brimmed straw cowboy hat perched on the back of his head. Katya, after some persuasion, was attired in the same outfit except she wore an electric pink wide-brimmed straw cowboy

hat and sported a pair of knee-length brown leather boots
with raised heels which made her tower over her colleague.
She was tall, thin, and straight as a broom handle with a long
horse-like face and long black hair, tied back in a ponytail.

It was a motley group of all shapes, sizes and ages that gathered for their first line dancing session. Peter, with a practised
smile fixed on his face, gave the rehearsed introduction.

'Howdy there, folks,' he said in an attempt at the accent of
someone from Texas. 'It's mighty fine to see y'all, ready and
a-rarin' to go line dancing with li'l ol' me, Pecos Pete, and my
cute li'l colleague, Kentucky Katya, bless her heart.'

His colleague was far from cute or little. She loomed a good
foot above him. Perhaps a more accurate description would
have been, 'Long Tall Sally'. She gave a fixed smile which
looked more like a rictus and waved half-heartedly. 'Howdy,'
she said with less than wholehearted enthusiasm.

'Welcome, those folks,' resumed Peter, 'who have line-
danced before and those who are novices and an itsy-bitsy,
teeny-weeny bit nervous. I hope y'all got those feet a-tappin
ready for the morning's hoedown.' He squeezed his fingers
into the pockets of his tight jeans. 'We are goin' to chassé and
pivot and slide and swivel.' His eyes were drawn to a couple
with stony faces, passengers he guessed would be the veteran line dancers who would give him the most trouble. He
could tell by what they wore: checked shirts, denim jeans and
lace-up ankle boots that they meant business. He also caught
sight of a thin woman with curly blond hair who was standing
apart from the other passengers with arms folded. She was
watching him as a zoologist might observe some rare creature hiding in the jungle undergrowth. With the fixed smile
still on his face Pecos Pete continued, 'Now, listen up folks.
If y'all would like to mosey on down here, line up in rows
facing li'l ol' me and Kentucky Katya, we're gonna take you
through a few of the basic steps. Remember folks, everyone

dances alone, side-by-side, facing the same direction, so no grabbin' an' a-gropin'.' Katya winced; the stony-faced couple breathed out noisily. 'The three dances we are to do this morning,' Peter carried on, 'are the "Hoedown Showdown", the "Western Shuffle", and the "Watermelon Crawl". Kentucky Katya and I will demonstrate the first, run through it a couple of times and then we will take you through the steps. Don't y'all get worried if you get things wrong, we'll show you what to do.'

'Pecos Pete,' called out Maureen. She was dressed appropriately for the class in a pair of fashionable jeans and a stylish checked shirt, which she had purchased from the ship's boutique.

'Yes, ma'am,' he replied, straining in the tight jeans.

'You will go slowly, won't you?'

'Dern tootin', I will, honey-pie. I'm a-fixin' to do just that.'

'Shall we make a start?' asked Kentucky Katya, thinking her colleague liked the sound of his own voice. She was getting irritated by his silly accent.

'Yup, surree, darlin',' said Pecos Pete. 'I'm a-rarin' to go.'

I wish I could say the same, she thought.

Pecos Pete turned to the bored-looking man standing behind the sound system, raised a thumb and soon the room was filled with the strains of "Achy Breaky Heart".

Despite the few predictable comments and unhelpful suggestions from the seasoned line dancers, the occasional moan from a novice that things were moving too fast, and a few with trodden-on toes, the session was relatively stress-free. The atmosphere was good-humoured and most in the class were enthusiastic and receptive. At the end of the session several passengers gathered around Peter and told him how they had enjoyed themselves.

'That didn't go so badly,' he said to Katya after the group had dispersed. 'In fact, I think it went pretty well. Everyone seemed to enjoy it and there were no complaints.' He wriggled in the too-tight jeans.

'Do you have to put on that fake American drawl?' she asked petulantly. 'It sounds absurd.' She found her colleague's jaunty, cocksure personality vexing.

'It's all part of the persona,' he replied. 'The punters like it.'

'Well, it sounds stupid and *I'm* not talking like that.'

'You don't talk much at all,' he said. 'You leave all the talking to me. You might open your mouth occasionally.'

'And would you mind not referring to me as your cute little colleague. It's patronising.' Katya blew out her cheeks. 'I hate this bloody line dancing. What is there to enjoy about stomping around the room like zombies to "Achy Breaky Heart"? I would sooner work with the screaming kids on the ship or do pool supervision than do this.'

'Well, it's only for this cruise,' Peter told her. 'We're down for the bingo on the next one.'

'Don't I know it,' she sighed. 'And, by the way, those jeans you are wearing are too tight,. You'll burst out of them if you're not careful.'

'Well, now we are sharing a few fashion tips,' replied Peter, 'would you mind not wearing those boots with the high heels. They make you a good head and shoulders above me.'

'It's all part of the persona.' She mimicked his voice.

Their exchange was interrupted by the passenger who had watched the class with keen interest but who had taken no part. She was a snub-nosed woman with curly blond hair which stuck out at the sides of her head like giant earmuffs and the glassy, staring eyes of a deep-sea fish behind large, black-framed glasses.

'Might I have a word?' she asked with a sharp edge to her voice.

'Yes, of course,' replied Peter.

'I am a fully-trained, professional teacher of line dancing and have my own dance studio back home.'

'Is that so,' said Peter.

'I've choreographed, coordinated and managed many line dancing events,' the woman continued.

Bully for you, thought Katya, who had taken an instant dislike to this strident woman and was desperate to get out of the boots that were pinching her toes.

'I should like to make a suggestion,' said the woman and without awaiting an answer, she carried on. 'I think a good idea would be for you to split up the group into the experienced dancers and those who are just learning the steps.'

'You weren't in the class,' said Peter.

'No, I was observing and, to be frank, I have to say I was not impressed. Now this is what I have in mind. I would be happy to take the more proficient dancers and instruct them in more advanced routines such as the "Hustle" and the "Catwalk Shuffle" and you and your partner can take the beginners.'

'That's very kind of you, but I think we'll keep things as they are,' replied Peter, with the smile still glued to his face.

The woman's eyes flared theatrically.

'What?'

'I said I think we'll keep things as they are.'

When he had first joined the Entertainment Team, he would respond to a passenger's suggestion on how things could be improved, by thanking them and saying he would certainly 'bear it in mind'. This usually resulted in the passenger pursuing him to find out if he were to take up the idea. Now, experience had taught him to dismiss such unsolicited advice – in a courteous way, of course.

'Thank you for the offer,' came in Katya sweetly, showing a set of teeth, 'but I think we will leave things as they are.' In reality, she wished the woman *would* take over.

The passenger's staring, fishy eyes opened wider. They looked as if they might pop out of her head. 'I see,' she said snappishly. 'I just thought, since you are both inexpert at teaching the intricacies and finer points of proper, traditional line dancing, you might have welcomed my help.' She strode from the room without another word.

'Well, that didn't go so badly,' said Katya sarcastically and mimicking her colleague's earlier words. 'In fact, I think it went pretty well. Everyone seemed to enjoy it and there were no complaints.' She gave an artful smile. 'Except, of course, for the fully trained, professional teacher of line dancing with the face like a wet weekend.'

6

'You cannot go down to dinner like that,' Maureen informed her husband. 'You look as if you've been sleeping in a ditch.' Albert was wearing a crumpled shirt and shapeless trousers, and a jacket which looked as if it had been left out in the rain and dried before an open fire.

'They will have to do,' he replied tetchily.

'They're all creased,' said his wife. 'You'll show me up. Take them off and go and get them ironed and don't be long.'

'And why are my shirt and trousers all creased?' he asked, not expecting an answer. 'I'll tell you why. It's because they've been crammed into the top shelf with the life jackets because you have taken up all the space in the bloody wardrobes and the drawers. That's why.'

'Will you stop using such language. I've told you before.'

'It's enough to make a saint swear,' he replied.

'Go on,' she told him, 'and don't be so long this time.'

'And while we're about it, why can't *you* iron my clothes like other wives? It's not a man's job.'

'I'm on holiday. I do enough ironing of your clothes at home.'

'*I'm* on holiday as well,' he answered.

'Look, are we going to stand here arguing all day?' She did not expect a response. 'If you don't frame yourself, we'll be late for dinner.'

Grumbling, Albert left the cabin and went in search of the nearest laundrette. He found it on the deck below at the end

of a long corridor where a red-cheeked man with a bristly
Stalin-style moustache and wisps of dry hair combed across
a bald head, was ironing with a vengeance. Next to him there
was a large plastic basket piled high with clothes.

'Have you nearly finished?' asked Albert.

'Does it look like it?' came the brusque reply.

'Well, how long are you going to be?'

The man stopped what he was doing and raised the iron. 'It
will take as long as it takes,' he replied. 'I've only just started.'

'Look,' said Albert, 'I've only got the one shirt, a pair of
pants and this jacket to press. Can I squeeze in?'

'Certainly not.'

'I'll only be a minute.'

'You will have to wait your turn.'

'But you've got a great pile of clothes. I've only got three
things. It won't take me a minute to iron them.'

'Look, I've told you, you will have to wait. If I let you jump
the queue, I'd have everyone wanting to do it.'

'What queue? I don't see any queue.'

'I want to get this lot done before dinner,' said the man,
resuming his ironing, 'and you are holding me up.'

'Well thanks very much!' cried Albert storming out of the
room.

Having tried the laundrette two decks below and finding a
line of people waiting at the ironing board, Albert returned
to his cabin clutching his creased clothes. He found his wife
standing at the door pulling a face and tapping her wristwatch.

'Don't start,' he told her.

Mrs De la Mare sat alone at her table for one in the exclusive
Diamond Grill restaurant and gazed over the empty ocean.
Never in her life had she felt so lonely and downcast as at that
moment. She thought of the one person she had really loved,
her mother, a woman who had endured such a wretched life

with her pitiless and malicious husband. Frances remembered her own abject childhood after her mother had died. She had loved her mother dearly and in losing her, she had felt an unbearable sorrow, unlike her father who lost little time in mourning his dead wife. He assumed that his fifteen-year-old daughter would leave school and take over the household duties once carried out by his compliant wife. But, although she had inherited her mother's good looks, Frances was not like her in temperament. In this she took after her father and when he was around, she gave like-for-like: bad-tempered, moody, lacking humour and with the volatile temper. She grew to hate him. There were ferocious arguments with her father, but the teenager held her own and shouted at him that she was no skivvy. She was fierce and obstinate. Once he had raised his hand to her. 'Just you dare!' she had spat in his face. 'Lay one finger on me and I'm down to the Social Services and have you done for child abuse.' He had lowered his balled fist and then stormed out of the house.

For the first few weeks after her mother's death, when he shouted and complained, she slammed doors, screamed at her father, threw things, and when he went out to the pub, she spent the evening doing her homework in her cramped bedroom. She was determined to make something of herself. Sometimes, when her father decided to stay at home, she would sit in simmering silence, reading a book, which infuriated him. The house became shabby and untidy, and he was left to his own devices to cook his meals. After a time, weary with the discord, he reluctantly admitted defeat and employed a woman to cook and clean, a woman who would later become his wife.

Frances's stepmother wasted no time in bundling up the clothes, bags, shoes and other things belonging to the first wife, stuffed them in plastic bags and took them to a charity shop, but she kept the few pieces of jewellery. She made it clear from the outset there was no place for the awkward, moody daughter in the house, so Frances, on leaving school, got a job waiting at tables, rented a room and worked at her studies. The only things she took from the house were a green silk scarf her mother used to wear (salvaged from the clothes destined for the charity shop) a small bottle of cheap perfume and a tea towel with a poem printed on the front which her mother had brought back from Ireland. She walked out of the house one bright Saturday morning and never said 'Good-bye'. When her father took his last sickly breath and expired with her by his bedside, she had shed no tears.

Frances had been driven with a compelling desire to bet-ter herself. Her neglected childhood after her mother's death explained much of her future way of life, her relations with others, her attitudes to men and it strengthened her resolve to succeed. Her future was not to become a domestic appli-ance, cooking, and cleaning. She expected something differ-ent from her life. At school she had no friends to distract her and boys kept their distance. The resident bully knew not to tangle with her. There was something unnerving about her. She worked hard and on leaving, with a string of respect-able O Levels, she went on to the local technical college to study shorthand and typing. She had no time for boyfriends. Independence was her foremost trait. From an early age she controlled every detail of her life and her image and avoiding emotional engagement became a habit with her. There was a raw determination to break clear of her background. She lis-tened to what were considered well-spoken people and taught herself painstakingly to speak without a trace of her accent.

Presentable, determined, and confident and with her newly awarded certificate from the technical college in a small attaché case, she presented herself at the plush offices of Dunsley, Dalby and De la Mare, financial planners, tax advis-ers, business consultants and stockbrokers on King George

Street. The salary for a clerical assistant was meagre and she could have commanded a better wage at another firm, but she wanted to work at the most prestigious of establishments in the town and would soon work her way up.

In a smart new black suit with a pleated skirt, plain white blouse buttoned up to the neck, black stockings, and highly polished court shoes with raised heels, she sat before the huge mahogany desk in Mr Julian Dalby's office with her hands primly folded on her lap. The senior partner, a conventional, solemn man near retirement, was immediately taken by this serious young woman who looked strangely old-fashioned in her black suit and white blouse. She was so different from the vacuous, mini-skirted young women in the typing pool.

'Well, young lady,' he had said, tapping Frances's letter of application before him, 'you've done adequately enough in your school exams, though not spectacularly well, got a good mark in your RSA examination, you appear a clear-headed and determined young woman, biddable and you are smartly turned-out.' What a pompous old buffer she had reflected. He had looked over the rims of his gold half-moon spectacles, which were perched on the end of his nose, and had scrutinised her. 'Do you reckon this sort of work will suit you?'

Stupid question, she had thought. Frances had considered asking the old fool would she have applied for the job if she had felt it would not suit her.

'Yes, sir,' she had replied meekly. 'It will suit me very well.'

'If your references are in order,' Mr Dalby had told her, 'I'm minded to give you a chance.'

'Does that mean I have been offered the post, sir?'

The senior partner had looked at her expectantly and had begun rotating his thumbs slowly around one another, clearly waiting for something further from her.

'Well, young lady, not so fast,' he had continued, after a long pause. 'Why should I take you on? Go ahead, sell yourself.'

Frances had known very well how to sell herself and could tell her responses were clearly very acceptable for the senior partner had smiled and nodded approvingly after each answer.

With questions over, Mr Dalby had emerged from behind his desk and shaken Frances's hand. 'Welcome to Dunsley, Dalby and De la Mare, Miss Goldsborough,' he had said.

As Mrs De la Mare sat at her lonely table thinking of her past life, eager passengers several decks below were flooding into the Sunset Restaurant to find where they were to sit for dinner. Five early arrivals sat at a table for six: the Reverend Christopher Hinderwell and his wife, the Port Lecturer and a formally dressed and earnest looking couple who had said little since sitting down. The waiter, who had come to take their order, was asked to wait awhile until the final passenger at the table had arrived.

'My wife and I are so looking forward to visiting Seville and Rome,' Mr Hinderwell was saying enthusiastically, 'and of course a trip to Naples is a real bonus. I think to walk along the ancient Moorish walls, to view the Roman ruins in Seville and visit the Baroque churches, to stand beneath the great dome in St Peter's and to stroll down the streets at Pompeii with Vesuvius looming above us, will indeed be memorable.'

'Yes,' assented Mr Carlin-How, 'the cruise will take us to some splendid places. I shall be describing some of the highlights in my lectures.'

'To look from one's cabin window when we approach the great rock of Gibraltar will be an added treat,' said Mr Hinderwell.

'It is, if one is fortunate enough to have a cabin window,' muttered the Port Lecturer pouting. He was still feeling a deep resentment about having a poky little cubicle while the other lecturer was enjoying the luxury of a passenger cabin with a balcony. My lectures will be just as important and interesting as hers, probably more so, he said to himself. And to think of all the time and effort I have spent preparing them, probably more than she has.

'We look forward to hearing you speak,' said the cleric.

'Pardon?' Mr Carlin-How, deep in thought, had not been listening.

'I was saying we are looking forward to hearing you speak,' repeated Mr Hinderwell. 'It must be a most interesting and rewarding life touring the world, lecturing on a cruise ship. You are very fortunate.'

'Oh yes, fortunate indeed,' repeated Mr Carlin-How sardonically, still thinking of his cramped cabin.

'We are so looking forward to hearing the other lecturer speak,' said Mrs Hinderwell. 'I've read some of Dr King's books and they are splendid. She's an Oxford professor, you know.'

'So I believe,' said Mr Carlin-How distantly.

'Have you heard her speak?' he was asked.

'No.'

'I gather she is a very inspirational speaker.'

'Is she really?'

Mr Hinderwell turned to the couple opposite. 'Did we see you earlier at lunch with a young man?' he asked.

'Yes,' replied the woman. 'That would be Oliver, our grandson.'

'Ah,' said Esmé, 'we had a most stimulating conversation with him the morning we boarded the ship. He is a very polite boy, and we were most impressed watching him read. It takes a deal of perseverance and a strong command of the English language to tackle a Dickens' novel.'

'My wife was a teacher,' explained the clergyman.

'Sooner you than me,' remarked Mr Carlin-How. 'I couldn't teach children. Today's youth don't seem to do very much at all. They have it far too easy. Of course, it was different in my day. Standards in education have dropped, as indeed has behaviour in schools and, sadly, in society generally. I find many young people these days lack manners. I teach older students and adults.'

The speaker, having never taught children, thought Mrs Hinderwell, was in no position to know much about the education and behaviour of the young.

'Adults have always taken a dim view of today's youth,' the clergyman remarked. 'We reminisce about a golden age, usually centred on our own childhood when we had the misguided belief that things were thought to be better. It has been ever thus. Wasn't it Aristotle who said that when he looked at the younger generation, he despaired of the future of civilisation and it was Plato I believe who bemoaned the behaviour of the young whom he said disrespected their elders, no longer listened to their parents, and ignored the law? I am sure you are familiar with the classical scholars, Mr Carlin-How.'

The Port Lecturer remained silent. He was not that well-up on classical scholars.

'I think if you were to meet the young man we are talking about, Mr Carlin-How,' said Esmé, 'you might moderate your views about the youth of today and not tar them all with the same brush. I have taught children for many years and am optimistic about the future in their hands. Young Oliver is a case in point. He is a most delightful child.'

'I can only speak from my experience,' the Port Lecturer replied. 'In the town where I live, I frequently see youths hanging about the streets during the day with cans of lager when they should be attending school or working.'

Oliver's grandmother turned to her husband, not wishing to pursue this topic of conversation. It was getting rather too intense. 'Yes, our grandson is a great reader, isn't he Charles?' she said.

'He enjoys books, amongst other things,' her husband agreed. 'It was Oliver who persuaded my wife and I to come on this cruise. It's his birthday very soon. He will be thirteen next month although he doesn't act his age.'

'My husband means that Oliver is more grown-up than most twelve-year-olds.'

'He loves history and is particularly interested in the Romans,' added Mr Champion. 'I'm sure he will enjoy your lectures, Mr Carlin-How.'

'I look forward to meeting him,' said the Port Lecturer. 'It is good to hear that a young person enjoys history. I have much to say about the Romans.'

'Oliver is an unusual young man,' said the boy's grandmother. 'He is a determined and thoughtful child, rather different from boys of his age. Old beyond his years, one might say. At school we have been told he is something of a loner, but he seems to enjoy his own company and is content enough. He is well-behaved and never gives us cause for concern.'

'You are very lucky,' observed Mr Carlin-How.

'Yes, we are,' she agreed.

'His parents were killed when he was small,' added her husband. 'A car crash. It was a terrible time. Fortunately, Oliver was strapped securely on the back seat and was unhurt. We have brought him up. Of course, it is not the same as having a mother and father, but we have done our best. I sometimes wonder if we have treated him as an adult long before he is one.'

'I think you have done a fine job,' said Mr Hinderwell. 'He is a most personable, well-behaved young man and a credit to you both. You must be enormously proud of him.'

'Where is Oliver this evening?' asked the clergyman's wife.

'He'll be eating in the buffet,' she was told. 'He prefers to do that rather than sit at a table of adults. I guess he will then return to the cabin or go to the library to read his Dickens.'

'It is a grievous thing to lose one's parents when one is so young,' pondered the clergyman. 'I once was called upon to counsel a young woman whose mother—'

He was stopped mid-sentence with the arrival of a flat-faced man with close cut hair.

'Good evening, folks,' he said loudly, plonking himself down and scratching his neck. 'Sorry, I'm late. I got talking to the Staff Captain. My name's Neville.' He looked around the table. 'So, how many of you have cruised before?'

While his grandparents were subjected to the irksome affability and garrulousness of Neville at the dinner table, Oliver sat in the Galleon Buffet. A young waiter approached him.

'Is there anything I can get you?' he asked.

'No, nothing, thank you,' replied the boy cheerfully.

'You eat alone?'

'Yes, my grandparents are dining in the restaurant, but I prefer to eat up here by myself. It's quiet and I can look out over the sea from this table.'

'I have seen you on deck reading,' said the waiter.

'Yes, I like books. My grandfather calls me a bibliophile.'

The waiter looked perplexed. 'I do not know that word.'

'It's someone who always has his nose in a book,' explained the boy.

'You don't play sports with the other boys?' he asked.

'No, I'm a bit of a loner.'

'A loner?'

'I don't mix very well with other children.'

'I was like that when I was at school,' said the waiter. 'I too was a bit of a loner. Will you be going ashore?'

'Certainly,' replied Oliver. 'I'm very keen on seeing all the historical sites and Rome in particular. Have you been to Rome?'

'No, no, but I would like to visit. On this cruise I have to stay working on the ship. Perhaps next time.'

'Might I ask you something?'

'Of course.'

'I've noticed that many of the waiters and stewards have a small tattoo of a cross at the base of their right thumb. Why is that?'

'It is a common practice in Goa, where I come from.'

'Where is Goa? I have never heard of it.'

'It is the smallest state in India. When you grow up you should visit. It is a most beautiful place with forests and jungles, waterfalls, and long sandy beaches. There are amazing, coloured birds and giant squirrels and Indian macaques.'

'You sound homesick,' said Oliver. 'When will you go home?'

'Not be for some time. I stay on the ship for another two months.'

'But what is the tattoo for?' he was asked.

'It is to remind us of our faith and shows we believe in Jesus Christ. Many people in Goa are Catholics. You can see why I wish to visit Rome.'

Oliver nodded thoughtfully. 'Yes, I can see that.'

'My name is Benedict,' said the waiter.

'I'm pleased to meet you. I'm Oliver.'

Earlier that day Neville had visited the Ocean Spa salon where Becky, the beauty therapist and hairdresser worked. He liked Becky, this slim young woman with the bright eyes, springy blond hair, and relentless perkiness. She was outgoing and chatty and different from Bianca, the other therapist, in that she always had time for her clients and seemed genuinely interested in what they had to say. Becky loved working at the Ocean Spa unlike her tall, slim colleague with the unnaturally shiny, jet-black hair, startling, glossy red lips, long red nails, and large heavily made-up eyes. Bianca was not given to much smiling. She was invariably poker-faced and cranky and not cut out for working on a cruise ship. She revelled in complaining and spent a great deal of her time criticising the passengers. One might have thought that she would have been envious of Becky whom the clients preferred but she was indifferent; after all it made less work for her. She made no secret that life on the high seas didn't suit her and after this cruise she was to open her own beauty parlour in Rotherham. That morning she looked through the smoked glass in the hairdressing salon and pulled a face on seeing Neville sitting in the reception area scratching his neck. He was wearing an electric blue shirt with dancing penguins on the front, red cotton shorts and sandals with grey socks.

'Oh, God,' she said, heaving a sigh. 'Look what the cat's dragged in.'

Becky peered through the glass. 'Oh, it's only Neville,' she answered. 'He just likes to talk.'

'Likes to talk!' huffed her colleague. 'He's like a gramophone record. He will not shut up. You shouldn't encourage him. He was a pain in the backside on the last cruise jabbering on and on. He's so boring.'

'Oh, he's harmless,' said Becky. 'I feel sorry for him. He's just lonely.'

'Am I surprised? Well, get rid of him. We don't want him cluttering up the place and putting off the clients.'

Becky, all smiles, went into the reception area.

'Hi, Neville,' she said brightly.

'Oh hello, Becky,' he replied giving a crooked grin. He stood up and wiped the palms of his hands down his shorts.

'What's it to be then, a thermal charcoal detox or a daily glow facial and skin rejuvenation, a deep-sea mud mask or a Brazilian foot soak?' He stared at her mystified. 'Only joking.'

He laughed showing a set of discoloured teeth. 'Oh, I see. I don't think any of those would do me any good. I . . . I just popped up to say "Hello".'

'That's nice.' She continued to smile. 'So, you're here again on another cruise.'

'Here again,' he repeated.

'How many have you been on this year?'

'This is my third.'

'Wow! You're very keen on your cruises, aren't you?'

'Yes, I've another booked on this ship for later this year to go through the Suez Canal.'

'You'll be quite the expert on cruising with all the voyages you take.'

'Oh, there's nothing much you can tell me about cruise ships,' he started his spiel. 'You see, cruising for me isn't a holiday, it's more of a mindset.'

'It's a way of life,' said Becky.

'Pardon?'

'You told me the last time. You said it was a way of life.'

'Oh, did I?'

'You certainly know a lot about cruising. You should write a book.'

'It's funny you should mention that,' he said, becoming enlivened. 'I *have* thought about writing about my experiences and giving would-be passengers the benefit of my advice. I have a lot of material. I've been having a word with Martin and I'm hoping I can be taken on as a member of the Entertainment Team.'

'Oh, right.'

'So, you might be seeing a whole lot more of me.'

'That's nice,' she replied, trying to sound pleased. She thought it had not been such a good idea after all to be so friendly with this passenger. It was proving difficult for her to shake off his attentions.

'I wonder if you might like to join me for a drink in the Jolly Sailor Tavern this evening?' asked Neville.

'I'm afraid I'm working tonight,' said Becky.

'What about tomorrow?'

She was saved from answering by the appearance of Bianca. Her colleague, with arms folded high across her chest, glanced at Neville, and didn't trouble to hide her pained expression. 'Becky, you haven't forgotten, have you?' she said in a toneless voice. 'You have a client in a few minutes who wants a shampoo and set.'

'Oh yes,' replied Becky. 'It's been good talking to you, Neville. You have a nice day.' Then she followed Bianca through the smoked glass door and into the salon.

7

There are individuals in the world – narrow, limited people, who cut sad and pitiful figures; Neville was numbered amongst those. He was not a bad person, not unscrupulous or cruel, it was just that he was a man of little consequence. Those with whom he engaged in conversation very soon tired of hearing his nasal voice, his wearisome and repetitive accounts. He had the habit of making those around him squirm. At first, they started eyeing him sideways, looking distracted but soon they became irritated by his know-it-all attitude and his boasting. It had been the story of his life: people just couldn't be bothered to listen to him. He had not been his mother's idea of what a son should be nor was she his idea of a good mother. She was a miserable, embittered woman who had been deserted by her feckless boyfriend on hearing of her pregnancy. She had taken little notice of her son, girls emphatically didn't. To his teachers at school Neville had been an annoying chatter-box, to his fellow pupils tiresome. If only someone could have taken him aside and told him honestly how he sounded, that he should talk less and listen more, he might have changed, but there was no one. Neville appeared oblivious to the effect he was having on others and persisted in rambling on unre-mittingly.

On leaving school, he had taken a poorly paid job as a packer in a large warehouse. He was punctual, reliable, never off sick, hard-working, and uncomplaining. Had his personality been different, the management would have singled him out for promotion, however they could see he did not possess the qualities needed to be a foreman. The men wouldn't listen to him. His fellow workers had little time for Neville. They didn't tease him or laugh behind his back; they just paid no attention to him and his annoying waffle. He was insignificant, a sad man who possessed a markedly insubstantial quality, someone easily ignored, easily forgotten.

Neville lived alone in the small, terraced house which had been his mother's. It was clearly the home of a solitary male occupant. The sparsely furnished interior was drab with walls the colour of sour cream, faded, threadbare brown carpets and creaky stairs. There was a cheap and shabby three-piece suite, coffee table and small bookshelf containing magazines and a dog-eared collection of paperbacks. There were few personal touches; no photographs were on display, no pictures on the walls, no ornaments. The television had seen better days.

He was a creature of habit and would rise at seven, shower, get dressed, have breakfast (always cornflakes and one slice of toast) and then set off for work. Monday evening was when he washed and dried his clothes, Tuesday was for ironing, Wednesday when he did his shopping at the corner convenience store, Thursday was for putting the bins out and Friday to clean the house. Saturday was his exercise day when he walked the same route in the park. On Sunday he stayed in bed late and spent most of the rest of the day watching television. His daily routine had been etched in stone. Then, his life changed unexpectedly.

An uncle, who had no children of his own, died and left him a row of terraced houses, which were being rented through a letting agent. Neville's new and not insubstantial income meant he could give up his job and take to cruising, which, as he told those inclined to listen, became a way of life.

In the Diamond Grill Mrs De la Mare, having ordered her dinner, sipped her vermouth in a diamanté, long-stemmed crystal glass and stared across the vast and empty ocean. This cruise had been a mistake, she mused. She should never have listened to her friend who had bullied her into booking it. Standards had unquestionably fallen. First, she had been plagued by the tedious be-smocked and garrulous woman on the sun deck and then obliged to listen to a tiresome conversation when she took afternoon tea in the Sunshine Restaurant. It had annoyed her that the Diamond Grill did not serve afternoon tea and she had been obliged to join the hoi polloi. The place had been noisy and crowded with people rushing about, balancing plates of heaped food and mugs of tea. She had sat at a table and had been compelled to listen to the whingeing of a head teacher about how overworked he was, the interminable accounts about pensions and investments from a retired bank manager, and the dreary family saga from a chattering woman. She had made no effort to be included in the conversation. When an obese passenger had joined the table and proceeded to tell everyone in detail about her gastric bypass surgery, Mrs De la Mare had left her tea and departed in a bad mood. But something more niggled her. On the cruise to the Norwegian fjords with Giles, a bottle of champagne, a welcome hamper and a bouquet of flowers had awaited them in their stateroom with a personal note from the Captain welcoming them aboard. Later in the week there had also been a card, edged in red, requesting the pleasure of their company for dinner at the Captain's table on the first formal evening. No champagne, hamper or flowers awaited her on this cruise and no invitation had been forthcoming to join the Captain at his table. Things were not unfolding as she had anticipated. She determined to mention this to the Purser when he condescended to make his appearance.

As she sat now nursing her grievances, her thoughts were disturbed with the arrival of two passengers who were shown to the neighbouring table. The man was a tall, bald individual in a loud suit and a flamboyant tie and was accompanied by a plump, round-faced little woman. She had seen this couple earlier in the first-class lounge at the terminal and assumed they had wandered in. Now they were gate-crashing the Diamond Grill.

'Good evening, sir,' said the wine waiter, approaching the couple and giving a slight bow.

'Evenin',' replied the man gruffly.

Mrs De la Mare sighed. It is a truism that as soon as a person opens his or her mouth some other person will make a judgement about the speaker. Mrs De la Mare, who had changed her tone of voice overnight when she realised a regional accent would hold her back, quickly made her assessment of the couple on the next table, which was far from favourable.

'May I get you and your companion an aperitif, sir?' asked the sommelier.

'A what?'

'A pre-dinner drink, sir.'

'Oh aye, that'd be champion. I'll 'ave a glass of lager an' a G and T for t'wife.'

Mrs De la Mare bristled. This was too much. Now she was compelled to share her evening dinner with a couple of disagreeable passengers. Where had the standards gone, she asked herself, that such people should force their way into the select restaurant reserved for those travelling in first class? She was about to summon the maître d'hôtel to request that he remind these people on the next table that the Diamond Grill was for the exclusive use of the privileged passengers and to ask them to leave, when the man produced a gold cruise card. She was taken aback at the sight of it.

'And can we 'ave a bottle o' champagne fer later, young man?' he asked. 'Just purrit on t'tab. We're in t'Manhattan Suite.' This stateroom was the one adjacent to Mrs De la Mare's.

'May I suggest the Dom Pérignon or the Louis Roederer Cristal, sir,' said the sommelier. 'Both are very popular.'

'Aye, well gerrus one of those,' answered the man. 'We might as well push t'boat out.'

'Might as well,' echoed his wife.

As the sommelier left to get the champagne, Mrs De la Mare was minded to leave but remained glued to her chair intrigued. She stayed long enough to hear the man place the order with the waiter for dinner.

'We'll start off wi' t'soup,' he told the waiter. 'What is it?'

'Mushroom velouté, sir, flavoured with ceps, goat's curd and tarragon.'

'Bit fancy,' said the man. 'Do you do oxtail?'

'I'm afraid not, sir, but the mushroom velouté is the chef's speciality. I can recommend it.'

'Sounds good. All right. Then mi wife'll 'ave t'glazed salmon an' can I have a steak?'

'The Côte de Boeuf is another one of the chef's specialities sir,' the waiter told him.

'Champion,' said the man rubbing his large hands together. 'Right, I'll 'ave that. Can I 'ave it well done an' could I 'ave it wi' chips an' peas an' some tomato sauce, please?'

'Of course, sir,' said the waiter.

Mrs De la Mare rose and told the maître d'hôtel to cancel her order. She would dine in her cabin.

Sandra had just got out of the lift, when she realised she had left her spectacles on the dinner table.

'Oh dear,' she said out loud.

Oliver was passing.

'Is there anything the matter?' he asked.

'I've left my glasses in the restaurant. I shall have to go and get them.'

'I'll get them for you,' offered Oliver.

'Would you? They've got red frames. I was on table twelve.'

'No problem,' he said and hurried off.

He returned five minutes later clutching the spectacles.

'Oh, thank you very much, young man,' said Sandra. 'That was very considerate of you. It's saved my legs. Do you know, I'd lose my head if it wasn't screwed on.'

'That's what my grandfather says,' Oliver told her. 'He uses lots of expressions like "You are a sight for sore eyes" and "We are off on our jollies".'

'That's a sign of old age,' said Sandra.

'Sometimes the things he says don't make much sense such as "There's no peace for the wicked" and "I'll go to the foot of our stairs". My grandmother's favourite is "It's neither here nor there". If it's not here and it's not there, then where is it?'

Sandra chuckled. He reminded her of her own son, Gerald, when he was about this boy's age: bright, friendly, and confident and always full of questions. 'You're a bit of a deep thinker,' she said.

'Yes,' nodded Oliver thoughtfully, 'I have been told so.'

On his way back to the library Oliver encountered the pimply faced youth and his sidekick.

'Well now, look who it is,' announced the bully, blocking Oliver's path. 'It's Ginger Nut. I said I'd catch up with you, didn't I?'

'Leave it, Lewis,' said the other boy. 'I thought we were going to play table tennis.'

'Not before I've had a word with Carrot Top?'

Oliver sighed. 'What sort of person gets pleasure by trying to make others unhappy?' he asked.

Pimply face grabbed Oliver's collar and pulled him forward so that he was close to his face. 'I do!' he spat.

'Lewis, leave it, will you,' said the other boy.

A large, red-faced man appeared. 'What's going on here?' he asked.

'Nothing, Dad,' said pimply face. He ruffled Oliver's hair. 'Just speaking to one of my pals.'

'Well shift your arse and stop mucking about.'

'Are you coming, George?' pimply face asked the other boy.

The following afternoon Mr Carlin-How arrived early at the ship's Excelsior Theatre to give his first talk.

'Are you sure you want it dark when you show your photographs?' asked the technician.

'I'm quite sure.'

'It's just that when the lights are dimmed some of the passengers are likely to fall asleep.'

'Yes,' replied the Port Lecturer sighing, 'the Entertainment Manager has already acquainted me with the fact. However, I would like the lights turned down. I need to show a number of photographs on the screen.' Then he added, 'And I don't imagine that people will fall asleep in my lecture.'

The technician shrugged. 'OK,' he said. 'You're the boss.'

There was no one in the theatre save for a small boy with red hair who sat in the middle of the front row intent on his reading book.

'I think I've been hearing a great deal about you,' said the Port Lecturer.

'Really?' replied Oliver, looking up.

'I guess your name is Oliver.'

'Yes, that's right.'

'I had dinner with your grandparents last night. I guess your ears were burning.'

Oliver glanced at him curiously. 'Oh,' he said.

'I believe you are interested in history.'

'It's my favourite subject at school.'

'It was mine. And what period interests you the most?'

Oliver thought for a moment. 'I should say the Romans. I'm looking forward to visiting Pompeii and Cartagena and, of course, Rome.'

'It will be quite an experience,' the Port Lecturer told him. 'My talk today is about the locations we are to visit, and I shall be mentioning those places in which you are interested. I hope you enjoy my talk.'

'I am sure I will,' replied the boy.

'Well, I must get on. If you will excuse me.'

Mr Carlin-How climbed onto the stage and proceeded to set up his notes on a table. Oliver returned to his book. When he had prepared his lecture, the Port Lecturer looked down at the boy. 'You know, young man,' he said, 'I am pleased to hear that some youngsters such as yourself are interested in history. We must talk further.'

'I should enjoy that,' replied Oliver, looking up.

The passengers began to file in. Most of them filled in seats near the back. Albert and Maureen sat on the front row next to Oliver and beside him the two sisters parked themselves.

'It had better be good,' observed Edna to her sister in a voice loud enough to be heard by the speaker. She turned to Oliver. 'You should be out in the sunshine with the other children enjoying yourself instead of sitting in the theatre.'

Oliver gave her a forbearing look. 'I'd rather be here,' he informed her. 'It promises to be very interesting.'

Edna cocked an eyebrow and exchanged a look with her sister.

Mr Carlin-How, dressed in a smart linen suit, pale blue silk tie with a matching handkerchief billowing from his breast pocket, a paisley patterned waistcoat and bright brown shoes polished like conkers, took centre stage and the chatter in the audience ceased. He cleared his throat several times and then rested his hands on the lectern like a vicar about to deliver a sermon. 'Good afternoon,' he said managing a small smile. 'My name is Hubert Carlin-How, and I shall be giving a series of illustrated lectures on the days when we are at sea. I shall be describing the locations we are to visit, the castles, palaces, churches, and their historical significance. This afternoon I shall be giving an overview and devote subsequent lectures to each of these places. I shall speak for forty or so minutes and then take questions. Lights please.'

Albert made no attempt to hide his yawn. Maureen prodded him in his side.

Mr Carlin-How stared in the direction of the noise for a moment before continuing. 'There are eight ports of call on our itinerary: Cádiz (when you can, if you wish, visit Seville) Mallorca, Valetta in Malta, Messina in Sicily, Naples (where a visit to Pompeii is a must) Civitavecchia (when you can visit Rome) Cartagena and finally Gibraltar. All these towns and cities have great historical significance. Here are the very cradles of civilisation.' He signalled to the technician and the lights were dimmed.

Things seemed to be going smoothly until Mr Carlin-How was halfway through his presentation when there was a snort, several guttural sighs and some heavy breathing that were soon accompanied by further exhalations. A chorus of snorts, snuffles and snores increased in such volume that the Port Lecturer could stand no more. 'Lights please,' he called to the technician. The theatre was illuminated. Some of those slumbering jolted awake in the brightness, but others slept on. Edna awoke with a start.

'Has he finished yet?' she asked her sister.

'He has,' replied Miriam in an undertone, 'but he doesn't know it yet.'

Albert on the front row, his head resting on the back of the seat, yawned so widely that his jaw clicked. It wasn't long before he was dead to the world and snoring loudly. Mr Carlin-How stiffened. He stared sharply at Maureen.

'Is this gentleman with you, madam?' he asked.

'Yes, he's my husband,' Maureen replied.

'Would you wake him up?'

There was a slight pause before she answered. 'Well,' she said, 'you put him to sleep, you wake him up.'

The Port Lecturer would gladly have throttled her with his bare hands.

As the theatre emptied after the lecture and Mr Carlin-How was packing away his notes, Edna clumped past with Miriam in tow.

'"There was a star in the East" when you were speaking,' Edna informed him.

'I beg your pardon?'

'It was an expression that our father used when his barn door was open.'

'I have no idea what you are talking about,' said Mr Carlin-How.

Miriam shook her head. 'She means your flies were open.'

'Did you not know?' Edna asked him.

'Had I known,' the Port Lecturer responded crossly and immediately addressed the problem, 'I should have seen to it.'

'Just thought I'd mention it,' said Edna nonchalantly before waddling off.

Oliver had remained behind. 'Thank you,' he told the Port Lecturer. 'Your talk was fascinating.'

'Well, at least somebody thought so,' the boy was told.

'I'm looking forward to the next one.'

Martin met Mr Carlin-How as he was leaving the theatre to ask him how the lecture had gone.

'I should have taken your advice,' bemoaned the Port Lecturer. 'You were quite right that when the lights go down, half of the audience fall asleep. I shall not make that mistake again. Having said that, even with the lights on, some would still stay comatose.' He gestured to the front row where Albert remained slumped in his seat, dead to the world. Maureen had left him there to go line dancing.

Following the lecture, Sandra settled into a comfortable chair in one of the lounges. The couple who had dined the previous evening at the Diamond Grill approached. The man asked if they might join her.

'Of course,' Sandra replied. 'I'd be glad of the company.'

'Were you in t'lecture?' the man asked.

'Yes, I was,' she answered. 'It was a bit of a rum do, wasn't it? Half the audience fell asleep when he put off the lights. I felt very sorry for the poor chap.'

'I nodded off myself,' said the man. 'Connie 'ere 'ad to dig me in t'ribs a couple o' times to wake me up, didn't you, love?'

'I did,' said the woman. 'I had to dig him in the ribs. Snoring like a trooper he was.'

'I can't say 'e was all that attention-grabbin',' said the man.

'Mind you,' said Sandra, 'it was out of order what the woman on the front row said, telling the lecturer to wake her husband up. It was very rude of her.'

'Aye, it were,' concurred the man. 'But you know what they say: "There's nowt as queer as folk".'

'"Nowt as queer as folk",' repeated his wife with a flutter of a laugh.

'That's true enough,' agreed Sandra.

'I'm Cyril, by the way,' said the man, 'and this is my missus, Connie.'

'I'm pleased to meet you. I'm Sandra.'

'Travelling alone then are you, Sandra?' he asked.

'I am. I lost my husband two years ago.'

'Oh, I am sorry,' said Connie.

'He'd been ill for a long time,' explained Sandra. 'We had thirty-five years together and never a cross word. Not many married couples can say that. I do miss him, of course, but as my son Eddie says, life must go on.'

'It does,' agreed Cyril.

'It was my son Eddie who persuaded me to come on the cruise. He's a good lad. To be truthful, I wasn't keen, but he said, "You're going, mother, and that's that." He booked everything – a lovely deluxe cabin with a balcony, private sun deck, eating in the Diamond Grill, a posh restaurant at the top of the ship.'

'So, you're in one o' them fancy suites, are you?'

'I am.'

'Aye, so are we. How the other 'alf live, eh? We were in t'Diamond Grill last night, weren't we love,' said Cyril.

'We were, we were there only last night.'

'I went up for dinner,' Sandra told him, lowering her voice, 'but I didn't like the look of it to be honest. Bit too posh for me and the people seemed a bit stand-offish. I felt, well, out of place.'

'Isn't it t'exact same thing I said to you, Connie?' stated the man. 'I said it were a bit too posh.'

'You did. You said it was a bit snooty.'

'I went and had my dinner in the main restaurant,' Sandra told them, 'and I met some lovely people, and we had such an interesting conversation. We were the last to leave the restaurant.'

Sandra soon learned that life on a cruise ship centred around the dinner table. Questions are asked, conversations repeated, excursions discussed, politics aired, lies told and truths occasionally revealed. Gossip caught fire like a bushfire in the breeze.

'I sat at a table with a lovely couple from Nottingham,' she continued, 'a chiropodist and her husband who sold insurance and two nice young men from London. They were doctors. I told them to keep quiet about what they did, or they would have queues asking them for medical advice. There was another man on the table with only one arm. He'd had some sort of accident, but he didn't go into it, and you don't like to ask, do you? He had a false arm which looked very realistic. I really couldn't tell when we all sat down. It was only when his wife started to cut up his meat for him that I realised.'

'These false limbs look very lifelike,' remarked Cyril. 'I used to work at an 'ousehold waste recyclin' centre an' one day we found a leg in t'skip.'

'A leg!' exclaimed Sandra.

'Aye, it were stickin' up from all t'rubbish.' He chuckled throatily. 'It 'ad a shoe on an' a sock, an' all. I thought at furst it were a real leg like, an' there were a body attached an' buried under all t'rubbish. Any road, it turned out it were a false leg, plastic, and metal. Very realistic. It gev me quite a turn, I can tell you.'

'Well, I never,' said Sandra.

'We used to find all sorts in t'skips. There was t'usual stuff like old rugs, garden refuse, chipped plates, broken chairs, piles o' books, wicker baskets, prams, sinks, televisions, computers, but there was other stuff. Once we found a dead dog an' two dead rabbits, a wedding album wi' t'photographs defaced an' a wad o' cash in a shoebox. There were no end o' false teeth. You wouldn't believe what some people chuck out,' Cyril carried on. 'Once we found a row o' medals. Now who would want to chuck away something special like that?' He leaned back in his chair. 'Now, I bet you're wonderin' 'ow someone like me who worked at a council waste disposal an' recyclin' centre, can afford a fancy cruise like this an' 'ave one o' t'posh cabins.'

'It's none of my business,' replied Sandra. She was, how-ever, very much intrigued to know.

'Aye, well. I'll tell you,' he said, dropping his voice into a whisper as if there had been a death. 'Connie an' me 'ave come into a bit o' brass.'

'We did,' said his wife, 'into quite a bit of money.'

He kept his voice low. 'We won on t'lottery. Four million quid.'

'We did,' said Connie, 'we won four million pounds.'

'Gracious me!' cried Sandra. 'Whatever could you do with all that money?'

'Well, we bought a little bungalow an' a new car – nothing fancy mind – an' booked this cruise. Then we gev 'alf of it to a kiddies' charity.'

'We did,' said his wife.

'We 'aven't kids of our own.'

'Not been blessed,' disclosed Connie.

'I mean, you just need enough cash to be comfortable,' he said. 'We don't need so much money at our time o' life. Fust thing I did was give up me job. Now, you might find this 'ard to believe, Sandra, but I miss it.'

'He does,' said his wife.

'People think if you win a load of money an' can pack in your job an' retire, you'll be as 'appy as a pig in muck. Well, it's not true. I miss workin' wi' me mates, I miss gerrin' up in t'mornin' an' goin' to work, I miss t'routine an' doin' summat worthwhile. Now I feel as if I'm at a loose end wi' too much time on me 'ands. I'm not t'sort o' bloke who wants to sit around all day doin' nowt; I like to be doin' [doin'] summat. Can you understand what I'm saying?'

'Yes, I can,' replied Sandra. 'Money doesn't always lead to happiness. You're right, you just need enough to be com-fortable. If I were asked what makes for a happy life, I'd say a healthy body, a cheerful mind, a peaceful rest, and good company, as my husband Frank, God rest his soul, used to say.'

The man sighed. 'Aye, you're right enough there,' he said.

They were quiet for a while.

'Are you goin' ashore in Cádiz?' asked Cyril.

'I'm in two minds,' replied Sandra. 'I'm a bit apprehensive about walking around a foreign city on my own and when I tried to book a tour, they were all full up.'

'Well, come around with us.'

'Yes do,' said Connie. 'Come around with us. You don't want to be wandering around by yourself.'

'We're going to tek a taxi into Seville,' Cyril told her. 'They'll be plenty o' room for you.'

'Plenty,' said his wife.

'That's very good of you,' said Sandra. 'Are you sure?'

'Course we are,' said Cyril. 'We'll be glad o' your company, won't we Connie?'

'We will,' echoed his wife. 'Glad of the company.'

8

Sandra sat in the Galleon Buffet enjoying her afternoon tea. There was something so undeniably pleasurable about sitting in the sunshine on a luxury liner. She thought fondly of her husband and wished he could have shared such contentment. Frank had been a quiet, gentle-natured man who never had a bad word to say about anyone and who had endured his illness with stoicism. Sandra had nursed him in the last few months of his life, refusing to let him go into a hospice. She had fed him and changed him and cared for him and loved him. She smiled as she remembered when it was suggested by their son that a stair lift could be installed in their small house.

'There's no way I'm having a stair lift!' Frank had exclaimed, with a laugh. 'It'd drive me up the wall.'

Sandra felt blessed to have such a close and supportive family, all of whom had done so well in the world.

Rosa, a waitress, came over. She had taken quite a shine to this passenger. Most of those on the ship were pleasant and civil enough, but Sandra went out of her way to be polite and friendly to the staff and she took the time to ask about the young woman's family in the Philippines.

One person who was less agreeable was the line dancing queen with the fishy eyes and earmuffs hair who suddenly appeared and plonked herself at the table.

Rosa had been asked when she would be going home to see her family and was telling Sandra when the woman rudely cut in. The waitress might have been invisible. Sandra was minded to tell the intruder that she was disturbing a private conversation, but she bit her lip. She never liked confrontations.

'I was wanting to have a word—' began the woman.

Sandra didn't turn her head and continued to look at the waitress.

'We'll catch up later, Rosa,' she said. 'Do bring the photographs of your family, I'd love to see them.' She now looked at the woman. 'I was talking to Rosa, the waitress, about her family.'

'Yes, yes,' answered the woman dismissively.

'She won't be seeing her husband and children for two months. It must be awfully hard on her.'

'Yes, I am sure it is.' There was the same indifferent tone of voice. 'You were at the line dancing if I'm not mistaken?'

'Yes, I was.'

'What did you think of it?'

'I thought it was very enjoyable.'

'Really?' The speaker was clearly hoping for a negative response so she could report to the Entertainment Manager that the session had been a fiasco and the passengers dissatisfied. She had been very put-out by the reaction from Peter and Katya when she had offered her services.

'I thoroughly enjoyed it,' said Sandra. 'It was such a hoot.'

'I suppose you could say that,' responded the woman, disappointed that there was no hint of a criticism in the reply.

'I thought Peter and Katya were excellent.'

'On that, I beg to differ,' said the woman, regarding Sandra owlishly through her large, black-framed spectacles.

'In what way?'

'They got the steps wrong in the "Hoedown Showdown" for one thing and the music they played for the "Watermelon Crawl" was inappropriate.'

'You seem to know a lot about line dancing,' observed Sandra languidly.

'I speak from years of experience,' said the woman portentously. 'I am a qualified, professional line-dance instructor with my own dance studio back home.'

'Fancy that.' Sandra looked out of the window.

'The session was amateurish, to say the least,' the woman carried on. 'I thought the instructor didn't know the correct steps and his putting on that ridiculous mock-American accent and dressing up like some fake cowboy was puerile.'

'I thought it was funny and we all enjoyed it.'

'He didn't take it all seriously.'

'I suppose if he had done that,' riposted Sandra, peeved by the woman's carping, 'it would have put off people like me who have come to line dancing for the first time. I thought he put everyone at ease and went through the steps really well.'

The woman chose not to respond. 'I did offer to take a class of the more experienced dancers, but it was thrown back in my face.'

Sandra felt like throwing the contents of her plate in the woman's face.

'Well, as I've mentioned, I thoroughly enjoyed the session and I shall be going again,' she said with a show of nonchalance. 'It was fun, and I don't suppose that in the great scheme of things, getting a few steps wrong is the end of the world.'

'Line dancing is a serious business,' the woman informed her. 'It involves complex patterns and position changes and requires intense concentration. It is vitally important to get right the steps specified in the dance and not start changing them or making them up as you go along. If you start doing this it confuses everybody and it ends up as a free-for-all.'

'It wasn't a free-for-all today,' remarked Sandra, wearying of the woman's company, 'and I wouldn't know if he made any of the steps up.'

'The instructors were way out of their depth.'

'Well, I wouldn't know,' said Sandra unconcerned.

'I've choreographed, coordinated and managed many line dancing events for all sorts of occasions. Last year it was a wedding. The bride and groom, both very keen line dancers, wanted the appropriately named "Cupid Shuffle" in the church and the "Tush Push" at the reception.'

'In the church!' cried Sandra. 'They line-danced in a church?'

'Yes. Of course, I had to adapt the steps in their chosen line dance because the aisle in the church was too narrow.'

'I thought you said it was important to get the steps right that are specified in the dance and not start changing them otherwise it would become a free-for-all.'

The woman looked slightly uncomfortable. 'Well, yes, I did say that, but this was a necessity. I was constrained by the narrowness of the aisle. I worked out the steps very carefully and rehearsed the dancers.'

'And the bride and groom line-danced into the church?' asked Sandra.

'Yes.'

'And down the aisle?'

'Yes. The bride, her father and the bridesmaids sashayed down to the altar to "Stand by Your Man" by Tammy Wynette. Everyone was dressed in Western-style clothes, even the old people.'

'Like Peter and Katya.'

'I beg your pardon?'

'Like Peter and Katya. They were wearing Western-style clothes.'

The woman didn't respond. 'It was a highly successful wedding, even if I do say so myself.' Sandra tried to visualise this bizarre scene. 'Then they arrived at the altar and the vicar took over.'

'Did the vicar line-dance?' asked Sandra, who had found her voice. She tried to picture it – a line dancing vicar.

'Oh, no, no, he just conducted the service.'

'He wasn't dressed as a cowboy, was he?'

'Oh no, although it was suggested. When it was over, the bride and groom, the bridesmaids and the parents of the happy couple all sashayed back down the aisle to "Forever and Ever, Amen" by Randy Travis. It was a very impressive event, even if I do say so myself.'

The words of Cyril came into Sandra's mind: "There's nowt as queer as folk." She shook her head in disbelief.

'Sadly,' continued the woman staring out of the window, her glassy, fish eyes magnified behind the black frames, 'the marriage didn't last forever and ever. The bride, rather than standing by her man, ran off with her personal trainer after three months.'

Dr Elodie King was a most unusual looking woman: uncommonly tall, statuesque and lithe, with gingery eyebrows and a flaming mane of curly hair the colour of copper-beech leaves. She had a pale freckled face and a porcelain skin which often comes with red hair. When she walked around the ship, she seldom went unnoticed. Heads turned that afternoon as this conspicuous young woman trod down the deck with an air of determination. She was dressed in an unfashionable, ankle length, bright green linen dress, a multicoloured scarf tied around her neck and beige mock crocodile ankle boots. She was on her way to give her first lecture.

'She'll be the author,' observed Edna as Elodie passed. 'She might not win a fashion contest in that outfit, but no one can say she doesn't inspire confidence.'

To hear Edna holding forth on the dress sense of others, the words "pot", "kettle" and "black" might come to the hearer's mind.

'She looks like Boudica,' observed Miriam.

'Who?'

'She was some Celtic princess who fought the Romans. Don't you remember we had a talk on "Famous British Battle-axes" at the WI? She was supposed to be tall and thin with long red hair.'

'Who was?'

'Boudica.'

'I can't remember,' replied her sister. 'I must have been putting on the tea urn at the time. I must say she's a funny looking woman and no mistake.' Her sister opened her mouth to comment but clearly Edna had more to say and wittered on. 'She's so thin you could pull her through a flute, and it wouldn't stop playing. I've seen more fat on a butcher's knife. She's thin to the point of emancipation.'

'Emaciation,' mumbled Miriam.

'And what *is* she wearing? I mean, that washed-out frock has seen better days. It's like a wigwam. I don't know about her looking like a Celtic princess, in that outfit she reminds me of some large, colourful erotic bird.'

'Exotic,' corrected Miriam.

'A very usual looking woman.'

'And it's not the weather to be wearing boots,' remarked her sister.

'Actually, I quite like them,' said Edna. 'They look very comfy. You know the trouble I have getting comfortable footwear what with my bunions and fallen arches. I'm a martyr to my swollen feet and the pain worsens with walking.' Her sister uttered a faint moan, closed her eyes but said nothing. 'Of course, boots like those are more suitable for winter wear than summer. You would have thought she'd have worn something more appropriate for this weather.'

'Edna,' snapped Miriam. 'I have just said that. Sometimes you just don't listen.'

'What?'

'Oh, it doesn't matter,' muttered Miriam with a kind of despairing gesture. Her sister, who had a penchant for turning a deaf ear, was not easy to tolerate and at times like this, she thought, Edna could be so maddening.

'Of course, a lot of creatively inclined people are on the eccentric side,' stated Edna, chattering on. 'You remember Miss Lythe who taught us English at the girls' high who once came to school without her bottom set of false teeth and wearing a flowery apron. She used to wear those thick brown bulletproof stockings and some very odd shoes – those heavy brogues with the percolated toecaps.'

'Perforated,' muttered Miriam.

'Poor woman ended up in a sanitation hospital,' said Edna.

'Sanitorium,' muttered her sister.

Edna, the mistress of the malapropism, ignored the correction. 'Are we going to hear her?'

'What are you talking about?' asked Miriam. 'She's been dead for donkey's years.'

'I don't mean Miss Lythe, I mean the writer,' explained her sister. 'She's giving a lecture in fifteen minutes.'

'Well, there's nothing else on, unless you want to go to the "Puffy Eyes Seminar".'

'Do you think she's wearing a wig?'

'Who?'

'The author.'

'I shouldn't think so.'

'Mr Ellerby wore a wig, but no one knew,' said Edna. 'I don't think it's natural.'

'Well, of course it's not natural. It's a wig. It's artificial.'

'No, I don't mean Mr Ellerby's wig, I mean the colour of the author's red hair. It's the colour of the hair on Mr Birtwistle's Irish setter and full of dizzy ringlets. I reckon it comes out of a bottle. Speaking of hair, when I went up to the Ocean Spa to make an appointment, that Becky, the slip of a girl with the bouncy blond hair, burst out laughing when I asked her if I could book in for a wash and a blow.'

'You asked her for a what?' cried Miriam.

'I didn't want my hair cut, I just a wanted a wash and a blow-job.'

'You wanted a blow-dry,' her sister informed her. She squeezed her eyes together like someone wincing at some inward pain.

'That's what Becky said. She couldn't stop laughing.'

'Well don't go using the other term,' advised Miriam. 'It's . . . well it's not at all appropriate. It means something completely different.'

'What?'

Miriam was about to say something and then thought better of it. 'Forget it,' she said, supressing a sigh. 'Just don't use that term.'

'Sometimes I don't have the faintest idea what you are talking about,' said Edna who was thoroughly baffled.

'Bless your innocent heart,' muttered Miriam, smiling and shaking her head and, before her ingenuous sister could pursue this line of conversation, she changed the subject abruptly, eager to steer the conversation elsewhere. 'If you do go and have your hair done make sure that Becky does it. The other woman at the Ocean Spa, that Bianca, is a disaster from what I've heard. There was a woman I met in the ladies' toilets who had had her hair done by her, and she resembled a frizzy-haired scarecrow on a windy day.'

'I'm not having it cut,' said Edna, patting her hair. 'Just a wash and blow-job.'

'Edna, it's a blow-dry,' her sister informed her again impatiently. 'I wish you would listen.'

'Whatever. Anyway, it might be worth going to hear the author after we've had a coffee but let's sit near the back and if it gets boring, we can slope out.'

Miriam put her arm around Edna in a fleeting gesture of sisterly affection. 'Very well,' she said.

There was no one in the theatre when Elodie arrived, save for a small boy with red hair who sat in the middle of the front row reading a book.

'Hello,' she said brightly going up to join him.

'Good afternoon,' said Oliver, glancing up.

'Are you here to listen to my lecture or are you just wanting somewhere quiet to concentrate on your reading?'

'I am here for your lecture,' he replied. 'I'm Oliver.' There was not a sign of a smile or a trace of nervousness.

'I'm pleased to meet you, Oliver,' she said.

'Could I ask you something, Dr King?'

'Of course.

'Are you a proper doctor?'

Elodie laughed. 'Yes, I'm a proper doctor but not a medical doctor so if you hurt yourself, I'm afraid I would not be of much help. My doctorate was awarded for original research and scholarship. I wrote something very long, very, very long and it took me six years.'

'Gosh,' said Oliver. 'Six years. That's half my age. Well, I'm pleased to meet you, Dr King.'

'I must say it's good to have a young person in the audience. I don't imagine that many children would be interested in a lecture on historical writing. Most boys of your age, I guess, are happier making use of the many activities on the ship or behind a computer screen playing games or in the swimming pool.'

'I'm not like most boys,' he responded.

True enough, she thought. He seemed such a serious, intense, and confident young man and was dressed most inappropriately for a Mediterranean cruise.

'You're here early,' she said.

'I wanted to get a good seat,' he replied.

She smiled. 'A front-row seat?'

'You see and hear more at the front. That's what my grandfather says.'

'And there's less likelihood of someone falling asleep,' Elodie added.

'Oh, I shall not do that. Actually, there was a person on the front row at the last lecture who did fall asleep,' Oliver informed her, 'and he snored very loudly.'

'Oh dear.'

'If I may suggest something, Dr King, it's not a good idea to turn off the lights.'

'Really?'

'The last speaker did and quite a number of the passengers fell asleep.'

'Thank you for the tip,' she said. The Entertainment Manager had already advised her to speak in a well-lit theatre. 'Well, I won't be turning off the lights and I hope I won't put anyone to sleep. May I ask you what is the title of the book that you are reading?'

'*Great Expectations* by Charles Dickens,' replied the boy. 'Have you read it?'

'My father read the opening part of it to me when I was about your age,' she said. 'He was a great storyteller. He came up to my bedroom, sat on the end of the bed and read the opening of the novel. This whetted my appetite and encouraged me to read the book myself. I recall being completely spellbound by the vividness of the language, the descriptions, and the range of voices he used for the different characters.

Dickens knew the importance of suspense in a story. My father reached a most exciting part where young Pip meets the convict in the cemetery. I listened entranced. Then, he stood up, snapped the book closed and said, "Well, goodnight," and departed. I would fall asleep dreaming of the misty cemetery, the dark fields beyond, the crouching shape of the toothless convict who suddenly emerges from behind a gravestone. As my father hoped, I read the rest of the book myself.'

'I think reading a small, exciting extract of a book is rather like eating a piece of cake,' remarked Oliver. 'If you eat a small slice, you are tempted to eat the whole lot.'

The author smiled at the analogy. *What an unusual boy*, she thought. 'You are quite right.'

'The beginning of the novel is quite a frightening passage,' said Oliver. He gave a small smile. 'I can see, Dr King, why you are a writer. You are very imaginative.'

'Books like *Great Expectations* inspired me to become a writer,' she told him. 'One learns a great deal from reading other authors. As I tell my students, on the back of reading is writing. Now, if you will excuse me, Oliver, I have to prepare for my talk. I can see people are already arriving.'

'Would you like any help?'

'That's kind of you but I think I can manage.'

'My full name is Oliver Richard Champion,' the boy informed her. 'Champion is a Huguenot name. My ancestors came over with the weavers from France many years' ago. They were persecuted. My grandparents haven't quite got over it.' He didn't smile when he said this but still, thought Elodie, he might be joking. It was hard to tell. 'Do you know anything about the Huguenots, Dr King?'

'I know quite a lot about them, as a matter of fact,' she replied. 'We must have a conversation while we are on the cruise, and I'll share with you what I know.'

'I should like that,' said the boy, his mouth curling into a hesitant smile. 'We must do lunch.' He then looked down at his book not aware of the amused expression on the writer's face.

Elodie had been advised by the Entertainment Manager to mingle with the audience before her talks, to ask the passengers where they came from, if they were enjoying the cruise, and what places they had seen. This, he told her, is really appreciated and was a useful way of getting the listeners on her side from the start. She approached a couple sitting to the side of the theatre: a slim, elegant middle-aged woman and a distinguished, elderly man, with the face of a Roman senator.

'Good afternoon,' she said.

'Good afternoon,' answered the woman. 'I am so looking forward to your lecture, Dr King. I am a great fan of your books. I was delighted when I learned you were on the ship. Your novels are so perceptive and engaging, the sort of books one has to start re-reading the moment one has finished them.'

'That's most kind,' said Elodie. 'Are you and your husband going ashore at the next port of call?'

'Oh, good gracious,' laughed the woman. 'This gentleman is not my husband. We don't know each other.'

'Well, that can be easily remedied,' she was told. 'May I know your name?'

'Henrietta Easington.'

'And yours?' she asked the man.

'I'm Royston Boulby.'

'Henrietta,' said Elodie, 'may I introduce Royston, Royston may I introduce Henrietta.'

The couple smiled at each other and shook hands.

The theatre was full when the Entertainment Manager took to the stage to introduce the speaker. Elodie stood behind the lectern, resting her hands on the top and looking at ease.

'Good afternoon, ladies and gentlemen,' he said. 'It's good to see such a splendid turnout. I am sure we are in for a most interesting, entertaining and informative talk from a wonderful, renowned speaker.'

'No pressure then,' said Elodie into the microphone.

There was a ripple of laughter from the audience.

'Our special guest,' said the Entertainment Manager, 'is Miss Elodie King. Dr King, I should say. Before I introduce her, I just need to mention that if you wish to purchase one or more of her books, they will be available on sale at the rear of the theatre after the lecture and I am sure she will be willing to sign and dedicate them for you.' He cleared his throat with a small cough and took a small card from his pocket. '"Dr King",' he read, '"has spent a number of years as an academic, lecturing at universities in the United Kingdom and in America. She holds a doctorate in medieval history, is an associate professor and a widely published, best-selling author with over a dozen books to her name. Last year she won the prestigious Donna Elsey Prize for historical fiction".'

Elodie held up a hand and laughed. 'Please, please, don't go on. You will put everyone off. It is most kind of you to give me such a fulsome introduction, Martin, but I am finding this acutely embarrassing.' She looked at the audience and whispered into the microphone. 'He makes me sound like a right old clever dick, doesn't he?' There was more laughter. 'Let me say "Good afternoon" to everyone and thank you for coming to my lecture. After the Entertainment Manager's overgenerous introduction, I cannot wait to hear what I am about to say.'

There was more laughter.

Elodie looked out at the full theatre, row after row of people staring at her and waiting for her to begin. She had read somewhere that most people feared standing up in public and speaking, more than they feared death but she revelled in it.

Relaxed, self-assured, and in full command of the subject, she was in her element in front of an audience. She gave a fascinating account of what it was like to be an author, reading short extracts from her books, punctuated by amusing anecdotes and answering questions adeptly and with assurance.

As she spoke, she noticed Oliver sitting straight-backed on the front row. He didn't laugh and he seldom smiled but he listened with rapt, sympathetic attention to what was being said and on occasions jotted things down in a small black notebook.

Dr King concluded her talk by asking if there were any questions. The first to raise a hand was Edna, who was sitting directly beneath the stage.

'I have a question,' she called out.

'Yes?'

'Could you tell me where you bought your boots from?'

As the audience left the theatre, Elodie noticed that the couple she had introduced to each other were still in their seats and seemed to be getting on extremely well.

'I wanted to come on this cruise because the ship stops at Gibraltar,' Henrietta was explaining. 'My late husband was an officer in the Royal Navy based in Gibraltar. I thought it would be interesting to go and see where he was posted.'

'We had a villa in Mallorca,' Royston told her. 'I sold it when my wife died.' He looked sad. 'She had a lingering illness. I really couldn't face going there alone. I thought I might go and see the place again and remember the good times.'

They were interrupted by the Entertainment Manager.

'I'm sorry to butt in,' apologised Martin, 'but could I please ask you to vacate the theatre. There's a rehearsal of the theatre group in a few minutes. Perhaps you might like to continue your conversation in the Rainbow Lounge.'

'If this good lady will do me the honour of joining me,' said Royston.

'I should like that very much,' she replied.

Elodie sat at the table outside the theatre to sign books. Oliver waited until the crowd of passengers had dispersed before he approached her. She was talking to the Entertainment Manager but broke off when she saw the boy, waiting patiently to speak to her.

'Hello Oliver,' she said.

'I very much enjoyed your lecture, Dr King,' he told her. 'I just wanted to tell you.'

'Well thank you very much,' she replied. 'Did you notice if anyone fell asleep?'

'Not one,' he replied. 'It was too interesting.'

As he turned to go, she called him back. 'One moment.' She opened a book and wrote something on the flyleaf. 'This is for you. I hope you enjoy reading it.'

'That's very kind,' he replied, taking the book from her. 'Thank you very much.'

'You've made quite a hit with that young man,' the Entertainment Manager told her. It was clear she had made quite a hit with the audience as well.

9

When Peter had told Katya after the first line dancing class that he thought that things had not gone so badly, it had been an understatement for generally the session had been remarkably well received. Martin had been approached by several passengers who were most complimentary about the class and about Peter in particular. There was just the one complaint – from the woman with the fishy eyes and ear-muffs hair.

'I have to say,' she had told him, stiff with indignation, 'that I was more than a little surprised that I was not taken up on my offer. I am a fully-qualified, very experienced, professional line dancing teacher. I have cups.'

'I'm sorry, you have what?' Martin had asked.

'Awards for my line dancing.'

'Congratulations,' Martin had said tongue-in-cheek.

The woman had carried on, now well into her stride.

'And I have to say that the young man adopting that ridicu-lous mock-American accent was quite unnecessary. Line dancing is a serious business.'

The woman had continued to find fault.

The Entertainment Manager had listened to her grumbles, and going into role, nodded sympathetically and gave her his full attention. Then with the fixed smile, he had told her that he was disappointed she had not enjoyed the class for it was extremely popular and passengers seemed to have enjoyed it. In fact, numbers had increased.

'I should explain,' he had continued with his set smile, 'that unless you have the appropriate liability insurance, you are not allowed to teach a class on the ship. Of course, if you happen to be fully covered for work on a cruise ship, I will have a word with the dance tutors and see if something could be arranged.' This was something he had no intention of doing. She departed, muttering under her breath.

Martin had heard no more from the disgruntled passenger. He did, however, have to smile when he saw her later in the cruise hobbling along the quayside. She had sprained her ankle attempting the Argentine tango at the ballroom dancing class.

Word soon circulated around the ship that the line dancing activity was good fun and the male instructor, in particular, was excellent. Apart from a couple of old hands who felt the class was too basic and beneath them, everyone who had attended the first session turned up for the subsequent ones and they were supplemented each time by a good number of newcomers.

Peter, in his too-tight denim jeans (which restricted him from executing anything too exacting on the dance floor) checked shirt, kerchief and bright blue, wide-brimmed straw cowboy hat, gathered the group about him with Katya posing by his side. His accent seemed to have undergone a transformation since the first session for he now sounded like someone from the Australian outback.

'G'day folks,' he said. 'What a beaut turnout it is this morning for a bonzer shindig with me, fair dinkum Pete and snake hips Katya. I see there are a few new faces here this morning. If you've not line-danced before, no worries, we'll show you the ropes and soon have you a-steppin' and a-struttin', a-stridin' and a-stompin'.'

Katya sighed inwardly but retained the frozen smile on her face.

'Now today, folks,' said Peter, 'we're goin' to learn the "Nut-bush", a line dance which is popular Down Under.'

'Down under where?' asked Maureen.

'Australia,' Peter informed her. 'It's all the rage in the out-back. Why even the kangaroos are doing it.'

'He's such a card, isn't he?' said Sandra to Katya.

'Oh yes, he's that all right,' she replied tartly.

At the end of the class a gaggle of elderly ladies, including Sandra and Maureen, surrounded Peter to tell him how much they were enjoying the session and how good he was at teaching the steps. Katya had been cornered by a grey-bearded pensioner who had not been all that steady on his feet, to be asked if she could give him a few private lessons to get him up to scratch. She had politely declined.

The Entertainment Manager had surreptitiously observed the session and been pleased to see how popular it had been. He nodded with obvious appreciation of the efforts of Peter. As the dancers departed, he approached the instructors, all smiles.

'Well done,' he congratulated them. 'You two are definitely drawing in the crowds. Victims of your own success. It appears you have a few groupies, Peter.'

Katya grimaced.

Peter smiled.

'Now, since your classes have been so successful and numbers have increased, it occurs to me that that we could offer an extra session.'

'What!' Katya exclaimed.

'And you might like to continue teaching the line dancing on the next cruise. You two make a first-class team. What do you think?'

'I'm up for it,' replied Peter.

His colleague remained in stunned silence.

The Entertainment Manager had recognised the stooped passenger with the long, gaunt face, drawn and lined, shambling through the Rainbow Lounge. He had seen him board the ship in Southampton and avoided making contact. It had been over twenty years since he had last seen Mr Seaton, his former teacher, pacing up and down at the front of the classroom like a caged lion, snarling at the pupils and making scathing comments. Martin had not been a high-flyer at school. He was not one of the bright boys in the top stream who had received more attention from their teachers than the less able pupils, such as the likes of him. He had been an average scholar, one of the unremarkable majority, the big hump in the academic bell, but he had been well-behaved and tried his best and he had been popular with his peers. The man he now saw, he had hated. His heart had begun to beat as he recalled the treatment he had suffered at his hands. The teacher had been a bully who liked the sound of his own voice; a lazy, pompous, cynical man who had no business being in charge of children. Martin recalled many occasions when he and some of his classmates had been humiliated by Mr Seaton, but one had remained vividly in his mind, the time he had written an essay on what he wanted to be when he left school. He was eleven and had recently started at the secondary school, excited and keen and had spent a deal of time writing about his dream to travel the world, see exciting places, meet different people. His composition had been torn from his exercise book and he had been told his effort was drivel, badly written and full of mistakes.

By nature, Martin had been a cheerful and biddable child, so it was out of character for him to answer back but on that occasion, he had been so incensed and felt the injustice deeply.

'It's not drivel, sir,' he had replied quietly. 'I spent a long time writing the essay. You shouldn't have torn it up.'

A silence had descended in the classroom. The pupils had stared open-mouthed at the teacher, awaiting the explosion which would inevitably follow. None of the pupils had dared to challenge this teacher.

'How dare you speak to me like that!' Mr Seaton had shouted angrily, his face flushed with anger. 'It *is* drivel, and you will do it again.'

The teacher had then embarrassed Martin in front of the class, telling him there was no chance of him ever realising his fanciful ambition. There had been a mocking curl of the lip.

'You need to lower your sights, lad,' he had told the pupil. The teacher's expression had said it all: this boy would amount to nothing in life.

Under different circumstances, for example if he had come across him in the street after leaving school, Martin might have approached his former teacher and told him some home truths but as the Entertainment Manager, who had to always remain polite and respectful to passengers, however galling or demanding they might be, he knew that this was not the time nor the place to speak to him, so he had ignored him.

It was as Martin was making his way back to his office following the line dancing class, that the man in question approached him.

'Might I have a word?' asked the ex-teacher.

'Of course,' Martin replied coldly.

'You are the entertainment chap, aren't you?'

'The Entertainment Manager.'

'Yes, yes. Well, the thing is, I have been speaking to a couple of the passengers who like me are keen to play bridge. Nothing has been arranged for us. On the last cruise there were two professional bridge players who ran courses.' When Martin didn't reply, the man continued. 'Now it occurred to me, that since nothing has been organised, you could find us a quiet room on the ship where we could meet and play and also to put a notice in the daily newsletter asking like-minded people to join us.'

Face to face with his tormentor, Martin decided that he *would* say something. 'Yes, of course, Mr Seaton,' he replied, stiffening his jaw. He looked directly into the man's rheumy, oyster-coloured eyes.

'Oh, you know my name. That's very impressive. Do you know all the passengers' names?'

'No, but I know yours,' said Martin. He stared him full in the face not angrily, nor with a smile, but with a penetrating and unsettling gaze. 'You used to teach me. Seeing you boarding the ship brought back many memories of when I was in your class.'

'That was some time ago.'

'More than twenty years. My name is Martin Roxby. I guess you don't recognise me.'

Mr Seaton looked up, screwing up his eyes and squinted. 'I have taught so many. I'm afraid I don't remember you.'

'No, but I remember you,' said Martin. 'When I saw you, I was reminded of an essay I once wrote for you in which I said it was my dream to travel the world, visit exotic places and meet interesting people. You told me there was no chance of my ever realising such fanciful ambition and advised me to lower my sights.' He spoke calmly but bluntly like a doctor telling a patient some bad news. 'You told me my essay was drivel.'

'I don't recall,' the man muttered, not meeting Martin's eyes but gazing resolutely ahead. He was clearly ill at ease.

'I do,' said Martin. 'Well, here I am, Mr Seaton, travelling around the world, visiting exotic places, and meeting interesting people and in charge of a large Entertainment Team. I am sure you are pleased that I proved you wrong.' The man's face became flushed. He stared open-mouthed, blinking rapidly and did not utter a word. Martin rather relished the man's discomfort. 'I shall arrange a room for you and the bridge players and put a request in the daily newsletter for interested people to join you as you have requested.' And, without waiting for a response, the boy who had been told that he would amount to nothing in life departed, his buoyant spirits giving his step a lively bounce.

At the "Travelling-Alone Get-Together" a melancholy faced woman of indeterminate age with a heavily lined face and wispy, straw-like hair, sat in the corner of the room. Her eyes were a pale grey and watery like those of fish glimpsed at the bottom of a pond. Sandra came and sat next to her and started chatting.

'Are you all right, dear?' she asked.

Her quiet words belied the deep lines of sadness Sandra could see on the woman's face.

'Don't you want to mingle and meet some people?' she was asked.

She shook her head dully. 'Not really. I'm not keen. I don't mix very well. Never have done. I'm quite happy watching.'

'You might make some new friends.'

'Oh, I don't want any new friends,' answered the woman. 'I'm not a very sociable person.'

Sandra got up to go. 'I'll leave you in peace then,' she said. 'I'm sorry to have disturbed you.'

'No, no,' said the woman, reaching out and touching Sandra's arm. 'You don't need to go. It's kind of you to ask if I'm all right. I don't mean to be unfriendly, it's just that I'm not an outgoing sort of person.'

Sandra sat down again. 'Don't you find it a touch lonely travelling all by yourself with no one to pass the time with?'

'I'm not really alone. I've got my husband with me,' the woman told her. 'I never travel anywhere without him.'

'Then you're not travelling alone?' asked Sandra, looking puzzled.

'No, as I said, I've got my husband with me.'

'Where is he?'

The woman held up a wrinkled hand displaying a large silver ring with a coloured stone. She touched it and gave a slow, wistful smile. 'This is my husband, Eric. When he passed over, I had some of his ashes made into a ring. I wear it all the time. It's a comfort.'

'That's nice,' muttered Sandra.

'I was given a choice of making Eric into a picture frame,' the woman said sadly, 'or a paper weight or bird bath.'

'A bird bath,' repeated Sandra.

'Or I could have had him preserved for posterity in an urn to display on my mantlepiece, but I settled for the ring. You see he can be with me wherever I go.'

It takes all sorts, Sandra thought to herself. She recalled Cyril's words yet again that 'There's nowt as queer as folk.' 'I'm off to hear the concert pianist this afternoon. I wonder if you might like to join me. I hear he's very good.'

'It's kind of you to ask me,' replied the woman, 'but I don't think I'll bother.'

Around the grand piano in the plush Consort Suite twenty or so passengers sat on comfortable, pink upholstered chairs in a half circle waiting for the afternoon recital to begin. Mr Carlin-How listened to the conversation of two passengers who were on the row in front of his.

'The author's talk was wonderful,' one of the women was saying. 'Didn't you think so?'

'Oh yes,' replied the other, 'it was so interesting and entertaining, and full of fascinating information. I've bought her book and shall certainly be getting the others when I get home.'

'It was a whole lot better than the other lecture,' stated her companion. 'It was as dull as ditch water. It's no wonder people fell asleep.'

Mr Carlin-How curled a lip and glowered with irritation. It was undeniable that his lecture had been a failure, he knew that. An unsettling number of his audience had fallen asleep and, apart from the comment by the young boy, he had received no positive feedback. The Entertainment Manager, who hadn't even had the courtesy to introduce him or to listen to his lecture, had been tight-lipped. He had heard that he had given Dr King a most fulsome introduction and remained for her talk and, no doubt, would be singing the woman's praises around the ship. Mr Carlin-How knew it was rather childish of him to harbour such bitterness against the other speaker, but he couldn't help but feel jealous and hard done by. He noticed Oliver, the boy who had thanked him, sitting with his grandparents next to a smartly dressed woman in an acid-green silk dress, bedecked in an assortment of heavy gold jewellery. *I must have a word with that young man*, he thought. The boy displayed more interest in history than most of the students at the college where he taught. At the other end of the row sat the two sisters, one of whom had pointed out to him that his flies had been open during his lecture. He glared at her.

'Can you see the woman at the other end of the row?' Edna asked Miriam, oblivious of the Port Lecturer's icy stare. She had examined the person in question with shameless curiosity. 'Her in the green dress and decorated like a Christmas tree.'

'What about her?'

'Do you remember I mentioned her before we got on board, swanning around in reception as if she owned the ship' – she paused for a telling simile – 'with a face like a smacked bottom.'

'Yes, I recall you said something of the sort, but I didn't take much notice.'

'*You* might not have taken much notice, but you can certainly hear her, bedecked in all that jewellery. Every time she moves, she sounds like a wind charm in a gale.'

During this conversation, Mr Champion had turned to the woman who was the subject of the sisters' discussion and had remarked that there was not a great turnout to hear the concert pianist.

'I beg your pardon?' Mrs De la Mare replied, turning her face to the speaker. 'Were you addressing me?'

'I was just making a general comment,' Mr Champion explained. 'I was saying there are not many people here. I'm surprised the recital isn't more popular.'

'It doesn't surprise *me*,' she pronounced offhandedly. 'I am afraid classical music does not appeal to those of little education or intelligence. The intellectual level of most people in society these days and any appreciation of culture are deplorably low. One only has to view the dross screened on the television to see that.'

Mr Champion sighed inwardly but persevered. 'Do you play yourself?' she was asked.

'I have a Steinway grand.'

Mrs De la Mare was indeed in possession of such an instrument, but she had never been known to touch the keyboard. Giles had inherited the house in which he and his wife lived, from his father (an accomplished pianist) with a music room and the piano.

'I play a little,' said Mr Champion, 'but am not that proficient.' He turned to Oliver. 'My grandson here is quite a talented pianist.'

'Really,' she said, in the sort of absent-minded voice which indicated that she was not paying any attention to him at all. She glanced at her expensive-looking watch.

Chatter in the room ceased when the Entertainment Manager stepped forward to introduce the performer.

'Good afternoon . . . er . . . ' he began but stopped abruptly. He was momentarily lost for words.

His eyes were drawn to a beautiful woman sitting cross-legged on the front row wearing a crimson dress and high-heeled sandals. Her beauty was heightened by her striking green eyes and dark wavy hair. Such a woman had magnetism.

'I'm sorry,' Martin apologised. 'Let me start again. Good afternoon, ladies and gentlemen. It's good to see you here today for what promises to be a magical recital by a renowned maestro and celebrated performer on the keyboard. Please welcome Mr Stanley Mulgrave.' He started the clapping and then took his seat.

The concert pianist made his appearance. Stanley Mulgrave was not most people's idea of what a concert pianist should look like: namely a man with slender, delicate hands, someone tall, distinguished-looking, serious-minded with a sophisticated poise, dressed in a black tailcoat and white bow tie. This pianist was a rotund, bearded little individual with a ruddy complexion, bright brown eyes, and a thick head of woolly chestnut coloured hair. He resembled a benevolent old lion. His mode of dress was a simple white shirt, strawberry coloured cotton trousers and canvas shoes.

Mrs De la Mare's mantra that standards had fallen came to her mind.

'Good afternoon,' he said. 'Thank you for coming to my recital. I shall be playing a varied programme of popular classical pieces and one or two little-known compositions. Should there be a particular favourite of yours that you wish me to play, I should be pleased to do so. Have a word with me afterwards. The first piano piece I shall be playing today is "La Campanella", composed by Franz Liszt, who is one of my favourite composers. Liszt was a child prodigy who became the greatest piano virtuoso of his time. At nine years old, he was performing in concert halls. As an adult, he toured extensively throughout Europe and his recitals evoked such frenzies that it was reported that women threw their undergarments at him during his concerts. I would ask you to refrain from doing the same during my recital.'

The audience tittered.

'My second piece,' continued Mr Mulgrave, 'is part of Charles-Valentin Alkan's "Concerto for Solo Piano". Alkan was another child prodigy. He entered the Conservatoire de Paris at an unusually early age and studied both piano and organ. At his piano audition in 1820, when he was nearly seven, the examiner commented that, "This child has amazing abilities." I shall then play Chopin's haunting and continuous "Nocturne in A Minor". This composer, perhaps the most famous of the three, was another child star; he was writing and composing poetry at age six and performed his first public concerto at age eight. I am sure you will be familiar with this piece. I now invite you to sit back as I take you into a world of the most breathtaking music.'

Mr Mulgrave sat at the piano, scratched his woolly head, stared for a moment at the keys to compose himself and then he began to play. His musical dexterity was astonishing. He concluded his recital with a stirring rendering of part of Schumann's "Piano Concerto in A Minor" which generated effusive applause.

Following the performance, the concert pianist chatted amiably to members of his appreciative audience and signed CDs. Mrs De la Mare waited until the queue had died away and then approached.

'Shall I dedicate the disc for you?' asked Mr Mulgrave.

'Thank you, no,' she replied. 'I won't purchase one. I have a large collection of compact discs of classical music featuring the great concert pianists – Ashkenazy, Daniel Barenboim, Myra Hess.'

'Indeed.'

'I merely wanted a word about your performance.'

'My recital?'

'Yes, yes, your recital. I am something of an aficionado of classical pianoforte music.'

'Are you really? Do you play yourself, Mrs . . . ?'

'De la Mare. I have a piano at home, a Steinway grand.'

'A very fine instrument.'

'I hope you won't mind my mentioning this, Mr Mulgrave but, while I thought the Liszt was very competently played, I did feel a little more work is needed with the Chopin. I thought it was rather on the slow side.'

The concert pianist looked at her as if she had grown an extra head. Then he gave a small derisive smile. 'You felt what?' he asked.

'I thought the Chopin could have been a little more *vivace*.'

He shut his eyes momentarily, as if composing himself before he spoke.

'Mrs Mare,' he said, remaining perfectly calm but inside seething, 'as an aficionado of classical pianoforte music and a pianist yourself, with a Steinway grand, you will no doubt be aware that a nocturne features a melancholy mood and a clear melody floating over a left-hand accompaniment of arpeggios or broken chords and must not be rushed.'

'Well, I—' she began.

'And as regards my rendering of the piece, it was said by Stephen Heller, the composer's friend who was a prolific composer for the piano himself, that Chopin never played his works twice in the same way.'

'I was merely—' she began.

'But thank you for giving me the benefit of your opinion. Perhaps at the next recital you may care to demonstrate your extensive knowledge of pianoforte composition on the grand piano here and show me how you think a Chopin nocturne *should* be played.'

'No, no, I have—' she began again, then lapsed into offended silence.

'Come, come, Mrs Mare, don't be modest. You should share your obvious musical expertise and indisputable talent with the passengers. I shall ask, no I shall insist, that at the next recital you play for us.'

Mrs De la Mare stared for a moment and then walked away. She looked around the room for the Entertainment Manager to complain to him about the rude and blatantly sarcastic comments of the concert pianist but Martin had made a quick exit, having gone in search of the woman in the red dress. He found her sitting quietly by herself in the Rainbow Lounge.

'Hello,' he said.

She gave a stunning smile. 'Oh hello.'

'May I join you?'

'Yes, of course.'

'I saw you at the recital. Did you enjoy it?'

'Oh yes, I always do. It doesn't matter how many times I've heard him play, I'm still in awe. He's quite brilliant.'

'You've heard him play before?' asked Martin.

'Many times. Did you not know, I'm with him on the cruise.'

'Oh, I see.' Martin's heart sank.

Having searched unsuccessfully for the Entertainment Manager, Mrs De la Mare went looking for the Purser. She confronted him as he was leaving the reception desk.

'A word, if I may,' she said, blocking his path. Her manner and bearing were stiff and formal.

'Yes, madam?' he enquired, granting her a blithe smile. He was a small man with a shiny bald head and large ears.

'My name is Mrs De la Mare and I occupy the Bermuda Suite.' She waited for the information to sink in and for the Purser to be suitably impressed and deferential to such a VIP, but he seemed indifferent and remained silent and smiling.

'The Bermuda Suite on Deck A,' she repeated abruptly, in an imperious tone of voice.

'Yes, madam,' he said. 'I do know it. How may I be of assistance?'

'As a rather special and valued passenger on this ship,' she told him, 'I had expected that I would have received a request from the Captain by now to join him at his table one evening. No invitation has been forthcoming. Perhaps he was not aware I am on board and ought to be acquainted of the fact. I assume this is an oversight on someone's part.'

'I hope everyone on the ship feels special and valued, madam,' he replied, a smile still set firmly on his face, 'but be sure I will mention your presence to the Captain. I am certain he will want to know you are aboard.' She failed to detect the hint of sarcasm in the tone of his reply.

He could have told her that first-class passengers were likely to receive an invitation to dine with the Captain in due course but remained tight-lipped. He took exception to her manner.

'Please do so,' she said. 'I also wish to lodge a complaint about the concert pianist.'

'For that you will need to speak to the Entertainment Manager.'

'I shall most certainly do that,' she answered and departed.

The Purser shook his head and chuckled. He had met passengers like this one during his many years working on cruise ships, people who considered themselves a cut above the rest, who demanded immediate attention because they had some sort of status, position in life, or lots of money in the bank. He was more amused by them than irritated. He would, of course, ignore the silly woman's request.

10

Elodie found Mr Carlin-How, having finished his lunch, sitting alone in the Galleon Buffet staring out of the window at the vast and empty ocean.

'May I sit here?' she asked, approaching his table, carrying her meal on a tray.

'Yes of course,' the Port Lecturer replied frostily. He stood.

'You looked very pensive.'

'Did I?'

'I admit that I do tend to sometimes get lost in thoughts myself,' she told him.

'If you will excuse me, Dr King,' said Mr Carlin-How pushing his chair beneath the table, 'I have finished my lunch and have things to do.'

'Do call me Elodie,' she replied smiling. 'I was hoping to have a word with you.'

'Oh, yes?'

'I wanted to say how much I enjoyed your lecture.'

'Oh, you attended it?'

He had decided to give her talk a miss, feeling piqued that she had secured a passenger cabin while he had been consigned to the bowels of the ship. He was minded to tell her now of his annoyance but, looking at the friendly, open face before him, he thought it would be churlish to do so.

'Yes, I found what you had to say most interesting,' Elodie said.

He made a face. 'You numbered amongst the few that did,' he told her morosely. 'Most of the audience fell asleep.'

'No, it was just a few. They had probably enjoyed substantial lunches and being in the dark didn't help. Martin advised me not to put off the lights when I gave my talk.'

'Yes, he advised I do the same. I should have listened. Well, I must be away. As I've said, I have things to do.'

'Do please sit down,' she said, her eyes lingering on his face. 'There is so much I wish to talk to you about. I'm sure the things you have to do can wait.'

'Well, er . . . '

'Oh dear, I must sound very bossy. Of course, I won't detain you if you have important business to attend to.'

'I wouldn't say it is *important* business,' he told her.

'So, you could deal with it later?'

'Yes, I suppose I could.'

'Then don't rush off and do come and join me.'

'Very well,' he said. He pulled out the chair and sat down. Her manner, he found, was disarming. *She is making a real effort to be gracious and amiable*, he thought, *and I am acting peevishly*. After all it wasn't her fault about his cabin. His gaze travelled slowly around her face. She was a remarkable-looking woman; the bright eyes, pale porcelain skin and hair glinting copper in the bright sunlight quite captivated him.

'Do you mind if I continue with my lunch?' she asked.

'I beg your pardon?' He had been miles away.

'My lunch. Do you mind if I continue with it?'

'Not at all.'

Mr Carlin-How soon discovered that Elodie was most pleasant company. She was lively and interesting and shared his love of history. They sat for quite a time chatting. He watched intrigued when she had finished her lunch. She dabbed the corners of her mouth with a napkin before folding it into a perfect square. Then she straightened the tray and placed the cutlery carefully together on the plate.

Elodie smiled. 'It drives some people mad,' she told him.

'I'm sorry?'

'I'm a bit of a perfectionist. I have this sort of compulsion to keep things neat and tidy. I can't explain it really because my parents were the untidiest people you might imagine. Perhaps my obsession with tidiness is a reaction to being brought up in a topsy-turvy house. At the university where I work, the professor's room is full of clutter: piles of papers and books all over the floor, half-drunk cups of coffee, a desk covered in pens and broken pencils, bookcases crammed with more books and journals, magazines, and files, his coat and academic gown thrown carelessly on a chair. I don't know how he manages to find anything. It looks as if a bomb has exploded at a jumble sale. I have this urge to straighten the whole place up. I did offer once, but he told me it was the way he liked it and that genius is seldom tidy.'

Mr Carlin-How's face lit up; his eyes were uncannily bright. This charming, considerate, and amusing woman was a kindred spirit. 'Do you know,' he said, 'I feel exactly the same as you. I cannot endure untidiness.'

Martin, the Entertainment Manager discovered Oliver in the Games' Room playing chess with Mr Hinderwell. The boy's face was serious and intent, his forehead creased in concentration.

'Who's winning?' he asked.

'It's stalemate at the moment,' said the cleric. 'My young player here is giving me a run for my money. He has got me in rather a tight corner.'

'I wonder if you are letting me win,' piped up Oliver.

'Not at all,' replied the cleric.

'I thought you might be with the other youngsters,' said the Entertainment Manager to Oliver. 'There are lots of activities for young people going on around the ship: games, competitions, an art class, a craft workshop, table tennis, choir, plenty of sports and there's a disco tonight. We have an excellent Youth Team, and you will be made very welcome. You really don't have to be shy about joining in with the other young people.'

Oliver looked up solemnly and blinked at him. 'I'm not shy,' he answered. 'It's just that these things don't appeal to me. Thank you for your concern, but you don't need to worry about me. I am quite happy and am thoroughly enjoying the cruise and really looking forward to visiting all the different places. It's the reason why I wanted to come on this cruise – to go to Pompeii and Rome.'

'Well, I just thought I'd ask.'

The youngster was like no other he had met on the cruises, Martin thought. The boy speaks in such an adult manner and appears to get along better with grown-ups rather than with his peers. Other boys of his age were running around the deck, making new friends, splashing in the pool, playing games, bubbling with excitement. This one preferred to play chess with an elderly clergyman. He summoned a smile. It takes all sorts, he said to himself, as he thought of the sullen-faced boy, about the same age as this one at the chessboard, he had spoken to. He had asked the teenager if he was looking forward to visiting Pompeii. 'I don't get off the ship,' the boy had answered with a surly pout. 'Who wants to look at boring old ruins?'

'I was wondering,' said Oliver, 'how much does the ship weigh?'

'Oh, in the region of eighty thousand tons,' Martin answered.

'And how many passengers are on board?'

'About two thousand, five hundred. Look, I have just had a bright idea. Would you like to go up on the bridge if I could arrange it? The Captain sometimes allows interested passengers to join him up there. He'll be able to give you the exact details about the ship.'

The boy nodded. 'I should like that very much. Thank you.'

'Well, you drop off your cabin number at the reception desk for me and I'll see what I can do. I'll be in touch.'

When the Entertainment Manager had left, Oliver looked down at the chessboard with a fixed expression and then moved a piece. 'Checkmate, I think,' he said.

The following morning a young ship's officer met Oliver at the reception desk to take him up to the bridge.

'Hello,' he said cheerfully.

'Good morning,' replied the boy, looking at him expressionlessly.

'I'm Roger and will be taking you onto the bridge.'

'What do you do on the ship?' asked Oliver.

'I'm an apprentice deck officer.'

'Does it mean you're in training?'

'Yes, I'm a sort of cadet. I'm learning the ropes.'

'I see.'

'So, you want to be an officer on a cruise ship, do you?' he was asked.

'No,' replied Oliver. 'I have no ambitions to go to sea.'

'I thought—'

'I've not considered a future career. I'm too young to decide what I wish to do and am keeping my options open. It's just that I am interested in the ship.'

Strange lad, thought the young officer.

Soon they were on the bridge of the ship. Oliver had been told not to touch anything, a warning he thought to be quite unnecessary.

'Excuse me, sir,' said the apprentice deck officer to the master of the *Empress of the Ocean*, colouring a little, 'this is the boy who is interested in hearing how the ship works.' He was in awe of the Captain since his first social blunder on joining the ship.

When he had first boarded, the apprentice deck officer, wet behind the ears, had made the great mistake of calling the Captain by his first name. The other officers, who had over-heard, had tried to hide their amusement.

'Tell me,' the Captain had said to him, 'are we related?'

'Well, no,' the young man had replied.

'Are we friends by any chance?'

'No.'

'Are we married?'

The apprentice deck officer's face had turned crimson.

'N . . . n . . . no . . . ' he had stuttered.

'Then when you speak to me,' the Captain had told him, 'you call me "sir".'

'Yes, sir, sorry sir,' the young man had replied, giving a salute.

Now on the bridge, the Captain shook Oliver's hand. 'So, young man,' he said, 'you wanted to know about the ship.'

'Yes, please, sir,' answered Oliver. 'I keep a notebook you see, and I like to record things of interest. It's good of you to let me come up here.'

'It's a pleasure. So, how are you enjoying the cruise?'

'So far so good,' replied the boy, sounding like someone well beyond his years. 'I am very much looking forward to visiting Pompeii and Rome and I think Gibraltar will be very interesting.'

'Well, let me tell you a little about the *Empress of the Ocean*,' the Captain told him. 'The ship is eighty-eight thousand, four hundred and seven tons, it is ninety-one feet in length, has two thousand, five hundred and fifteen passengers aboard and nearly nine hundred crew. This is a very popular cruise and there isn't a spare cabin. Here on the bridge, which is at the front of the ship or the forward and on the upper deck, we have a clear view ahead and it is here that the direction and speed of the ship are managed as well as other functions of the vessel. The Staff Captain there, is the head of the Deck Department. He knows everything there is to know about the ship. On the bridge this morning is the Safety Officer, an important member of the crew. The First Officer sitting at the computer, oversees the navigation of the vessel. The high-tech computer equipment controls and reports on the ship's mechanical, electronic and communications systems. It also shows us our global position and the route to our next destination and provides information about any other vessels we might come across at sea.' The Captain stopped. 'Is this a bit too technical for you?' he asked.

'Not at all, sir,' replied Oliver. 'It seems a very sophisticated system.'

The Captain and the First Officer exchanged amused glances.

'Have you any questions?' asked the Captain.

'Yes,' replied Oliver. 'If you wanted to contact the other ship that we can see on the horizon, say in case of an emergency, I guess you would use a radio.'

'Yes, that's right.'

'But what if the radio doesn't work or there's interference or if the radio operator on the other ship couldn't speak English.'

'That would be tricky. I would have to stand on the top deck with a megaphone and shout, "Ahoy there"!' There was a touch of mischief dancing in the corners of the Captain's mouth.

'I don't think so,' said Oliver, giving an impish grin. 'I think you are pulling my leg.'

'You are quite right,' laughed the Captain. *What a surprisingly mature young man,* he thought, *with his lack of boyishness.*

He could not imagine him larking about or behaving as most boys of his age are supposed to do. 'If, for some reason, the radio message isn't getting through, signals can be sent by flag hoist, signal lamp or flag semaphore. There is a wide variety of maritime flags used for signalling.'

'Like the one Nelson used at Trafalgar,' stated Oliver. '"England expects that every man will do his duty".'

'Exactly. We have what is called the "International Code of Signals" which is used by vessels to communicate important messages regarding safety of navigation and related matters. I'll give you a copy and then you will be able to understand what a flag on a ship signifies.'

'Thank you, I should like that,' replied Oliver.

'You may be puzzled,' said the Captain, 'by what the member of the crew is doing, looking out to sea with the binoculars.'

'I guess he's there to make sure there is nothing in the water ahead, things which may get caught in the ship's propellers,' answered Oliver.

'That's correct,' replied the Captain smiling at the response of this precocious child. 'So, you see, everyone on the ship has a certain assigned task, various responsibilities and duties.'

Oliver nodded and thought for a moment. 'So, what exactly do you do, sir?' he asked the Captain.

Mrs De la Mare, on her way for lunch in the exclusive Diamond Grill, caught sight of the woman who she had met on the sun deck; the small, talkative woman with the thick wavy hair. She immediately swivelled around not wishing to get into conversation with her, only to come face-to-face with the concert pianist.

'Ah, Mrs Mare,' he said, smiling like a hungry vampire about to sink its teeth into a victim, 'the very person I wished to see.'

'I can't stop. I'm rather in a hurry and—' she began hastily but was cut off.

'I shall be rehearsing for tomorrow's recital at the grand piano this afternoon in the Consort Suite,' he told her. 'If you would care to come along you can practise your piece.'

'My piece?' she repeated.

'I thought we had agreed that you would delight us with a rendering of a nocturne by Chopin and show me how you feel it should be played.' She was lost for words. The dripping sarcasm was not lost on her. 'So, until this afternoon then,' he said, before walking away smiling. Needless to say, Mrs De la Mare did not make an appearance at the grand piano in the Consort Suite the following afternoon, nor did she attend any more piano recitals.

That evening she sat at a table for one in the Diamond Grill thinking about the confrontation. She considered having another word with the Entertainment Manager about the conduct of the concert pianist but reflected that perhaps she had been rather indecorous in criticising his playing. This was not the first occasion she had said something which she later regretted. However, she determined to go in search of the Purser to enquire about the invitation to the Captain's table which had so far not been forthcoming. As she sipped her vermouth in the crystal glass before dinner, she glanced around the restaurant relieved to see that the rough-and-ready couple who had dined there before were not to be seen. On the next table sitting alone was an elegant, middle-aged woman dressed in an expensive chartreuse-coloured dress and wearing delicate peridot earrings and a matching pendant. She also wore a spectacular ring set with a large red stone surrounded by diamonds. Her make-up was faultless, her long nails were impeccably manicured and not a hair on her head was out of place. She listened with interest as the woman, having finished her meal, got up to go. In a genteel accent, she thanked the waiter. *This is the sort of passenger I should meet,* thought Mrs De la Mare, *someone stylish and cultured who, no doubt, shared her opinions.* When the woman passed her table, Mrs De la Mare made her move.

'Good evening,' she said, affecting a rather cut-glass accent.

The woman stopped and examined the speaker for a moment before replying. 'Good evening.' She gave a polite if somewhat forced smile.

'Are you enjoying the cruise?' enquired Mrs De la Mare.

'Very much, thank you,' replied the woman. 'There is so much to do and so many places to see. We are very fortunate, are we not, to have the opportunity of such an experience.' She made to go but Mrs De la Mare detained her.

'Have you cruised before?' she was asked.

'This is only my second but it certainly will not be my last.'

'Will you be going ashore?'

'But, of course. I am so looking forward to visiting Rome. It's such a wonderful city.'

'Oh, I don't imagine I will venture ashore in Rome,' said Mrs De la Mare.

'Not venture ashore?' the woman repeated, sounding surprised.

'The heat will be quite unbearable. I have decided to remain on the ship.'

'My dear lady, you must visit Rome. I think it was Lord Byron who said it is the city of the soul.'

'I have visited Rome before,' Mrs De la Mare informed her.

'One can never see enough of Rome.'

'To be honest, I find it a rather oppressive place.'

'I see. Well, if you will excuse me,' said the woman, thinking what an odd person this was, 'the Italian tenor is singing this evening in the theatre, and I am eager to hear him.'

'I do hope we might catch up with each other before the end of the cruise. My name is Frances De la Mare, by the way.'

'I am Lady Staithes,' came the reply.

The theatre was full for the performance of Lorenzo Barritino. The Italian tenor was a small, tubby man with thick black curls slicked back in rippling waves, high cheekbones, and large dark eyes. In his youth he would have been a striking looking man with his brilliant white, even teeth, olive skin and green eyes. Now in middle-age, he had put on a few pounds in weight, dyed his greying hair and had his teeth capped. The exotic olive colouring had faded. His voice, however, had, if anything, improved with age and he had become a celebrated performer in his home country and abroad. His repertoire that evening included several popular songs and some classical favourites. He finished the concert with a stirring rendering of "Che gelida manina" by Puccini and was rewarded with enthusiastic clapping. As Signor Barritino basked in the reaction of his audience, his eyes were suddenly drawn to a man sitting in the middle of the front row who didn't clap once but stared fixedly ahead of him. The tenor was rather unnerved by this but continued to bow several times before leaving the stage. There were continued clapping and shouts of "Bravo, Bravo" and "Encore! Encore!" from the audience. Signor Barritino returned to the stage, bowing and beaming. His eyes were immediately drawn again to the same stony-faced man in the middle of the front row. At the conclusion of the concert his singing of "Nessun Dorma" was received with tumultuous applause. Several in the audience got to their feet to clap. The man on the front row, however, did not clap once but maintained the unsmiling expression.

Off stage the Entertainment Manager rushed up to congratulate the singer on the success of the concert.

'I think you could tell from the response of the passengers how well your performance was received,' he said. 'It was outstanding. Everyone so much enjoyed it.'

'Nota everyone,' answered Lorenzo, waving his hand in a dramatic gesture. 'There was a man ona the front row, he no clap me once. Not once. How you say, I give my all, onea hundred and tena per cent and I geta not one clap. I singa in the great opera houses of the world – the Teatro alla Scala in Milan, the Metropolitan Opera House in New York, the Royal Opera House in London. I singa before the Pope in Rome and he clap me. The Holy Father himself he claps me but this man, he don'ta clap me one time.'

The Entertainment Manager rested a hand on the singer's shoulder. 'Look, Lorenzo,' he said, 'I have worked on cruise ships long enough not to try and understand the behaviour of some of the passengers. Most are really appreciative and full of praise for the excellent service, the superb meals, the top-class entertainment and the amazing places we visit, but there is always someone for whom nothing is right.' He thought of Mrs De la Mare who had been to see him about the concert pianist before tackling the Restaurant Manager to complain about the lowering of standards in the Diamond Grill. He had told her politely that he would mention her complaints. Of course, he did no such thing. 'They make complaining an art form,' he continued. 'They delight in fault-finding. Nothing seems to please them. I have learned to take their criticisms in my stride and not let them get to me. I suggest you do the same and ignore the man. Your performance was outstanding.'

But the Italian tenor could not take such a snub in his stride. It niggled him, so when he saw the passenger in question sitting on a bar stool in the Jolly Sailor Tavern later that evening, he approached him.

'Oh hello,' said the man cheerfully. 'Can I get you a drink?'

'No, no, thank you,' said Lorenzo. He puffed out his chest like a turkey. 'You camea to my concert.'

'I did and very much enjoyed it.'

'You enjoyed it?' Lorenzo looked puzzled.

'Oh yes indeed. I thought your singing was wonderful. You have a superb voice. It was a real treat to hear you.'

'But you no clap me.'

'No.'

'Why you no clap me?'

'I've only got the one arm,' explained the man.

11

The *Empress of the Ocean* arrived in Cádiz, the first port of call. Most excited about the visit was Mr Carlin-How. Dressed in a stylish pale blue linen jacket with a silk handkerchief spilling flamboyantly from his breast pocket, pristine, white cotton razor-creased trousers, and smart espadrilles, he was the first to get off the ship keen to take the coach to Seville and explore the city. He had invited Elodie to accompany him, but she was keen to remain in Cádiz for the morning to undertake some research for her new book and travel to Seville later that day. They agreed to meet later in the Jolly Sailor Tavern for a pre-dinner drink.

Having visited the Basilica de la Macarena, Seville Cathedral and La Gironda and viewed the extraordinary Mudejar, Gothic and Renaissance architecture, the Port Lecturer wandered along the tiny streets of Barrio Santa Cruz, dotted with orange-tree-filled plazas, taking photographs and buying postcards. He then rested in a quiet, shady corner on a tiled bench. He sighed with pleasure, closed his eyes, and felt the sun on his face. His peace was disturbed by the arrival of the two sisters.

'We thought it was you,' said Edna bustling up and sitting next to him. She parked her walking frame and sat down. 'We're not disturbing you, are we?'

'No, not at all,' he lied.

'Budge up, will you, and let my sister sit down,' she said.

He did as he was instructed. 'Are you not seeing something of the city?' he enquired, hoping they might soon depart.

'It's too hot,' said Edna, wafting away a fly. 'This heat is enough to blister your eyeballs.'

'The sun is certainly dazzling today,' he admitted, 'but that is to be expected in this part of the world and at this time of year.'

'I'm roasting,' she moaned.

'Now I am sure you would complain if it were pouring down with rain,' he told her.

'I'm sure a bit of rain would be very welcome,' she remarked. 'You know what they say, an hour's steady rain would do more good in a week now, than a week's rain would do a month later on.'

'Well, there's no answer to that,' uttered the Port Lecturer, baffled by the observation.

'It's too dry and dusty,' persisted Edna, 'and far too hot and there's all these wretched flies.' She waved her hand again.

'It *is* mid-summer,' said Mr Carlin-How, making a visible attempt to summon up a greater degree of attentiveness. 'One must expect such heat in southern Spain at this time of year.'

'I shall have to do something about my head,' Edna announced absent-mindedly, clearly not listening.

'What's wrong with it?' asked her sister. 'You haven't got one of your migraines coming on, have you?'

'No, I haven't. When I say, I shall have to do something about my head, I mean I shall have to cover it up.'

'Cover up your head?' asked Mr Carlin-How. He thought of her with a large brown paper bag over her head and smiled unkindly.

'What do you mean cover your head up?' asked Miriam.

'I mean it's too hot.'

'Your head is too hot?'

'No, the weather is too hot.'

'What you mean is you need a hat?'

'Yes, I should think that's self-evidential,' announced Edna. 'I'll wait until we're in Mallorca to buy one there. I'm not wandering around Seville in this heat.'

The Port Lecturer made his escape. 'Well, I shall have to make tracks,' he said. 'Enjoy the rest of your day.'

'He's very dapper, isn't he,' remarked Miriam. 'Those smart pumps and the way he pulls up his trousers at the knees before he sits down, are sure signs of good breeding.'

'Yes, Mr Ellerby used to do that,' observed her sister. 'I will admit that Mr Double-barrelled does scrub up well but he's well short of handsome and likes the sound of his own voice and he's certainly not one to underestimate himself.'

As Edna continued to consider the failings of the Port Lecturer, Cyril, Connie and Sandra were strolling around the bustling streets before sitting in the San Lorenzo Plaza, shaded by banana trees, to listen to a street guitarist play flamenco music. They then took a horse-drawn carriage around the city and ate tapas at a plush pavement restaurant overlooking the river.

'Enjoyin' yerself, Sandra?' Cyril asked.

'Oh, yes,' she replied. 'It's wonderful.'

'It is, it's wonderful,' echoed Connie.

'So, are you up for comin' wi' us in Mallorca?' asked Cyril.

'That's most kind, but I don't want to impose.'

'Don't talk daft,' laughed Cyril, 'it'll be a pleasure to 'ave you wi' us, won't it, Connie?'

'A pleasure,' echoed his wife.

'Look, isn't that the young man from the ship?' Sandra suddenly piped up.

Oliver was walking down the street as if in a hurry. He looked smart in his linen trousers and a loose plain white shirt. The straw trilby-style hat was perched on his head.

Cyril called out. 'Are you lost?'

Oliver stopped, looked around and seeing some fellow passengers from the ship went to join them.

'Hello,' he said.

'We was wonderin' if you was lost,' asked Cyril.

'No, I'm not lost,' replied the boy. 'I have a map.'

Having studied the guidebook the evening before, he had planned his trip to Seville, circling the places he wished to visit and devised the route. He had assured his grandparents, who were anxious about his visiting the city alone, that he would be fine. He had his passport, sufficient money, an emergency number and assured them that he would be careful and would get a taxi back to the ship should he get lost.

'Are you by yourself?' asked Sandra.

'Oh yes,' replied Oliver. 'My grandparents are on a coach tour of the city, but I didn't want to join them. I prefer to see the sights myself. I'm off to visit the Real Alcázar Palace.'

'Would tha like to join us fer a drink, young man?' asked Cyril.

'No thank you. I have some water in my rucksack. Well, I must make tracks. I've much yet to see.'

''E's a grand little lad, isn't 'e?' said Cyril as he watched the boy stride off.

'He is,' agreed his wife, 'a grand little lad.' She thought that had she been blessed with a child of her own, it would have been nice to have had a son like Oliver.

On the journey back from Seville, Elodie sat with Oliver.

'Do you mind me sitting here?' she asked the boy.

'Not at all,' he replied. 'I was hoping to bump into you, Dr King. I thought you might be on the coach to Seville this morning, but I didn't see you.'

'No, I took a later coach to Seville. I spent the morning in Cádiz.'

'I enjoyed your book,' said Oliver.

'You've read it already?'

'Oh yes. I couldn't put it down. I had a bit of a rest from the Dickens. You really bring history to life and tell a rattling good story. I thought I knew quite a bit about the Tudors, but you know so much more, and you make it really interesting.'

'Well, I'm pleased you enjoyed it,' she said. 'So, what did you think of Seville?'

'It was tip-top,' replied the boy, his eyes bright with enthusiasm. He reached into his pocket and produced his small notebook and consulted a page. 'I went to the Real Alcázar Palace, the Casa de Murillo and the cathedral. I saw the tomb of Christopher Columbus and watched some flamenco dancing in the Plaza de España. There was so much to see. I couldn't fit it all in.'

She looked around. 'Are your parents not with you?'

'My parents are dead,' Oliver told her. 'They were killed in a car crash when I was small.' He didn't appear to exhibit any emotion but stared ahead fixedly.

'Oh dear,' said Elodie. 'I am so sorry.' She put her hand on his arm and rested it there.

'Of course, I miss not having a mother and a father,' he said in a matter-of-fact tone of voice. 'I think about them every day.' He was quiet for a moment. 'I never really knew them. I have pictures of them, of course, and my grandparents tell me about them. I often wonder what my parents would have been like. I guess my mother would have spoiled me, as most mothers tend to do with their sons, and my father would be full of advice, the sort of guidance a father would give to a son. I miss that. I used to watch the boys at school and wish I had parents like them. My grandparents have brought me up and they do their best but it's not the same as having a mother and a father.'

'I'm sure they would have been enormously proud of you,' Elodie told him.

'I hope so,' he replied. 'I'm on the cruise with my grandparents. They know how interested I am in history and this trip is my birthday present. They are getting on in life, so they didn't feel like going into Seville in all the heat and doing a lot of walking.'

'You went around the city by yourself?' she asked, sounding surprised.

'Yes.'

'How old are you, Oliver.'

'I'm twelve, going on thirteen.'

'It was very brave of you to go into Seville on your own.'

'Not really. I had a map. I'm quite an independent person.'

'I'm impressed. There's not many boys of your age who would have gone around a busy foreign city by themselves.'

'I'm not like other boys, Dr King,' he replied. *No*, she thought, *you are not.* 'Did *you* have an interesting day?'

'I did,' Elodie replied. 'I had a wonderful morning in Cádiz and spent the afternoon in Seville. I'm writing a novel set at the time of Elizabeth I and wanted to do some research about the attacks against the Spanish during her reign. Cádiz was one place that was raided. I am sure you have heard of Sir Francis Drake.'

'Yes, he defeated the Spanish Armada,' said Oliver.

'He didn't defeat the Armada single-handedly, although some history books make out that he did,' explained Elodie, 'but he played an important part.'

'My history teacher told us that he was playing bowls, with the Spanish Armada in sight, and he said that Drake said that he had time to finish the game and lick the Spaniards too.'

'When you study history in some depth, Oliver,' Elodie told him, 'you will find there has been a great deal of hearsay; there are lots of myths and legends. Drake probably knew that there was plenty of time to finish his game. With the tide flooding into Plymouth Sound and a stiff south-west breeze blowing, no British ship could have left the harbour until the tide ebbed. I hope I'm not boring you.'

'Not at all,' replied the boy. 'It's really interesting.'

In the lecture theatre at Oxford weeks' later when she looked at the faces of the students, many of whom appeared less than interested, she visualised this earnest young man's shiny face as if it had just been scrubbed and his wide-eyed wonder.

'In 1587,' she continued, 'Drake led a raid on Cádiz. You see the Spanish were getting ready to invade England and were building up a great fleet of ships. They were assembling in the Bay of Cádiz. I visited it today. It was thrilling for a historian to see exactly where Drake led the daring expedition and destroyed or captured over a hundred Spanish vessels.'

'He must have been very brave.'

'He was a dare-devil and took a great risk and he was a bit of a show-off. When he got back to England, he boasted that he had "singed the King of Spain's beard".'

'My teacher at school told us about it,' Oliver told her. 'He said Drake was a pirate.'

'He was right, but the queen turned a blind eye because he brought her chests of Spanish treasure and kept the Spanish navy in check. He was known in Spain as *El Draque*. King Philip of Spain offered a reward of twenty-thousand ducats for his capture. That's about six million pounds in modern currency.'

'I should have liked to have seen where his ships sailed into the harbour.'

'And a little over two hundred years later just off Cádiz,' Elodie continued, 'Admiral Nelson won a decisive victory at the Cape of St Vincent and captured two French warships.'

'He was killed by a French sniper at Trafalgar, wasn't he?'

'Yes, he was. When we get to Gibraltar you might like to visit the Trafalgar Cemetery where two of the officers killed in the battle are buried.'

'Yes, I shall do that.'

'I can tell you like history, Oliver,' she said.

'It's one of the subjects I do enjoy at school. I tend to be a bit of an all-rounder, but history is my favourite.'

She guessed he would be a bit of a loner too, this serious little boy with the intense expression and grown-up way of speaking.

'My history teacher, Mr Ruswarp, is very good,' Oliver continued to tell her. 'I like to listen to the stories he tells of the past, of the kings and queens, the great battles, and voyages of exploration. He told us about Drake's expedition. Mr Ruswarp is a bit odd, overweight with a bushy beard and a roar like a lion and when he shouts his false teeth wobble. Of course, some of the boys find him a bit strange and make fun of him behind his back. He ties his trousers up with a piece of string and wears open-toed sandals in winter. He is a bit eccentric, I suppose, but I like him.'

'The enthusiasm of an eccentric teacher has an enormous influence on pupils, and it makes a lasting impression,' Elodie told him. 'Many a good teacher, in my opinion, tends to be a bit out of the ordinary. Don't you agree?'

Oliver thought for a minute. 'Yes, I do. It's not a bad thing to be a bit different, is it Dr King?'

'No, it isn't. Throughout history, many men and women who have been labelled different or eccentric during their lifetimes have gone on to be seen by later generations as amazing people, with originality and vision. Some think them arrogant, outspoken and opinionated, unconventional people who didn't care what others thought of them and who didn't stick to the rules. I reckon Drake and Nelson were a bit like that.'

She found she was talking to the boy as if to one of her students at the university where she lectured.

'The boys at school don't really take to me because *I'm* a bit different,' Oliver told her. 'I guess they think that *I'm* outspoken and opinionated. I don't have any friends, but I am not that bothered. I like my own company.'

'Are you bullied, Oliver?' she asked.

'I am, but I just ignore the bullies.' When he was taunted or laughed at by his classmates, Oliver never got angry or showed that he was upset, because he knew that is what bullies enjoyed. He remained cool and distant, and they soon tired of trying to provoke him and looked for another victim to torment.

'Bullies are sad and ignorant people,' she told him.

'Of course, my red hair doesn't help,' Oliver said, thinking of the pimply faced boy on the ship. 'At school they call me silly names like "Brick-top", "Carrots", and "Copper-nob". It's very childish. I take no notice of them.'

'Foolish people have always joked or said unpleasant things about those of us with red hair,' Elodie told him. 'It's a bit out of the ordinary. I was called names at school too because of the colour of my hair but I am proud of it. And do you know why some people say cruel things about red-headed people?'

'No.'

'It's because there is a superstition surrounding people with red hair, the misguided belief that Judas had red hair. It was thought to be unlucky to have a sailor with red hair aboard a ship. He was regarded as a jinx. Silly prejudice isn't it and rather ironic because Drake had ginger hair and Nelson had a thick shock of bright red hair when he was young. Both these sailors were different from those around them – risk takers, tenacious men of independent views.' She was talking as if the listener were an educated adult and not a small boy. 'A lot of great historical figures were the same: people who were unusual, out of the ordinary, who didn't always follow the rules: Boudica, Galileo, Leonardo da Vinci, Christopher Columbus, Henry VIII, Catherine of Aragon, Elizabeth I, Oliver Cromwell, Catherine the Great, Van Gogh, and the men we were talking about – Sir Francis Drake and Admiral Nelson. And do you know something, Oliver, they all had red hair, so you and I are in good company, aren't we?'

The boy nodded. 'Yes, I guess we are,' he said thoughtfully.

In Oliver, Elodie recognised so much of herself. When she was his age, like him, she had been regarded as something of an oddity, old beyond her years, extremely bright ('too clever by half', some of her teachers had remarked), fascinated by history, a child who showed little interest in what her peers were getting up to or what they thought of her. Everything about this bright-eyed, red-headed girl with the sharp, curious mind and her candour, spoke of her set-apartness. And like Oliver's experience, her unusual carroty frizzy hair, didn't help. But there was nothing shy or humble about her; she was disconcertingly confident and self-contained which, of course, did not endear her to some of her teachers or to her classmates. She guessed Oliver experienced the same sort of thing at his school. Elodie recognised in the boy the same strength of character, determination and self - confidence, the unwillingness to let the tormenting get to him. He was like her too – a rare being who had an unconcerned disregard of how others viewed him or expected him to lead his life. She often wondered what her future would have been like if the people around her could have accepted how different she was, not bully her and laugh at her appearance and her quirks, understand that being out of the ordinary was something special and to be valued.

She had never harboured any doubt that she would be accepted when she applied to study at Oxford. She knew she had performed well on the entrance paper and regarded the interview as a mere formality.

'Don't be too disappointed if you're not accepted,' Miss Liverton, the headmistress had told the sixth-former begrudgingly when Elodie had informed her that she had been called for interview. The headmistress's tone of voice had been far from reassuring. She had been unsuccessful in gaining a place at Oxford when she was Elodie's age, had never liked this headstrong pupil and had hoped that she would not be accepted. In her opinion, the girl needed knocking down a peg or two.

'So, what are you reading at the moment?' the Oxford don had asked Elodie at her interview. He had leaned back in his chair and had smiled like a shark.

'*Watership Down*,' she had replied.

He had raised an eyebrow. 'A children's book?'

'Is it?' she had asked, looking into his eyes.

'Is it not? A story about talking rabbits?'

'Have you read it?' Elodie had asked.

The tutor had continued to smile. He was used to asking the questions and not answering them. 'Well, no, actually, I haven't.'

'Then how are you in a position to make the assumption that it is a children's book? I wonder if you regard *Animal Farm,* with the talking animals, as a children's book, or *Metamorphosis* by Franz Kafka.'

'You have read Kafka?' He had leaned forward and sat up, intrigued by this self-possessed young woman.

'Yes. Have you?'

'Yes, I have read Kafka.'

'And you don't think this book is for children?'

She had met his gaze. 'No.' The tutor leaned back in his chair again. 'What do imagine *Metamorphosis* is about?'

She had considered the question and eventually responded. 'I think the point of the story is that conflict and confrontation don't make us tougher. In fact, they make us weak and pitiful.'

The lecturer had sat up again and grinned. 'Do you consider yourself to be clever, Miss King?' he had asked.

'Do you mean that I'm too full of my own importance?' She had given a small, wry smile.

'No, I mean do you think you are intelligent, knowledgeable, someone who can tackle challenging ideas.'

'Well, I have a good memory and feel I can communicate my opinions well. Of course, you will be the judge of that. I do tend to pick things up quickly and I can stand my ground in discussions.' She had smiled again and looked intently into his eyes. 'I'm sure that must sound arrogant.'

'Not at all,' he had replied. He had been impressed by this very perceptive and self-assured young woman who had the faculty of seeing to the heart of things and was not afraid of expressing them. An inner light of certainty and confidence had shone in her eyes. Of course, she had been accepted and had gone on to study for her degree. Her tutors were delighted with her. They saw by the jut of her chin and the intensity of her gaze that she was a young woman of determination with an independent and perceptive mind. She had studied to gain a doctorate and had been asked to lecture at her former college.

'Dr King,' Oliver said now, 'could I ask you something?'

'You can, but it depends on the question whether or not I answer you.'

'Are *you* eccentric?'

Elodie threw back her head and laughed so loud the other passengers on the coach looked around. 'Do you know, Oliver, I rather think I am.'

Oliver smiled. His freckled face glowed. 'I think maybe I am too.'

'Well stay as you are,' she told him. 'Don't let people try to change you. Be yourself and continue to take no notice of ignorant things they might say. Put it down to envy. Control of your own life should rest with you. I think you're a very clever, observant, and courteous young man.'

A faint blush of pleasure crept across the boy's face. 'Do you know Dr King,' Oliver told her, giving a small smile, 'we've had a most interesting conversation, haven't we?'

She laughed again. 'We certainly have,' she said. 'We certainly have.'

Back in his cabin later that evening, Oliver reflected on the heart-to-heart with Elodie. 'We are not all made the same,' she had said. 'I think it's good to be different.' She had told him he should be himself and take no notice of the ignorant things people might say. 'Some of the world's greatest minds and bravest people were a bit different.' No one had ever spoken to him like that before, nobody had made him feel so reassured and gladdened, that there were others in the world like him. She had made him feel better about himself. That conversation with the author on the coach back from Seville on a gloriously bright, sunny afternoon would stand out in the boy's mind for long after the cruise had ended and, in some small way, help to change the course of his life. That night he read that part in *Great Expectations* where Pip returns from the visit to Miss Havisham's ruined mansion. It struck a chord.

That was a memorable day to me, for it made great changes in me. But it is the same with any life. Imagine one selected day struck out of it! and think how different its course would have been.

12

That evening Mr Carlin-How met Elodie for drinks in the Jolly Sailor Tavern.

'I hope I'm not being presumptuous,' he said, 'but I hope I might prevail upon you to join me for dinner. I have taken the liberty of booking a table in the L'Epicureo Italian restaurant.'

'I should be delighted,' she replied. 'I love Italian food.'

Something else we have in common, he thought, looking at her over his drink. She could be habit-forming. With her long copper hair cascading over her perfect shoulders, those bright eyes and mischievously arched mouth, she left him spellbound. 'That's splendid,' he managed to say.

'I'm so glad that we have met, Hubert,' she said. 'We have so many shared interests.'

'I feel the same,' he told her beaming.

'Now you must tell me what you did in Seville today and I'm dying to tell you all about my trip to Cádiz.'

Watching them chattering and laughing and exchanging stories, Edna, who was sitting nursing a large gin and tonic, nudged her sister.

'Look at those two, Miriam,' she said.

'Which two, dear?'

'The author and Mr Double-barrelled sat sitting over by the window, billing and cooing like a pair of smitten lovebirds. It didn't take long for those two to get together.'

'I think they're well-suited,' remarked her sister. 'They make a nice couple.'

Edna took a gulp of her drink and thought for a moment. 'Yes, I suppose they do,' she said.

Elodie lay awake in bed the following morning watching as dawn broke and pellucid sunlight filtered through the curtains lighting up the cabin.

She listened to the screeching of the gulls and the slap of the waves against the side of the liner as it made its steady progress to the next destination of Mallorca, and she thought of what her life would now be like. She never imagined when she agreed to lecture on the ship that she would meet someone to whom she would be attracted, someone who was attentive and considerate, who shared her passion for history and had the same preoccupation for tidiness and order. It was clear to her that the attraction was mutual. Having escorted her to her cabin that evening, he had kissed her gently on the mouth before wishing her 'Goodnight.'

Elodie had lived with Adrian, another academic, in what could best be described as a comfortable arrangement. It wasn't a passionate Mr Darcy–Elizabeth Bennet sort of romance, a union of souls, but it had sustained a staying power for they had been together for nearly two years. Neither of them was much bothered about the physical side of things; they just enjoyed each other's company and shared the same interests – music, ballet, opera, the theatre, reading – and both spent much of their time lecturing, attending conferences and seminars, undertaking research and writing books. Neither had mentioned marriage and children, both knowing this was not what either of them wanted at this stage in their careers.

The week before Elodie was due to set sail on the cruise, she decided that she would tell Adrian that she wanted to break off their relationship. It was going nowhere. Of late, he had become increasingly petulant, complaining that those at the university where he worked did not appreciate him and recognise his talent. She had been offered an associate professorship and knew that he would find this difficult to accept. He had been hoping for such a post himself, but none had been forthcoming, and she could well imagine what his reaction would be when she told him of her promotion. He would try not to look surprised at first and congratulate her somewhat half-heartedly, but then resentment would set in. She had secured the post he had so desired and for which he had been passed over. She decided not to tell him. Elodie felt the time was right for her to move on in her life. She had been undertaking research for her latest novel and came across a letter, dated 1560, from Elizabeth I to King Eric XIV of Sweden, who had sought her hand in marriage: 'We do not conceive, in our heart to take a husband,' she wrote, 'but highly recommend the single life.' Elodie thought, as she read the words, that all things considered, a single life for *her* was to be recommended.

They had been uncharacteristically quiet one evening over dinner. Adrian had barely touched the meal and had stared thoughtfully at his half-drunk glass of wine. Elodie had said little, thinking that perhaps he had got wind of her promotion. Perhaps this might be the moment to tell him that she thought their relationship should end.

'Is something on your mind?' she had asked after a while.

'Well . . . er . . . yes, there is actually,' he had replied, looking up. 'There is a matter I need to speak to you about.'

'Oh?'

'I've been meaning to tell you for a few days but there has never seemed to be the right time.'

'Is it another woman?' she had asked calmly.

'God no!'

'What is it then?'

He had taken a deep breath. 'You are aware that I shoot off to the States during the university vacations to run those masterclasses.'

'Yes.' She had taken a sip of wine.

'As I've mentioned before, they value the work I do a great deal more than those at the university here.'

How many times had she heard this gripe, she had thought.

'Well, the thing is, I got a call from the university in Washington last week to ask if I was interested in an associate professorship.'

'I see.'

'It came out of the blue. They are really interested in my research and have offered generous funding. It's a fantastic opportunity, Elodie.' His eyes had lit up. 'I mean I would never get a chair of a faculty over here at the moment. I also got wind that they have offered the associate professorship to someone. It would be waiting to step into a dead man's shoes and there would be so much competition.'

'Yes, I suppose so.'

'Trying to get funding for my research has been well-nigh impossible,' he had told her. 'So, the thing is—'

'You have accepted.'

'Pardon?'

'You have said yes to the associate professorship in America.'

'I have ... er ... yes. It's too good an invitation to turn down.'

'I see,' she had said again.

'I know I should have mentioned it to you before, but we have both been so busy.'

'I'm happy for you.'

'Pardon?'

'I'm sure you will be a great success.'

'Oh.' He had expected rather a different reaction. 'So, you don't mind?'

'Of course I don't mind,' she had replied. 'Why should I mind? As you have said, it's too good an opportunity to turn down.'

'You could come with me.'

'No, Adrian, that would not be possible. I like my work here in Oxford. I feel I am good at it and have my own writing and research commitments.'

'Yes, but you will be waiting for a promotion as I have been. There's greater prospects over in the States.'

She had been minded to tell him that she had been offered the associate professorship he had so coveted but kept it to herself. 'I have no intention of following you halfway across the world away from family and friends and abandoning my career on the off chance of securing a post in America.'

'With your qualifications and references and your published works you would walk into a university position in the States without a problem. I could have a word with—'

She had interrupted. 'It is out of the question. I do wish you well, Adrian. I really do. As I have said, I am sure, you will be highly successful.'

'You're taking this awfully well,' he had answered.

'These things happen,' she had told him. 'Both of us knew our relationship would not last forever. We are not some sort of love story, are we? We have enjoyed each other's company, but I think it is the right time for us to call it a day. Your moving to America has come at an opportune time. Whatever we feel for each other, it isn't quite enough, is it?'

He had lifted his eyes. 'No, I don't suppose it is.' Silence had hung in the air. Adrian had looked genuinely stunned by her response. He might have expected some shock or bewilderment, at the very least that she would have looked a tiny bit sad. One small part of him had thought that she might have begged him to stay. Elodie, however, seemed remarkably composed and not in the least upset. 'Well, I suppose that's it, then.'

'Yes, I suppose that's it,' she had replied.

He had not anticipated this unemotional reaction. He had opened his mouth to continue but then thought better of it and had looked down at his glass. After a moment, he had swallowed a mouthful of wine in an audible gulp, hoping to diffuse the silence that now fell between them.

'Of course, I'll move out of the flat and find somewhere before I fly to Washington at the end of the month,' he had said at last.

'You don't need to do that,' she had told him. 'Next week I shall be away for a fortnight. I think I mentioned that I will be lecturing on a cruise ship.'

There had been an uncomfortable silence.

'I shall miss you,' he had said at last.

'I shall miss you too, Adrian,' she had replied, before taking another sip of wine. There didn't sound much conviction in her voice.

Walking down the deck, chatting to the passengers, the Entertainment Manager came across Edna and Miriam in the Photograph Gallery.

'Good afternoon,' he said brightly.

'Oh hello,' said Edna. 'I was just saying how this picture of us taken by the ship's photographer does us no favours. He's made us look like a pair of old bookends.'

'Speak for yourself,' said Miriam.

'Oh, I don't know,' said Martin, scrutinising the portrait of the two sisters posing by a lifebelt. 'I think it's er . . . er . . .very fetching.'

'Well, I shan't be fetching it home, and that's for sure.'

In truth the Entertainment Manager thought the photograph of two ageing and overweight women in heavy make-up and with tightly permed hair, grimacing at the camera, would never appear in the brochure advertising the delights of cruising.

'Having your walking frame in the picture spoils it,' said Miriam to her sister. 'You should have put it out of sight behind the lifeboat. The sooner you have your hip replaced, the sooner you'll get rid of that damned contraption. You nearly had that poor man with the crutch falling full length over it in the restaurant last night.'

'Now look here—' Edna began.

'So how did you ladies enjoy Lorenzo Barritino's evening concert?' asked Martin, not wishing to be in the middle of a domestic disagreement.

'It was most enjoyable,' answered Edna. 'He has a lovely voice.'

'A lot of Italians do,' said Miriam.

'And he was very striking looking.'

'A lot of Italians are.'

'No, they're not,' contradicted her sister. 'What about Mussolini. He was no oil painting, and I don't suppose he could sing a note.'

'Mind you, he could do with losing a few pounds,' remarked Miriam.

'Mussolini?' said Edna.

'The Italian singer.'

'Yes, he was a bit on the tubby side. That'll be the pasta. They do like their pasta and piazzas the Italians.' She turned to her sister. 'You remember I mentioned Mrs Fattatori, who had the corner shop, she was a size, well-upholstered as our mother, God rest her soul, would say.'

'Her size didn't seem to put off the owner of the shop where you used to work,' remarked her sister. 'That Mr Ellerby was always in and out of her mini-mart like a rat up a drainpipe from what you've told me, and it wasn't to do his weekly shopping.'

'I told you that they were just friends—' began Edna.

'And how did you find Dr King's lecture?' the Entertainment Manager asked, managing at last to get his say in.

'She was very interesting,' replied Edna, 'a very artificated young woman. We're not great readers, but we bought two of her books which she signed for us. They'll do as presents. However, I can't say we were very enhamoured with the other lecturer, Mr Double-barrelled.'

'He needed to speak up,' added her sister. 'I could hardly hear a word he said.'

'It might be the agnostics in the theatre,' said Edna.

'Agnostics?' repeated a puzzled Entertainment Manager.

'She means acoustics,' explained Miriam sotto voce. 'She sometimes gets words mixed up.'

'Ah, I see.'

Miriam looked at Martin.

'If I might venture to give you some advice,' said Edna.

'Of course,' he said smiling.

'You ought to tell those who lecture not to have a dark theatre. People go to sleep, particularly after a four-course lunch. When he turned off the lights most of the audience dropped off.'

'I shall bear it in mind,' he replied.

'We quite enjoyed the pianist,' said Edna, 'although he could do with playing a few more popular tunes. Classical music is a required taste. You might have a word in his ear.'

'Did you go ashore in Seville?' asked the Entertainment Manager, wishing to receive no more unsolicited advice.

'We did,' replied Edna, scowling, 'but it was a bit of a damp squid, ridiculously hot and everything was shut. It's very inconsiderate of them to close all the shops in the afternoon.'

'The siesta is the tradition in Spain,' explained Martin. 'Everyone takes a nap midday when it's the hottest.'

'When I managed a store which sold specialist appliances,' Edna informed him, 'I didn't shut up shop in the afternoon to take a siesta. Of course, they wouldn't need to take a nap in the afternoon if they went to bed in good time. I've noticed these continentals stay up all hours. We were looking to buy some proper biscuits – custard creams, chocolate digestives or garibaldis – but the place was like a ghost town with everything locked up. We did manage to find a café open for a cup of tea, but it tasted like dishwater and the biscuits were like cardboard. I can't stand the sight of weak tea. It should be strong enough to trot a mouse across it, as our grandmother used to say.' She looked at her sister. 'And tell him what happened when we were coming back to the coach.'

'We were accosted,' said Miriam.

'Accosted?' repeated the Entertainment Manager.

Edna enlightened him. 'This bald little man with bad teeth kept running after us, pestering us to buy an apartment with a sea view, jabbering on in broken English. I told him to sling his hook. "We don't speak English," I said, "we're German."' Speaking of the sea, is it likely to get rough on this cruise?'

'My sister gets seasick very easily,' explained Miriam. 'The sight of water makes her queasy.'

Martin was minded to mention that a cruise might not be the best way to spend a holiday for someone for whom the sight of water made them queasy, but before he could manage to squeeze in a word, Edna carried on. 'I mean you read about people in the middle of the ocean being swept away on a salami.'

'A salami?' He imagined a giant sausage crashing out of the sea and flattening everything in its path.

'She means a tsunami,' Miriam informed him.

The Entertainment Manager laughed. 'I can assure you there is no likelihood of any tsunami happening on this cruise. The forecast is very promising, and we can look forward to fine weather and calm seas.'

As he said this, he recalled the last cruise when a force-ten storm had rocked the ship in the Bay of Biscay. The vessel had listed violently amongst mountainous waves and crockery and glasses could be heard crashing to the floor. The Captain had addressed the passengers over the public address system reassuring them that everything was under control; that the ship was designed to deal with such eventualities. He had explained that the course had been altered to compensate for the rough conditions. Suddenly there had been an almighty crack followed by the Captain's cry of 'Oh! Shit!' as a powerful wave bounced the ship like a cork. This had been followed by a whispered, 'Captain, you are still broadcasting,' and then by a loud click as the public address system had been switched off.

Edna now looked at Martin doubtfully. 'Well, I've seen a lot of sick bags about,' she said. 'That doesn't fill me with a deal of confidence.'

'Just a small precaution,' he told her. 'Actually, we call them motion discomfort receptacles.'

'You can call them what you like, young man, but all the fancy words don't butter no parsnips,' said Edna, threading her arm through her sister's. 'Come along, Miriam, the bingo starts in a minute.'

The following afternoon the red-cheeked man with the fierce moustache and short cropped hair who had antagonised Albert in the laundrette, found Mr Hinderwell in the library. The clergyman was busy with a crossword in the newspaper.

'I wonder if I could trouble you and borrow the sports' page in your paper?' asked the man. 'I meant to go ashore to get one but never got around to it.'

'You may have the whole newspaper,' said the clergyman, handing it over. 'I've finished with it.'

'Thanks. I do like to keep up with the cricket.' He sat down. 'Are you into cricket?'

'I used to play a little at university,' Mr Hinderwell replied diffidently, not mentioning that he was an Oxford Blue, the highest honour granted to individual sportspeople and a highly sought-after achievement. 'These days I do follow the cricket on the television. Did you say you didn't go ashore in Seville?'

'Yes, it was too hot, and the place would no doubt be crowded,' the man told him, 'and, to be honest, I'm not that keen on wandering around all those ruins and gloomy churches.'

The clergyman wondered why such people came on a cruise which took them to the most amazing locations in the world if they didn't bother to go ashore.

'You can't walk anywhere in Spain or Italy without coming across a whole lot of churches,' carried on the man. 'I'm afraid I don't have much time for religion. To my mind it's all superstition.'

'One piece of particularly good advice I was once given,' said Mr Hinderwell, looking like the benevolent priest that he was, 'is not to discuss politics or religion. It is sure to lead to a falling-out.'

The man was not deterred. He leaned back in his chair.

'In my view, most of the trouble of the world is caused by religious people,' he pronounced.

'I must take issue with you,' said Mr Hinderwell. 'What Hitler, Stalin, Pol Pot, Mao Tse-Tung, Idi Amin, Slobodan Milosevic and numerous other despots did, was not motivated by religion.'

'All the trouble in the Middle East is down to religion,' said the man, brushing a hand over his bristly moustache.

'Sometimes, I will own,' admitted the cleric, 'that some misguided people, who profess to be religious, can be unkind and sometimes cruel but they ignore the teachings of their faith. It is a fact that all the world's great religions have the same ideology if only their adherents lived by it. Hinduism, Buddhism, Judaism, Christianity and Islam, they all have the same creed which is to do to others as you would have them do to you. The Talmud says that is the entire law, the rest is commentary. The Koran says the same, as does the Bible.'

'You speak like a vicar,' laughed the man.

'It is because I am an Anglican priest,' Mr Hinderwell informed him. 'I imagine I sounded as if I were in the pulpit. You must forgive me. I have a tendency to sermonise. It gets to be something of a habit.'

'I didn't mean to cause any offence,' said the man.

'None taken.'

With his long oval face, aquiline nose and crop of dark hair neatly brushed back and with the soft voice, solicitous and kindly manner, the speaker was the red-faced man's idea of a typical vicar.

'Don't get me wrong,' said the man. 'I'm sure that *you* don't do anyone any harm and that you are caring and well-meaning.'

Mr Hinderwell, a gentle, modest man with a reserved sincerity and quiet dignity, smiled. 'Well, thank you for that. I try to be caring and well-meaning.'

'I have no doubt that you're a compassionate sort of chap but vicars, in my experience, tend to be unworldly, tucked away in some little country parish. I guess those in your profession don't have much of an idea what it is like in the real world – all the violence and conflict. With respect, I was in the police force, and I can tell you I've seen my fair share of fighting and bloodshed.'

Mr Hinderwell did not respond. He could have told the man that he had seen *his* fair share of fighting and bloodshed, probably much more than the man had experienced. He had been an army chaplain for twenty-five years. On retirement he and his wife had moved to a small village in rural Yorkshire, 'tucked away in some little country parish' as the man had said. He had anticipated a peaceful and an uneventful life. He assisted the vicar, set up a charity for homeless people, became a school governor and the chaplain at the local care home and took up gardening. His wife had secured a part-time post at the nearby preparatory school. He would often stand at the cottage window looking out at the tranquil scene which unfolded before him: silvered clouds stretching across a pale blue sky, green pastures, and dark woodland. There was the garden with its neat hedges, a crazy-paving path, trimmed lilac and buddleia bushes, a velvety, weed-free lawn, and a profusion of bright scented flowers. Behind the high, red brick wall there was the vegetable plot with the rich black soil, rows of fat cabbages, slender runner beans hanging from a wigwam of canes, courgettes, carrots, beetroot, spinach and herbs. The ancient oak tree with its gnarled branches and the sturdy Norman church with its spire spearing the sky had been there undisturbed for centuries. Everything was so soothing and tranquil. How different was this world from the one he remembered when he had served as a chaplain with the British Army in the Middle East: burned-out rusting vehicles, baked earth, shell holes, arid depressions, crumbling ruins, an obstacle course of craters and dugouts, endless stretches of sand and shrivelled scrub and the interminable heat and flies and, of course, the dreadfulness of war.

He would never forget the horrors he had witnessed and sometimes would wake up in the night shaking and sweating and calling out after a dreadful nightmare. One image came back to him time and again. It was the picture of the young soldier who had been fatally wounded. Mr Hinderwell had sat by the young man's bed as the soldier's life had ebbed away.

'I'm going to die, aren't I, Padre?' the dying man had whispered. He had gripped the chaplain's hand.

'Rest now,' Mr Hinderwell had told him looking into the pained eyes. His words had sounded so feeble.

'Will you write to my mum and dad?' the soldier had asked. 'Will you tell them I love them, that I'm sorry for some of the things I said.' There had been a scared and profound sorrow in his eyes.

'Of course.'

'And when I am gone, will you light a candle for me?'

Mr Hinderwell had tried to bite back his tears of grief. 'Of course, I will,' he had replied as the soldier had taken his last breath.

He had been resolute in keeping that promise and every time he had visited a church, he had lit a candle and said a prayer, not just for that soldier, but for all who had died in the conflict.

'When someone begins a sentence with the phrase "with respect",' said Mr Hinderwell to the red-cheeked man now, 'it invariably means the very opposite, but I assure you I am in no way offended. I am indeed tucked away in a little country parish, but it was not always the case, and I am not quite as unworldly as you might imagine.'

With that, the Reverend Christopher Hinderwell, MC, wished the man a 'Good morning' and left the library.

13

The Entertainment Manager, heading down the deck, caught sight of Neville, one of the most boring and long-winded of the passengers it had been his misfortune to meet, a man who spoke *at* people, rather than converse with them. He knew he should feel sorry for him for Neville was a sad and lonely figure who wandered the deck trying to engage people in conversation, but it was difficult to raise any sympathy for someone who constantly demanded his attention and never stopped talking. The last time he had been buttonholed by this particular passenger on the promenade deck, Martin had nearly been talked into a stupor and, looking over the side of the ship, had contemplated jumping overboard. Neville had asked him how he might become a member of the Entertainment Team; he had offered his services as a lecturer on future cruises and spoke at length about his proposed book on the pleasures of cruising. The Entertainment Manager had pretended to spot someone he needed to speak to and had mouthed an excuse before making his escape. Now, he noticed that an unsuspecting couple sitting by a window had been cornered and Neville was in his stride, expounding. Martin sucked in his breath, nodded, and smiled in Neville's direction and then hurried off to the Jolly Sailor Tavern for a meeting with Katya who was unhappy about continuing with the line dancing class.

Martin sat with Katya at a corner table in the Jolly Sailor Tavern.

'But you're very good at line dancing,' he flattered her. 'The feedback from the passengers who attended your classes has been really positive.'

'Spare me the flannel, Martin,' she huffed, tossing her head. 'You know as well as I do that I am not cut out for it. Peter is in his element surrounded by all those doting old women, strutting about the room putting on those silly accents, but I'm just like a spare part.'

'Not at all. You add a certain *je ne sais quoi.*'

Katya gave a wry smile.

'You complement Peter really well,' flattered Martin, 'and we do need a female member of the team at the classes and—'

He stopped mid-sentence on hearing a raised voice.

'Look just get the drinks, will you.'

The speaker was a loud, flop-eared, portly individual sitting at a nearby table. His shirt collar strained around a roll of flesh. He was accompanied by a thin woman with a face short of expression and a lanky, pasty, pustulant-faced youth with black spiky hair that stood up like a lavatory brush. He wore silver studs in the side of his nose and in his ear lobes. The man had attracted the waiter's attention by clicking his fingers repeatedly and calling out, his uncouth behaviour noted unfavourably by those in the bar. It was clear he had drunk more than his fair share of alcohol.

'I'm sorry, sir,' explained the young waiter calmly, 'I am afraid I am not allowed to serve alcoholic drinks to underage passengers.'

'How do you know the beer is for him?' asked the man in a low, grating voice.

'Well, sir, the young man drank the last beer I brought to your table.'

'Oh, for God's sake,' the man countered angrily, 'get the lad a beer. He's fifteen. What harm is a beer going to do him? He's on holiday.' He waved a hand. 'Just get the drinks.'

'I'm sorry, sir, but it is the rule. I would get into great trouble if I knowingly served alcohol to someone underage.'

'Just leave it, Sid,' said the woman.

'No, Cynthia, I will *not* leave it!' he snapped. 'I'm only asking for a glass of beer for the lad. He's not going on a drunken rampage.'

'Shall I get the young man a soft drink?' asked the waiter.

'No, you bloody won't. You can get him a glass of beer.'

'I'm afraid not, sir.'

'What's happened to the customer is always right?' demanded the man.

'Not in this case, sir.'

'I don't like your tone. Get me your boss. I want to talk to the organ grinder not the monkey.'

Martin got up and went over.

'There seems to be a problem,' he said.

'And who the hell are you?' demanded the man.

'The Entertainment Manager and I would ask you to lower your voice and be more civil.'

'Oh, do you?'

'For God's sake,' muttered the woman noticing that several of the passengers had turned their heads and were watching.

'All I want is a glass of beer for my lad and the waiter, Abdul or whatever his name is, refuses to get one for him.'

'Would you mind lowering your voice?' said Martin.

'Yes,' agreed the man's wife. 'Just give it a rest will you Sid.'

'I just want to get the lad a drink, Cynthia,' he replied, turning on her. 'Is that too much to ask?'

'Dad, I'm not that bothered,' said the youth, looking uncomfortable. 'Just leave it, will you.'

'No, I won't leave it!' snapped his father.

'Cruise lines don't tolerate the consumption of alcohol to those under eighteen or anyone aiding and abetting an underage person to acquire alcohol,' the man was told by Martin.

At the Captain's Table   171

'Aiding and abetting?' repeated the man. 'It's a glass of beer for God's sake, not a bottle of whisky. There was no problem when we were ashore. He got served then with no problem.'

'I'll just have an orange juice,' said the boy.

'No, you bloody well won't!' cried his father who had now got the bit firmly between his teeth.

'Will you leave it, Sid,' pleaded the woman. 'People are looking.'

'Let them bloody look. We've paid good money for this cruise and I'm not having some jobsworth laying down the law.'

'I'm sorry, but it *is* the law,' said Martin remaining calm. 'It may not be the law ashore, but it is on the ship. All cruise liners have Codes of Conduct, and passengers agree to abide by them when they sign their cruise contracts, one rule being that alcohol cannot be served to anyone under the age of eighteen.'

'I don't believe this!' shouted the man.

More passengers' heads turned.

'He's only doing his job,' said Albert who was sitting with Maureen at the next table. 'Give it a rest.'

'Bugger off! Nobody asked you to stick your neb in.'

'You're disturbing the other passengers, so just put a sock in it.'

'I'll come over there and disturb you in a minute.'

'Leave it, Albert,' said Maureen. 'Don't get involved.'

He ignored her and challenged the man. 'You can try.'

'Right,' said the objectionable passenger getting to his feet. His hands were tightened into fists.

Martin blocked his way. 'I wouldn't do that if I were you.'

'Sid, will you shut up!' cried the woman, jumping to her feet and gripping her husband's arm. 'You've had too much to drink.' She looked at Martin apologetically. 'He always gets like this when he's had too much.'

'Perhaps you should return to your cabin,' Martin told the man.

'Perhaps I might suggest to you to get stuffed.'

'If you persist in disrespectful and disruptive behaviour towards crew members and other guests, sir, I shall have to call security. You could be confined to your cabin and then you and your family will be put off the ship at the next port of call.'

The man gave a hollow laugh. 'What, chuck us overboard? Make us walk the plank? Don't make me laugh.' He pulled the boy up by the arm. 'Get up, Duane, let's go. Come on, Cynthia.' He pushed back his chair which clattered to the floor, then lurched to the exit followed by his red-faced wife and son. His departure was accompanied by clapping from the passengers.

'That was most impressive,' came a voice from behind Martin.

He turned to find the femme fatale in the red dress sitting with the concert pianist with her hand on his arm. The woman had occupied Martin's thoughts since he first saw her at the recital. She had captivated him. Why was such a beautiful, spontaneous and charming woman such as she be the mistress of this strange little man. Of course, he could guess. He had seen many a couple on cruises in the past where young women were with men old enough to be their fathers. Money, power, celebrity, lifestyle were all powerful attractions. He stumbled to find the words.

'Oh . . . er . . . well . . . it's part of the job.'

'Would you like to join us for a drink?' she asked.

How he wished that she were alone, that she was unattached. Had she been, he would have jumped at the chance.

'No, thank you,' he said, 'I'm with my colleagues and we have business to discuss. Thank you for asking.'

'Perhaps another time,' she said. She smiled bashfully.

'Yes, that would nice.' His ears went pink.

'What will happen to that boorish passenger?' asked Stanley.

'That will be for the Captain to decide,' Martin told him. 'He won't tolerate that sort of behaviour, so I guess the man and his family will be put ashore in Mallorca.'

And that is what happened, for when the ship arrived in port, the flop-eared man, his furious wife, and the acne-ridden youth were put ashore. As they walked down the dockside pulling their cases, Albert, a smug expression on his round face, watched from the upper deck. There was the gleam of satisfaction in his eyes, a characteristic of those who enjoy the misfortune of others.

Albert formed his hands into a megaphone. 'Have a good trip home,' he shouted.

'Whatever came over you, buying that ridiculous hat?' asked Miriam.

The sisters had been shopping in Palma.

'It's a sombrero,' Edna told her. 'That's what Spanish people wear.'

'I know what it's called,' said her sister. 'It looks outlandish, and I never saw one Spanish person wearing one, but I did notice that you were getting some very funny looks.'

'I couldn't give two hoots,' said Edna. 'You will soon wish you had bought one when the sun burns the back of your neck and your face ends up like an over-ripe tomato with all the sun.'

'I wouldn't be seen dead in it.'

As they walked around the city Edna began to find the flies, which she seems to attract, and the heat, unbearable and, added to this, her feet and hip started to ache. Miriam suggested that while she looked around the nearby shops, her sister should rest for a while in the small church they had passed, and they would meet up in an hour. Edna agreed.

The small church was beautifully proportioned, the shadowy, white-walled interior quiet and pleasantly cool. Edna

installed herself on the front pew and soon she felt her eyelids beginning to droop. The flickering candles near the altar
seemed to have a mesmerising effect and she soon nodded
off. Sometime later she awoke with a jolt and found herself
staring at a large, doe-eyed statue of the Madonna in a pale
blue cloak and with pink plaster cheeks. The figure had a bea-
tific expression and slender hands that were held out before
her. Above the altar was the pale figure of Christ on the cross
with a faraway look and lifelike drops of blood on his arms
and legs. Edna glanced around to discover that the church
was packed to the seams, and she was sandwiched between
an elderly woman and a younger man, both dressed in black.
In fact, she noticed that most of the people in the church were
attired in black. Edna in her flimsy looking sandals and long
patchwork cotton skirt and nursing on her lap the bright red
sombrero embroidered with gaudy flowers, appeared singularly out of place. With alarm, she saw a coffin on an elaborate
catafalque at the front of the church and heard a priest, robed
in a black cope, chanting something in Spanish. Edna had
found herself in the middle of a requiem mass. She appreciated that to get up and leave would be the height of insensitivity, so she stayed glued to her seat, feeling conspicuous and
aware that she was getting a good few puzzling looks from
those in the congregation. She tried to join in with the prayers
and the hymns, listened to the priest giving a lengthy homily
and when it came to 'the sign of peace' she shook hands with
those on the front pew, those who were sitting behind and the
priest and altar boys who had come down from the altar.

At the end of the mass the weeping woman next to her,
whom Edna assumed was the grieving widow, approached
the coffin, bent over, and kissed the body inside. She then
went to join the priest at the door ready to shake the hands
of the mourners as they left the church. Edna would have
waited until the place had cleared but the man sitting next

to her, rose to his feet, took her arm and, without a word, escorted her, walking frame and all, to the coffin. Edna stared for a moment at the corpse and then headed for the exit on the arm of her escort. The widow grasped her hand, kissed her on the cheek and said something in Spanish. Edna gave a sympathetic smile.

'Well dear,' she said, 'he's passed to his eternal reward now and gone to meet his maker. Gone, but not forgotten.'

The widow stared at her blankly.

Later when she related the episode to her sister, Miriam commented, 'I'd have liked to have been a fly on the wall at the funeral reception. I'm sure the strange woman with the red sombrero and the walking frame would have been the main topic of conversation.'

There was a welcome surprise awaiting the Port Lecturer when he boarded the ship in Palma. Mr Carlin-How was in a particularly good mood when he walked along the dockside with Elodie. They had spent a very pleasant morning together in the city, visiting the Moorish Almudaina royal palace, the thirteenth century Santa María Cathedral and the stone-built village of Pollença. They had enjoyed a leisurely lunch at the exclusive Sadrassana restaurant and never stopped talking. The Entertainment Manager greeted him at the top of the gangplank.

'Ah, Mr Carlin-How,' he said, 'I have some good news for you. A family have left the ship and as a result, a passenger cabin has become available so if you would like to move into it you would be—'

Mr Carlin-How cut in before the sentence was finished.

'Yes, yes, indeed,' he interrupted, 'that would be splendid.'

'The cabin is on Deck B and, you will be pleased to know, it has a balcony.'

'Even better.'

'It will be available this evening. If you speak to Bimla at the reception desk you can collect the details,' he was told.

Mr Carlin-How shook Martin's hand vigorously. *Things*, he said to himself, *are looking up.*

'Many thanks,' he said, and giving his apologies to Elodie after inviting her to join him for a drink before dinner, he rushed off to the reception desk.

Later the Port Lecturer wasted no time in vacating his cramped berth at the bottom of the ship and installing himself in his new cabin. He unpacked, rearranged things to his liking and introduced himself to the steward. Later, as the sun sank over the sea and lit up the horizon in purest gold, he stood with Elodie on the balcony, drinking a glass of well-chilled champagne in slow and stress-free pleasure.

'I owe you an apology,' he said, turning to face her.

'Whatever for?' she asked.

'When I first met you, I was crass,' he admitted. 'I feel quite ashamed. It was very rude of me to have behaved in such a manner, sharp and offhand, and I can assure you it is out of character. I am sorry I was so ill-mannered.'

'Hubert, there is nothing to apologise for,' she interjected. 'I just thought you were a bit stiff and stand-offish that's all, but you loosened up and we had a delightful talk. Today has been lovely.'

'It was the cabin you see,' he told her.

'The cabin?'

'I was indignant that you had been given a passenger cabin like this one with a balcony, and I had been assigned little more than a cubicle at the bottom of the ship.'

'Why were you given such a small cabin?'

'That is what I asked the Entertainment Manager, but he said that you are a celebrity, widely published, a professor and so forth, and I am just well . . . I suppose I'm thought a bit of a nobody by comparison.'

Elodie took his hand, reached up and kissed his cheek.
'But not to me, you're not, Hubert.'

Stanley Mulgrave's second piano recital was better attended
than the first, although there was still a half row of empty seats
at the rear of the Consort Suite. The musician played a selection of well-known classical pieces ending with a bravura performance of the beginning of Rachmaninoff's Third Piano
Concerto, a dazzling finger twisting triumph. He received a
standing ovation. As his audience dispersed, he caught sight
of Oliver, sitting at the end of the front row with crossed legs
and his hands on his lap, a pensive expression on his young
face. He resembled a little old man. He had listened to the
music in rapt attention, staring at the pianist with his sharp
green eyes.

'Still here,' said Mr Mulgrave.

'Yes,' replied the boy. 'I just wanted to say how much I
enjoyed your recital. It was superb. I have never heard piano
music played so brilliantly.'

'My goodness,' the pianist replied. His smile crinkled the
corners of his eyes. 'Praise indeed and from one so young. I
shall have to employ you as my agent. I saw you at my first
recital. I can see that you enjoy piano music.'

'Yes, very much.'

'But I guess you prefer pop music.'

'Not at all,' Oliver told him. 'I prefer classical music and I
like folk music.'

'I'm pleased to hear it.' Oliver hoped he wouldn't say that
he was unusual, not like other boys of his age. He heard that
all the time.

'I was the same when I was your age,' Mr Mulgrave told him.

'You were?'

'I loved classical music. I was a bit different. I think the
other fellows in my class at school thought I was a bit weird.'

'I know what you mean,' declared Oliver. 'It's not a bad thing to be a bit different, Mr Mulgrave, is it?' He recalled Elodie's words.

'No, it isn't,' agreed the pianist. 'And do you play the piano yourself?'

'I do, but I am not awfully good.'

'And what sort of music do you play?'

'Mostly the pieces for my grade exams, although I have just learned to play the "Moonlight Sonata", well the easy part of it anyway.'

'Ah, the first movement of Beethoven's "Piano Sonata in C-sharp Minor". It's quite a challenging piece for one so young.'

'I don't play it very well though,' he said modestly.

'Why don't you come up here to the piano and let me hear you play.'

'I couldn't possibly,' replied Oliver, shaking his head. 'I should be far too embarrassed playing for such as you.'

Mr Mulgrave smiled. 'I don't bite,' he said.

Oliver looked doubtful.

'Do you need the score?' asked Mr Mulgrave.

'No,' replied Oliver. 'I've practised it so many times, I know it.'

'Come along then, let me hear you.'

So, Oliver played part of the 'Moonlight Sonata' for the concert pianist.

'You are a modest young man,' said Mr Mulgrave. 'Your playing was good.'

'Thank you,' the boy answered shyly.

'You have a sensitive touch. Of course, like all pianists, you do need to practise. That is the secret of playing well. It's the same with any other endeavour in life, practice makes perfect.'

'How often do you practise?' asked Oliver.

'Several hours every day,' replied the concert pianist.

'Golly.'

A smile crept over Mr Mulgrave's face. *Did schoolboys still say 'Golly'*, he thought. It sounded so quaintly old-fashioned; the sort of expression used by characters in a comic of the 1950s. He left the piano, reached into his briefcase and produced a CD.

'This is for you,' he said. 'You may enjoy my rendering of the complete "Piano Sonata in C-sharp Minor" and various other pieces.'

'That's most kind of you,' replied Oliver. 'Thank you very much.'

Miriam and Edna had decided, after some discussion, that they would attend the piano recital.

'Well, we might as well give it a go,' Edna had told her sister, 'since there's nothing much on unless you want to go to the quiz.'

'No thank you,' her sister had huffed. 'Listen to all of those know-it-alls showing off?'

Following the recital, they had left the Consort Suite and were now having a coffee in one of the lounges when they caught sight of the concert pianist heading down the deck. He was accompanied by the young woman in a dark, dramatically cut red dress and high-heeled sandals they had seen before boarding the ship.

Edna got to her feet and shuffling in his direction with her walking frame, blocked their path. If Edna had been asked to describe what she considered to be her good qualities, she might have claimed the virtue of being plain-speaking – 'not backward in coming forwards' as her sainted mother would have said. If her sister had been asked to add to the list of Edna's assets, tact and delicacy of feeling would not have been on it, for she was a woman who was not afraid of voicing her opinions and judged people without prevaricating or vacillating. Thus, Edna felt obliged to share with the concert pianist her assessment of his performance.

'Your session was most enjoyable,' she told him. 'I must say you're very good at tickling the ivories.'

'Thank you,' he replied, 'I am pleased you enjoyed it.'

'I did, but I reckon your fingers must ache after all that thumping at the piano.'

The concert pianist found it hard to know what to say in reply. He glanced at his companion sideways and gave a wearisome sigh.

'Now you did say that at your first gig that if anyone had suggestions for tunes, they should have a word,' continued Edna.

At the mention of the words 'gig' and 'tunes' Mr Mulgrave pulled a pained face.

'Yes indeed, I did say that. Have you any suggestions?'

'My sister and I were wondering if you could play a few more modern tunes, something a tad more popular, a bit catchier, you know, something a bit easier on the ear with not too many notes.'

He fixed her with a penetrating stare and smiled mirthlessly. 'Such as?' At least this passenger, unlike the dreadful Mrs Mare, was not seeking to criticise his playing. However, it did irritate the celebrated musician who had performed with some of the most prestigious orchestras in the world to be asked to play something "a bit catchier" and "something easier on the ear".

Edna rested a hand on his arm. 'A few selections from the musicals like *The Sound of Music*, *The King and I* and *My Fair Lady*. I'm sure you are up to it and if you played something a bit trendier, you'd get a bigger audience.'

'You see the classical stuff is not everyone's cup of tea,' stated her sister, as if she had imparted some great words of wisdom. 'Most people like—'

'Something a bit catchier and easier on the ear,' he repeated.

'Exactly. You see—'

'I would agree with you there,' cut in the concert pianist. 'The "classical stuff", as you term it, is not everyone's cup of tea. It is something of an acquired taste.'

'In the town where we live,' Edna informed him, 'they used to play classical music over the tannoy in the bus station.'

'Really?' he replied. 'Quite a novel idea.'

'It's a pity they stopped doing it because it had the effect of getting rid of the pigeons, the down-and-outs and the good-for-nothing teenagers who congregated there and got up to no good. They couldn't stand hearing it.'

'Thank you for sharing such a fascinating piece of information with me,' the concert pianist told the two women sardonically. He turned to his young companion who was stifling a smile. 'Did you catch that, Antonia, I have now seen Mozart's piano concertos and Beethoven's "Rondo a Capriccio" in a completely new light – as the deterrents of pigeons, down-and-outs and feckless teenagers.'

14

Bruce and Babs, the dance tutors, were having one of their weekly spats. They had been together for nearly three years in unmarried antipathy and had been instructors on cruise ships for two. They rented a small apartment in Southampton but were rarely there, spending most of the year at sea. Although they both found the work relatively undemanding and not without interest, they had become jaded with each other, and both wanted a change. At first it had been exciting, travelling around the world together, meeting different people, having accommodation and food provided and, in addition, a comfortable cabin, but they had become weary of each other's company. Neither had considered the notion of marriage. Their relationship had become more volatile of late, and each wondered why they stayed together. To the passengers they appeared a happy, affectionate couple but behind the façade, in the confines of their cabin, they were different characters.

'Oh really, Bruce,' complained Babs, applying some scarlet nail varnish, 'do we really have to go through all this again. It is what I have to do. It's part of my professional duty. It keeps the passengers happy.'

'Yes, but he is not a passenger, is he?' answered Bruce. 'He's the ship's singer and you're always waltzing round the floor with him when you're supposed to be dancing with the passengers. It's embarrassing.'

'You make Lorenzo sound like a club singer. He is a famous classically trained opera vocalist for your information. What's more, he knows how to speak to a woman. You could take a leaf out of his book.'

'Yes, I bet he knows how to speak to women,' scoffed Bruce. 'They're all the same these Latins. Smooth - talkers, gigolos. The last thing I want to do is take a leaf out of *his* book.'

'You make it sound as if I dance with him all the time,' said Babs, painting another long nail.

'Well, you spend a lot of the time in the class prancing about the floor with him in a clinch.'

'I don't prance,' she told him. 'For your information, Lorenzo happens to be an exceptionally good dancer.'

'Rubbish! He's got legs like India-rubber and, for someone who is supposed to know something about rhythm and tim-ing, he's all over the place on the dance floor.'

'Nonsense.'

'Anyway, he shouldn't be at the class. It's for passengers and not for the likes of him. He's an employee.'

'He's a celebrity guest entertainer,' Babs informed him, 'and he is perfectly entitled to take full advantage of all the activities on offer.'

'Well, he's certainly taking full advantage of you, chatting you up. I've seen the way he looks at you and noticed him clamping onto you like a limpet when you're doing the tango.'

'Don't be ridiculous,' she reacted. She stopped painting her nails and wafted a hand to dry the polish.

'Anyway, it'll not be for much longer,' Bruce informed her. 'He'll be getting off the ship in Rome so we'll soon be saying "*Arrivederci*" and I, for one, will be glad to see the back of him.'

Babs did not share this sentiment for she had become enamoured with the smooth-talking Italian and would miss him.

'And speaking of noticing things,' she said, 'it hasn't escaped *my* notice that you never pick the old women who are shaky on their feet to demonstrate with. It's always that young tarty one with the ridiculous blond fringe and the tight-fitting T-shirt and shorts. Your hands are all over her like an octopus's tentacles.'

'Now *you* are being ridiculous. Firstly, the older ladies could not manage the more expressive dances and secondly it just so happens that Vanessa has the energy and picks things up easily.'

'She picked you up easily enough, I'll say that,' said Babs.

'The lambada is a very tactile dance. It's not like the "Military Twostep". The physical contact is very important. And you're not one to speak, cavorting across the dance floor clamped in a tango with the little, touchy-feely Italian.'

'Speaking of the tango, I only dance with Lorenzo because you don't seem to have the stamina for it anymore.'

'What?'

'You sounded like an old carthorse clomping about the floor puffing and blowing when you last tried to dance it with me. I think you should stick to the waltz or the foxtrot, something less challenging. You can just about manage those.'

'Not have the stamina!' Bruce cried. 'I've a damn sight more stamina than you and I'm lighter on my feet. Of course, I suppose your varicose veins are taking their toll. I've noticed you are slowing down in the cha-cha-cha.'

'Well, at least I can remember the steps.' They remained in starched silence for a while. 'And it's a bit rich you complaining about me and Lorenzo when you are up in the Jolly Sailor Tavern with that Melissa.'

'It's Vanessa actually and we were discussing the bolero.'

'I bet you were.'

There was another stubborn silence.

'You need to get another dinner jacket,' Babs told him eventually. 'You've put on so much weight recently, the buttons don't fasten at the front and you're bursting out of the trousers. Perhaps you ought to think of getting a corset.'

'You're one to talk,' he huffed. 'You need to do something about what *you* wear. That frothy bilious green dress with the big round puffy sleeves that you put on last night for the quickstep demonstration, made you look like a peripatetic sprout.'

'And you're thinning on top,' she said, a grim smile flicking across her face. She thought of Lorenzo's black-satin curls. 'You perhaps ought to think about getting a wig.'

'Well, I don't dye my hair, like you,' he countered, 'or, for that matter, like the little Italian.'

There was silence again.

Babs sighed and looked at her watch. 'We'd better make a move. We have a class in ten minutes.'

'What is it today?' he asked.

'The paso doble,' she said, 'and do try and keep in time with the music.'

On the promenade deck Neville approached the melancholy faced woman with the wispy hair who was sitting at a table by herself. She was staring out to sea, her face creased and her expression unutterably sad.

'Do you mind if I join you?' he asked. 'All the tables seem to be occupied.' Before she could answer he slid into a chair opposite her. 'I say, you were at the "Travelling-Alone Get-Together", weren't you?' he stated. 'You were sitting by yourself. You should have mingled.'

'I didn't feel like mingling,' she told him tersely, twisting the ring on her finger round and round. This was a special day for her, and she wished to be alone. She stared at him with emotionless eyes. Who was he to tell her what to do? Of course, it was the story of her life – people always telling her to do this or to do that and it had got worse since her husband's death.

'You ought to get out more,' she was told. 'You should join a support group', 'You ought to take up a hobby', 'You should do some charity work.' Eric was the one person who never made any demands on her or try to run her life. He accepted her as she was and now, he was gone.

'That's the idea of the get-together,' Neville was rambling on. 'It's to meet other passengers and make new friends. There's really no need to feel nervous or shy. Everyone's very friendly.' The woman didn't answer but stared impassively out at the empty ocean and the gulls wheeling and diving. She continued to twist the ring on her finger. 'I'm the opposite,' said Neville, leaning back in his chair and crossing his legs. 'I'm a very sociable person. I like meeting people and learn-ing about their lives.' The woman turned and looked at him wearily but said nothing. 'The thing about cruising is you can get to know a lot of different and interesting people, that's if you make the effort.'

Why don't you make an effort and leave me alone, she thought.

'I could go on for hours talking about some of the charac-ters I've met while I've been on the high seas,' Neville told her. 'I'm thinking seriously about writing a book about my experi-ences on a cruise ship. I reckon it could well be a best-seller. It will be informative and include amusing anecdotes and stories and lots of advice for would-be cruisers. Of course, I might take to lecturing about my experiences. I'm sure my accounts will be of great interest. I've been on over twenty voyages all over the world and have got a lot of the material.' He rested his head on the back of the chair, closed his eyes, and felt the warmth of the sun on his face. 'I reckon I could do as well as the lecturers on this cruise.' When he opened his eyes, he saw that the woman had gone.

When she had returned from breakfast that morning, the woman had found a vase of salmon pink roses and a card wishing her 'Happy Birthday' in her cabin. It had been such a shock and she had had to sit on the bed for a moment to compose herself. Her husband had always bought her roses for her birthday. She would come downstairs on the morning of her special day to find just the one card with 'To my darling Wife' written in coloured letters on the front. There would be a bouquet of roses and her carefully wrapped present and Eric would be standing there beaming. They had been a shy, reclusive but happy couple who never sought other people's company. Neighbours thought them odd, keeping to themselves and barely passing the time of day. 'A pair of timid little mice,' one of the neighbours remarked. They weren't deliberately unfriendly; it was just that they were nervous in company and had little to say. They had each other, which was enough. Her parents hadn't approved of Eric, of course – this unattractive, insignificant little man who stammered and coloured up if anyone spoke to him.

Jean had taken Eric home to meet her parents. Her father with his large, broad nose and prominent chin and with an intimidating expression and folded arms, had sat on the sofa next to her mother, resembling an Easter Island statue. He stared at the poor man before firing questions at him. When Eric had gone, Jean's parents had given their opinion in no uncertain terms.

Her mother, with a look of distaste on her pinched features, had told her sharply. 'You can do a whole lot better than him, Jean. He sits there like a stuffed dummy and when he does open his mouth you can't hear a word he says, mumbling and spluttering.'

'And what does he do for a living?' her father had held forth. The question was rhetorical. 'He works at a council rubbish tip. What sort of job is that I ask you?'

'Eric's a waste disposal operative,' his daughter had told him.

Her father had given a snorting sniff, indicating his disapproval. 'Rubbish collector, you mean.'

She had answered back in a rare show of feeling. 'It's not as if *I* have a high-powered job, is it, making ham sandwiches in the back of a baker's shop?' She could have added that her father didn't have a high-powered job either but she stayed silent.

'Yes, well if you had applied yourself more at school you might have made something of yourself,' her father had declared.

'The teachers said you made little effort with your schoolwork, and you never opened your mouth in lessons,' her mother had nagged. 'And you had no friends to speak of.'

Jean had known that both parents had not applied themselves at school and had no friends, but she had bitten her lip.

'And if you smartened yourself up a bit, like your cousin Angela,' her father had added, 'you might meet somebody better than a bin man. She's set up in life marrying an executive.'

'He's a shop assistant in a shoe shop,' Jean had muttered.

'Well, that's better than being a refuse collector,' her mother had countered. 'I mean it's an embarrassment telling people who you are walking out with.'

There had been another sudden uncharacteristic flare of anger. 'Will you both shut up!' their daughter had cried. 'I'm going to marry Eric, so you can both like it or lump it.'

They had not gone to the wedding.

Jean had experienced an unbearable time at school. A group of pupils had found great pleasure in bullying this plain, nervous, mousy-haired girl with the thick-framed glasses. Her teachers had been unaware of the treatment meted out or had turned a blind eye. They did nothing. Most parents would have realised how unhappy their daughter had been but not hers. Her father was self-centred and humourless, her mother domineering and fault-finding; neither displayed any real affection for this dull and withdrawn child. It was clear she was a sad disappointment to them. If she had been blessed with caring, supportive parents, she sometimes wondered, she might have turned out differently – more confident and sociable. She had opened up to Eric about her childhood which replicated his own – bossy parents, bullying at school, no friends. 'They thought I was dreary and pathetic,' she had told him.

'I don't find you dreary or pathetic,' he had replied, taking her hand in his.

She had loved Eric's calm, quiet manner, his thoughtfulness and sensitivity. She had met him at the council waste disposal and recycling centre – not the most romantic of places to meet your future husband. He had helped her carry a bag of garden refuse to the skip. She had liked this reticent, rather nervous man with a stutter from their first meeting. Subsequent visits to dispose of her rubbish were really not necessary but she was keen to see him again and she could tell he liked her. They had struck up conversations and finally he had asked her out. After they were married, they rented a small flat above a corner shop and looked forward to a long and happy life together. They hoped they would have children, but it was not to be. She saw nothing of her parents. Her eyes now were blurred with tears. She sniffed and twisted the ring on her finger. 'Oh Eric,' she said, 'I do miss you.'

They had saved up and planned the cruise together but then there had been the accident. The police officers had called one dark, rainy evening and told her that her husband had been killed while crossing the road with their dog, knocked down by a drunk driver who had skidded across the road. At the funeral, the manager of the baker's where she worked had made a short appearance and one of Eric's workmates had offered his sympathies but it was all a blur. So strong was their hostility towards Eric that her parents refused to attend the funeral or send any message of condolence. For that she never forgave them. Then some young woman from a bereavement counselling service had called at the house. She was advised to 'move on' as if Eric had been some kind of obstacle in her life. All Jean had wanted was to be left alone with her grief, so she had closed the curtains, locked the door, and stayed in her bedroom, not answering knocks or the ringing of the telephone. After a week she had gone back to work but the manager of the baker's, noticing that her mind was not on the job, had suggested she take some time off. It was then that she had decided to go on the cruise and get away from it all. The train tickets had been bought and the holiday all paid for.

There was a knock now at the cabin door. She took a deep soulful breath and went to answer it. Outside stood the stewardess who held an envelope.

'Excuse me, madam, but I have been asked to deliver this.'

'Did you put the card and the flowers in my cabin, Maria?' Jean asked.

'Yes, madam.'

'How did anyone know it was my birthday today?' she asked.

'Your details are on your passport, madam. Those at reception always look through the passports when the passengers leave them there, to see if it is anyone's birthday during the cruise. The flowers are with the Captain's compliments.'

'I see.' Jean took the envelope and opened it. The card, edged in red, was a request for her to dine at the Captain's table that evening.

'Happy birthday, madam,' said the stewardess.

Jean's heart fluttered. At first she felt too weak, too shy, too apprehensive to sit with the great and the good at the

Captain's table but inadequate and fearful though she was, she thought, after some consideration, it would be churlish to refuse the invitation. So, at the appointed time she presented herself at the Sunset Restaurant and was shown to the top table by the Restaurant Manager. She had made an effort with her appearance, choosing her best dress, and calling at the Ocean Spa to have her hair washed and set. Becky had persuaded her to have a facial and applied some light make-up.

'You have lovely eyes,' Becky had told her.

The comment had made her cry. Eric had been the only one to tell her that.

As Jean approached the Captain's table that evening, she felt butterflies of nerves in her stomach, but she managed a small smile. The other guests at the table included a tall, bald individual with a rugged face and a dumpy, round-faced little woman with thick springy hair, the Italian tenor and the aged couple who held hands. The Captain stood and welcomed her warmly before pulling out a chair for her to sit down. He then introduced the other guests.

'Thank you for the flowers and the card,' said Jean, her mouth curling into a hesitant smile. There was a slight tremble in her voice. She was unused to such company with all eyes upon her. 'It was a very kind thought.' She twisted the ring on her finger.

'Not at all,' said the Captain, smiling widely. 'May I wish you a very "Happy birthday"?'

'That goes for us all at t'table, I'm sure,' said Cyril.

'It does,' agreed his wife.

After some polite conversation, in which Jean contributed little, Pat turned to her. 'That's an unusual ring,' she remarked. She held up her own – the large square-cut emerald set in a circle of diamonds. 'My husband got this for me for my birthday.'

'It's lovely,' said Jean. 'My ring is not valuable but it's very special. I never take it off.'

While the aged couple chatted to each other and the Captain enquired how the singer was enjoying the cruise, Cyril looked at Jean.

'You know we 'ave met afore, Missis Borrowby,' he said.

'Have we?'

'At Eric's funeral. I was 'is boss.'

She looked at the smiling face for a moment. 'Oh yes, of course, it's Mr Ugthorpe, isn't it,' she said. 'I'm sorry I didn't recognise you. My mind was elsewhere at the funeral and . . .' Her voiced tailed off.

'I did call around to your 'ouse a week after t'funeral to see 'ow you were gerrin on,' said Cyril, 'but there was nob'dy in an' you weren't answerin' t'telephone.'

'No,' she told him. 'I just wanted to be left alone.'

'I can quite understand that,' said Connie. 'You needed time on your own to grieve.'

'I only saw you on t'deck this morning, Missis Borrowby,' said Cyril, 'an' was goin' to 'ave a word wi' you but you'd gone afore I could. I said to t'wife I'd catch up wi' you afore t'end o' t'cruise.'

'He did,' said Connie. 'He said he'd catch up with you.'

'I've kept very much to myself,' she told her.

'We were all so sorry at work to 'ear about your 'usband's death,' said Cyril. 'Eric were a grand chap, salt o' t'earth. Never 'ad a day off in 'is life. Nowt too much trouble for 'im.'

Jean felt tears clouding her eyes.

'Stop it at once, Cyril,' chided his wife. 'Look how you're upsetting the poor woman and her on her birthday as well.'

'No, please,' insisted Jean. 'It's a great comfort to hear about Eric, particularly today, and to know how much he was liked. I've not spoken to anyone about him since the funeral. It's good to talk.'

Something shifted in Jean that evening. In the company of such kind and good-humoured people who didn't judge her or nag her, she had not felt as relaxed and contented since Eric's death. Her eyes were full of gratitude. She looked around the table and a smile stretched across her face for the first time for many weeks. The evening concluded when the Italian tenor rose to his feet, clapped his hands, and sang 'Happy Birthday', which generated generous applause from the other diners. Then a waiter arrived with a cake.

In the laundrette Albert was at the ironing board. Beside him he had a large pile of washing in a basket. Ernesto, who had noticed that this passenger was a frequent visitor to the laundrette with just a few items to press each time, suggested that Albert iron all his clothes and then he could put them on hangers and keep them in the storeroom opposite his cabin and save them getting creased. This suggestion was well received.

A young woman in a smart grey suit appeared holding a clipboard.

'Good morning,' she said brightly.

'Morning,' Albert replied.

'I'm Christine, the Chief Housekeeper,' she said.

'I'm Albert. I'm pleased to meet you.'

'I won't disturb you, Albert. This is just a spot-check to make sure that the laundrette is up to standard. Sometimes it's left in a bit of a state. It looks fine this morning. Have you everything you need?'

'Yes, thank you.'

'And how's your cabin?'

'It's very comfortable.'

'And your steward?'

'Ernesto is first class. He can't do enough for us.'

'You might recommend him for a commendation. Staff are rewarded for excellent service.'

'I shall do that. To be frank I wasn't that keen on coming on this cruise, but I am really enjoying it.' *I'd enjoy it a whole lot more without the nagging wife,* he thought.

She smiled. 'We aim to please, Albert,' she said.

She had gone but a moment when Sandra arrived with a dress over her arm.

'Oh, I can see that you're busy,' she said to Albert. 'I'll call back.'

'Have you the one item?' he asked.

'Yes, just the dress.'

'Come along, love, you can squeeze in. I've got a mountain of stuff to iron here.'

'That's very kind of you Mr . . . ?'

'Albert.'

'I'm Sandra.'

As she ironed her dress they chattered away. Why couldn't Maureen be as agreeable as this woman, he reflected, instead of finding fault with whatever he did. When she had gone and Albert was about to return to the ironing, Edna trundled in followed by her sister who was carrying a large bag of clothes.

'I know there's a laundry service on the ship,' she was saying huffily, 'but I'm not shelling out all that money, not when I can do it myself.'

'Yes, but you don't do it yourself, do you,' retorted her sister. 'It's left to me.'

Albert greeted them with a cheery, 'Good morning.'

'Good morning,' answered Edna. Miriam began furiously loading the washing, then she added the washing powder and turned on the machine, watched by her sister.

'Excuse me, young man,' said Edna, manoeuvring her walking frame closer to Albert. 'Would you be kind enough to keep an eye on our washing for us and if we're not back when it's finished, could you unload it and pop it in the dryer and when it's dry, put it in this bag and leave it over there on the table. We don't want to be waiting around.' She patted her walking frame and adopted her martyred face. 'As you will no doubt have noticed, I'm physically disabled with a painful hip, and I experience a lot of discomfort having to stand and my sister has a bad back.' Miriam looked around. It was the first she had heard of this. 'So, would you mind?'

Albert was tempted to ask if she wanted her clothes ironing as well, but he just smiled and agreed.

'Of course, love. I'll deal with it.'

'Thank you very much Mr . . . ?'

'Albert.'

'I'm Edna and this is my sister Miriam.' The two women departed.

The red-cheeked man with a bristly Stalin-style moustache and short cropped hair appeared before Albert could resume his ironing. He was holding a shirt.

'Have you nearly finished?' he asked.

'Does it look like it?' answered Albert echoing the words the man had used at their last encounter in the laundrette.

'Well, how long are you going to be?'

Albert stopped what he was doing and raised the iron. 'It will take as long as it takes,' he replied. 'I've only just started.'

The man smiled weakly, suddenly recognising this passenger and the earlier exchange he had had with him. 'I've just got the one shirt,' he said meekly.

'Really?'

'I'll only be a minute.'

'You want to jump the queue?'

The man chose not to announce, as Albert had done previously to him, that there was no queue. He coughed awkwardly.

'You see, if I let you jump the queue,' said Albert, 'I'd have everyone wanting to do it.'

The man turned to go, deciding he would call later.
Albert put down the iron and stood back.
'Be my guest,' he said.
'Pardon?'
'You can iron your shirt.'
'Well thanks very much!' said the man, in a thin voice.

15

Mr Carlin-How was sitting with a group of passengers in the Galleon Buffet when his eyes were drawn to two boys of about fourteen years of age who were on the next table. He found their behaviour intensely annoying. One boy, a pimply faced youth with an unruly thatch of mousy brown hair, was flicking food at the other and laughing loudly. The table and floor were littered with bits of pizza and chips.

'I say!' shouted the Port Lecturer. 'Will you desist from doing that.'

The pimply faced youth stopped what he was doing and stared at him, brazen-faced.

'Doing what?' he challenged.

'Making such a mess. You need to clear it up.'

'What's it got to do with you?' the boy asked belligerently.

'It has a lot to do with me,' he was told. 'Your conduct is appalling, and you are disturbing other passengers.'

'The staff should not be expected to have to clean up after you,' said Sandra.

'Course they should,' said the boy grinning. 'That's what they're there for.'

The other boy looked suitably chastened and began to pick up the detritus. 'Come on, George,' said the spotty-faced youth, standing up. 'Leave it.'

'You should show more consideration,' said Sandra.

'And you should mind your own business, grandma,' said the boy.

'How dare you speak to this lady like that,' barked Mr Carlin-How, rising from his chair. 'Now clear up the mess you have made.'

'Get a life,' said the boy, getting up to go. 'Come on, George.' He left, leaving most of the mess untouched. His pal followed.

'I shall have a word with the Purser,' said Mr Carlin-How to Sandra. 'Such behaviour is intolerable.'

'Leave it with me,' she replied, '*I* shall have a word with the Captain.'

'If it is any help,' said a passenger who had witnessed the exchange, 'I would be happy to make a statement.'

The following morning the boys and their fathers were summoned to the Purser's office. The incident in the Galleon Buffet had been reported. Sandra had had a word with the Captain.

The two parents and their sons stood before the large desk behind which sat the Captain, the Purser and Roger, the young officer, with his pen poised there to take notes. One of the parents, a ruddy-faced, sandy-haired man had a face decorated with irritation and impatience. His planned game of snooker that morning had had to be cancelled. The tenor of the short, sharp letter from the Captain requesting he attend this interview over 'a matter of some concern', had annoyed him. The other man was clearly perplexed. For some seconds the Captain gave no sign that he was aware of the new occupants in the room. He was studying the papers before him.

'You wanted to see us,' said the annoyed man with a sour expression. He blinked, his jaw tightened, and he bit his lip momentarily.

The Captain raised his head slowly and studied the speaker with the directness of a searchlight. He interlaced his fingers slowly and set them just beneath his chin, resting his elbows on the desktop. 'Just to let you know,' he said, 'this interview is being recorded.'

'What's this all about?' demanded the ruddy-faced individual.

'Perhaps your son would care to explain why I have sent to see him and you,' answered the Captain, sitting up and placing his hands on the desk.

The father of the pimply faced youth turned to his son. 'Well, Lewis?' he asked. 'What's this all about?'

'I don't know,' was the best the boy could manage.

'You don't know?' asked the Captain.

'No,' grunted the boy, shrugging.

'Then let me refresh your memory,' said the Captain, his face darkening. 'What about yesterday lunchtime in the Galleon Buffet?'

'What about it?' mumbled the boy, staring mulishly at his feet. The other boy shifted uncomfortably from foot to foot, licked his lips nervously and wrinkled his nose.

'I suggest you don't speak to me in that tone of voice, young man,' said the Captain sharply. 'Look at me when I'm talking to you and take your hands out of your pockets.'

The boy did as he was told. The Captain sounded like an angry headmaster.

'Could you tell us what this is all about?' repeated the ruddy-faced father impatiently. 'What's he supposed to have done?'

The Captain passed across the desk a sheet of paper. 'You might like to read what it says on here.'

'I don't follow,' said the parent, leaving the paper on the desk. 'What's this got to do with my lad?'

'This describes the state these two . . . youths left the table in at lunchtime yesterday in the Galleon Buffet.' He scanned the pad on his desk. 'I have here several other statements from passengers and the Port Lecturer who witnessed what happened. I also have a report from the Restaurant Manager. Since you do not wish to read what it says I shall inform you of the contents. When told by the Port Lecturer to stop flinging food at each other and leaving such a mess, one of these' – he pointed with his index finger at the miscreants – 'asked rudely, and I quote, "What's it got to do with you?" When an elderly lady asked these two to show more consideration she was told, "Mind your own business, grandma." I think that is a fair summary of what happened.'

'Oh,' was all the quieter parent could find to say. He licked his lips and there was a trickle of sweat at the side of his forehead and he looked suitably embarrassed. Then he turned to his son. 'Is this true, George?'

'Yes, Dad,' replied the boy. 'I'm sorry.' He could have informed his father that he was not the one to flick food and leave the mess and had started to clear it up, but he kept this to himself. His father picked up the paper on the desk and read the report of the incident.

'Look, I've got things to do,' the ruddy-faced parent blustered. 'I can't see why we have been summoned here over a messy table. It's not as if my lad has damaged anything. It's not a hanging offence, is it?'

'So, you think it is quite acceptable then for your son to leave the floor covered in food and the table in this state?' asked the Captain.

'From what you say, I admit it sounds a bit messy but surely it's the waiter's job to clear up after the passengers, or am I mistaken?'

'Yes, I think that is what your son thinks. When one of the boys was told by a passenger that the staff should not be expected to have to clean up after them, one of the boys replied, "That's what they're there for." I guess then that you are quite happy for your slovenly son to throw food on the floor at home and you or your wife to clear up after the mess he leaves?' The parent didn't respond. 'The restaurant staff do amazing work on this ship,' he was told, 'and they deserve to be treated with respect and courtesy. They work incredibly hard and are invariably polite and good-humoured. They warrant, as the passenger said, to be treated with consideration.'

'Could I say, Captain,' said the other parent, who had remained in virtual shocked silence until this point, 'I don't think what my son did is at all acceptable. It was disgraceful and what he said to the passengers, if indeed he is the guilty one, was rude and offensive. I am ashamed of him, and I will have a few words to say to him when we are alone. Furthermore, I shall see to it that he apologises to the restaurant staff and to the passengers he offended.' He turned and glared again at his son. 'Is that clear, George?'

'Yes, Dad,' muttered the boy.

'I should like to point out—' began the ruddy-faced parent.

'One moment,' the Captain cut him off, holding up a hand. 'I have not finished. You will, no doubt, have heard that a family was put off the ship in Mallorca, following a passenger's unacceptable behaviour.'

'Yes, I heard something of the sort,' replied the man.

The Captain drew in a deep determined breath. 'I am minded doing the same with you and your family.'

'What?'

'Nothing escapes my notice on this ship,' said the Captain in a flat, matter-of-fact tone. 'The happiness and well-being of the passengers is my main priority. I will not tolerate such behaviour from these . . . reprobates. You do your son no favours by taking his part.'

The individual opened his mouth to speak but the other parent cut him off.

'I certainly do not take my son's part in this, Captain,' he said. 'George's behaviour was unacceptable, and I am ashamed of him. I'm sure he has something to say.'

'I'm sorry,' mumbled the boy.

'Now let me make myself perfectly clear,' said the Captain, speaking calmly and precisely, 'if there is a reoccurrence of their rude and boorish conduct, then I shall put them and their families off the ship at the next port of call.'

'I don't think you can do that,' said the sour-faced man half-heartedly.

'Oh yes, I can,' replied the Captain, 'and I will. On board this ship, my word is law.' The man stared at him but said nothing. The other parent refused to meet the Captain's eyes. 'Do I make myself plain?' he asked the boys.

They both nodded and mumbled.

'I didn't quite catch that.'

'Yes, sir,' they replied.

He turned to their fathers. 'I shall ask the restaurant staff to keep a close eye on these two and if their table is not left tidy and their behaviour is faultless in future, then we will be seeing each other again and I shall have no qualms about putting them and their parents off the ship. That is all.' He looked down.

The sour-faced man opened his mouth to speak but the other parent gripped his arm. 'For God's sake, leave it!' he said.

The sisters were relaxing on the promenade deck when Edna, with unconcealed interest, leaned forward in her recliner when she caught sight of the concert pianist and the tall, strikingly good-looking young woman in the red dress who had accompanied him after the last recital. She watched them hungrily like a bright-eyed cat might stare at a bird or a goldfish in a bowl. She made a little clucking noise and then nudged Miriam.

'What is it?' asked her sister, jumping up on her recliner, startled at being prodded out of her sleep.

'It was that piano player who's just walked past,' said Edna, lowering her voice melodramatically. 'Did you see who he was with?'

'How could I see who he was with?' replied her sister. 'I was fast asleep until you jabbed me in the ribs.'

'He was with that young woman in the red dress who sat on the front row when he did his concert and who followed him out.'

'Was he?' sighed Miriam.

'She's called Antonia.'

'Who is?'

'The woman the pianist was with.'

'Well, what about it?'

'I *thought* there was something going on between them two, the way he kept looking at her and smirking. He's just walked past, all lovey-dovey, as bold as brass, with his arm around her waist.'

'She's probably a fan of his music,' said Miriam yawning.

'You're barking up the wrong street there,' announced Edna. 'They were having breakfast together this morning and yesterday I saw them sitting at the same table later in the Rainbow Lounge as thick as thieves. I mean what is an attractive young woman doing with the likes of a small, unfortunate-looking, overweight, middle-aged man who is old enough to be her father?' Before her sister could venture an opinion, Edna provided the answer. 'I'll tell you what it is and it's not his plinky-plonky music that's attracted her, it's money. He'll not be badly off. I bet that piano player's long-suffering wife is stuck at home while he's sowing his wild oats aboard a cruise ship with his fancy woman. Of course, what makes it worse is the way he flaunts her. It's the same the whole world over: a man like him, past his prime, is thinking he can recapture his youth by taking up with a younger woman, an old dog up to his new tricks.'

'It happened with the owner of that medical supplies' shop where you worked,' teased Miriam, knowing full well her sister would come to the defence of her former employer. 'Mr Ellerby was no oil painting, but he had his bit on the side – the little Italian woman who ran the corner mini-mart.'

'There was nothing going on of that nature with Mr Ellerby and Mrs Fattatori. They were just good friends.'

'Really?' She did not disguise the mischief in her voice.

'There was some spectaculating by the woman in the fish-monger's that there was more to it than meets the eye, but I never believed Mr Ellerby was carrying on with Mrs Fattatori and if it was mentioned I soon put them right.'

'I'm sure you did,' muttered Miriam.

'As you well know, I'm not the sort of person who gossips about somebody else's dirty washing in public. You can say what you like about me, Miriam, but I pride myself at being an exceptionally good listener and very discreet. I'm the last person to pay any attention to tittle-tattle.'

Her sister's eyelids began to droop.

'Anyway,' Edna continued, 'Mr Ellerby didn't make an exhibition of himself parading Mrs Fattatori in public. And another thing—' Edna stopped mid-sentence when she heard snoring. Her sister had fallen back asleep.

After a substantial meal the sisters retired to the Rainbow Lounge for coffee.

'What do you want to do now?' asked Edna.

'I thought I might try my hand at line dancing this afternoon,' replied her sister.

'Line dancing!'

'I was speaking to a woman who said it was fun. There's a young man in the Entertainment Team who takes the class and I heard he's a laugh a minute.'

'Do you think you're up to it?'

'I'm not quite in my dotage yet, thank you very much.'

'Well, there is no way I could go line dancing what with my medical conditions,' said Edna.

'I'm not suggesting that *you* go line dancing. You could come and watch.'

'What, a lot of geriatrics strutting about like constipated turkeys,' huffed her sister tritely. 'I'd sooner watch paint dry.'

Miriam was quiet for a moment.

'You don't mind me going, do you?' she asked.

'Of course not.'

Miriam flicked through her daily newsletter. 'Well, there's quite a bit to occupy you while I'm gone. There's a craft workshop this afternoon where the tutor is teaching bead weaving, which might be of interest, or an art class on watercolour painting or there's a film on at the cinema. It's called *Death Wish.*'

Edna shook her head in exasperation but didn't deign to reply.

Miriam consulted the newsletter and read. 'You might like to go to the seminar "Living Longer and Looking Better". It shows you how to reduce the signs of ageing and how to live a happy and contented life through weight loss, daily exercise, stress control and sleep management which will reduce the risk of dementia.'

'No, thank you.'

'And a dance demonstration—'

Edna interrupted noisily. 'You go to your line dancing,' she said. 'You don't need to worry about me.'

'Will you be all right by yourself?'

'Of course I will. We're not joined at the hip.'

Thank goodness for small mercies, thought her sister. She could not imagine anything worse than being joined to Edna's legendary hip.

Later that afternoon, Miriam found her sister still sitting in the same spot in the Rainbow Lounge.

'So how was your line dancing?' she was asked.

'Oh, it was really good,' bubbled Miriam. 'Peter – he was the teacher – said I had natural rhythm after we'd danced the "Boot Scootin' Boogie". He said I had the agility and timing of a seasoned dancer and the lightness of a bubble.'

Enda snorted. 'He'll say that to everyone,' she remarked disparagingly.

'Have you been sitting here all the time?' asked Miriam.

'No, I haven't,' replied Edna. 'I went to the casino.'

'The casino?'

'Yes, I had a little flutter. There was a very nice gentleman who showed me how to play blackjack. He won thirty pounds and said I brought him luck.'

'It's a mug's game is gambling,' stated Miriam. 'People rarely win anything.'

'I did,' said Edna smugly.

'You won?'

'A hundred pounds.'

'A hundred pounds.'

'Will you stop repeating me. You sound like an echo. Percy asked me to meet him for afternoon tea.'

'Who's Percy?'

'The man who taught me how to play blackjack. He said he'd explain the rules of baccarat, show me the rudiments. I shan't meet him. I think he had other things on his mind than showing me how to play cards.' She took a breath. 'I don't want to get entangled with men at my time of life.'

That evening it was a formal occasion on the cruise and the Ocean Spa and hairdressing salon was solidly booked by women wanting to look their best for this special occasion.

Edna and Miriam, having booked hairdressing appointments, were sitting in the reception area.

'This pew is most uncomfortable,' complained Edna, shuffling in the seat. 'It's too narrow and there are no armrests.'

'It's not a pew,' her sister informed her, 'it's called a banquette. We used to have them in the first-class lounge at the station where I worked.'

'It's a what?'

'It's a banquette, an upholstered seat. It's French. It's a very fashionable piece of furniture.'

'Well, the French are welcome to it because it's like sitting on a garden bench. You would have thought—'

She stopped mid-sentence as Maureen made an appearance from the hairdressing salon. She was red-faced, panting, and yelling at Bianca who was following her.

'Just look at it!' Maureen shouted at Bianca, pointing to her head. 'I look as if I've been dragged through a hedge backwards. All I wanted was a trim, a quick wash and my roots doing, and my hair looks as if it's been cut with a pair of garden shears and the colour's all wrong. It's frightful.'

It was a fact that Maureen's hair was a mess. She resembled the survivor of a road crash who had struggled up the embankment of a motorway after the road accident. Her bright dyed hair stood up from her scalp in wiry tufts.

The sisters watched fascinated.

Bianca remained remarkably calm. 'You have very unmanageable hair,' she said. 'It was the best I could do.'

'Well, it wasn't good enough,' complained Maureen. 'I look like a freak.' She turned to Edna. 'What do you think?'

Most people asked for their opinion would have poured oil on troubled waters, perhaps remarking reassuringly that the hair wasn't all that bad, but Edna did not number amongst those, nor was she one to refrain from a forthright comment.

'Well, she's done you no favours and that's for sure,' she remarked carelessly.

Her sister, the well-practised appeaser when it came to her sister's comments, opened her mouth to placate the passenger and sounded a reassuring note. 'Oh, it's not too bad,' she said.

'Not too bad,' echoed her sister. 'It's a shambles.'

'I beg your pardon?' asked Bianca in a sharp defensive tone of voice and with a direct and stern-eyed gaze. Her equanimity had disappeared with this intervention. 'I suggest you keep your comments to yourself.'

Miriam shot her sister a glance. 'Leave it,' she warned, under her breath.

'I was asked for my opinion,' responded Edna, unabashed and in a sharp voice. 'I'm a plain-speaking sort of woman and I speak as I find. I say what I mean, and I mean what I say unlike some folk. Anyone can see that this poor woman's hair is a disaster. It looks as if she's had her hair cut by a blind person with a pair of blunt scissors.'

Bianca, lost for words, breathed in the manner of a goldfish.

'You see!' barked Maureen. 'It's a disaster. Am I supposed to go into dinner on a formal night with hair looking like this?'

'Well, I wouldn't want to go down to dinner with my hair like that,' remarked Edna blithely, rubbing salt in the wound.

Bianca now seemed less composed and was feeling under threat as she noticed that other passengers, who were waiting in the reception area, were listening to the exchange. Her dogmatic tone faltered. 'I could have another go, I suppose,' she said.

'Over my dead body!' cried Maureen.

'My sister and I are booked in with Becky,' Edna told the distraught passenger. 'You want to see if she can do some remedial work on your hair though she's probably all booked up and by the looks of it I don't suppose she could do an awful lot.'

Bianca gave her a look that would have turned milk sour.

'It's a pity they don't sell wigs in the shop,' remarked Edna.

'Ever the diplomat,' muttered Miriam, shaking her head.

16

The formal night was a highlight of the cruise and passengers were dressed for the occasion. The men wore dinner jackets or tuxedos, the women were resplendent in evening gowns and the Captain and officers wore their dress uniforms. Mrs De la Mare, dressed in a flattering and dramatic petrol-blue dress and bedecked in an assortment of expensive gold jewellery attracted a deal of attention. She stood on the gallery holding her head proudly and peered austerely at the passengers who had gathered in the atrium for the Captain's reception with the look on her face of a woman quite aware that she was being admired. She had arrived late and missed the Captain's speech. Drinking from her champagne flute in little bird-like sips, she caught sight of Lady Staithes who stood out in the middle of a knot of people, dressed in an exquisite lilac satin gown. She was listening to the author. This was the sort of passenger with whom Mrs De la Mare wished to mix, someone of refinement and importance with that quiet aristocratic bearing. She descended the stairs and went to join her. Unquestionably, she assumed here was a kindred spirit.

The group, in the centre of which was Lady Staithes, consisted of the Reverend Christopher Hinderwell and his wife Esmé, Dr Elodie King and Oliver's grandparents.

'Good evening,' announced Mrs De la Mare, approaching with a full-frontal assault, and rudely interrupting the speaker. Her face wore a contrived smile.

Lady Staithes arched an eyebrow but did not respond. On the cruise she had preserved that mysterious reticence which went well with her demeanour and appearance. A fleeting expression of annoyance passed across her face. How impolite of the woman to intrude, she thought.

'Good evening,' replied the other passengers in unison.

'I thought I might join you,' said Mrs De la Mare. She looked at Lady Staithes and allowed herself another small smile. 'We have met.' She cocked her head to the side as though she expected to receive a reply but when this was not forthcoming, she continued. 'We were both dining in the Diamond Grill, if you recall and—'

'Yes, I do remember,' replied Lady Staithes cutting her off and staring at her with calculated blankness. She turned back to Mr Hinderwell. 'You were saying?'

'I was just telling Mr and Mrs Champion here,' said the clergyman to Mrs De la Mare, 'that they must be most proud of their grandson. Oliver is travelling with them on the cruise and has made quite an impression.'

'Really?' she replied indifferently.

'He is a credit to them; such a polite young man, intelligent and full of self-confidence. Very unusual for someone of his age.'

'And extremely well-informed,' added Elodie. 'His knowledge of history is quite amazing.' She turned to Lady Staithes. 'We had a most interesting conversation on the coach when we returned from Seville. Do you know, he went around the city all by himself? That was quite an achievement for someone of his age.'

'How old is he?' she was asked.

'He's twelve, going on sixty,' said the boy's grandmother good-humouredly.

'I always feel that the young are more adventurous these days than we were at their age,' observed Lady Staithes.

'I don't know about Oliver being adventurous,' declared the boy's grandfather, 'but he is quite a character and has an independence of mind which some adults find rather disconcerting. I am so pleased that you like him, Dr King.'

'We did, however, tell him that going into Rome by himself is not a good idea and suggested he come on a tour with us,' said Mrs Champion. 'I'm afraid my husband and I are a bit too long in the tooth to go walking around in the heat. We find—'

'Yes, this weather tends to be too oppressive at this time of year in the Mediterranean,' interjected Mrs De la Mare. 'I shall not venture ashore. I have been to Rome on several occasions. I am informed the Pope will be giving a blessing while we are there so I guess the city will be awfully crowded. Rome also has the reputation of being a hotbed of pickpockets. I recall being told—'

'I should be delighted if Oliver wishes to accompany me,' said Elodie to Mr and Mrs Champion. She, like Lady Staithes, was wearying of the strident woman's moans. 'I am not very conversant with Roman history. It will be an education for me. Oliver I'm sure knows more than I.'

'That's most kind of you, Dr King,' said the boy's grandmother. 'I'm sure he would love to join you. Some adults do find our grandson . . . how can I say . . . a little precocious. I'm so pleased you like him.'

'There is nothing wrong in being precocious,' said the author. There was a sharpness in her voice. When she had been at school, the word had often been ascribed to her by her teachers as if it were something pejorative.

'Old for his years might be a better description,' remarked Mr Hinderwell. 'He is a most interesting young man. He managed to beat me at chess. He told me you taught him, Mr Champion.'

'Yes, but I soon found he was wiping the board with me.'

'I believe he owes his impeccable table manners to you and your good wife,' said the clergyman. 'Oliver and I were having lunch together yesterday and I commented upon them when he cleared away after himself and never once put his elbows on the table. He told me that if he did, his grandfather would say "all joints will be carved". It did so make me laugh.'

'Yes,' said Mr Champion laughing too. 'It sounds like Oliver.'

'We received a delightful note from the Captain,' added his wife, 'saying how taken he was with Oliver when he was invited to go on to the bridge of the ship. Evidently he asked—'

'Really?' interrupted Mrs De la Mare, her ears pricking up at the mention of the Captain. 'You received a note from the Captain?'

'Yes, it was good of him.'

'I have not seen him yet,' she remarked.

This was hardly surprising since she had spent most of her time in the stateroom or on the exclusive sun deck reserved for the VIP passengers.

'He was here earlier to formally welcome everyone aboard,' Mr Hinderwell informed her.

'I arrived late,' explained Mrs De la Mare.

'He gave a very witty speech,' said Mrs Hinderwell. 'I was surprised to see how young he was. Someone told me he is the youngest Captain in the fleet.'

'We can ask him over dinner,' said Lady Staithes inclining her head gracefully.

'You are dining with the Captain this evening?' enquired Mrs De la Mare. The revelation had shattered her composure and her face flashed with a sudden fierce grimace. It was clear the news was not well received.

'Yes, our group are to join him at his table,' said Mrs Hinderwell.

'You are *all* dining with the Captain tonight?' asked Mrs De la Mare, unable to disguise the surprise in her voice.

'We are,' Oliver's grandmother told her. 'It is so kind of him to invite us.'

'I don't know why my wife and I have been so favoured,' said Mr Hinderwell.

Neither can I, thought Mrs De la Mare.

'I think dinner is about to be announced,' said Elodie, 'so we should perhaps be making a move.'

To attract passengers into the Jolly Sailor Tavern before they headed for the restaurant for dinner, it was the 'Happy Hour' when all the cocktails were half price.

Bruce was at a corner table with one of the passengers who attended the dance class. The young woman, who was listening to him attentively, was tall and thin with a long, angular face and large wondering eyes half hidden behind a fiercely cut blond fringe.

'You have real talent, Vanessa,' said the dance tutor.

'Aahhh, go on,' she said, colouring a little.

'No, it's true, you're a natural on the dance floor. It's all very well knowing the right steps, but you respond to the subtleties and rhythms of the music like a professional.'

'Aahhh, go on.'

'No, really. You were most passionate in the tango today and in the Viennese waltz, your turns and pirouettes were superb. You glided across the floor like a swan on a tranquil lake.'

'Aahhh, go on.'

'No, really. I saw what a good dancer you were at the first lesson. I said to myself, "That young woman doesn't need any lessons." You dominated the floor and moved so deftly to the music.' He ran his eyes critically over her as a doctor might do when examining a patient. 'Of course, you must have trained as a dancer.'

'No.'

'That does surprise me.'

'I did a bit of ballet and tap when I was young, but it hurt my feet, so I gave it up and then went to RADA.'

'To RADA!' Bruce exclaimed. 'The Royal Academy of Dramatic Art. Now that is quite something.'

'No,' she tittered. 'René Arnold's Dance Academy. She taught ballroom dancing.'

'I knew you were a trained dancer.'

'Aahhh, go on.'

'I did.'

'We didn't do anything special, just the ordinary ballroom stuff. I've come to your classes to improve my mambo and learn the lambada.'

'I shall be delighted to show you the moves. Of course, it doesn't surprise me that you have experience dancing, Vanessa,' said Bruce. 'You have an innate gift.'

'Aahhh, go on.'

'So, what brings an attractive young woman like you travelling on a cruise ship all by herself?'

'It's a long story. You don't want to hear all about that.'

'No, I'm interested,' he told her, leaning forward. 'I'm a good listener.'

'Well, for a start I broke it off with my boyfriend.'

'Oh, I am sorry.'

'I'm not. He was a motor mechanic and he had dirty fingernails and smelled of petrol. I had a sneaking feeling he was seeing someone else.'

'The cad.'

'And I had another sneaking feeling he'd keyed my car when I dumped him. You know, scratched it down the side.'

'A nasty thing to do.'

'Then I got the sack from the "Salt and Battery Fish Restaurant" where I worked. I have a sneaking feeling that one of the other waitresses had been talking to the manager behind my back, saying I was giving certain favoured customers more chips.'

'Aahhh, go on.' Vanessa's catchphrase seemed to be infectious.

'I'm not sorry that I got the sack. Actually, between you and me, I didn't like the job. I always seemed to smell of chip fat. Then I lost my Shih Tzus.'

'You lost your what?'

'My dog, Pippin. He did tend to bark a bit and the neighbours were always complaining. I had a sneaking feeling that one of them put some rat poison down in my garden and it killed him.'

'Dreadful,' said Bruce. Vanessa seemed to have had a remarkable number of sneaky feelings, he thought. He wondered if she had a sneaky feeling about him.

'So, things got on top of me.'

'Things got on top of you?' he repeated.

'And I thought a holiday would do me good. Fresh air and a change of scene and all that. So, here I am, determined to make a new start.'

'To pick yourself up, dust yourself off, and start all over again,' sang Bruce.

'What?'

'It's a song,' he told her.

'What is?'

'It doesn't matter. I'm delighted you are on the cruise. Now, I guess you could do with another cocktail.'

'Ahhh, go on then.'

'Yours was a "Hanky Panky" wasn't it?'

Albert and Maureen sat by the bar.

'We should have come earlier,' Maureen grumbled, 'then we could have got a table by the window. It was you taking all your time in the laundrette. I don't know why it takes you so long to iron a few shirts.'

Albert decided not to respond. 'What do you want to drink?'

She looked at the list of cocktails. 'I'll have "Sex on the Beach".'

'You'll have what?'

'This cocktail. It's vodka, peach schnapps, orange, and cranberry juice. It's called "Sex on the Beach". Mrs Mickleby had it when she was on the cruise last year and she recommended it. She said it was very refreshing.'

'What sort of name is "Sex on the Beach"?' he asked.

'Just get the drinks, will you Albert,' she told him, sighing.

Having ordered the cocktail and a beer for himself, he returned to his table.

'Have you ordered the drinks?' Maureen asked.

'No, I've been ironing a shirt,' he replied sarcastically. 'What do you think I've been doing?'

Before his wife could answer back, the Chief Housekeeper passed.

'Hi, Albert,' she called.

'Oh hello, Christine,' he called back.

'Who was that?' asked Maureen.

'She's in charge of the housekeeping on the ship.'

'How do you know *her*?'

'I met her in the laundrette.'

A moment later Sandra passed.

'Good evening, Albert,' she said.

'Good evening, Sandra,' he replied.

'And *who's* that?'

'A woman I met in the laundrette.'

Edna and Miriam had decided they would avail themselves of sampling some cut-price cocktails and came and sat at the next table.

'Hello, Albert,' said Edna.

'Hello, Edna,' he replied.

'Hello, Albert,' said Miriam.

'Hello, Miriam,' he replied.

'Is this your wife?' asked Edna.

'Yes, this is Maureen,' he told her.

'You've got a real treasure there,' she said.

'A perfect gentleman,' added Miriam.

'And who are those two?' asked Maureen, lowering her voice. She held up a hand before he could reply. 'No, don't tell me, you met them in the laundrette.'

'I did, actually,' said Albert.

'What have you got down there, a harem? I shall have to come along with you tomorrow and see what you're getting up to with all these women.'

'I'd like that,' said Albert, 'and then happen you can do the bloody ironing while you're there.'

There followed a simmering silence.

Edna studied the drinks' menu.

'I think I might have a "Peniscoala" or a "Dark 'n' Stormy",' she said. 'What do you fancy?'

'I like the sound of "El Diablo",' replied her sister. 'It's ginger beer and lime juice or maybe I might try a "Brass Monkey".'

'There's one here called the "Corpse Reviver." I could do with something like that after traipsing around Mallorca all day. My feet are killing me, and I won't mention how my hip feels.'

'Please don't,' muttered her sister.

'All those people getting in the way.'

'If you'd been able to see where you were going and not wearing that silly sombrero,' said her sister, 'you wouldn't have banged into people.'

'The place was too crowded and too hot. We should have come back to the ship. I have seen enough castles, ruins and churches to last me a lifetime.'

'Well, it was you who insisted on going to the cathedral.'

'That was to get out of the sun.'

'At least you didn't gatecrash a funeral this time,' chuckled Miriam.

'Least said about that the better.'

'I've said it before, you're a menace with that walking frame. You nearly collided with that old priest and had the candles all over the floor. Then going out you nearly knocked the Virgin Mary off her plinth, and you would persist in plodding down the main street stopping at every blessed shop you came to. It's no wonder your feet and your hip are killing you. The sooner you decide to have that hip operation the better.'

'Firstly, Miriam, I did not gatecrash the funeral and secondly I do not plod,' answered Edna nettled. 'You make me sound like a tortoise. Thirdly having the hip operation is a big decision and I am still thinking it over.'

'And then you would go around the packed market with those scary looking fish staring from the slab, cutting through the crowds like a knife through butter.'

Edna ignored the comment and called the waiter over.

'Let's order a drink,' she said.

Several cocktails later, the women were the worse for wear and when it was announced dinner was now being served in the Sunset Restaurant they remained resolutely in their chairs as the room emptied.

The Entertainment Manager, seeing the inebriated condition of the two women, approached them. They had been knocking back the cocktails like lemonade on a hot day.

'Would you like me to escort you down for dinner, ladies?' he asked.

Edna looked up and blinked. 'What dinner?'

'Dinner is now being served in the restaurant,' he explained.

'Is it?'

'Would you like me to accompany you?'

'Where?'

'To dinner.'

'No. I would like another drink,' she said, slurring her words.

'I think perhaps you've had enough,' said the Entertainment Manager. 'The cocktails are very alcoholic.'

'Halcoholic? Are they?' hiccupped Edna, giving him a bleary-eyed look. 'I thought cockatails were mainly fruit juice.' She turned to her sister and nudged her. 'Did you know that these cockatails are halcoholic?'

Miriam didn't answer for she was well lubricated and dead to the world, slumped in her chair sound asleep, her head lolling back and her mouth open.

'I think we'll give dinner a mish,' Edna told him. She was experiencing some difficulty in pronouncing the words. 'I'm feeling a bit light-headed.'

'Could you tell me what cabin you are in?' asked the Entertainment Manager, bending closer to the tipsy passenger.

Edna jerked up in her seat and hiccupped again. 'What do you want to know what cabin I'm in for?' she asked brusquely.

'Because I shall make sure you get there safely, madam. You may have had rather too many cocktails. You have just had a bit too much to drink.'

'Have I?'

'I think so. It might be a good idea for you and your companion to rest for a while.' Without his help, he had visions of the woman staggering down the deck with the wretched walking frame, losing her balance and falling overboard. 'So could you tell me what cabin you are in?'

'I've no idea.'

'Well, what deck are you on?'

'I'm on E Deck,' Edna told him. '"E" for Edna.' Then, after a moment she added, 'I can't remember the cabin number.'

'Don't worry, the steward will know. Now let me help you.' He hauled her to her feet and looped an arm through hers.

'What about my sister?' she asked.

'I'll come back for her.'

'And my walking frame?'

'I'll fetch it later.'

Martin took Edna's arm and guided her to the lift. She swayed from side to side.

'The sea's getting rough,' she said. 'I can feel the boat rocking. I might need one of those sick bags.'

'It's not the ship that's rocking, madam,' he told her. 'It's you.'

On E Deck he discovered from the steward the number of the women's cabin.

'Where are we?' asked Edna hanging onto Martin's arm.

'At your cabin,' he told her.

She was asked for her card key to open the door. She rummaged in her handbag, plucked it from a pocket but before handing it over, she clutched it to her bosom and looking him straight in the eye, told him curtly, 'And you're not coming in, you know.'

While Bruce and Vanessa were enjoying their "Hanky Panky" and Edna and Miriam were out for the count in the Jolly Sailor Tavern, Babs was in the Piano Bar with the Italian tenor. She looked dreamily into his eyes.

'I so enjoyed your concert, Lorenzo,' she said. 'You have a wonderful voice.'

'Thank you,' he replied, bowing his head a little, in response to the flattering attention. 'That isa most kind.'

'On the last cruise,' Babs informed him, 'we had an opera singer with the most dreadfully high screeching voice. She sounded like a live bat being stapled to a wall. People walked out. Your concert was magical.'

Lorenzo looked at her and displayed his capped and crowned dazzling white teeth.

'Will you be getting offa the ship in Roma?' he asked.

'Oh yes, I wouldn't miss it for the world.'

'Ah, Roma, *la citta eterna*,' he said. 'It was called "the eternal city" back in the first century because of its splendour.'

'I shall be going ashore alone,' she confided, fluttering her lashes. 'Bruce and me have not been exactly hitting it off lately. He's been very difficult. I won't be coming with him on the next cruise. There'll be a parting of the ways.'

The Italian tenor rested his hand on hers and displayed a mouthful of sympathetic teeth. 'Perhaps you might allow me to takea you around. I could show you a thing or two.'

'Oh, I should like that very much,' Babs replied demurely, resisting adding that she was sure that he could.

17

Mrs De la Mare stood on her balcony inhaling the fresh night air. It was a warm evening. A bright, cold moon shone in a jet-black sky punctuated by pinpricks of stars. The only sound was the swish of the ocean as the great liner moved through the water. She was not a happy woman. How was it that *she* had not been asked to dine with the Captain? She could understand why such a passenger as Lady Staithes had been invited but what singled out the dusty old vicar and his simpering wife, the elderly couple, and the blue-stocking author?

She had decided to dine in her stateroom that evening but had hardly touched the meal. As the butler cleared the contents on the dinner table, she came into the cabin and asked if there had been a card or a letter from the Captain. She was told nothing had been left for her.

'Were you expecting something, madam?' he asked.

'I thought perhaps there might have been a communication from the Captain,' she said.

'No, madam, there is nothing.'

'I was rather anticipating a request to dine with him,' she said, her sense of injury deepening. 'On the last cruise I was invited to join the Captain at his table one evening. Perhaps it might have been mislaid.'

'Should I enquire for you, madam?'

'No, no, don't bother. It's of no great consequence.' But it *was* of great consequence, and she determined to have another word with the Purser.

'Is there anything else you require, madam?' he asked.

'No thank you, Dominic,' she replied.

After leaving her stateroom the butler went to see the Chief Housekeeper. Christine was in a particularly bad-tempered frame of mind. It was customary for a square of chocolate to be placed on the pillow of each passenger by the steward or stewardess each evening when the cabins were being cleaned. It was a practice about which the Chief Housekeeper had complained but her protests had gone unheeded. The evening before, several passengers, no doubt worse for drink from taking full advantage of the 'Happy Hour', had stumbled into their beds forgetting to remove the sweet. The following morning the stewards had discovered the sheets and pillowcases daubed in chocolate. This, of course, meant all the bedclothes and pillowcases had to be changed. Added to this, a passenger had deposited some foreign object down the cabin toilet and blocked the system, another had been sick on the carpet and a third somehow managed to break the bed. It had all meant extra work for her team and for herself, hence her bad mood.

'I am really busy at the moment, Dominic,' she told him irritably. 'Is it important?'

'I think so,' he replied.

'Well, what is it?'

'It's the passenger in the Bermuda Suite,' he said. 'She doesn't seem to be enjoying the cruise.'

There was an audible sigh. 'What's *her* problem?'

'She is a sad and I think a lonely woman,' said Dominic.

'More money than sense it sounds to me.'

'I feel sorry for her.'

'You don't need to, and she doesn't need to feel sad and lonely in one of the most luxurious staterooms on the ship, looked after by a butler, with all the activities on offer and surrounded by passengers. How is it possible to feel lonely on a ship full of people? I really don't think you should feel any sympathy for her with what she's got. *We* should be so lucky. She should get a life.'

'She was hoping she might have received an invitation to dine at the Captain's table,' Dominic told her.

The Chief Housekeeper scoffed. 'Is it all she has to moan about?'

'It seems important to her,' she was told.

'Not all the passengers can dine with the Captain,' Christine answered testily. 'It is up to him who he wishes to invite and, from what you have told me, she's not likely to be stimulating company.'

'I know,' he answered, 'but it seems she was really looking forward to it and—'

'Look, Dominic,' she interrupted. 'I appreciate your interest, but we can't have passengers demanding to sit at the Captain's table. As I've said, it's up to him who to ask.'

'No, no, she hasn't done that. She has not asked me to come and see you. She's mentioned she was hoping for an invitation and—'

'I am up to my eyes at the moment. I really have too much to do without dealing with some spoiled and disgruntled passenger's whim.'

'I just thought I would mention it,' he said, turning to go. 'I'm sorry to have bothered you.'

She mellowed and rested a hand on his arm. 'Oh, very well. Let me see what I can do. I'm not promising anything, but I'll have a word with the Purser. Passengers,' she mouthed, 'who would have them?'

At lunch in the Sunrise Restaurant the following day, Christopher and Esmé Hinderwell and Cyril and Connie were joined at the table by two smartly dressed young doctors. The group had a most interesting and good-humoured conversation during the meal until a couple arrived and put paid to that. The man was a broad, pugnacious-looking individual with the crease of a double chin, vast florid face, twisted with ill-temper, and close-set unsmiling eyes. His eyebrows flew outward like wings. Mrs Hinderwell pictured him standing behind a butcher's counter or hauling sacks of coal. The woman, in contrast, was small, wrinkled and careworn with a face set in a permanent frown. They sat down, the man leaning back expansively on his chair, stretching his fat legs underneath the table, and sucking in his teeth. His stomach pushed forcefully against his shirt which opened slightly to reveal a portion of white flesh. It was clear he liked his food and plenty of it. His diminutive companion perched on the end of her chair like a frightened mouse, clutching her handbag in front of her like a shield.

'I'm afraid we will prove poor company for you this lunchtime,' Mr Hinderwell informed the couple genially. 'We have all but finished our meal. Perhaps you may wish to sit with some passengers who, like yourself, have not eaten yet.'

'No, you're all right,' replied the man. 'We like this table by the window.'

A moment later the waiter approached. 'Good afternoon, sir,' he said. 'Are you ready to order?'

'We'll have what we had yesterday,' said the man. 'Tomato soup, cottage pie and treacle sponge and don't stint on the custard. Oh, and some cheese and biscuits for afters. Tell the wine waiter we'll have just the one glass of wine – the Chardonnay will do.'

Mrs Hinderwell bristled. As a teacher she had taught the children in her classes to always display good manners, to be polite and respectful and say 'please' and 'thank you'. She recalled the Port Lecturer's words that he found young people lacking manners. There were some adults, like this ignorant individual sitting opposite her, who needed a lesson in that respect. She felt like telling the boorish passenger to be more civil, but she bit her tongue.

The man looked at her husband. 'So, what have you been up to on the cruise?'

'Well quite a deal of things, really,' replied the clergyman pleasantly. 'My wife and I have been ashore, of course, and have very much enjoyed the opera singer, the lectures and the classical piano recital.'

'They're not our cup of tea,' stated the man dismissively.

'Each to 'is own,' said Cyril.

'What?'

'I said each to 'is own,' he repeated.

The wine arrived. 'I'm in cabin A 200,' the man told the wine waiter. 'Put it on my tab.' He took a large gulp before turning to his wife. 'She doesn't drink,' he explained. The soup arrived. The man finished his in four large and noisy spoonfuls, the woman sipped hers, bird like.

'So, what do you do for a living, then?' the man asked Mr Hinderwell.

'I'm an Anglican priest,' he was told, 'and my wife was a teacher.'

'One of the God squad, eh?'

'Yes, I suppose you might say that.'

'I've not much time for religion, myself,' he announced. 'Course, if I'm asked, I always say C of E. I mean you can believe anything can't you in the Church of England, not like the Catholics and the Jews.'

'I might take issue with you on that,' ventured Mr Hinderwell, raising a scholarly eyebrow. His wife rested a hand on his arm and shook her head. 'But this is not the time nor the place.'

'I don't have much time for teachers,' said the man.

'You don't say,' remarked Esmé, looking at him as she used to look at a troublesome pupil.

'I did nothing at school.'

'Perhaps you didn't make much of an effort to learn,' said Esmé acidly. 'It is an old axiom that a child who does not wish to learn cannot be taught.'

'Well, I was taught nothing,' replied the man, oblivious of the coolness in her remark, 'but I've done very well for myself.' His arms were folded and rested on his stomach. Then, like many a self-made man, he exuded a boastful confidence which comes with success in life. 'I left school without any susstifucates, and I don't have letters after my name like the vicar here, but I'll tell you this, I've done a whole sight better than the clever clogs who were in the top class. Not many of them would be able to afford an outside cabin with a double balcony like ours or drive a Merc. I left school at fifteen and started at the bottom and worked my way up from nothing. I got took on at the shoddy factory sorting fabric to be used for stuffing mattresses.' He drummed his stubby fingers on the tabletop.

'Fascinatin',' mouthed Cyril in a wearisome voice.

'In my book,' the man continued to hold forth, pompously and slowly as if he were addressing his workers, 'it's deter-mination, hard work, and discipline what lead to success in life.' He leaned back and rested his fat hands on the curve of his paunch. If he thought this monologue would impress his listeners, he was mistaken, for it had the very opposite effect. But he had not finished. He leaned forward, now in his stride. 'Too many people sit on their backsides these days and think the country owes them a living. You can't walk anywhere these days without seeing all these down-and-outs begging for money.' He drained his glass noisily.

'Sometimes it's not a homeless person's fault that they have to live on the street,' the clergyman told him. 'In my experience—'

'They should get a job,' cut in the man. 'I ended up owning the factory and I've done well, even if I do say so myself. There's a lot of brass in shoddy, you know.'

His table companions decided not to engage in any further conversation with him. When the main course arrived for the couple, the two young men, disinclined to listen to the dogmatic, loud-mouthed passenger, made their excuses and departed.

'So, what cabin have you got?' the man asked Mr Hinderwell before forking up a large portion of the cottage pie and devouring it greedily.

'Just an ordinary one,' said Mr Hinderwell. 'Nothing special.'

'Inside, is it?'

'Yes, it's inside, but very comfortable and perfectly adequate.'

'We're in an outside cabin, on A Deck.'

'Yes, we heard,' said Mrs Hinderwell with a certain tartness.

'Mavis suffers from claustrophobia,' said the man, tilting his head in his wife's direction.

The woman, who had remained as silent and expressionless as a graveyard statue, raised her head at the mention of her name with tired, long-suffering eyes. She gave a small wearisome sigh before returning to poke the food around on her plate like an archaeologist sifting through some ancient bones.

The man finished his lunch, wiped his mouth extravagantly on a napkin and now turned his attention to Cyril.

'So, what do you do for a living?'

'Nowt,' said Cyril. He had taken a strong dislike to this passenger and found something disconcerting in the man's close-set eyes.

'What?'

'I don't do owt. I'm retired.'

'What did you do before?'

'I worked at an 'ousehold waste an' recyclin' centre.'

'I wouldn't have liked doing that – sorting through other people's rubbish and cast-offs,' the man said throatily. It was clear that this passenger measured people by what they did for a living and how much money they had.

'Aye, well as I said, each to 'is own,' Cyril answered, 'I liked my job. I was good at it an' it were interestin' and different.'

'So, are you in an inside cabin like the vicar here?'

'No, we're in t'Manhattan Suite.'

'The Manhattan Suite?' cried the man. He sat up. 'It's one of them penthouses at the top of the ship, isn't it?'

'Aye, it is,' answered Cyril.

'Must have cost you an arm and a leg.'

'Aye, it did,' he was told. 'There's a lot of brass in 'ousehold waste, tha knows.'

The waiter cleared away the plates. The man had cleaned his, the woman had hardly touched her meal. No one spoke for a moment.

'You know those two blokes who was on our table,' said the man in a confidential tone of voice, 'well I reckon their gates swing the other way.'

'I'm sorry, I don't quite follow,' said Mr Hinderwell, genuinely mystified.

'They play for the other team,' the man told him.

'Lancashire?' enquired Cyril, knowing full well what the man meant.

'You know, members of the limp wrist brigade.' The man mouthed the next word, 'Gay.'

'Really,' said Cyril, feigning surprise. 'I would never 'ave guessed.'

'I mean, I'm not prejudiced or anything like that,' the man carried on, placing a meaty fist in the table. 'As you said, each to his own, but those sorts of people, well just let's say they aren't the sort I feel comfortable having lunch with.'

'And what do you mean by "those sorts of people"?' asked Esmé, piqued. A sharp look of disapproval came over her features. Her jaw was clenched involuntarily.

'You know, not normal.'

'We should go,' she said, nudging her husband. She placed her napkin on the table.

'I mean,' said the man, 'I could tell they were the other way inclined just by looking at them. For a start, they were wearing pink shirts.'

'Pink shirts,' repeated Cyril.

'They were both wearing pink shirts. It's a sure giveaway is that.'

'I think we should be going, Christopher,' persisted Esmé to her husband, resisting the urge to give the narrow-minded bigot who sat opposite her a smack in the face. Then, loud enough for the man to hear she said, 'I have heard quite enough of this.'

'Excuse us,' said Mr Hinderwell, and taking his wife's arm left the restaurant.

'An' we 'ad better mek a move, Connie,' said Cyril.

'I'm ready,' said his wife, getting to her feet, with a stony countenance. She had heard quite enough from the man as well.

'Pink shirts you say,' said Cyril thoughtfully, rubbing his chin. 'Well I never.'

Before dinner Mr and Mrs Hinderwell were invited up to the Manhattan Suite for drinks. Esmé stood with Connie on the double balcony looking out over the vast, empty sea, benign and calm and sparkling azure beneath a sky of vivid blue. She held a glass of chilled white wine which had been served to her on a silver tray by the butler. She was simmering over the comments of the lunchtime passenger with whom they had had the unfortunate experience of sharing a table.

'What a dreadful man,' she said.

'Yes,' said Connie. 'There's some silly, mindless people in the world.'

'I'm always amused by braggarts,' observed Mr Hinderwell, coming to join them. 'There is something rather absurd about people who constantly blow their own trumpets in the mistaken belief that their hearers will be impressed. Of course, it has the very opposite effect. It's best to ignore such people.'

'No, Christopher, I disagree,' said his wife crisply. 'It's best not to ignore them, it's best to tackle such prejudices head on. If people just stand by and listen to such views, then they will allow the cycle of prejudice to continue. It's all very well you advocating tolerance from the pulpit but that is not good enough when faced with such blatant homophobia. If I see that man again, I shall give him a piece of my mind.'

'But do you feel doing that will change his views?' asked her husband.

'Maybe not, but he needs to be told that his comments were deeply offensive and entirely unacceptable, and people don't have to sit and listen to his drivel.'

'I'm sure the man wasn't as bad as he sounded,' said her husband.

'You always look for the good in people, don't you, Christopher,' his wife remarked. It sounded like a criticism rather than a compliment.

It was true the clergyman always looked for the good in others, tried to be fair and see the other person's point of view. It was in his nature. He was a mild-mannered, unobtrusive man who eschewed altercations.

'I'm a priest, my dear,' he reminded her. 'I think it is what priests are supposed to do.'

'I know, my dear,' she said softening and taking his hand. Her love for him had not diminished after forty years of marriage. It was his gentle nature, sincerity and compassion that had first attracted her to him. Her mother, on first meeting the rather serious-minded young clergyman with the long oval face and heavy hooded eyes, had been far from impressed. 'You could do a whole lot better, Esmé,' she had told her daughter. 'You will soon tire of some dull vicar in an out of the way country parish.' But Esmé had never tired of him.

'I didn't tek to t'man as soon as 'e sat 'imself down,' said Cyril now, thinking that it was sensible to interrupt a conversation which looked as if it might develop into a domestic squabble. 'Chap wi' a big 'ead and a small brain. Course every ass likes to 'ear itself bray. I've met 'is type afore – too full of 'is own importance, t'sort that look down on t'likes o' Connie an' me. I've allus thought that them who could be snobbish aren't like that at all. It's people like that chap at the dinner table. He meks some money and then starts to think he's a cut above other folk.'

'When I was a cleaner in an office,' said his wife, 'I could count on the one hand those who actually knew my name, wished me "Good morning" or who appreciated what work I did. Some wouldn't talk to me. I might have been invisible. I could never understand why some people think that what you do for a living reflects their importance. Anyone going to work, whether they are some high-flying managing director or a cleaner deserve respect and to be treated civilly. I've seen that "I'm a lot better than you" attitude on the ship, the way that some of the passengers look down at the waiters and cabin stewards.'

'Like me in my job,' said Cyril. 'Some thought that those of us who worked at a waste disposal site were beneath 'em, of no importance, menials.' He laughed. 'It's funny 'ow money can change things. You would never believe 'ow many would-be friends and relations 'ave come knockin' at our door since we've got a bit o' brass.'

'You wouldn't believe it,' echoed Connie.

'That sort of bigotry is shameful,' said Esmé, still smarting over what she had heard at the lunch table. 'I so dislike snobs and, even more, I dislike narrow-minded, intolerant people like that dreadful man.'

'That's t'way o' things,' said Cyril. 'Some folks think they're better than others. People thinkin' they were better than us, didn't bother Connie an' me much. As my mother used to say when she came across one o' these social climbers, "They all 'ave to wipe their own bottoms".'

'Cyril!' exclaimed his wife, digging him in the ribs and giving him a disapproving look.

'I feel sorry for t'bloke's wife,' said Cyril. "Er face was like t'back end of a Barnsley bus on a wet day in 'Uddersfield. Fancy 'avin' to purrup wi' 'im.'

'Stop going on, Cyril,' instructed his wife. 'Now tell our guests why we invited them up.'

'Aye,' he said. 'Connie an' me 'ave a little something for you,' said Cyril to the clergyman. 'If you remember, I telled you afore t'arrival of Mester Shoddy ("I've worked my way up from nothing") barged in, that we've come into a fair bit o' money. Now, you was tellin' us about that charity fer 'omeless people what you've started. Well, we'd like to mek a donation.' He turned and put his arm around his wife. 'Give it to Christopher, love.' His wife pressed an envelope into Mr Hinderwell's hands.

'It's a little something from us to help,' she said.

Mr Hinderwell opened the envelope and took out a cheque. His eyes widened. 'My goodness,' he said. 'I'm lost for words.' He passed the cheque to Esmé.

'This is most generous of you both,' she said. 'We can't tell you what a difference this will make.'

'An' there's summat else,' said Cyril.

Connie presented Mr Hinderwell with an up-market carrier bag.

'We bought this at t'shop,' Cyril explained. 'I got one miself. I thought we might wear them tonight at dinner in case we come across a certain person.'

Later in the Sunset Restaurant the two men, on catching sight of Mr Shoddy ("I've worked my way up from nothing") approached his table.

'Good evening,' they both said, displaying their powder pink shirts.

The man's mouth became a thin line of suppressed anger.

18

The following day Mr Shoddy, the big, loud, self-made man was holding forth to Edna and Miriam in the Galleon Buffet at lunchtime. His large body spilled untidily in his chair. The sisters, busily eating, paid little attention to what he was saying. He was wearing a flashy shirt which was too short and too tight and revealed a couple of inches of convex stomach. His wife, still with the frown on her heavily lined face, sat beside him clutching her handbag to her chest, staring at an untouched slice of broccoli quiche on the table in front of her. The sisters seemed to have experienced no after-effects from drinking themselves into a state of oblivion in the Jolly Sailor Tavern. Both had enjoyed a prodigious breakfast and were now tucking into substantial lunches. Edna, despite her sister's exhortation to abandon the spicy food that was causing a problem for her sister 'in the downstairs' department', was making rapid inroads into a sizeable plate of Rogan Josh curry so that she could eat up and escape the man's rant. Miriam soon finished eating and regarded the man opposite with an air of weary disdain. He devoured food noisily with stubby but nimble fingers like someone starving, his fork travelling up and down to his mouth in a regular rhythmic movement.

The large forkful of fish and rice which Mr Shoddy had shovelled into his mouth, did not prevent him from blethering on. 'I worked myself up from nothing,' he spouted, pointing his fork at the sisters for emphasis, 'and I'll tell you this, ladies, the trouble is with some people these days is that

they can't stand hard work. Now, take me for example—'
He suddenly stopped mid-sentence. Something had caught
in his throat. His face became flushed, his eyes bulged,
and he began to choke. One might have expected his wife
to have jumped up in a panic to help, but she remained in
her seat looking at him with an oddly curious expression on
her creased face. She didn't appear at all distressed. Perhaps
her lifelong subordination by her boorish husband had left her
with little sympathy for him. The two sisters regarded the
gagging man with religious intensity as if they were watching some absorbing television programme. A passenger on
the neighbouring table jumped to his feet, rushed over, and
began thumping Mr Shoddy on his back but to no avail.
Fortunately for the self-made man, one of the two young
doctors with whom he had dined the previous lunchtime,
was in the restaurant and, seeing what was happening, he
hurried over. He quickly took charge, moving the helpful
passenger out of the way and dragging Mr Shoddy to his
feet. Then, standing behind him he thrust his fist between
the lower ribs, exerted sudden, sharp pressure with sufficient force that the casualty gave a great spluttering cough
and ejected a bone and a cascade of boiled rice, which
shot across the table and came to rest on Edna's shelf of a
bosom. Mr Shoddy, still coughing and gasping, slumped
heavily in his chair. Then he turned to look at his rescuer
and, on seeing him, gave a weak smile.

'Thank you very much,' he said feebly. The lobes of his big
fleshy ears turned crimson.

'My pleasure,' replied the young doctor smiling.

'Well, that was a right carry-on,' remarked Miriam. She was
accompanying her sister who was keen to change her clothes,
back to their cabin.

'I noticed none of the contents of that man's mouth touched
you,' said Edna sounding peeved.

'Fortunately, I was out of his line of fire,' replied Miriam in a rather self-satisfied tone of voice. She plucked a grain of rice from her sister's dress. 'At least we had our lunch.'

'You might have,' pronounced Edna, 'but I didn't have time to finish my poppadom.'

The following morning Albert arrived at the laundrette. He had ironed most of his clothes on his previous visit but had forgotten about the dress shirt he was to wear that evening at the formal dinner. Maureen, despite her threat to accompany him, had decided to go to the line dancing class. Albert found the damp, bleach-smelling place was full. All the tumble dryers were in action as were the washing machines except for one, on top of which was a printed official-looking notice which stated, 'OUT OF ORDER.' There was a small queue of passengers waiting to use them. On the stainless-steel table at the centre of the room were piles of laundry waiting to be put into the washing machines and the tumble dryers. There were also two passengers waiting to use the iron. Albert sighed as he saw that the woman at the ironing board had a basket full of clothes. He was about to leave when she called him back.

'Is it just the one shirt you want ironing?' she asked Albert, who hovered by the door.

'Yes, just the one,' he answered.

'Give it here,' said the woman, 'I'll do it for you. I'm sure these good people in the queue won't mind, seeing as you just have the one item. You don't want to be hanging around. I've got quite a bit to do.'

'Oh, that's very kind of you,' he said, passing her his shirt.

'I wish I could get my husband to do his own ironing,' remarked a tall, gaunt-looking woman to no one in particular. She had a mop of curly hair the colour and texture of wire wool, a long prominent nose, and alarming eyebrows. Little grey hairs sprouted at the corners of her down-turned mouth. The intimidating figure held her body stiffly upright. 'He wouldn't know one end of an iron from the other. It's an effort to raise himself out of bed on a morning.'

'Mine wouldn't know what to do with an iron either,' added another passenger. 'He can't even work the washing machine.'

'You would think someone would have been to fix *this* washing machine by now,' complained the tall, gaunt-looking woman, pointing to the 'OUT OF ORDER' sign. 'It was out of action when I called in here yesterday. I did mention it to my steward.'

'What's wrong with it?' asked Albert.

'Well, *I* don't know, do I?' responded the woman snappily. 'I'm not a plumber. It just says it's not working.'

'I'll have a look,' said Albert. 'It might be something simple.'

'Do you know what you're doing?'

'Yes, love, I do know what I'm doing,' Albert told her. 'I *am* a plumber.'

He opened the door to the machine and peered inside, then examined the pipes at the back. A small dumpy woman in a pink dressing gown and fluffy slippers entered the laundrette. She had a worried-looking face framed in untidy lustreless stringy hair.

'What are you doing?' she demanded, sounding like an angry head teacher who had surprised a pupil enjoying a surreptitious smoke behind the bicycle sheds.

'I'm seeing if I can fix the washing machine,' Albert told her.

'There's nothing wrong with it,' he was told, and without another word the woman picked up a basket of washing from the table, shifted Albert out of the way and began to load the contents into the machine on which the notice 'OUT OF ORDER' was displayed.

The other passengers eyed her curiously.

'It's out of order,' the tall, gaunt-looking woman told her. 'Can you not read the sign?'

'No, it's not,' came the reply. She poured in some washing powder, clicked the door shut and switched on the machine, which started immediately.

'There was a notice on the top which said it wasn't working,' said the woman at the ironing board. 'If they've fixed it, they should have removed the sign.'

'Oh that,' said small dumpy woman, giving her a steady look. '*I* put it on.'

'*You* put it there?' asked another woman.

'It saves me having to wait in a queue,' came the bold-faced reply.

Most of those in the laundrette stared open-mouthed, too amazed to speak.

'*You* put the notice on?' asked the woman at the ironing board.

'Yes.' The dumpy woman whirled around to face her. 'Have you a problem with that?'

'I should say I have,' she replied angrily, thumping down the iron and regarding the offender with unconcealed hostility.

'And so do I,' said another. 'I think it's very inconsiderate of you.'

The woman turned her head sharply sideways like a ventriloquist's dummy. 'You can think what you want,' she retorted.

'I don't believe what I'm hearing,' cried the tall, gaunt-looking woman who had so far remained speechless. An angry spot showed itself in her cheek and it was with difficulty that she controlled herself. 'I have never heard anything in my life so selfish and brazen-faced.'

'Oh, get over it,' said the small dumpy woman, and putting the notice under her arm, left the laundrette without uttering another word.

'It beggars belief,' said the woman at the ironing board.

'And if she thinks she can jump the queue,' declared the tall, gaunt-looking woman, 'she's got another think coming.'

With that, she turned off the washing machine and cancelled the setting. When the water had drained from the drum, she opened the door, scooped out the woman's wet washing and threw it on the table. She then loaded her own washing.

'I'm ever so sorry,' said the woman at the ironing board to Albert. 'I was too busy watching what was going on. I'm afraid I've scorched your shirt.'

Back in his cabin Albert threw the shirt angrily on the bed and slumped down beside it, breathing like a carthorse.

His wife, on returning from the line dancing class, examined the garment with the brown scorch mark down the front and tutted.

'Well, you've made a right pig's ear of that,' she scolded.

Albert remained in festering silence.

'Can't even iron a shirt without burning it. And this is the only dress shirt you've got. You'll have to go and buy another. I hope you've got a decent shirt to wear when we go ashore this afternoon. I'm not walking around Valetta with you in a creased shirt, showing me up.'

Maureen had been accustomed during their twenty-five years of marriage of being the dominant and most vociferous partner in the relationship, so the fearsome revolt to her authority which ensued was unprecedented and left her speechless.

'Will you just shut up, you stupid woman!' exploded Albert. 'I'm sick to the back teeth of hearing your grumbling and griping and I'm sick and tired of spending half my time in that bloody laundrette while you go line dancing, and as for going into Valetta, you can stick it, because I'm going to watch the football.' He stood, breathed in, then exhaled noisily and stormed out of the door.

Maureen was applying cold cream to her face at the cabin dressing table when she was interrupted in this task by the arrival of her husband later that day. She didn't turn around. She didn't speak. On the bed was a sizeable cardboard box. Albert broke the strained silence.

'What's that?' he asked.

'It's a box,' she said, tight-lipped.

'I can see it's a bloody box. What's in it?'

'Something I bought in Valetta,' she replied coldly.

'You went ashore then?' he asked.

'Yes, I did, and I could have done with you helping me to carry it back.' She began wiping the cream from her face.

'What is it?'

She turned to face him, still tight-lipped. 'If you must know, it's a set of hand-painted traditional Maltese ceramic mugs with matching coffee pot and sugar bowl. I shall have to put it in your case. They'll be no room in mine.'

Albert bit his tongue.

'Did you get me another dress shirt while you were ashore?' he asked.

'No, I didn't. You can get one at the shop on the ship and while you're there get one of those cummerbunds to hold your stomach in.'

'I'm going for a drink,' he replied.

At the bar in the Jolly Sailor Tavern, Albert was brooding. He had not wanted to come on this cruise. He knew it would be a disaster. His experience had focused his mind. Closeted in a small cabin with a continually bad-tempered, badgering, and forever-complaining wife had goaded him to breaking point. He was not going to spend the rest of his life with a woman who had become insufferable. Enough was enough. On the return home he would tell Maureen that he wanted a divorce.

Becky, on her evening off, had joined the sisters for a drink in the Jolly Sailor Tavern. She had mentioned to Edna, when washing, drying, and tinting this passenger's hair, that one of her hobbies was reading palms.

'You can tell an awful lot about a person's character and say what some of the future holds for them,' she had told Edna, who had become intrigued and begged her to do a reading. Becky had agreed.

'The lines in your hand tell your life's story,' she now pronounced unsmilingly as she examined Edna's palm. 'They reveal all.'

'What do they reveal?' asked Edna in a hushed voice; her eyes were wide with excitement and expectation.

'Give the woman a chance,' came in Miriam.

'What do they say?' said Edna ignoring her.

Becky thought for a moment as she traced a finger towards the top of the palm. She gazed at Edna's hand as if into a crystal ball. 'This is the "heart line" and represents love and attraction. It signifies romance and intimate relationships.'

'Well, there's nothing doing there,' interposed Miriam.

'Do you mind?' shushed Edna.

'I see a man,' said Becky, continuing to peer into the palm. 'It is someone who has played a big part in your life.'

'That will be Mr Ellerby,' stated Miriam.

'Shush!' snapped Edna.

'He is handsome, loyal, tender and passionate,' said Becky, 'but has never disclosed his love because at heart he is shy, and he fears rejection.'

'That is definitely not Mr Ellerby,' said Miriam. 'He can hardly be described as "handsome", "tender" and "passionate." He's small and tubby and wears false teeth and a wig. Anyway, he's too taken up with Mrs Fattatori.'

'Will you stop interrupting,' Edna told her sister crossly. 'It's my palm that's being read and not yours. Go on, Becky.'

'The next line, which flows across the palm towards the wrist, is the "head line". This represents your mind and the way it works including a thirst for knowledge, creativity and communication skills.'

'This should be interesting,' muttered Miriam.

'I see here,' said Becky, 'that you have a nobility of character, you are a caring and sympathetic person.'

'That's me to a tee,' announced Edna beaming. 'I do tend to look for the best in people.'

'An admirable quality,' said Becky.

'And diplomacy has always been my forte.'

There was an expressive roll of the eyes from her sister.

Becky continued, 'It also indicates that you are an optimistic person, never one to expect the worst in life, someone who always hopes for the best.'

'That's very true,' agreed Edna, nodding.

'You are patient and persevering and not someone who is given to self-pity.'

'I do always look on the bright side of life and I'm not one to complain. It would be false modesty to deny it.'

There was a snort from Miriam.

Edna glared at her sister.

'But you don't feel that you've achieved your true potential,' Becky continued. 'Am I right?'

'I do sometimes feel like that,' murmured Edna, spellbound.

'As you have walked down the highway of life you have missed opportunities that have come your way.'

'It's been difficult walking what with my bad hip.'

Becky ran her finger from the end of the palm in an arc towards the wrist. 'This is the "life line" and represents physical well-being. I see here that you are suffering at the moment.'

'That's very true,' announced Edna, assuming an air of noble suffering. 'Of course, I've not got what you might call a robust constitution, but I've learned to live with it.'

'I see you are bearing your pain with fortitude,' commented Becky peering at the hand.

'It's amazing how accurate that reading has been,' said Edna.

'Amazing,' muttered her sister mordantly.

'But things will improve,' said Becky, 'and you will return to a full and active life and live to a ripe old age.'

'When, that is, she decides to have the hip operation,' added Miriam, almost to herself.

'Finally,' said Becky running a finger from the bottom of the palm towards the middle finger, 'this is the "fate line" which reveals circumstances beyond your control.'

'What does it reveal?'

'I can't say,' replied Becky, 'because, as I've said, what will happen is beyond your control. We really don't know what lies ahead. No one can argue with what the future holds.'

'But if you don't know what lies ahead or what the future holds,' stated Miriam, 'how do you know things will improve and Edna will return to a full and active life and live to a ripe old age?'

'The fate line does reveal certain things,' said Becky defensively, 'but not a lot.'

'Well, as far as I'm concerned,' said Edna, 'what you've told me, Becky, was spot-on.'

Stanley Mulgrave had his arm in a sling.

'So, how did it happen?' asked the Entertainment Manager.

The concert pianist inhaled sharply. 'A mad woman with a walking frame and a ridiculous sombrero, forced her way in front of me as I headed for the gangplank in Valetta. I was pushed aside, grabbed the handrail and sprained my wrist. To add insult to injury she told me to watch where I was going and then tottered off without a by your leave.'

'I have an idea who that might be,' said Martin. 'Have you seen the doctor?'

'No, it's not too bad.'

'I guess I shall have to cancel your recital tomorrow afternoon.'

'Not at all. I shall have to play some left-handed pieces.'

'Are you able to?'

'But of course. I have a number of one-handed items in my repertoire. It is not uncommon for highly proficient pianists who have suffered an injury or even the loss of a hand to be able to tackle some very demanding pieces. I was at the Royal Academy with a man who had been born with only the one hand and he has made a very successful career for himself as a pianist. Many composers – Chopin and Bach, for example – created coherent pieces of music for a left-handed performer. I shall find playing with just my left hand an interesting challenge.'

'Excellent,' said Martin. 'I have to hand it to you.' He laughed. 'Excuse the pun.'

News of the concert pianist's accident spread around the ship. Passengers who had given his recitals a miss, now took an interest. It would be quite something, they thought, to see how he could play a piece of music with just the one hand. At the next concert, in the Consort Suite there was standing room only.

'You will no doubt have heard of my unfortunate mishap on the quayside,' Mr Mulgrave told his audience. He glanced at Edna, his assailant, who was sitting on the front row with her sister like a contented cat, oblivious of his acerbic look. She showed no pang of conscience, no sign of embarrassment. 'This regrettable accident, in which I lost my balance and sprained my wrist, necessitates my performing "*la mano sinistra*", which means, with the one hand. I should say at the outset that single-handed piano music can be of the same quality and be equally as interesting as two-handed music and sometimes more challenging. My first piece this afternoon is by Franz Liszt and was dedicated to his pupil and friend, Count Geza Zichy, who lost his right arm in a hunting accident early in his life. This will be followed by part of one of the best-known classical pieces of music for the left-hand only: part of the piano concerto by the French impressionist composer Ravel, written in 1929 for the Austrian concert pianist Paul Wittgenstein who tragically lost his right arm during combat in the First World War.'

At the conclusion of the concert the passengers rose to their feet and loudly applauded the extraordinary talent of the performer.

As the sisters made their unhurried way to the exit, people were careful to avoid going near the menace and her mobility appliance. Her reputation as a walking hazard had circulated around the ship.

'So much for more popular music,' said Edna. 'It was the same old plinky-plonky classical stuff.'

'To be fair,' said her sister, 'I don't think he could have played "Climb Every Mountain" with just the one hand.'

'Did you notice?' asked Edna.

'Notice what?'

'That woman in the red dress was with him again, sitting as large as life and twice as natural on the front row making eyes at him. It's a wonder he could keep his mind on his playing.' Edna had not been keeping her mind on the music. She had been watching the young woman with professional scrutiny. 'Of course, you know what they say about women who wear red dresses like that.'

'No, Edna, I don't, but I guess you're going to enlighten me.'

'That they're no better than they should be.' She dropped her voice. 'It's obvious there's something going on between those two.'

'You didn't seem to mind about Mr Ellerby's goings-on,' remarked Miriam, 'so why should the woman in the red dress and the pianist bother you so much?'

'Mr Ellerby did not carry on with a woman half his age, and anyway, I don't imagine there was anything physical in his relationship with Mrs Fattatori. I reckon it was purely plutonic.'

'You're very naïve,' commented her sister.

'I'm not naïve at all,' responded Edna. 'It's just that I don't listen to gossip and jump to conclusions. I tend to see the good in people. As Becky said, I'm a caring and sympathetic person.'

'Come along,' said Miriam, grasping her sister's arm, 'let's get to the afternoon tea before the crowds.'

As Mr Mulgrave collected his musical scores together a passenger approached.

'I should just like to say,' he said, 'that your playing this afternoon was brilliant, inspirational.'

'Thank you,' replied the concert pianist. 'I am pleased you enjoyed it, Mr . . .?'

'Matthew,' replied the man. 'It was quite astonishing how you managed to play with just the one hand.'

'Do you play the piano yourself, Matthew?' he was asked.

The passenger, who only had the one arm, extended his left hand, held up his prosthetic limb and smiled. 'I don't, but perhaps I should learn,' he said.

19

It is said that rumour has a thousand tongues and nothing in the world travels faster. It is a fact that anything interesting disclosed by one passenger to another on a cruise ship is likely to circulate like wildfire – with, of course, suitable exaggeration and embellishments. The heated exchange in the laundrette over the use of the washing machine was soon transformed into full-scale fights with the two women attacking each other like feral cats. The family that had been put off the ship in Mallorca at the beginning of the cruise was the main topic of conversation at the dinner tables and in the lounges. Some passengers applauded the Captain's action, others felt he had been too severe, and a stiff talking-to was all that was needed. The sour-faced man who had been summoned to the Purser's office with his son regarding the messy table in the Galleon Buffet, had complained about his treatment by 'Captain Bligh' to anyone who was inclined to listen. Few had any sympathy for him. The rumour spread that there was a titled woman on board who was a lady-in-waiting to the queen, and it was said the concert pianist, on the cruise with his mistress, had not really sprained his wrist; it was a publicity stunt to get more people to come and hear him play. Of course, the fact that there was a lottery millionaire on board was the talk on the dinner tables. The Italian tenor, it was reported, affected the Italian accent and in fact came from Huddersfield; he had been heard ordering a pint of bitter in the Jolly Sailor Tavern with a distinct Yorkshire accent and the elderly, loving couple who could be seen walking hand-in-hand around the ship, were said to have eloped from an old people's care home leaving their distracted families wondering where they had got to. News of 'the mad woman with the walking frame" who 'cocked-up the lift', tripped up the concert pianist and nearly had a man with a crutch falling full length in the restaurant, soon circulated. It was not long, however, for the event which caused the greatest gossip, to spread around the ship.

A man and a boy waited in the Excelsior Theatre to speak to the Port Lecturer following the talk. Mr Carlin-How recognised one of the rascals who had left the table in the Galleon Buffet in such a state. No doubt this was the father, there to harangue him for reporting the incident. It certainly appeared from the expression on the man's face that he was not best pleased. The Captain had acquainted the Port Lecturer of the interview with the boys and their fathers and described one of the parents as obstinate and disagreeable.

'Excuse me, Mr Carlin-How,' said the man.

The Port Lecturer drew a deep breath, preparing for the confrontation. 'Yes?'

'My son has something to say to you.' The boy, shamefaced, was pushed forward by his father. 'Well, go on, George.'

'I'm sorry for what happened in the Galleon Buffet,' said the boy. He was on the verge of tears.

'He has been to see the restaurant staff,' said the father, 'to say he is sorry for his disgraceful behaviour, and he has written a letter of apology to the Captain. He will also apologise to the passengers who witnessed the incident. I am extremely angry with him. As I said to the Captain, his conduct and that of the other boy was totally unacceptable. I have not brought my son up to be bad-mannered and disrespectful.'

Mr Carlin-How, having been prepared for an altercation, now felt pleasantly surprised.

'I have to say, in your son's defence,' he answered, 'that he was not the main culprit. It was the other boy who was largely to blame. He was the one who threw the food and was rude to the passengers. Your son should be careful of the company he keeps. I don't imagine that the other youth will be forthcoming with an apology.'

'No, I think not,' said the father. 'He is confined to his cabin, probably for the rest of the cruise from what I hear, so my son will have nothing further to do with him.'

'A little harsh, but it will no doubt teach him a lesson,' said the Port Lecturer.

'He's in isolation,' it was explained. 'He's down with mumps.'

'You are quite a hit with Oliver,' Mr Champion told Elodie. He had discovered her in the library poring over the notes for her next lecture.

'He is quite a hit with me,' she replied. 'I have never met a child so interested and well-informed in history. He is also very well-mannered.'

'I'm pleased you like him,' he said. 'I think I mentioned that some adults do find our grandson a bit of a smarty-pants.'

'I don't find him a smarty-pants at all,' she objected. 'Some adults feel intimidated by a very bright and articulate child. How does he get on at school?'

'The head teacher tells me that Oliver is the brightest child he has ever met,' Mr Champion replied. 'He describes him as an extremely clever boy, immensely knowledgeable, very polite, a dutiful student with an exceptional recall of facts and details but . . .' He paused for a moment to try to think of the most appropriate word. 'He said he finds him too serious for a boy of his age, a rather reclusive child who doesn't mix with the other children or share their interests. He told me at the parents' evening that the other boys come in from the playground with muddied knees, grubby hands and scuffed shoes, their hair like haystacks and shirts hanging out, but Oliver appears with not a hair out of place. It sounded like our grandson. I do wish he would kick a football around or play conkers or ride a bike or climb trees as other boys of his age do, but he prefers his own company and books. I was told that in summer he can be seen sitting reading quietly on the bench in the playground like an old man enjoying his retirement. I think part of the problem – if it is a problem – can be put at our door. We are, admittedly, somewhat old-fashioned and set in our ways. In many ways he is an amazing child; he's never subject to mood swings, does as he's told, is always helpful and incapable of deceit. The headmaster told me he is a determined boy with strong opinions, the sort of child who swims against the current.'

'As I have said to Oliver,' said Elodie, 'it's not a bad thing to be different from others and be something of a nonconformist, after all, only dead fish swim with the stream.'

'We are, of course, enormously proud of him,' said Mr Champion.

'I should imagine you are,' answered Elodie.

'Perhaps Oliver has told you why my wife and I are bringing him up.'

'Yes, he has. I was sorry to hear about his parents.'

'It was a tragedy from which my wife and I have never recovered. He was only two when he came to live with us. We were not of an age best suited to bringing up a growing child. Like many older people, we'd slowed down and wanted a quiet, unhurried life. We never anticipated raising a child again.'

'Quite a challenge.'

'Yes, indeed.'

'Is he bullied at school?' Elodie asked.

'Yes, I am afraid so but, surprisingly it doesn't seem to worry him much. I think the other boys think he's something of a smart alec. It's not that he's a show-off, it's just that if he knows the answers, he sees no reason why he should keep quiet. He's a stickler for facts, as you've probably gathered. Sometimes when he pulls up a teacher on some piece of inaccurate information, you can imagine this does not go down too well.'

'That's not Oliver's fault,' said Elodie, recalling the sharp reaction of one of her teachers when she corrected her. 'Teachers don't know everything. The good ones admit to their ignorance and error and with a very bright child they should show him or her the ropes and not feel threatened or surprised if that child is climbing higher.' She smiled. 'I should imagine that Oliver is making his own ropes. You should be immensely proud of him, Mr Champion.'

'Well, as I have said, Dr King, Oliver is very taken with you, and my wife and I would like to thank you for showing such an interest in him.'

'I shall say this, Mr Champion,' replied Elodie, 'I do not have children but if I had a son, I would wish him to be like Oliver.'

The man was lost for words.

The subject of their conversation was at that minute sitting reading in the shade on the promenade deck. The short grey trousers, white shirt, tie and knee-length grey socks that he had worn at the start of the cruise, had been replaced by a smart, short-sleeved checked shirt and pale blue shorts. Unlike the other boys on the cruise, who wore brightly coloured baseball caps (usually the wrong way around) Oliver had a straw trilby-style hat perched at a jaunty angle on his head. A wave of red hair escaped at the front.

'Hello.'

The speaker was a small, slight, willowy girl of about eleven or twelve with long, feathery blond hair and china-blue eyes between almost colourless lashes. She sat next to him and smiled, showing a set of teeth encased in braces.

Oliver looked up. 'Hello,' he replied, looking at her enquiringly.

'You're always reading,' she said brushing away a strand of hair from her face.

'I like books.'

'I like books too,' she said, 'but there's so much going on around the ship. There's lots of sports for example.'

'I'm not good at sports,' Oliver told her. He closed his book. 'The PE teacher at the school I attend says I lack dedication and have poor coordination.'

'I like your hair.'

'Pardon?'

'Your hair. When the sun shines, it looks golden.'

'It's ginger,' said Oliver.

'I know, but it looks like gold when the sun shines on it. I wish I had hair that colour.'

He eyed her searchingly. 'There's nothing wrong with your hair.'

'I wish I had hair like the author,' she said with a sigh. 'She has hair your colour.'

'Dr King?'

'My father says she looks as if she's walked out of a painting by some famous Victorian artist, like a medieval princess.'

'Yes, she does look something like that,' agreed Oliver.

'Are you going to the teen disco tonight?' she asked.

'No, I'm not,' replied Oliver determinedly. 'I'm not into dancing. As I said, I have poor coordination and I certainly lack the dedication for disco dancing.'

'You don't need to be a good dancer,' the girl told him. 'You just sort of wiggle your bottom about and move your arms and legs in time with the music.'

Oliver raised an eyebrow. He had the startled expression of a teacher who had overheard a rude remark from a pupil. 'I can't imagine anything sillier that wiggling my bottom about and moving my arms and legs. I'd look ridiculous.'

'You could always go to the line dancing. That's fun.'

'Not for someone like me with poor coordination. I'd be stepping on people's toes.'

'You are funny,' she said, giggling.

'So I have been told,' he said indifferently.

'I don't think I'll bother going to the teen disco,' said the girl. 'The boys there are so immature, and the girls all have a crush on Leon.'

'Who's Leon.'

'He's the fitness trainer. Have you not been to the gym?'

'Need you ask?'

'What time do you eat?'

'At about six,' he answered. 'I go to the Galleon Buffet. My grandparents, who I am on the cruise with, they eat later in the main restaurant. I prefer to eat by myself and I'm sure that the adults at the table don't want a child sitting with them.'

'Can I come and eat with you in the Galleon Buffet?' asked the girl.

Oliver regarded her for a moment. 'If you like,' he said.

'My name's Miranda,' she said.

'I'm Oliver.'

Edna was not alone in speculating about the association of the concert pianist and the woman in red. The Entertainment Manager, assumed like Edna and some of the other passengers, that the young woman was the man's mistress. He had watched as the couple strolled around the deck together, arm-in-arm, so affectionate with each other. He had noticed how they were engrossed in each other's company at the dinner table and how she often held his hand and kissed his cheek. After his brief conversation with her after the recital and meeting her again in the Jolly Sailor Tavern, Martin had kept his distance but one morning, when the cruise ship docked in Messina, he came across her sitting by herself in the Rainbow Lounge.

'I thought you did a splendid job,' she said as he passed her table. She was dressed in cream linen slacks, which emphasised her slim waist and feminine hips, a lilac collarless blouse with pearl buttons and open-toed sandals. She was a fine-looking woman, he thought.

'I'm sorry?' he said.

'With the two elderly women who were rather worse for drink.'

Martin smiled thinly. 'Ah yes, the bibulous cocktail ladies.'

He gripped the back of the chair and stared at this graceful and self-contained woman. She was not classically beautiful; her nose was a little too long, her forehead too broad, her mouth on the large side but she had striking jade green eyes with long and beautifully shaped lashes, dark wavy hair, and a flawless complexion. Such a woman had style and flair. She was aware that he was studying her, but she did not appear to mind the scrutiny. They held each other's stare for a moment.

'Did you manage to get them safely to their cabin?' she asked.

'I'm sorry?' he asked again.

'The two ladies who were worse for drink.'

'Just about. I think one thought I had lustful intentions.'

'How amusing.'

'I was—'

'As I said—'

They began speaking at the same time and then both stopped suddenly.

'I'm sorry,' she said.

'No, go ahead.'

'As I said, I thought you handled that objectionable passenger with great authority. I was most impressed. I gather he was put off the ship.'

'He was, yes, with his family. His wife and son were not best pleased.'

'Would you care to join me?' she asked.

'Well . . . I . . . '

'Of course, if you're busy.'

'No, no,' he said quickly, sitting down. 'I'm not busy. I'm not busy at all.' There was a discreet scent of perfume. 'Is Mr Mulgrave not with you this morning?' he asked.

'Stanley? Oh, he's practising. He spends hours in the day at the piano and this morning he is going through his repertoire for the next recital. I thought we might go ashore but I don't think we will manage it.'

'He did a magnificent job playing those superb pieces with just the one hand,' he said. 'It was the talk of the ship.'

'I shall let you into a little secret, but not a word to him.' She put a finger to her lips and dropped her voice to a conspirator's whisper. 'His wrist wasn't that badly sprained and he could have managed with the two hands, but he is a bit of a show-off and thought he'd demonstrate his undoubted talent. It's a bit of a party piece. Not many pianists could perform with the one hand as well as he. He'll be playing two-handed compositions from now on.'

'So how long have you known him?' Martin enquired.

'Pardon?' She sounded most surprised.

'Stanley. I was asking how long you have known him?'

She threw back her head and laughed. 'Why, all my life, of course.'

'All your life,' he repeated. It was his turn to sound most surprised.

'Yes, of course. He's my father.' She looked him in the eye.

'Your father!' he exclaimed.

'Yes, Stanley is my father. I have an idea, Mr Entertainment Manager, that you thought he was my sugar-daddy.'

Martin's face turned red. 'No . . . no . . . I didn't. Really. I'm sorry . . . I . . . I just thought you must be his agent or his secretary.'

She looked at him hard, taking in the strong face, dark eyes and high cheekbones. His heightened colour made him look young and handsome. Her eyes lingered a moment longer than they might. She tilted her head as if waiting for him to speak. A coquettish smile played on her lips.

'I never for a moment assumed you were—' he started.

'His bit on the side?'

'No ... no ...' he spluttered.

'I think you did,' she teased. 'I've noticed some of the passengers looking at us with disapproval. I guess they assume we are an item. I suppose my father should have said something to you. When he was asked to come and play on the cruise, he thought I might like to accompany him. I needed to get away. It's been a difficult time for me lately.'

'I'm sorry.'

'I've just gone through a rather unfortunate divorce. It's the same old story. My husband left me for a younger model.'

'He was a fool,' said Martin.

She smiled. 'Ah well, these things happen. I'm getting over it. My father thought sun, sea, chilled white wine and exotic places to visit would take me out of myself.'

'I've been in the same boat,' he told her.

'I'm sorry?'

'Divorce.' His eyes were trained squarely upon her. 'I've recently spit up with my wife. It was difficult to make the marriage work with me being at sea, away from home so often. We both knew pretty quickly that it was a mistake. We found when we were together that we had little in common. I arrived home after four weeks at sea and my wife said she'd found someone else.'

Her lips parted and her large eyes were fixed on his face. 'I'm sorry,' she said.

He shrugged. 'That's what she said, "I'm so very sorry." But, as you say, these things happen and I'm getting over it.'

'Any family?' she asked.

'No.'

'Neither have I.'

'That was one of the things we didn't agree about – wanting children. I did, she didn't.' Their eyes locked and then he looked away quickly. His breathing was tight, his heart missed a beat. *Why am I telling a stranger all this?* he asked himself. He had told her more about his failed marriage than he had previously told anyone. Perhaps his loneliness had left him with a need to share his feelings with someone. The woman's beauty was heightened by her grace of bearing and the warmth and softness of her voice induced confidence.

'I don't know why I am telling you this,' he said. 'I don't normally talk about my personal life.'

'I'm a good listener,' she answered, leaning over the table, 'and very discreet.' He felt her eyes linger on him and smelled again the delicate perfume. He looked down and wondered how long it had been since he felt so preoccupied by a woman. 'So, has the cruise taken you out of yourself?' he said cheerfully, looking up.

'Yes, I think it has, although I didn't get off the ship in Valetta. As I've said, my father spends a great deal of his time practising. It's not quite the same wandering around a place by oneself.'

'So, you are not intending to go ashore at out next port of call?' he asked.

'I think perhaps I'll give it a miss.'

'You cannot give Messina a miss,' he told her, sounding like a schoolteacher. 'It's the most fantastic city.'

'You obviously know it.'

'It's one of my favourite places. We sail through the Strait of Messina with Mount Etna towering over the island. It can be easily seen from the ship. Then we dock at the city with its wonderful panoramic views, great marble fountains and ancient buildings. There's this incredible bell tower with an astronomical clock. I was going to hire a car and take the scenic drive to Torre Faro later this morning. It's something I promised myself to do on the next visit.'

'Sounds nice.'

'But it's not half the fun doing it on one's own.'

'No, I guess not.' She tilted her head.

Martin chanced his arm. 'I wonder, would you care to keep me company?'

'That's very kind of you,' she said with undisguised alacrity, and rewarded him with a sincere and unguarded smile. 'I should like that very much.'

20

The Sunday morning service was conducted in the Excelsior Theatre by the Captain. After he had welcomed everyone, he read from his Bible:

They that go down to the sea in ships and occupy their business in great waters; These men see the works of the Lord, and his wonders in the deep. For at His word the stormy wind ariseth, which lifteth up the waves thereof. These see the works of the Lord, and His wonders in the deep. For He commandeth, and raiseth the stormy wind, which lifteth up the waves thereof.

There followed the hymn:

Eternal Father, strong to save,
Whose arm hath bound the restless wave,
Who bid'st the mighty ocean deep
Its own appointed limits keep;
Oh, hear us when we cry to Thee,
For those in peril on the sea!

During the rousing singing, Edna leaned towards her sister and whispered conspiratorially.

'I hope we're not in store for some of these restless waves and stormy winds or be in any peril on the seas,' she commented. 'I still worry about seeing those sick bags all over the ship.'

'Motion discomfort receptacles,' her sister reminded her with a smile.

There followed a passage from the Gospels, read in a most engaging voice by Lady Staithes. She had been prevailed upon by the Purser, who had taken quite a shine to her, to take part in the service.

On that day when evening came, a furious squall came up, and the waves broke over the boat, so that it was nearly swamped. Jesus was in the stern, sleeping on a cushion. The disciples woke him and said to him, 'Teacher, don't you care if we drown?' He got up, rebuked the wind, and said to the waves, 'Quiet! Be still!' Then the wind died down and it was completely calm. He said to his disciples, 'Why are you so afraid? Do you still have no faith?' They were terrified and asked each other, 'Who is this? Even the wind and the waves obey him!'

Following the reading, Edna leaned towards her sister again.

'She's very aristocratical, isn't she?' she observed, nodding in the direction of the speaker. 'It's no doubt she's titled. She certainly has the polish and charm of a high-bred lady. You can tell she's got blue blood.'

Miriam smiled. Her sister's experience of nobility was hardly extensive.

'I bet she's in one of the fancy cabins and gets prefermental treatment,' Edna continued.

'Preferential,' muttered her sister.

'And I'll tell you this,' remarked Edna, 'if we do get into a furious squall and we get swamped and *are* in peril on the seas and this ship starts to go down, I reckon she'll be the first to be shown to a lifeboat and those of us with an inside cabin are last to get off. It happened like that on the *Titanic*, the rich lot getting off before everyone else.'

Miriam had a sudden mental glimpse of the scene: passengers panicking to get off the sinking ship and her sister charging down the deck to be the first in the lifeboat and parting the crowds with her walking frame.

Mr Hinderwell gave a short homily. He noticed Mr Shoddy ('I've worked my way up from nothing') in the congregation with his long-suffering wife next to him. The cleric directed the first words in his direction.

'The *Empress of the Ocean*, like any cruise ship, is a microcosm,' he said. 'Aboard is the rich diversity of people who inhabit the world. In this world of ours we should try to think the best of each other and show an open friendship and acceptance for people of every kind, to draw others out by kindness and encouragement. We will soon be visiting Rome and have the chance of seeing one of the most beautiful masterpieces the world has ever seen. I refer, of course, to the Sistine Chapel. I hope Mr Carlin-How will forgive me for adding a small postscript to his very excellent lecture about "the eternal city". It was Michelangelo who said that "any beautiful thing raises the pure and just desire of man from earth to God, the eternal fount of all, such I believe my love." Someone once watched the great sculptor as he chipped away at a block of marble and asked him what he was making. "I'm not making anything," came the reply. "I'm releasing an angel from a lump of stone." When Michelangelo was going to Rome to see the Pope, prior to his being employed to build the great dome of St Peter's and paint the Sistine Chapel, he took with him a reference which said:

The bearer of these presents is the sculptor, Michelangelo. His nature is such that he requires to be drawn out by kindness and encouragement, but if love be shown him and he be treated kindly, he will accomplish things that will make the whole world wonder.'

Captain Smith concluded the service with a prayer:

May we always have a fair wind and a calm sea and a safe harbour for when we reach home.

'Hear! Hear!' exclaimed Edna.

Matthew remained behind after the service and approached Mr Hinderwell as he left the stage. He was accompanied by a small, shy looking woman.

'Padre,' he said.

'It's quite some years since I was called padre,' replied the cleric affably, going to meet the speaker.

'It is Mr Hinderwell, isn't it?'

'It is indeed.'

'I have seen you about the deck, but it was only when you spoke this morning that I recognised you. You have quite a distinctive voice. We served together in Iraq. I was in the Royal Army Medical Corps. You were the chaplain.'

'My dear fellow,' started the clergyman. 'How very good to see you.'

'Do you not remember me, Padre?'

Mr Hinderwell looked into the man's eyes and shook his head in bemusement. 'I'm afraid not,' he said apologetically. 'I met so many soldiers over my time as an army chaplain. It was some years' ago. Time and my imperfect memory have taken their toll.' He thought of the overweight pensioner he had seen on the coach going into Seville who had been wearing a tight-fitting T-shirt on the front of which was written 'Been there, Done that, Can't remember.' That, he had thought, sums me up these days. 'I'm sorry,' he said, 'I'm afraid I don't remember you.'

'I remember you, Padre,' said the man quietly. 'You are a legend in the regiment.'

'A legend,' laughed Mr Hinderwell. 'I've never been called a legend before. I was once—'

'You dragged a wounded soldier from a Warrior armoured vehicle that had triggered an IED, and you were shot in the back by a sniper.'

The smile had disappeared from the clergyman's face. The memory came back like a shockwave and a shadow fell across his face as he looked for a moment into his past. 'Yes, it is not something one forgets,' he said. 'It was a terrible time.'

'You went through hell.'

'It wasn't an experience I should wish to repeat,' the cleric told him. 'But, you know, many were not as fortunate as I was.' He sighed. 'Some never made it home.'

'I guess you wondered what happened to that soldier you saved.'

'I did try and find out how the young man that I helped was getting on,' Mr Hinderwell told him. 'Thank God he survived. He left the army I was told. I received a letter from him sometime after I got home but I was laid up in hospital for quite some time and it took a few months for it to finally reach me. I did write back but heard nothing. Corporal Loftus was his name. Did you know him at all?'

A lump rose in Matthew's throat and his eyes filled with tears. Awkwardly he rubbed them away with the heel of a hand as a small child might do, then he found his voice. 'I'm Corporal Loftus, Padre,' he said.

While Mr Hinderwell and Matthew recalled their time in the British Army, Edna, shuffling her way out of the theatre, bumped (literally) into Mr Shoddy ('I've worked my way up from nothing') catching his leg with her walking frame.

'Steady on,' he barked.

'You should watch where you're going,' snapped Edna, blaming him for her own clumsiness. She recognised the man.

'Oh, I want a word with you,' she told him as he bent down to rub his ankle.

'About what?' he asked gruffly, looking up.

'About emptying the contents of your mouth all over me.'

'I don't know what you're talking about.'

'You've got a short memory then. I'm talking about when you covered me with fish bones and boiled rice in the Galleon Buffet.'

'Oh that. It might have escaped your notice,' he said angrily, 'but I was choking at the time.'

'I'm aware of that,' stated Edna, clearly immune to the sarcasm. 'You wouldn't have been choking if you had stopped wittering on with a mouthful of food. I was always taught not to speak with my mouth full.' The man made to reply but Edna hadn't finished. 'You might have shown more consideration by turning away instead of facing me and disposing of the contents of your mouth all over my dress.'

The man might have responded that she should have shown more consideration by watching where she was going.

'And,' prompted Miriam, supporting her sister, 'you might have had the good manners and offered to pay for the cleaning.'

'And at the very least apologise,' added Edna in a loud voice. The man attempted to make an escape, but his path was blocked by the walking frame. Edna had not finished with him yet.

Passengers on their way out of the theatre stopped to listen. No doubt this confrontation would circulate around the ship in quick time.

'And I don't imagine you have had the good grace to thank the doctor who saved you from choking to death.' The man opened his mouth to speak but Edna waved a hand as if wafting away a fly. She looked at the small, wrinkled woman with the careworn expression who was standing next to him. 'Is he your husband?' she asked. The woman nodded. 'Well, you have my sympathies.' At that, with a theatrical flounce, she waddled past without waiting for a response from an open-mouthed Mr Shoddy, who on this rare occasion was speechless.

Later, in the Jolly Sailor Tavern, Edna shared with her sister an observation. 'You know, Miriam, when I see ignorant men like that fat man who nearly choked, I'm glad I never got married and remained celebrate. A husband would drive me up the wall with his funny habits. It's a fact that the complications of life begin at the altar.'

Miriam smiled. Her sister's experience of marriage was hardly extensive.

Edna thought for a moment, then gave a small chuckle. 'Of course, I might be on the shelf, but I've been taken down and dusted a few times.'

As Oliver made his way out of the theatre after the service, he came upon one of the bullies, the one with the spiky black hair and thin pale complexion.

'Could I have a word?' the boy asked looking uncomfortable.

'Of course,' replied Oliver steadily, staring him in the eye. 'What is it you want?'

'Look, I'm sorry for what Lewis said to you.'

'I'm used to it,' stated Oliver. 'I take no notice. Bullies are sad, spiteful people who have nothing better to do than make fun of others.'

The boy looked embarrassed and then down at his feet. 'I want you to know that it was wrong,' he mumbled. 'It was a mean and stupid thing to say, and I wouldn't have said that sort of thing. I'm not like Lewis.'

'You should pick your friends more carefully,' said Oliver, starting to walk away.

The boy didn't move. He raised his head. 'Do you fancy a game of quoits?'

'What?'

'Quoits.'

'I've never played.'

'It's good fun. You throw a rubber ring at a target and try and get as close as possible. It's dead easy. There's a junior competition later today. I need a partner.'

'I don't think I'll be any good,' said Oliver.

'There's not a lot to it. Well, will you?'

Oliver thought for a moment. 'All right,' he replied.

'Great. My name's George.'

'I'm Oliver.'

Mrs De la Mare had decided to give the Sunday morning service a miss. Later that morning she sat on the executive sun deck, closed her eyes, and gave a small wearisome sigh.

'Hello again.'

She opened her eyes and looked up to see the cheery face of the small woman with the thick wavy hair. She sighed. 'Good morning.'

'I've just been to the service in the theatre,' said Sandra. 'It was very moving.'

'I'm not a religious person,' Mrs De la Mare told her simply before closing her eyes again. She wished she could close her ears to the woman's incessant chatter.

'I'm busy writing my postcards,' Sandra told her. 'My family like me to keep in touch. My daughter in particular likes to hear from me. She's feeling a bit homesick. Janette's a dancer.'

A belly-dancer or a pole-dancer no doubt, thought Mrs De la Mare.

'She's in Russia at the moment touring with The Royal Ballet.'

Mrs De la Mare sat up. 'The Royal Ballet?' she repeated.

'I went to see her in *Swan Lake* when it was in London.'

A likely story, thought Mrs De la Mare.

'My other son, Gerald – of course I've told you about Eddie he works in America. He's a professor at New York University, married to a lovely American woman. Their son, Wesley, is in the Olympic wrestling team.'

'You have a very talented family,' remarked Mrs De la Mare sardonically.

'Yes, I am very blessed. Have you a family?'

'No.' She shuffled in her recliner. 'I'm sorry but I am not up to a conversation this morning,' she said curtly. 'I have a splitting headache and thought I might close my eyes for a minute.'

'Oh dear. Would you like me to get you an aspirin?'

'Thank you, no.'

'It's no trouble. I have some in my cabin.'

'No, really,' she said stiffly.

'Well, I'll leave you in peace and get on with writing my postcards.'

Thank goodness, thought Mrs De la Mare, closing her eyes. She gave a small cynical smile. At the dinner tables and in the lounges the second question usually asked by one passenger to another (the first being 'What did you pay for the cruise?') is: 'So, what do *you* do for a living?' When faced with this enquiry some people feel obliged to inflate their position in life, to massage the truth a little to make them sound more important and interesting. Others invent an entirely new persona. They could be eminent doctors, published writers, wealthy financiers, film directors, even titled personages who are on speaking terms with the Queen. I mean who is there to know? The thing about cruises is it is easy for passengers to pretend to be something they are not and to invent a more delectable world than the pedestrian one in which they live. It is very unlikely they will ever see the person again to whom they are telling such far-fetched stories after the cruise. *And here*, thought Mrs De la Mare was a case in point. *Ballet dancer, professor at an American university, Olympic athlete. Who did the woman think she was fooling?*

In the afternoon the Captain, dressed in a pristine white uniform, appeared on the executive sun deck. He was a tall distinguished-looking man. A carefully trimmed beard framed his smiling face. He looked every inch the ship's master. He glanced in the direction of the two women, grinned and waved. 'Good morning,' he called to them.

Mrs De la Mare sat up in the recliner and her face broke into the practised smile which she had perfected for when someone of importance came into view. She felt a small glow of satisfaction in the knowledge that the Captain had sought her out and she would, after all, be dining that evening on his table. The Purser had indeed, she imagined, had a quiet word. She rehearsed in her head what she would say. 'I should be delighted to join you.' She opened her mouth to graciously accept the invitation, but the Captain cut her off.

'It's a lovely day again, isn't it,' he said. 'I'm sorry I can't stop. I'll catch up with you later.'

When Albert arrived at the laundrette to iron his clothes, he entered a war zone. The floor was littered with shirts and socks, vests and underpants, skirts and bras, jumpers and dresses. A small, wrinkled individual with wisps of wiry white hair combed across his otherwise bald pate, was shouting at a large man with pendulous ears and a moustache which drooped limply on either side of his lips.

'Oi, oi!' Albert shouted. 'What's going on?'

Both men stopped what they were doing.

'It's him,' said the small man, in the voice of a petulant child. 'He's chucked all my clothes on the floor.'

'And you've chucked mine on the floor,' said the other.

'You started it.'

'No, I didn't.'

'Yes, you did.'

'No, I didn't.

'Yes, you did.'

They sounded like fractious schoolboys.

'You took all my washing out of the dryer,' complained the small man, with a feeble attempt at belligerence. 'You had no business interfering with my things and gawping at my wife's personal items.'

'Are you having a laugh?' The big man snorted. 'I've got better things to do than gawp at your wife's knickers. I wanted to get my clothes dry but you left your stuff in the machine and walked off and made other folk have to wait until you decided to wander back.'

'Not again,' sighed Albert.

'Look here,' said the small man, 'you're asking for a good hiding.'

The big man huffed. 'From you and whose army? Come on then.'

'You'll get put off the ship,' Albert told them calmly.

'What?' they said simultaneously.

'There was a family put off in Mallorca after a chap in the Jolly Sailor Tavern caused a ruckus, and another two women were nearly put ashore following an argument in this very place. They were hauled up before the Captain and given a warning. You two had better watch your step or you will be the next ones to be packing your bags. I suggest you calm down and pick up your things.'

This had the desired effect and the two combatants calmed down. Both men surveyed the washing strewn on the floor.

'I'm not exactly sure which are my clothes, and which are his,' said the small man, shaking his head.

'Neither am I,' said the large man, brushing a hand through his bristly moustache, 'but I'm quite sure this is not *my* wife's.' He had picked up a large greyish pink bra with giant cups which resembled a piece of bullet-proof body armour rather than an article of clothing.

'Do you mind!' shouted the small man, snatching the bra from him. 'That happens to be my wife's. You have no business touching her underwear.'

'I think those are mine,' said the large man reaching down to pick up a large pair of baggy white underpants.

'Well, they're certainly not mine,' the small man told him. 'You could get an elephant into them.'

'You look here, you little pipsqueak—' began the large man.

'Listen to me,' said Albert impatiently, 'you both had better tidy up these clothes and then go and find your wives and let them sort things out. I've said you could be put off the ship if you carry on arguing.'

Having recovered a certain degree of calm, the two men gathered the garments, placed them on the table, and then departed to fetch their wives to sort out the jumble. While Albert had been talking to the men, a woman had sidled into the laundrette carrying a great pile of clothes. She had ignored what was transpiring, stepped around the washing on the table and commandeered the iron.

21

When he saw the motley collection of passengers heading, in no great hurry, for the coach, Mr Carlin-How's face blanched and a cloud of gloom settled around his head. Such was the popularity of the visit to Pompeii that several extra coaches had been commissioned to take the passengers to the site and, as a result, there was a shortage of escorts. Mr Carlin-How had been pressed into being one of them. He had hoped that he could spend the day with Elodie, but she too had been dragooned into being an escort.

'It really doesn't involve very much at all,' the Tour Manager had explained casually. 'You tell the passengers about some of the things they are likely to see, warn them to take care, wear sun cream, be wary of pickpockets, make sure they have plenty of water and tell them the time they need to be back at the coach.'

'It sounds as if you're talking about a lot of schoolchildren. Surely all that is common sense.'

'From my experience,' the Tour Manager had replied, 'they do need reminding. Take my word for it. So, there it is. It's as easy as that, like shelling peas.'

'Really.' The Port Lecturer had sounded unconvinced.

'You won't be taking them around the ruins,' he had been told. 'There will be official guides there if people want to use them. You will be free to wander around. It's just a matter of counting the passengers on and off the bus, making sure you don't leave anyone behind, and dealing with any small problems which might arise.'

'Any small problems which might arise,' the Port Lecturer had reiterated, raising an eyebrow. 'And what small problems might these turn out to be?'

'Oh . . . helping to find someone who has got lost, looking for a mislaid item. Nothing to worry about.' He had been disinclined to mention the occasion when a couple had decided to make their own way back to the ship without informing the escort and left the coach waiting for them for over an hour, or the time a woman had had her handbag snatched or the incident when a passenger had tripped and broken his wrist. 'Oh, and you'll have a first-aid kit in case of an accident.'

'I don't like the sound of a first-aid kit,' Mr Carlin-How had blustered.

'The likelihood is that you will not need it,' he had ben reassured. The would-be escort had looked markedly unpersuaded. 'It does mean, of course, that you will not have to pay for the excursion and entry to Pompeii and you will be provided with a voucher to get a drink.'

The Port Lecturer had agreed grudgingly.

As bad luck would have it, it seemed that all the old and infirm were on Mr Carlin-How's coach. There was the aged couple, holding hands, tottering towards him, several others with sticks, a man with a crutch and two large women, one of whom, wearing an outlandish sombrero, was shuffling along pushing a sizeable walking frame. It was like an outing for the walking wounded. He sighed despairingly as if he was watching a group of children misbehaving. In his mind came visions of rushing around Pompeii with his first-aid kit tending to the broken bones, cut heads and sprained ankles of the elderly and frail who were now heading his way. At his lecture on the previous afternoon, he had strongly advised those passengers who were 'not good on their feet' to opt for another less demanding tour for there were stone outcrops and much uneven ground at the Roman remains, which might prove hazardous for those who find walking difficult. Clearly his advice had been ignored by this party of invalids. He had also mentioned that those intending going on the trip should wear appropriate footwear. Most he could see had ignored his advice and wore sandals; one woman sported shoes with heels and a man was in flip-flops. He felt a stirring of tension and dread when he caught sight of the ignorant man who had fallen asleep in his first lecture – the fat-faced individual with the bald patch – and his boorish wife. He was attired in the most unbecoming checked shorts and a bulging T-shirt on the front of which was printed 'PLUMBERS NEVER DIE. THEY JUST GO DOWN THE DRAIN' in bold letters. She was wearing a shapeless floral tent of a dress like a converted curtain and sporting a ridiculous straw hat shaped like a bucket which covered up her bedraggled hair. She held a coloured parasol before her like a weapon. Mr Carlin-How made a mental note to avoid the couple at all costs when he got to Pompeii.

The tour did not get off to a good start.

'I think you will find that these seats are reserved for disabled people such as myself,' Edna told Maureen who had installed herself with Albert at the front of the coach.

'I wasn't aware of that,' came a sharp retort.

'Well, they are.' Edna turned to Mr Carlin-How. 'Would you ask this couple to vacate these seats?' she instructed him. 'They are set aside for the incapacitated.'

The Port Lecturer drew a slow and thoughtful breath and exhaled. He was not aware that these were reserved seats, no more than Edna was, but he did what he was asked. 'I wonder if I might trouble you to move to another seat and let this lady sit here?' he asked Maureen.

'I can't see why we have to move,' she answered angrily.

'Because I'm disabled, that's why!' snapped Edna.

Albert stood up. 'Just move will you,' he told his wife. 'You're holding everybody up. There are seats behind.'

Maureen, looking daggers at Edna, reluctantly gave up her seat.

When the coach had made its way out of the dock, the Port Lecturer stood at the front and picked up the microphone. He blew on it and then tapped it to check if it was working. 'Testing, testing. Can you all hear me?'

'I can,' Albert said in an undertone but just loud enough for the Port Lecturer to hear, 'but I'm prepared to change with someone who can't.'

Mr Carlin-How glared at him and breathed heavily through his nose. 'May I have your attention, please?' he announced. 'This morning our tour takes us to Pompeii, which is about twenty kilometres from the city of Naples through which we will be passing presently, so we have a short journey to the site. Now, a word of warning before we arrive at our destination. The Roman ruins are full of potential hazards – irregular outcrops, potholes, areas of rough ground, broken masonry and there are likely to be crowds of people milling around. So please, I urge you to watch your step.' He caught sight of the new white trainers on Albert's feet. Clearly this passenger, like many on the coach, had not heeded the advice given at the lecture or read the guidance in the cruise newsletter recommending suitable footwear. Mr Carlin-How allowed himself a small smile of satisfaction knowing that the loud-mouthed man's new white trainers would be covered in red Vesuvius dust by the end of the day.

'In a moment,' he continued, 'I will tell you something of the history of Pompeii, the cataclysmic eruption of Vesuvius and describe some of the interesting things you will see in the ruins.' He sat down.

Maureen and Albert had broken into their usual bickering and had largely ignored the Port Lecturer.

'Sounds a barrel of laughs,' chuntered Albert to his wife but again loud enough to be overheard by the Port Lecturer. 'I don't know why you wanted to see a load of old rubble, Maureen. It sounds as if we're visiting a bloody building site.'

'There you go again grumbling,' said Maureen, 'and keep your voice down. You've done nothing but complain since you got up. Mrs Mickleby said it was an interesting place to visit. She said it's very historical and you can get a nice cup of coffee and a Danish pastry at one of the cafés. She asked me to get her a Roman urn while we are there.'

'A what?'

'A Roman urn. The one she bought when she came here, her cat knocked off the mantelpiece.'

'She wants you to get her a Roman urn?' exclaimed her husband. 'Give me strength.'

'I've asked you once, keep your voice down,' she told him. 'Yes, I've told you, she wants me to get her a Roman urn, not an actual one, a reproduction. Do I have to keep repeating myself?'

'It's the first I've heard about some Roman urn.'

'You just don't listen.'

'And how are we going to fit a bloody great Roman urn in the case what with all that china you bought in Valetta and all your stuff?'

'The Roman urn won't go in the case and anyway it won't be a big one. It will have to be carried.'

'If you think I'm lugging all the cases off the ship and carrying a bloody great Roman urn on my shoulder, you've got another think coming.'

Before Maureen could respond the Port Lecturer rose to his feet and raised his voice to gain the attention of some chattering passengers.

'Now a further word about our destination,' he said. 'At the time of the volcanic disaster, Pompeii was a relatively small community by Roman standards with a population of around eleven thousand. In AD 79 during the reign of the Emperor Titus, Mount Vesuvius erupted, covering the town and the inhabitants with layers of volcanic materials, mostly ash and pumice, to a depth of twenty-five metres. The lost city proved to be a dream come true for archaeologists, with its rich trove of intact artefacts that have remained in near-perfect condition, undisturbed for centuries. Not only has the city structure been preserved right down to the graffiti, but the excavations at Pompeii provide a truly unique archaeological treasure: actual Romans who—' He broke off, noticing that more of the passengers were beginning to lose interest. Albert gave a great yawn; the aged couple had fallen asleep, and Edna and Miriam had begun a lively conversation. Seeing he had lost the attention of most of his audience, Mr Carlin-How decided to give up the ghost. If people are not prepared to listen, he told himself, then I am not prepared to give them the benefit of my knowledge. 'If you require any further information,' he said haughtily, 'I suggest you purchase a guidebook.' He then sat down on the front seat next to a small boy.

'I found what you said most interesting,' Oliver told him.

'Thank you. I'm glad at least someone was listening.'

'I should have liked it if you had carried on.'

'I would have provided more information if the passengers had showed the slightest bit of interest.'

'I was fascinated,' Oliver told him.

'You are the young man who came to my lecture and made notes, are you not?' stated the Port Lecturer.

'Yes, I think I told you I like history.'

'Well, you will be spellbound by Pompeii. It is a remarkable place. So much we know about the Romans was preserved under all the ash. Of course, a great many artefacts are housed in the National Archaeological Museum in Naples, including a number of important mosaics recovered from the ruins of Pompeii and the other Vesuvian cities. This includes the Alexander Mosaic, dating from circa 100 BC, originally from the House of the Faun in Pompeii. It depicts a battle between the armies of Alexander the Great and Darius III of Persia. It's a pity we can't visit the museum, but I guess not many on this coach would be interested.'

'I would be,' answered Oliver.

'The next time you visit Naples, make sure you go. The exhibition is mind-blowing.'

'Mr Carlin-How,' said Oliver, 'you mentioned the volcano erupted at the time of Emperor Titus. Isn't he best known for completing the Colosseum?'

'He was indeed,' replied the Port Lecturer, surprised by the boy's knowledge.

'I read it in the guidebook, but it didn't say he was famous for anything else, just that he had quite a short reign.'

'Titus was known for his generosity in relieving the suffering caused by two disasters: the eruption of Mount Vesuvius and a fire in Rome the following year,' Mr Carlin-How told him, warming to his theme and pleased someone at least was interested. 'After barely two years in office, he died of a fever in AD 81 and was made a god by the Roman Senate.'

'Who came after him?' asked Oliver.

'His younger brother Domitian succeeded him.'

'What sort of emperor was he?'

'Not a very good one by all accounts, in fact, he was known for being one of the worst Roman emperors in history. His suspicion of others made his actions cruel and unjust. He came to a bad end. He was hacked to death.'

With such a captive audience the Port Lecturer became animated and continued to give his young companion a personal seminar on Roman history. When the coach arrived at Pompeii, Oliver thanked him for a most fascinating account, saying he was looking forward to the next lecture.

'It was a pleasure,' replied Mr Carlin-How, greatly cheered by the conversation. The boy knew more about history than most of the students at the college where he lectured. And he showed a great deal more interest in the subject. 'You are a very unusual young man,' he said.

'Yes, so I've been told,' replied the boy nonchalantly.

'Now, when you get into Pompeii you must spend a few moments looking up at Vesuvius, which towers above the city, and try to imagine what it must have been like when the volcano erupted. Try and picture the terrified inhabitants trembling at seeing the sky being turned black by the ashes as it covered them, and then running to escape the melted burning rock. Some of them managed to escape, others just tried to protect themselves in whatever way they could, but it was hopeless. Don't miss the figures which have been preserved by the ash. They have been dead for eighteen centuries, but you can see them as they were at the time of their death. It is very moving, something, I guess, you will not forget.'

At Pompeii, the Port Lecturer reminded everyone to be back at the coach for four o'clock, to take plenty of water with them and be careful not to spend too long in the sun. He stressed again the need for them taking extra care on the uneven ground. Oliver remained in his seat until all the passengers had left the coach and dispersed. He then climbed down the steps and consulted his guidebook.

'Are you not with someone?' asked Mr Carlin-How.

'No, I'm by myself,' explained Oliver. 'I'm on the cruise with my grandparents but they decided, after hearing what you said at your lecture, the excursion was unsuitable for those not too good on their feet, so they have gone on a coach tour of Naples.'

'Very sensible. I'm glad someone at least took my advice,' he replied, seeing the driver struggling to remove a substantial walking frame from the storage space under the coach.

'But I was keen to visit Pompeii,' Oliver told him smiling. 'I'm really excited.'

'Well now, since you are by yourself, you might like to see some of the places of interest with me and I could tell you more about this astonishing city.'

'Oh, yes please,' answered Oliver, with grateful alacrity. His smile broadened. 'I should like that very much.'

Edna, who had overheard the conversation, manoeuvred her walking frame, and approached. She wore flimsy looking blue sandals beneath a shapeless canary yellow cotton skirt and the bright red sombrero. Her sister was clad in a wide tent of a dress which displayed large patterned pink poppies on a bright green background. It made her look like an upholstered settee. To complete the ensemble, a flower-pot straw hat with an artificial daisy pinned to the front was perched on her head.

'Can us two tag along?' asked Edna.

'I beg your pardon?' answered the Port Lecturer.

'Could my sister and I join you?' She batted away a fly that had landed on her nose.

'We're a bit nervous about getting lost,' said Miriam.

'And being mugged by pickpockets,' added her sister.

The sight of the flint-faced, light-heavyweight pensioner behind the sizeable metal contraption and wearing the bizarre sombrero, thought Mr Carlin-How, *would deter an armed gang of blood-thirsty brigands, never mind a pickpocket.*

'I am sure that if you have heeded my advice given at my lecture there is no danger of you being mugged,' he told her. 'I did mention that one has to keep alert at all times, and it is not a good idea to bring valuables such as jewellery on the excursions and to keep any money well out of sight.'

'Oh, I've secreted my money,' replied Edna, patting her stomach. 'All my cash I've got in my body bag.'

'Body belt,' mouthed her sister.

'So, can we come along with you?' asked Edna.

'Going around Pompeii with your mobility aid might not be such a good idea,' Mr Carlin-How told her. 'As I mentioned in my lecture and reiterated just now on the coach, a visit to the site might prove hazardous for those, such as yourself, who find walking difficult, particularly in those sandals.'

'Well, the only other excursion that wasn't booked up was a walking tour round the seven hills of Rome or a trip up Mount Vesuvius and I certainly couldn't have managed either of them what with the state of my hip.'

'But this visit might prove rather demanding for you,' he said, attempting to dissuade her.

'Oh, don't worry your head about me,' replied Edna. 'I'll burn that bridge when I get to it.'

'I ... er ... I intended to see as much of the city as possible,' answered the Port Lecturer, with a tentative smile, 'and this might prove difficult with—'

'With us holding you up,' said Miriam, finishing the sentence.

'Well yes.'

'Oh, we won't hold you up,' Edna told him. 'We'll just see a bit of the ruins and then you can park us in a café and collect us later.'

'I suppose so,' he replied, feeling suitably manipulated. He gave a sigh of resignation.

'I wonder if you might carry this for me,' said Edna, reaching for a large and battered canvas shopping bag with a picture of a parrot on the front. Her bosom strained against the material of her cotton dress. She thrust the bag into his hands. 'It's difficult to manage with my walking frame.' She waved away another fly.

22

And so, Mr Carlin-How, accompanied by two elderly ladies and a boy, made his way into Pompeii with a white-hot Mediterranean sun beating down on them and not a breath of wind. He stopped every so often to call the sisters' attention to the sights in the ancient city, but they showed little interest.

'You would have thought they'd have tidied the place up a bit,' remarked Edna shuffling down the main street behind her walking frame and struggling to stay perpendicular. She groaned with the effort. 'It's the devil's own job keeping upright with all these gullies. They should be filled in.' She wafted a fly that had settled on her nose.

'Those are the ruts worn down by the chariot wheels,' Mr Carlin-How objected, throwing back his head in frustration.

'That may be so, but they're playing havoc with my bunions and fallen arches and I'm a martyr to my bad hip and what with the trouble I'm having in the downstairs department, I can't say this trip is a barrel of laughs.'

Miriam said nothing but wondered how many infirmities her sister would be adding to her list before the cruise ended. Edna accumulated ailments like charms on a bracelet.

'It's very painful walking over this uneven ground,' continued Edna. 'My feet are getting bruised, and these sandals are chafing.' She slapped at another fly on the side of her cheek.

'I did say at my lecture that the ground would be uneven, and it is advisable to wear sensible walking shoes,' said Mr Carlin-How irascibly.

'Well, I shouldn't imagine that the Romans wore sensible walking shoes,' Edna answered back.

'Actually,' responded the Port Lecturer complacently and in the style of a sermon, 'the Romans wore most appropriate footwear: a light shoe of leather called a solea, the soccus, a loose leather slipper, and the sandalium, a wooden-soled sandal.' Edna scowled. 'Perhaps you should have given this excursion a miss.'

'And look at all these crumbling walls,' she told him, ignoring the comment. 'It looks as if a bomb's hit it.'

'It was a volcano,' the Port Lecturer pointed out. He took a deep, frustrated breath, looked at Oliver, who had remained silent, and shook his head. 'As for the walls, they have been preserved as they were discovered. It would be a desecration to repair them.'

'Well, it's not user-friendly for disabled people,' grumbled Edna, 'that's all I can say.'

'Look at this, Mr Carlin-How,' said Oliver, squatting and staring at a carving on a rock.

The Port Lecturer examined the bas-relief. His eyes widened. It was not something he felt inclined to explain to two elderly women and a young boy. 'Oh, it's . . . er . . . a sort of road sign,' he said casually. 'Let's move on.' He knew exactly what the street stone was – the depiction of a phallus acting as an arrow pointing in the direction of the brothel.

'Funny sort of road sign,' remarked Edna. 'It looks like a pair of scissors.'

'I don't think the Romans had scissors,' offered Oliver grinning. He was not so innocent that he did not know what the carving represented.

'Oh dear,' sighed Mr Carlin-How, shaking his head again. He remained outwardly placid which belied his inner exasperation.

'What are those people queuing for?' asked Miriam catching sight of a line of tourists outside a stone building ahead of them.

'It's not somewhere you ladies would wish to visit,' he told her, trying to move her on.

'Why?' Edna cast a curious look in his direction.

'It's not suitable for women such as yourselves, with . . . with delicate sensibilities.'

'Well, why are all those people queuing?' asked Edna undeterred. 'There must be something of interest inside.'

'Oliver,' said Mr Carlin-How, 'could you do me a favour and sit over there in the shade for a moment and look in your guidebook. I would like to visit the Amphitheatre and the Forum. Perhaps you can find out where they are located.' He didn't want the boy to overhear the conversation he was about to have with the two women. When the boy was out of hearing, he turned back to Miriam. 'This is the Lupanar,' he told her in a hushed voice. 'It was the most famous brothel in Pompeii. I'm sure it is not a place you ladies would be comfortable in visiting.'

'Why not?' asked Edna.

He coughed. 'It's somewhat indecorous.'

'It's what?' asked Edna.

'Scandalous,' he informed her, under his breath. 'The walls in there are covered with very lewd and explicit frescoes and extremely obscene graffiti, not that you would be able to understand the latter, it being scratched on the walls in Latin. Nevertheless, it is not somewhere—'

'I'm up for it,' piped up Edna, taking her bag from the Port Lecturer. 'Get in the queue, Miriam.'

'I really think—' he started.

'You stay with your young friend,' he was commanded, 'and we'll see you in an hour in the café.'

'In an hour!' exclaimed the Port Lecturer. 'You are surely not intending to spend an hour in there?'

'There's probably some very interesting things to see,' said Edna.

'I don't doubt it,' he muttered, more to himself than to the woman.

Oliver came to join them.

'Now you behave yourself, young man,' she said to him, placing a patronising hand on his shoulder and then affectionately pinching a cheek and ruffling his hair. 'Don't do anything I wouldn't do.'

The boy looked up at her sharply, clearly annoyed by the gesture and the comment, then he sighed with weary sufferance.

'We'll see you in a bit,' Edna told the Port Lecturer. 'Come along, Miriam.'

'Yes, unfortunately,' he said under his breath and with a shrug of the shoulders. He watched the terrible two waddle off.

So, while the sisters joined the queue, Mr Carlin-How and Oliver went in search of the Temple of Jupiter, the Odeon, and the Garden of the Fugitives.

When Edna and her sister were nearly at the front of the queue at the Lupanar, the aged couple emerged from the building. The man was shaking his head good-humouredly; the woman was laughing.

'Oh hello,' said Edna.

'Good morning,' replied the man.

'Is it worth seeing?' he was asked.

'Oh yes,' he answered, forcing a grin, 'I think you will find it most ... er ... educational.'

The woman slid her hand through her companion's arm and they departed.

'I hope we don't have to wait in the queue for very much longer,' complained Miriam. 'It's like being in an oven out here.'

'I'm not feeling the heat,' her sister told her with an air of piety. 'My hat keeps the sun off me and—' She was interrupted by a

large American woman, waving a small red flag above her head
and leading a party of tourists to the front. She wore a voluminous yellow frock and immense rhinestone earrings. Her face
was dominated by heavy, black-rimmed oversized sunglasses.

'Down here, folks,' she cried. 'Come right down to the front.'

'And where do you think *you're* going?' demanded Edna,
placing her walking frame in front of the entrance like a bar-
rier.

'Could we squeeze in?' the woman asked Edna in a shrill
voice.

'Certainly not. Join the queue. And would you mind not
waving that flag in my face.'

'We're on a very tight schedule,' said the woman, lowering
the flag. 'Our coach will be here to collect us in half an hour.'

'I can't help that. You should have planned your time better.'

'You might not queue where you come from,' added
Miriam, 'but we are British, and we do.'

The woman looked as if she had been smacked. She pulled
a face and took a deep breath.

'Could you move out of the way and let us through?' she
asked piqued. Then she made a move forward as if to push in.

Edna studied her like a wolf closing in for the kill. She took
exception to the woman's tone of voice and her attempt to
jump the queue. 'Have you some problem with understand-
ing plain English? You are not pushing in.'

'What's the hold-up down there, Myra?' came a booming
voice from the back.

'There's a woman up here, Chuck, who won't let us go in
before her.'

'Let me deal with it,' came the reply.

A moment later a large, pudding-faced man in a baseball
cap and baggy checked shorts, came striding forward. He
clutched a clipboard.

'What's the problem here?' he asked.

'There's no problem,' Edna informed him with heavy emphasis on the last word. She lifted the brim of her sombrero, swiped a fly away that was buzzing around her face and gave the man a glare of Gorgon ferocity.

'Well, could you stand aside and let our party in?' asked the man.

'No, I could not,' she said with a burst of sudden anger.

'We are on a very tight schedule.'

'So I have been told.' She squinted at him.

'Our coach will be arriving to collect us in an hour,' announced the man. 'The driver won't wait and—'

'Look!' snapped Edna, her lips moving like a pair of scissors, 'you are not pushing in. If you think my sister and I are going to wait out here in this sweltering heat surrounded by annoying flies while you lot traipse in before us, then you have another think coming. Get to the back of the queue.' Having delivered the rebuke, she turned her back on the man and pulled down the brim of her sombrero.

'I really think—' began the man.

'Do you not understand plain English?' asked Edna, swivelling around, and speaking slowly like a nurse to a senile person.

'Well, he's American,' said Miriam, shading her eyes against the glaring sunlight. 'They don't speak proper English, do they.'

'Let me spell it out for you,' said her sister to the man, with a tone of finality. 'You will get in here before me and my sister over our dead bodies.'

The gleam in the woman's eye was one of the most disagreeable and menacing the man had ever encountered. Knowing any further appeals would be futile, he closed his mouth. Then he turned to his companion.

'I guess, we'll have to give the brothel a miss, Myra,' he told his companion with the red flag, and they departed, followed by a crocodile of grumbling Americans.

'Colonials,' muttered Edna, with a gleam of triumph in her eyes.

The sisters entered the brothel. After a good half hour in the building, during which they spent a deal of time examining the salacious wall paintings, the two women emerged into the glaringly bright sunlight.

'Well, that was an education and a half,' observed Miriam. 'It left nothing to the imagination.'

'You know the big picture of the nude man on the wall when we went in?' Edna asked her sister.

'You couldn't really miss him, could you?' Miriam replied. 'He did tend to . . . stand out.'

'Did you notice his feet?'

'His feet!'

'Yes, did you notice his feet?'

'I wasn't looking at his feet.'

'Well, he was wearing a pair of sandals exactly like the ones I bought before we came on the cruise. Fancy that.'

Her sister stared at her blankly.

An hour and a half later Mr Carlin-How and Oliver went in search of the two women. Having looked in several cafés and restaurants without success, they found them in the Scavi di Pompeii café behind the Temple of the Capitoline Triad in the Forum. A muscle twitched in the Port Lecturer's jaw as he noticed the odd couple in the restaurant – the fat-faced individual with the bald patch and his wife – sitting at a table by the window. The man was tucking into a sizeable pizza with a large glass of beer before him.

'We wondered where you had got to,' remonstrated Edna, as Mr Carlin-How approached her. He looked hot and sticky. He mopped his brow with a handkerchief.

'It would have been useful,' he replied irritably, dropping into a chair, and breathing out noisily, 'to have agreed on the café to which you were intending to go. I assumed it would be the one by the entrance. We have looked for you in three restaurants and—'

'Well, you're here now,' she interrupted. 'Sit down, you're blocking the light.'

With a look of weary sufferance, he did as he was told. 'So, what were your impressions of Pompeii?' he asked, wiping his forehead again.

'I've seen better.'

'Really?' he said despairingly.

'Well, it was all right if you like ruins,' stated Edna. 'Of course, we have our own ruins back in Yorkshire and they're in much better condition than the ones here.'

Mr Carlin-How decided it would be fruitless to respond. He addressed Oliver. 'I wonder if you might get me a bottle of water and get yourself a drink.' He took out his wallet and plucked a note from it.

'Yes, of course,' said the boy.

'While you're there,' said Edna, 'I'd like another cup of tea. This one was like dishwater. Tell the woman behind the counter, I'd like two teabags in the cup. I like it strong. I fancy a biscuit, but these foreign ones taste like sawdust, not like the ones we get from Bettys in Harrogate. What about you, Miriam, do you want anything?'

'Just a glass of orange juice for me,' said her sister, 'with plenty of ice.'

Since there was no sign of either woman dipping into her bag for a purse, the Port Lecturer sighed and took another note from his wallet.

'And how did you find the Lupanar?' Edna was asked when Oliver had gone to get the drinks.

'We've never seen anything like it, have we, Miriam?' Her sister nodded. 'I mean what was painted on those walls was shocking. None of the people had a stitch of clothing on them.'

'I did warn you,' Mr Carlin-How told her. 'In the recent past women were not allowed to enter the Lupanar. The paintings were thought to be far too explicit.'

Edna leaned closer so as not to be overheard by those on the next table. 'People in their birthday suits, cavorting in all those neurotic drawings. It's beyond my apprehension why anyone would have that sort of thing displayed on the walls. They got up to some things did the Romans and no mistake.'

'As I said, I did warn you,' said Mr Carlin-How.

'You never mentioned anything like that in your lecture or showed any pictures,' Edna carried on priggishly.

'It would have been more interesting if you had have done,' piped up Miriam. 'Mind you, the last time you turned off the lights to show us the pictures, people fell asleep.'

'Nobody would have fallen asleep if he'd have shown some of those pictures of what was on the walls in that . . . that place,' remarked Edna. 'What the Romans got up to is nobody's business. It made my toes curl.'

Oliver returned with the drinks on a tray.

'*Bustina di tè,*' he said.

'What?' cried Edna.

'It's Italian for a teabag,' explained the boy. 'I asked the lady to put two in your cup.'

'That's useful to know,' said Miriam. 'Thank you, love.'

'Apropos what you were saying,' said Mr Carlin-How, 'I didn't think it was at all appropriate in my lecture to go into detail of what was on the walls in the Lupanar, bearing in mind some of the passengers with the more sensitive dispositions.' He looked at Oliver and then added, lowering is voice, 'And younger members of the audience.'

'Well, those drawings left nothing to the imagination,' said Edna primly.

Oliver looked up from his drink. He had read about the Lupanar in his guidebook and overheard the conversation.

'I suppose you might expect to find that sort of lubricious painting on the walls of a brothel,' said the worldly-wise boy with alarming directness.

The three adults were incapable of speech.

While counting the passengers as they boarded the coach to take the party back to the cruise ship, Mr Carlin-How discovered two were unaccounted for. He climbed aboard, walked down the aisle, and did a recount. He then stood at the front, picked up the microphone, blew into it and then tapped it to check if was working. 'It appears that two of our party are missing,' he said. 'Does anyone know who they are?'

'It's the fat man in the T-shirt and the baggy coloured shorts and the woman in the straw hat with the umbrella,' Edna shouted out. 'They were sitting on the seat behind us.'

'Does anyone know where this couple might have got to?' he asked.

'We saw them in the café,' Miriam informed him. 'He was eating a pizza.'

'This is all I need,' moaned the Port Lecturer. A vein in his temple stood out and beat angrily.

'Would you like me to go and look for them?' volunteered Oliver.

'No, no,' answered Mr Carlin-How. 'I had better go myself.'

When he returned ten minutes' later minus the absentees, he discovered the passengers had grown impatient and tempers were becoming frayed.

'Could we make a move?' asked Edna. 'I need to have a shower before dinner. I'm covered in dust.'

'Make a move!' cried Mr Carlin-How. 'Are you suggesting we leave this couple stranded in Pompeii?'

'They were told pacifically we should be back at the coach at four o'clock. It is now twenty-five minutes after the hour. If they are so disconsiderate as to have us all waiting for them to saunter back, then it's their fault. I think we should leave them here.'

There were a few mumbled agreements from some of the passengers.

'It is out of the question for us to go without them,' he replied. 'I shall go and have another look.'

'Well, don't be too long,' Edna shouted unhelpfully.

Moments after Mr Carlin-How had departed to go in search, the two truants wandered back to the coach. They were greeted with several handclaps. Albert clambered aboard after his wife carrying an earthenware pot with two handles to the side.

'Sorry we're a bit late,' Maureen informed the stony-faced passengers with no trace of embarrassment, 'there was a long queue in the gift shop.'

'Now we've got to wait for the guide,' grumbled Edna, looking fiercely at the couple.

'Where is he?' asked Albert.

'Gone looking for you two,' Miriam told him shrilly.

Mr Carlin-How, hot and flustered, was not in the best of moods on arriving back at the coach and seeing the missing pair sitting comfortably in their seats.

'Where did you two get to?' he asked crossly.

'We got held up in the gift shop,' replied Maureen.

'She wanted to buy a Roman urn,' Albert told him, tapping the vessel which had been deposited on his lap.

'Can we get going?' asked Maureen. 'I'd like to have a shower before dinner.'

The Port Lecturer had the sudden urge to throttle her.

As the coach made its way back to the ship, Albert, nursing the rust-coloured earthenware pot on his lap, turned to his wife. 'It was you what held everyone up,' he said. 'I don't know why you had to go in the bloody gift shop just before we were supposed to meet at the coach.'

'I'd have gone there earlier but you spent far too long gawping at those filthy pictures in the brothel.'

'What did you buy this ugly great thing for anyway?'

'I told you, I promised Mrs Mickleby I'd get her a Roman urn. I think you're going deaf or losing your memory or your marbles or you just don't listen.'

'Give me strength,' he muttered.

She suddenly jolted up in her seat as if she had been bitten. 'Oh, my goodness!' she cried.

Albert nearly dropped the urn. 'Now what?'

'I've left the parasol in the gift shop. See if you can stop the coach and go and get it.'

'Do you want me to get lynched?' he told her.

'I borrowed it from Mrs Mickleby,' said Maureen. 'I don't know what I shall say to her when we get back.'

'Tell her you lost it and you'll get her another one. I don't know why you wanted to bring it with you in the first place. You've never put the bloody thing up.'

'She'll not be best pleased.'

'Well, she'll have to make do with the Roman urn.'

Later as she strode hastily down the dockside to the cruise ship, Maureen, who had taken charge of the Roman urn and put it in her bag, collided with Edna, who accomplished a sort of pincer movement with her walking frame to get on the gangplank. She dropped her bag. There was the sound of shattering pottery.

'You want to be careful where you're going with that contraption,' she barked, reaching down to retrieve her bag. 'You've made me drop my Roman urn.'

Edna fixed her with a penetrating, unwavering stare. 'And you want to buy a watch,' she declared, 'and then the next time you might get back to the coach when you're supposed to and not hold everyone up.'

'And then none of us would be in a hurry to get back to the ship,' added her sister in a tone of rebuke.

'You can't see where you're going with that silly great hat,' began Maureen, 'and you're a walking hazard with that—'

'Leave it,' warned Albert, gripping her arm. 'Just leave it will you.'

Mr Carlin-How, hearing the disagreement, approached the two women. 'Is there a problem?' he enquired.

'It's this woman,' Maureen told him, stabbing the air with a finger. 'She's a menace with that metal appliance. She blocked my way and then knocked my bag out of my hands, and I dropped my Roman urn. It's in pieces.'

'Your Roman urn?' said the Port Lecturer.

'It's a replica that I bought at the gift shop,' she told him. 'A friend of mine asked me to get it for her. Now what am I going to tell her?'

'I suggest you stick it,' he told her with a wry smile.

'What?' she snapped.

'Stick your urn back together and say it's an original Roman antiquity.'

Before she could respond he swept on ahead with the grin fixed on his face.

23

Cyril and Connie were enjoying afternoon tea in the Rainbow Lounge when they were approached by Lady Staithes. She wore a plain but clearly expensive fuchsia cotton dress. As a ways she looked immaculate, every inch a woman of quality and position.

'May I join you?' she asked.

Cyril jumped to his feet as if he had been poked with a cattle prod. 'Yes, yes, of course.'

'I hope I am not disturbing you,' she said sitting down.

'No, no, not at all.'

Connie, too dumbfounded to speak, stared open-mouthed. She had never met a titled lady before.

'I think we are neighbours,' said Lady Staithes.

'Neighbours?' repeated Cyril dropping back into his seat.

'I believe you occupy the stateroom next to mine on A Deck.'

'Oh, yes.' Cyril, not a man to be unforthcoming was now tongue-tied in the presence of the aristocracy.

'You're in the Manhattan Suite,' she declared.

'We are.'

'The accommodation is quite splendid, is it not?'

'Yes, yes,' agreed Cyril, 'we think so.'

'We do,' echoed Connie who had now found her voice.

'One could not wish for anything more.'

'Very true,' Cyril concurred.

'I'm Lady Staithes.'

She had little need to introduce herself for she was well known on the ship: the graceful and mysterious aristocrat who was rumoured to be a lady-in-waiting to the Queen, lived on a vast estate and was the widow of some belted earl.

'I'm Cyril Ugthorpe an' this is mi wife, Connie.'

'I'm pleased to meet you both,' said Lady Staithes.

'Likewise, I'm sure,' said Connie, managing a small smile.

'I've never met a lady afore,' admitted Cyril.

'I've never met a Cyril before,' she answered.

He gave a nervous laugh.

'I guess you 'ave been on a lot o' cruises, Lady Staithes,' he said.

'No, this is only my second. I enjoyed the last one so much that I decided to splash out on another. I find cruising most satisfactory, particularly for a woman travelling on her own. It is most relaxing and secure, and one gets to meet interesting people and see so many different places. How about you and Connie? Are you both veteran cruisers?'

'No, it's our fust,' Cyril told her. 'To tell you t'truth, Lady Staithes, we never in our wildest dreams imagined that we'd one day end up sailing on a luxury liner. We came into a bit o' money an', like you, thought we'd splash out.'

'And why not,' she said.

'Will you be goin' ashore in Rome tomorra?' she was asked.

'Yes, indeed, I would not miss Rome. It is said that one should see Rome and die not that I am intending to depart this life quite yet.'

'I 'ope none of us does that,' said Cyril laughing.

'I did want to go on a tour,' Lady Staithes told him, 'but they were all fully booked up. I guess I shall have to make my own way around the city.'

Cyril looked at Connie. She smiled and nodded. 'Well, if I'm not bein' presumptuous, you are very welcome to cum around wi' us.'

'Very welcome,' echoed Connie.

'We're goin' to tek a taxi into t'city,' said Cyril, 'stoppin' at all the sights an' mebbe having a bite to eat. We 'ave a friend comin' wi' us, but they'll be plenty o' room for you.'

'Yes, do come with us,' said Connie. 'They'll be plenty of room.'

'How very kind of you,' said Lady Staithes, 'but I really would not wish to impose.'

'You'll not be himposin',' cried Cyril. 'We'll be glad o' your company, won't we Connie?'

'We will, glad of your company,' echoed his wife.

'Then, in that case, I should be delighted to join you,' replied Lady Staithes.

That evening Lorenzo Barritino gave his second bravura concert. Dressed in white tie and tails, he strode onto the stage to rapturous applause. His white teeth sparkled, and his black hair shone like polished jet under the bright lights. With a flourish, he gave several low bows and then, looking directly at Matthew, who sat with his wife on the front row, he smiled and held out his arms as if preparing to embrace him. Matthew nodded and smiled back.

'Tonighta is a nighta of love and romance,' the tenor told the audience. 'Tonighta, I perform for you some of opera's most beautiful and powerful arias. The first is "La Donna E Mobile" from *Rigoletto* by Giuseppe Verdi. The Duke of Mantua sings that woman isa fickle like a feather ina the wind.' The music began and he sang in a deep, rich voice:

La donna è mobile
Qual piuma al vento
Muta d'accento
E di pensiero.

And so, the evening continued, each aria receiving an enthusiastic reception.

'Now I come to my last aria ofa the evening,' said Lorenzo. There was an audible 'Ahhhh.' 'I singa for you, "Di Quella Pira" from *Il Travatore* by Giuseppe Verdi.'

Following his performance, he bowed, kissed his hands, and left the stage. There were shouts of 'Encore! Encore!' and a few moments later he returned, basking in the accolade.

'You area very kind,' he said. 'For my encore. I need *il mio amato*, my beloved.' He tripped down the steps to the side of the theatre, ran with impressive speed along the front row, took the hand of a speechless Maureen, raised her from her seat and, before she could protest, drew her up and onto the stage and under the bright lights. Fortunately, she had managed to book an appointment with Becky in the Ocean Spa, so her hair looked a little better. She squinted, wrinkled her nose, and looked dazed. As Albert remarked later to a passenger in the laundrette, 'The wife was too gobsmacked to argue.'

Lorenzo, still holding Maureen's hand, told the audience, 'I nowa sing for you "The Flower Song" from *Carmen* by Georges Bizet. The opera is set in Seville, where many of you havea visited, and is about the beautiful, sultry gypsy heroine Carmen.' Maureen affected what she thought would look like a coy little smile, but it resembled more of a grimace. Inside her chest her heart was thumping.

Martin appeared on stage and passed the singer a red rose which the tenor presented to Maureen. He then raised her hand to his lips, kissed it lightly and said, '*Bella Donna*.' Then he sang.

'Did you recognise her?' Edna asked her sister as she shuffled up the aisle of the theatre after the performance.

'Recognise who?'

'The woman with the dyed blond hair the colour of marmalade, and nose like a beak who the singer dragged onto the stage. She was the one who had the set-to with the hard-faced hairdresser in the Ocean Spa. I see she's had a makeover, but her hair still looks a mess.'

'She was the woman who you barged into with your walking frame when we were coming back from Pompeii and broke her urn.'

'Excuse me!' exclaimed Edna. 'I've already told you, I did not barge into her. It was her who barged into me. She was in such an almighty hurry to get aboard the ship, charging down the dockside like a cat with its tail on fire, that she impeded my passage. I don't know why with all the people in the theatre the singer had to pick her out.'

'*Bella donna*,' said Miriam.

'What?'

'That's what the opera singer called her: *Bella donna*. It's Italian. It means beautiful woman.'

Edna gave a snort of uncompromising disapproval. 'Well, he wants his eyes testing. A beautiful sultry gypsy heroine? He must be kidding.'

'I notice she's been to have her hair redone,' remarked her sister.

'I've just said that, Miriam. Sometimes you just don't listen. I think you're going a bit deaf. Anyway, I can't say that the investment in her looks has paid off.' She stopped and leaned on her walking frame and thought for a moment. 'As I recall, belladonna is a poisonous plant.'

Miriam chuckled, 'Well, the way she looked at you when you made her shift her seat on the coach to Pompeii and then knocked her Roman urn out of her hands, that was venomous all right.'

Albert and Maureen sat at a table in the Sunset Restaurant for dinner. Neither was in a good mood.

'Will you stop going on about the bloody Roman urn,' moaned Albert. 'It was a bit of cheap pottery. You could get something like that from Doncaster market and at half the price. Anyone would think it was a piece of priceless antique china the way you keep harping on about it.'

'I promised Mrs Mickleby I'd take her one back,' said his wife.

'Aye, so you keep on telling me.'

'If it hadn't have been for that doddery old woman wobbling along with the silly walking frame and the ridiculous hat, getting in my way, I wouldn't have dropped my bag and broke my Roman urn.'

'And if you hadn't spent so long in the bloody gift shop buying it, we'd have got to the coach on time, and nobody would have been in such a rush to get back to the ship.'

'I'd wanted to go there earlier but couldn't drag you out of the brothel and then you took your time stuffing you face with pizza in the café.'

'Oh, so it was my fault, was it?'

'You were as much help as a chamber pot with a hole in,' declared Maureen, 'telling me to leave it.'

'You were causing a scene.'

'And the Port Lecturer poking his big nose in and telling me to stick it. I promised Mrs Mickleby I would get her a Roman urn. Now what am I going to tell her? And then there's her parasol which she lent me that we left behind in Pompeii.'

'What's with the "we"?' asked her husband. 'It was *you* who would insist on bringing it along and you never used the bloody thing.'

'I shall have to get Mrs Mickleby another one,' said Maureen, who appeared not to have heard.

Albert sighed. 'I'm sick and tired of hearing about Mrs Mickleby and her bloody Roman urn and her parasol. I'll tell you this, Maureen, if you come on another cruise, you can come with Mrs bloody Mickleby because I shan't be coming.'

Well on that we can be agreed, she thought. *I most certainly shan't be coming on another cruise with you.* He'd been more of a pain in the neck since they got on the ship. The thought of returning home with him filled her with dismay.

For once Albert was of the same mind. The idea of going back to a life with Maureen filled him with the same dread. Being on a cruise ship in a confined space can have the effect of bringing some people closer together. It can also, as in the case of this couple, drive people further apart.

Maureen's thoughts were interrupted when they were joined at the table by the aged couple they had met when having afternoon tea.

'Do you mind if we join you?' asked the man.

'Not at all,' replied Maureen, her sour expression suddenly transformed into a bright, artificial smile. She watched the elderly man as he pulled a chair out from the table, helped his companion into it and kissed her close to the mouth before sitting down himself. His wife smiled at him and stroked his cheek.

'Thank you, darling,' she said.

'We met in the Galleon Buffet if you recall,' said the man looking across the table, 'and we had a most interesting conversation.'

'That's right,' replied Maureen.

'You are the lady who the Italian tenor singled out, aren't you?' asked the woman.

'That's right,' replied Maureen, her face warranting a small, self-satisfied smile. 'Of all the people he could have picked, he had to pick me. I was lost for words.'

Makes a change, thought Albert.

'*Bella donna,*' said the man. 'Beautiful woman.' He reached over to his companion and kissed her on the cheek. 'And here is my *bella donna.*'

Maureen hoped the starry-eyed pensioners were not going to do this sort of thing during dinner. She had had enough of watching their canoodling when she'd met them in the Galleon Buffet. It would quite put her off her meal.

The waiter arrived with the menus.

'I must apologise for my husband,' she told the couple.

'What have I done now?' asked Albert.

'He's in a bit of a bad mood. He's had an accident with his dress shirt,' she told the couple pointing to Albert's chest. 'You can see the scorch mark there. He took it to the laundrette to iron it and came back with it all creased and with a big burn right in the middle.' She made a face at her husband and shook her head.

'We didn't notice,' the woman told her.

'Not, that is, until it was pointed out,' said Albert.

'It was his only dress shirt as well,' said Maureen. 'He went to the ship boutique to see if he could get another one, but they didn't stock ones in his size. He's XXL.'

'Why don't you speak a bit louder and tell all the restaurant,' her husband muttered.

'I can't even trust him to iron one piece of clothing,' said Maureen, shaking her head again.

'*You* should have done it then,' he said in a peevish tone of voice. 'I did explain to you, that there was a rumpus in the laundrette and the woman who very kindly offered to iron my shirt got distracted and burned it.'

'Yes, we heard about the argument in the laundrette,' said the elderly woman, attempting to change the subject and lighten the tone. 'Evidently two of the passengers got into a fight over the washing machine, didn't they?'

After Albert had returned to his cabin, the small dumpy woman had returned to the laundrette to retrieve her washing to find it still damp and screwed up on the table. The tall, gaunt-looking woman who had thrown it there, had now commandeered the washing machine. An altercation had ensued in which the two women started shouting at each other until a steward had been called by a passenger and he had managed to separate them. The incident had been reported.

'They both had to go and see the Captain, I gather,' said the man now, 'and rumour has it he threatened to put them off the ship if there was a recurrence. Fancy getting into a fight over a washing machine.'

'It was quite a carry-on,' Albert told him. 'I witnessed what started it all when I went into the laundrette—'

'They don't want to hear all about that,' cut in his wife.

'Actually,' said the woman, 'we would be quite interested to know what started it all off.'

So, Albert regaled the couple with a blow-by-blow account of what had happened before turning to his wife who was studying the menu. 'And that is why, as I explained to Maureen, who clearly wasn't listening, why I ended up with a creased shirt with a scorch mark down the front. Perhaps next time she might like to iron my clothes like all the other wives do for their husbands.'

'If you think—' began Maureen.

The arrival of the waiter to take their orders, stopped her mid-sentence.

'My name's Jimmy, by the way,' the elderly man said, 'and my wife is called Pat.'

'We're pleased to meet you. I'm Maureen.' She cocked her head to one side and scowled. 'He's Albert.'

'I wonder if you would like to join us for a glass of bubbly this evening?' asked Jimmy. 'We're celebrating. You see, it's Pat's birthday.'

'Yes, we'd like that very much,' replied Maureen. 'Happy birthday, Pat.'

'Jimmy has ordered a bottle of champagne,' she was told.

'Champagne! There's posh, as my mother would say.' Maureen looked at her husband. 'It'll be wasted on him,' she said. 'He only drinks ale.'

'If you would prefer a glass of beer, Albert,' began Jimmy.

'No, no, the champagne will be fine,' he replied.

'I hope you don't mind me enquiring,' Maureen asked Pat, looking across the table, 'but might I ask how old you are today?'

The elderly woman gave a small smile. 'I'm ninety-two,' she whispered.

'And I'm ninety-four,' added her husband, 'but we don't let old age get us down. At our time of life, it's too hard to get back up.'

'Well, I hope I look as good when I'm your age,' Albert told them. He gave his wife a sidelong glance. 'Though I don't think I'll ever manage to get to seventy, never mind ninety-four.' He was minded adding, "what with what I have to put up with," but refrained.

'If you went steady with the drink and the food and took more exercise,' said his wife, 'then you might manage to last a bit longer.'

It was the opinion of the aged couple that the speaker had favoured her husband with this opinion on more than one occasion.

During the meal they ate little while Albert tucked into a substantial plate of steak and chips. Maureen leaned across the table again. 'You know people are talking about you two,' she revealed.

'Really?' replied Jimmy.

'You've become quite the topic of conversation on the ship. Everyone thinks you are such a devoted couple; they say it's lovely to see how you treat one another after all those years you've spent together – holding hands and showing such affection.' She looked accusingly at her husband. She couldn't recall the last time he had held her hand or shown her much affection.

'We are in love,' said the elderly man, giving his wife a tender look. 'It's as simple as that.'

'Jimmy's a romantic,' said the woman. 'We were sitting in the sunshine on a bench in the municipal park when he proposed. It was so pretty and peaceful, with all the bright flowers and the sun shining on the boating lake.' She touched his cheek. 'He looked so sweet and earnest in his Royal British Legion blazer. It seems like yesterday.'

Jimmy gazed at her tenderly. 'Pat made me the happiest man in the world when she said "Yes".' He looked at Albert. 'Can you imagine what I feel like to have got a wife who shows so much love, care, and affection.'

No, I can't, thought Albert.

'Might I ask you how long you've been married?' asked Maureen.

'A month,' answered Jimmy, patting his wife's hand.

'A month!' Albert spluttered. 'Is that all?'

'Yes,' said the man, 'we met in the care home earlier this year and our hearts took flight. We fell head over heels for each other. Didn't we, sweetheart?'

'We did.'

'Love at first sight,' said Jimmy. 'I asked her to marry me, and she said she would.'

'My husband's a great believer in the institution of marriage.' She chuckled. 'He loves it so much, I'm his third wife.'

'Third time lucky, sweetheart,' he said, patting her hand again.

'I divorced just the once,' said Pat. 'I've a daughter, Jimmy's got a son. They were both dead against us tying the knot. They did everything they could to stop us. They didn't even come to the wedding.'

'My son arrived at the care home with a Power of Attorney document for me to sign,' said Jimmy. 'He said I wasn't thinking straight, and I was losing my marbles and said he would take care of all my affairs. I told him to stuff it.'

'My daughter said I was not in my right mind,' said his wife, 'and she said that if I married Jimmy, she wouldn't speak to me again. I told her I wouldn't lose any sleep over it.'

'But as I said to Pat,' stated her husband. 'I said bugger them both and we've started spending their inheritance.'

'And do you know,' said his wife, 'it costs less to come on a cruise for a month than it does in the care home, so we might spend the rest of our lives sailing around the world.'

Her husband grinned. 'Life's too short,' he said, 'so you might as well smile while you've still got your teeth.' He leaned over and kissed his wife. 'Am I right, sweetheart?'

'You are, darling,' she replied smiling.

Albert and Maureen were lost for words.

'And here's the champagne,' said Jimmy, rubbing his hands.

24

The day was excessively hot, unbroken, and bright as metal. As the coaches lined up on the quayside to take the passengers into Rome, the Port Lecturer stopped Oliver at the bottom of the gangplank. He wore a fetching Panama fedora and was dressed in a smart pale oatmeal linen suit and matching canvas shoes. Oliver wore a plain cotton shirt and pale blue trousers, with his straw trilby-style hat pushed back jauntily on his head. For their visit to Rome, Mr Carlin-How had cautioned the passengers who had attended his lecture, to be appropriately dressed if they intended visiting St Peter's Basilica. 'No shorts, short trousers, short skirts, sleeveless shirts or bare shoulders are acceptable,' he had warned them.

Mr Carlin-How had hoped that he could spend the day with Elodie but she informed him that she had made other plans. He was disappointed, even more so when the two sisters had latched onto him again. He prayed that Edna would not make an appearance in the ridiculous sombrero.

'I don't think it's a good idea for you to go into the city by yourself if that is what you intend to do,' he advised the boy. 'It will be extremely busy today with the Pope giving a blessing and it's not the safest place for a young man to be by himself. You are very welcome to come around the city with me, but I guess we will see little because the two ladies who were with us in Pompeii have asked to accompany me again.'

'My grandparents said the same, that it's not sensible for me to go off by myself today,' answered Oliver. 'It's kind of you to ask me, but Dr King has said I could accompany her.'

'Ah, well, that's an excellent idea. You will see far more of the city with Dr King who will, no doubt, share with you her considerable historical knowledge. Now you must try and visit—'

'Are you ready, Mr Carlin-How?' asked Edna, who had stepped into the full glare of the morning sunshine and was keen to be away. 'We've been stood standing here like spare parts for ten minutes.'

She cut a dash in a brightly coloured floral print dress as shapeless as a sack of potatoes and wore a rope of large grass-green beads. She now wore a spotted bandanna on her head knotted at the back of her neck and earrings the size of onion rings. She resembled a gypsy fortune teller. Her sister was equally bizarre in appearance, dressed in a voluminous, peas-ant style blouse with great balloon sleeves and a flouncy red skirt. She looked like an ageing Heidi. Both carried capacious handbags.

He sighed. 'Yes. I'm about as ready as I will ever be,' he told them muttering morosely. 'I'll catch up with you later, Oliver,' he told the boy.

Rome was full of life, sound, and sensation. As Mr Carlin-How looked around he breathed in deeply, intoxicated by the breathtaking beauty around him. Edna was not similarly inspired and complained about the heat, the noise, the crowds, the exhaust fumes, and the maddening flies.

She sniffed dubiously as if there were an unpleasant smell in the air. 'I'm not all that impressed with Rome,' she con-cluded.

'We'll not stay too long,' said her sister, her comment falling well short of enthusiasm. 'It's too oppressive for comfort.'

'For goodness' sake,' muttered the Port Lecturer, controlling his annoyance.

'Beg pardon?' asked Edna.

'We have only just arrived,' he told the sisters with uncontrolled severity in his voice. 'This is the most beautiful city in the world. "How is it possible to say an unkind or irreverential word of Rome? The city of all time and of all the world." Not my words, dear ladies, but those of Nathaniel Hawthorne.'

'I've never heard of him,' remarked Edna indifferently. 'I think we ought to stop for a cup of coffee, my hip's started playing up.'

'But we have not seen anything yet,' said Mr Carlin-How, 'and we have precious little time here.'

'I can't say I'm over keen on foot-slogging around a lot of gloomy churches,' announced Edna. 'You might just as well buy the postcards.'

'When you've seen one church, you've seen the lot,' said Miriam.

'No, my dear lady, that is patently not the case,' he replied. 'There are over nine hundred churches in Rome and each one is unique.'

'They're far too fancy for me,' said Edna. 'All these coloured statues and candles and crucifixes and big black tombs give me the creeps.'

Mr Carlin-How shook his head. Why had he lumbered himself with these two? Why hadn't he been firmer when they had asked to accompany him and suggested they should go on a guided tour? He had planned to visit the Colosseum, the Pantheon, and the Villa Borghese Gardens. Fat chance of that with these two hangers-on. He determined to shake them off.

'I shall have to sit down,' said Edna. 'These sandals are chafing.'

'I'll find a café,' the Port Lecturer told her, pleased that
he could escape, 'and meet you back there in a couple of
hours. Get a drink and sit in the shade and don't wander
off too far.'

'Are you going to leave us then?' asked Edna, shielding her
eyes against the bright sunlight, and then batting away a fly.

'Yes, I have not come to Rome to sit in a café all day. I
shall leave you just for a short time. I particularly wish to see
the Roman Forum, the Trevi Fountain and the Santa Maria
Sopra Minerva with its stained-glass windows.'

'That will be the pigeons,' remarked Edna.

'What?'

'The stains on the glass. It will be the pigeons. They're
everywhere.'

Mr Carlin-How bit back a reply.

'We'll sit over there,' Edna told him, 'in the Flamin gobar.'

'Flamingo,' he corrected. 'It's the Flamingo Bar.'

'I don't know how it's pronounced,' she declared curtly. 'I
don't happen to be fluid in Italian.' She flapped at another fly
that was buzzing around her nose.

Having, with great relief, installed the two women in the
café, the Port Lecturer strode off to find the places in which
he was interested. He did not intend to rush back.

On his way to the Colosseum, he caught a glimpse of two
of the disagreeable passengers sitting at a pavement café. He
hurried on.

Albert had just ordered his lunch.

'Do you remember what you said to me before we got on
the ship?' Maureen was asking complacently.

'Having to lug all those cases, you mean?' Albert answered.

'I said we will probably want to eat out on some occasions
and you said I should forget about that. "This cruise has cost
me an arm and a leg," you said.' She mimicked his voice. '"I'm

not shelling out any more money. All the food is included anyway".'

'So?'

'So, what are you doing here then ordering a meal?'

'I happen to be hungry, Maureen.'

'It's not even lunchtime yet and you're tucking into fish and chips.'

'Give it a rest.'

'You need to lose weight and cut down on the drink.'

'I *am* on holiday,' he told her.

'The trouble with you,' said his wife, 'is that you say one thing and do another.'

'I thought you were going shopping?'

'I am.'

'Well, don't let me keep you. And don't buy more heavy stuff to cart back home,' he grumbled.

'I'm looking for a particular item.'

'What?'

'I want to see if I can get something similar to the Roman urn that got knocked out of my hands when we were coming back from Pompeii.'

'Give me strength,' muttered Albert. 'Not the bloody Roman urn again.'

When his wife had gone, Albert brooded over his beer. He would wait until they got home and then he would tell Maureen that he had had enough. He would ask for a divorce. He pictured a life without her nagging. He could get up late, go to the football or down to the pub, do as he pleased, without the constant complaining. Yes, he thought life would be sweeter.

Two hours' later Mr Carlin-How found the two sisters still in the café. Edna was complaining about the price of the coffee and the tasteless biscuits.

'In light of your earlier comment,' he said, 'I guess you will probably want to give the Vatican a miss. The Pope is giving a blessing today so the place will be heaving. I shall go myself and meet you back—'

'We've not come all the way to Rome,' she said, 'to miss meeting the Pope.'

He sighed. 'You won't actually meet him,' she was told. 'He'll appear as a small figure in white on a balcony a long way off and there will be hundreds and hundreds of people there.'

He could not, however, dissuade them.

Edna got to her feet. 'Come along, Mr Carlin-How,' she commanded, in a hectoring tone as if talking to a recalcitrant child. 'I've not come all the way to Rome to spend all my time in a café. Let's make a move. We've been sitting here long enough waiting for you to return.'

She made him feel like a naughty boy as she waddled off, followed by her sister.

'Very well.' He exhaled noisily, attempting not to sound as exasperated as he felt and, like an obedient child, he too followed her.

St Peter's Square was crowded with tourists and pilgrims awaiting the appearance of the Pope.

'I've never seen so many people,' remarked Edna. She waved away a fly which was hovering around her nose.

'I did say,' muttered Mr Carlin-How. He plucked a handkerchief from his breast pocket and dabbed at his forehead.

'I can't stand in the sun for too long,' complained Edna. She poked the Port Lecturer. 'When is he coming out?' she asked in a loud peremptorily high-pitched voice, which attracted the attention of the people around her.

'I don't know,' replied Mr Carlin-How. 'I don't happen to have the Pope's itinerary handy.'

'Do you think he'll be long?'

'I really couldn't say.'

At this point the Pontiff appeared on the balcony. There were cheers and shouts, clapping and the waving of flags.

'Oh look,' announced Edna to her sister in a loud voice, 'speak of the devil.'

Two nuns standing in front of her swivelled around and gave her merciless Medusa stares.

Mr Carlin-How closed his eyes and stifled a wince.

It was impossible to see the end of the queue of people waiting to visit St Peter's Basilica. Edna and Miriam surveyed the long line of people.

'I'm not joining the queue,' announced Edna, batting away another fly.

'A very wise decision,' agreed the Port Lecturer. 'I am sure, having heard what you have said about the churches, you won't feel you will be missing much.'

'Oh, we want to go inside,' announced Edna and, without waiting for an answer set off. Despite the bad hip, chafing sandals, the bunions and the fallen arches and the inconvenience of manoeuvring the walking frame, she advanced in a remarkably brisk and business-like manner. 'Come along. Follow me.' She addressed Mr Carlin-How as a teacher might a disobedient child.

Pushing her walking frame at considerable speed and with a stern purposefulness on her face, she rocked her way through the crowds which parted before her and arrived at the very front of the queue. Her sister and a reluctant Mr Carlin-How followed.

Adopting an authoritative voice, she addressed the first person in the queue, a smartly dressed man in a light cotton suit, who sported a wide-brimmed straw hat which sat rather rakishly on his head.

'Excuse me,' she said, 'do you speak English?' She spoke loudly and slowly as a person might speak to someone hard of hearing.

'Yes,' replied the man. 'I speak English.'

'Oh, are you an American?'

'That's right, from Tennessee.'

'Oh, I *do* like the Americans,' she flattered. 'They are so friendly. As you will notice, I'm physically disabled and am in some pain standing, and the heat is making me feel quite faint.' She adopted the pious face of reverend mother.

'I'm sorry,' replied the man. 'Is there anything I can do?'

'As a matter of fact, yes. I do so much want to see the church and light a candle and say a prayer for my dear departed mother, God rest her soul, but I can't wait all that time in the queue with my infirmity. I wonder, could I squeeze in?'

'Squeeze in?' repeated the man.

'Go in before you.' She sighed, wiping her brow, and pulling a tragic face.

'Well . . . I . . . suppose so,' he replied.

Edna gave an arch little smile. 'Come along, Miriam,' she shouted to her sister. 'This Good Samarian is making room for us.' With the smile still glued on her face, she gave the man a measured look. 'This is my sister,' she explained, 'and the person with her, he is my carer.'

Mr Carlin-How closed his eyes and breathed in deeply.

'Chop, chop, Mr Carlin-How,' said Edna smiling at him as if he were an infant.

The three interlopers entered the great basilica of St Peter's.

'I must say it's good to get out of the heat,' announced Edna, 'and those annoying flies which seem to make a beeline for me.'

Then the two women set off around the church at a cracking pace. The Port Lecturer had never seen anyone move so swiftly around the building with a walking frame or heard anyone talk so loudly in a place of worship. After a quick tour of the church, the sisters joined Mr Carlin-How who stood before the great altar. The Port Lecturer stared upwards with the reverence of a barefoot pilgrim approaching the Pope. Wide-eyed, his gaze lingered on the great domed roof and lavishly decorated marble, the towering pillars, reliefs, architectural sculptures and gilding like a lover viewing the woman he adored. He was spellbound. After a while he was moved to speak.

'What do you think of that?' he asked.

'Of what?' asked Edna.

'The altar.'

'I have seen an altar before, you know,' answered Edna.

'Not like this one,' she was told. 'This is the most renowned work of Renaissance architecture ever built, the largest and most beautiful ecclesiastical masterpiece in the world.'

'It's certainly big enough,' remarked Miriam, with a deadpan expression.

Mr Carlin-How, aware that Miriam and her sister did not share his apparent enthusiasm, went into lecture mode, attempting to explain why this was a work of genius. 'This pavilion-like structure with the four huge barley-sugar columns decorated ornately with laurel leaves and bees, which stands beneath the dome, is by Bernini and is over ninety feet tall. It is claimed to be the largest piece of bronze in the world.'

The two women scrutinised the ornate altar.

'Exquisite, isn't it?' he said, in a hushed and reverential voice.

The great altar piece of St Peter's Basilica elicited little more than a shrug of indifference from Miriam.

Mr Carlin-How turned to Edna. 'Have you ever seen anything made by man more wonderful than this?' he asked. 'Don't you relish the unparalleled beauty?'

'Well, I wouldn't like to dust it,' replied Edna.

The Port Lecturer let his breath out slowly between his teeth and bit back a response.

'Well, I think we've seen enough,' stated Edna. Emerging from the church into the bright sunlight she informed Mr Carlin-How, 'I think we'll give the Sixteenth Chapel a miss.'

'The Sistine Chapel,' he answered perfunctorily.

'I saw a picture postcard of it,' Edna rattled on, 'and there's far too many naked men cavorting on the walls for my liking. I saw enough of that in Pompeii.'

'One can scarcely compare the brothel at Pompeii with the Sistine Chapel,' Mr Carlin-How told her in an exasperated tone of voice. 'It is one of the world's—'

Edna ignored him and took her sister's arm. 'Watch your bag, Miriam.' She cast her eyes around her as if looking for some undesirable character lurking in a side street. 'There's a lot of pickpockets about.'

As Edna and Miriam tagged along behind the Port Lecturer, Mr Hinderwell, in St Peter's Basilica, searched for somewhere to light a candle in commemoration of the young soldiers who had died hundreds of miles away from home and family. He asked a friendly looking priest but was told that to protect the church against smoke or the risk of fire, sadly no candles could be lit. He could, however, light a candle bulb in remembrance. 'Like a lit candle,' he was told, 'it will signify that the memory of a loved one still lives on and shines bright.'

And in Bernini's Chapel of the Sacrament, which marked the place of the death of St Peter, Mr Hinderwell knelt in prayer and thought of the young soldiers and their families. On either side were angels; one gazed in rapt adoration, the other looked towards him as if in welcome.

'"Therefore, you too have grief now",' murmured the clergyman, '"but you will see each other again and your hearts will rejoice, and no one will take your joy away from you".'

Oliver and Elodie explored the city. They visited the Colosseum, the Parthenon and the Vatican but also places off the tourist trail: the Basilica of St Clements with the archaeological excavations, the Villa Doria Pamphili with its Roman antiquities and the Appia Antica, the paved Roman Road. They stood in awe in the Forum amidst the ruins of Rome.

'Try and picture,' said Elodie, 'what it must have been like many centuries ago, when Julius Caesar and the senators walked here. Imagine the triumphal processions and elections; the public speeches, criminal trials, and gladiatorial matches. This site has been called the most celebrated meeting place in the world, and in all history.'

'Amazing,' whispered Oliver.

Elodie saw the boy's sense of exuberance, his joy and fascination at what he was seeing. There was an eager sparkle in his eyes.

On the way back to the ship on the coach after a tiring day walking around the city, Oliver fell asleep with peaceful exhaustion, his head resting on Elodie's shoulder. She glanced down at him and smiled affectionately without moving for fear of waking the boy. *What an amazing child*, she thought.

Later that day, as Oliver sat at his usual table in the Galleon Buffet for dinner, Benedict approached.

'Hello,' said the waiter.

'Oh, hello,' replied Oliver.

'So how did you like Rome?'

'It was magnificent. There was so much to see. I hope you will get the opportunity to visit one day.'

'Ah, that might be some time. The next cruise is to the Caribbean and then I have two months in the Baltic, but some day perhaps . . . ' His voice tailed off.

'I have something for you,' Oliver told him. He slid a small box across the table.

'For me?'

'Yes, I was told it has been blessed by the Pope. It's a St Benedict medal with a Latin inscription, *Vade retro Satana*. Mr Hinderwell – he's a priest on the ship – translated it for me. It means, "Get thee behind me, Satan." I should have preferred something a bit more cheerful myself. It has a chain so you can wear it if you like.'

Benedict opened the box and took out the medal which he held up to examine. 'But it's silver,' he said. 'It must have cost a lot of money.'

'Not that much,' the boy told him. 'I have an allowance and I've spent very little. I should like you to have it. It's not the same as visiting Rome, I know, but it's something you might like to keep.'

The young waiter looked at him for what seemed a long time, without speaking. 'Thank you,' he said at last, cradling the gift. 'I shall always wear it.'

25

The morning after the call at Rome, Bruce sat in the office of the Entertainment Manager. He leaned back casually in his chair with his fingers laced behind the back of his head.

'This must have come as quite a shock,' said Martin.

'Well, I will admit it was rather surprising,' replied the dance tutor matter-of-factly, 'but not entirely unexpected. Babs has always been a creature of whim.'

'But to run off with the Italian tenor,' said Martin.

'Things between myself and Babs have not been going all that well of late,' Bruce informed the Entertainment Manager. 'In fact, our association, such as it was, had just about come to the end of the line.' He appeared remarkably composed, bearing in mind the startling news he had received.

'You're taking this very well.'

'Nothing I can do about it,' said Bruce shrugging. '*C'est la vie*. These things happen. To be perfectly honest I did feel that our relationship was running on empty.'

'From my point of view, this is a most unfortunate turn of events,' said Martin.

'How so?'

'Well, I shall have to cancel your dance classes,' he said.

'Not at all,' Bruce replied, sitting up on the chair.

'But how will you manage without Babs?'

'Actually, I shall manage perfectly well. One of the passengers will be able to take over.'

'One of the passengers?'

'Vanessa is a trained dancer, and I am sure she is more than capable, with a little coaching from me, of stepping into Babs's shoes. I feel sure she will be happy to do so. Babs was getting a bit past it on the dance floor. She hadn't the stamina for the more demanding dances.'

'I never found her to be so.'

'Oh, some of the more adventurous dances like the salsa and the mamba were beyond her. She had trouble with her varicose veins.'

'I should have thought that the salsa and the mamba are well beyond most of the passengers in your class,' observed Martin, thinking of the largely elderly women who attended the dance sessions. 'I imagine that the waltz and the foxtrot are more in their line.'

'Quite so, but we do various demonstration dances,' explained Bruce. 'Anyway, Vanessa is certainly up for it.'

'Well, if you are sure.'

'Perfectly.'

Before leaving the ship in Rome, Babs had packed her things, collected her passport from reception and informed Martin that she would be remaining in Rome. She had handed him a letter to give to Bruce.

'I think it might be better not to mention this to those in your dance class,' suggested Martin now. 'Perhaps just say that Babs is indisposed. You know how gossip and rumour travel around the ship.'

'A good idea,' agreed Bruce. 'After all, we only have another two ports of call so I'm sure Babs will not be missed.'

'I guess without a partner, this will be the last occasion you will be working on a cruise ship,' ventured the Entertainment Manager.

'Not at all,' countered Bruce. 'I think I will be able to persuade Vanessa to partner me in future. As I said, I am sure she's up for it.'

While this conversation was taking place, Maureen sat by herself in the poolside pizzeria, nursing a large glass of Cabernet Sauvignon, looking wistful, when she was joined by the aged couple.

'By yourself this lunchtime?' asked Pat cheerfully.

Maureen pulled a doleful face. 'I've lost Albert,' she replied.

'We get lost on the ship, don't we, sweetheart?' said Jimmy. 'There's so many cabins and decks and corridors. It's like a maze. He'll soon turn up.'

'No, he won't,' said Maureen. 'I lost him in Rome.'

'Lost him in Rome! You mean he's still ashore?'

'Well, yes, if you put it like that,' she said. 'He'd just tucked into a plate of sardines and chips at a café, when he felt light-headed and short of breath, then he had these chest pains. Next thing he was flat out on the pavement. Heart attack it was.' She sighed. 'I was always telling him to cut down on the food intake, but he wouldn't listen.' She took a swallow of her wine. 'When he collapsed a passing nun rushed over and tried to revive him. She blessed Albert and said a prayer which was very nice. They were very concerned at the restaurant and sent for an ambulance and gave me a glass of brandy to calm my nerves. They didn't ask to be paid for the meal which was very nice of them and got me a taxi to take me to the hospital.'

'How is he?' asked Pat.

'As I say,' replied Maureen. 'I lost him.' She took another mouthful of her drink. 'He's reached his final destination.'

'You mean . . . he's . . . dead?' said Jimmy.

'I'm afraid so.' She made no attempt to feign a remorse which she clearly did not feel.

The aged couple stared but said nothing. They had expected her to be stunned, bewildered, wide-eyed with shock but the recently bereaved widow seemed to be taking things with remarkable *savoir faire*.

'They've been very good on the ship,' Maureen said. 'They're sorting everything out – all the paperwork and the arrangements to fly Albert back home. I was going to stay in Rome but there was really nothing I could do. And, of course, I can't speak a word of Italian. Anyway, Albert would have wanted me to stay on the cruise.' She knocked back another mouthful of wine.

'Oh, we are so sorry,' said Pat, in a quavering, concerned voice. She reached over and squeezed the grieving woman's hand. 'You must be devastated.'

'Terrible thing to happen,' murmured Jimmy.

'It was, but thankfully it was quick, and he felt no pain, well not much at any rate,' said Maureen dispassionately. The words 'devastated' and 'terrible' were not ones which would accurately describe her demeanour. 'It was the best way to go. As I've said, Albert wouldn't have felt much. I mean, one minute he was there tucking into a plate of sardines and chips and the next he was . . . gone. I'm pleased we took out insurance which should cover the costs. Albert didn't think we needed it, but my friend Mrs Mickleby said it was best to get covered to be on the safe side. I'm glad I took her advice.'

'Your poor heart must be broken,' comforted Pat soothingly, 'but you were blessed to have been together in a close and loving relationship for so long and have many happy memories. He's now sleeping in the sleep of the peaceful.'

'Yes,' agreed Maureen thinking of Albert's thunderous snoring, 'many happy memories.' Then, as an afterthought she added, 'Poor Albert. He went before his time.' It was the kindest remark she had made about the man she had been married to for twenty-five years. She sighed, finished her drink in one great unladylike gulp and set the glass down on the table. 'Well, I had better make a move. There's line dancing this afternoon.'

The sisters were sitting down for lunch in the conservatory bistro the following day.

'So, did those tablets you bought from the pharmacist in Rome do the trick?'

'No, they didn't,' replied Edna. 'I reckon he gave me the wrong ones. I tried to explain that' – she lowered her voice – 'I had this problem in the downstairs' department, but he didn't understand.'

'I'm not surprised,' said Miriam. 'A problem in the downstairs' department could be anything and anyway he probably spoke no English.'

'And I have to say you were no help in explaining to the pharmacist what I wanted.'

'What could I have done?' responded her sister. 'I don't speak Italian any more than you do.'

'You were too busy stocking up on cotton buds,' said Edna.

'They're a lot cheaper in Italy than at home.'

'Am I bothered?'

'You should have said you wanted a laxative or told him you'd got constipation or a bowel problem instead of beating about the bush. They're probably the same words in Italian.'

'Shush! I don't want the whole restaurant to hear.'

'Why didn't you go and see the doctor on the ship? He would have given you something.'

'Yes, with the benefit of ironside I should have done, but the last time I went down to the suppository to get the seasick tablets there was a queue a mile long.'

'Dispensary.'

'What?'

'It's a dispensary. A suppository is something . . . oh, it doesn't matter. You want to have a bowl of prunes for breakfast tomorrow. There's nothing like prunes to get things moving. You know what mother used to say: they are Nature's little workers.'

'Yes, I'll try the prunes.'

'Of course, it's all this foreign food you've been eating. That Rogan Josh curry you had in the Galleon Buffet and the Mexican spicy nachos and Japanese shishito peppers you had yesterday for instance. It's no wonder you've got an upset stomach. I've told you, you would be better off with the steak and kidney pudding or the cottage pie but you wouldn't listen. Your body's not used to it. All the spicy food has infected your digestive system.'

'I was telling Becky in the Ocean Spa about my upset stomach,' said Edna, 'and she thought I might be a celeriac.'

'A turnip?'

'No, it's someone who is allergenic to certain foods like wheat and barley, but a wrinkled passenger who was waiting to have a deep tissue hydro-facial and lip pumping treatment, which she certainly needed, said it could be the change in the water. We were sitting on that uncomfortable baguette and got into talking.'

'Banquette,' muttered Miriam. 'It's called a banquette.'

'My goodness, she could talk,' pronounced the woman whose loquacity knew no limits. 'I couldn't shut her up.'

'If the prunes don't do the trick, you had better go and see the doctor tomorrow,' said her sister, scanning the menu.

The waiter approached. 'Are you ready to order, madam?' he asked.

'Yes,' said Edna. 'Is the soup hot today?'

'It is, madam.'

'Because it wasn't yesterday. The Gestapo was stone cold.'

'That was the gazpacho,' the waiter informed her. 'It's a Spanish dish, always served chilled. Today's soup is spiced carrot and lentil.' Then he added, 'And it's very hot.'

'I'll have that then,' said Edna. 'I'm minded having the Mexican hot sizzling spare ribs to follow but I've not quite made up my mind yet. Are they chicken?'

'Are what, madam?'

'The spare ribs.'

'They are pork, madam.' The waiter attempted to hide his amusement.

'What fish is it?'

'Pollock, madam.'

'What?'

'The fish. It's pollock or you could have striped sea bass if you prefer.'

'Are these fish very fishy?' he was asked.

'They are fish, madam, and therefore are likely to be fishy,' she was told. He rolled his eyes in a display of amused forbearance. 'They come out of the sea.'

'Yes, I am aware of that, but I find very strong fish indelible. Are these very fishy, moderately fishy or not very fishy at all?'

'I really couldn't tell you, madam.'

'Well, pop in and ask the chef, will you? If the fish is very fishy, I don't want it and I'll have the Jamaican jerk chicken as a main.'

When the waiter had taken Miriam's order and departed Edna leaned across the table.

'I don't intend to go around Cartagenica with Mr Double-barrelled. He was a liability rushing us around Rome and he never stopped talking, going on and on about the history of every blessed place we visited. He's all jaw, like a sheep's head is Mr Double-barrelled with a mouth like a barn door on a windy day. His tongue's too big for his mouth that's his trouble.' The most voluble passenger on the ship, who preferred a silent audience when she was speaking, didn't pause for breath. 'I've always thought talking is overrated,' she declared.

'I'll have a word with him and tell him we're going on a guided tour,' said Miriam.

As luck would have it, the sisters caught sight of Mr Carlin-How leaving the restaurant.

'Coo-ee!' shouted Edna.

The Port Lecturer turned and pulled a pained face when he saw the sisters waving at him. The trip with the two of them to Pompeii was bad enough but their visit to Rome had been a nightmare. In the gift shop Miriam had complained crossly that the necklaces were far too small to fit over her head.

'These Italian women must have very small heads,' she had remarked, oblivious that people were staring.

'They are not necklaces,' Mr Carlin-How had pointed out in a hushed voice. 'They are rosary beads.'

On the way back to the coach Edna had insisted she needed something for her queasy stomach. Outside the pharmacist's she had told Mr Carlin-How to, 'Wait here,' as if she had been talking to a dog. He had smiled weakly with noble resignation.

Thus delayed, when the three of them arrived back at the coach they had to face an angry bus driver, an indignant tour guide and a phalanx of disgruntled passengers.

'We thought we might bump into you,' said Edna now, as Mr Carlin-How approached their table. *Well, why not*, he thought, *she's bumped into nearly every person she's encountered with that wretched walking contraption of hers: the concert pianist, two waiters, the man with a crutch, a priest in Seville Cathedral, a Swiss Guard at the Vatican, and the woman with the Roman urn.*

'We wanted to see you about going ashore at the next port of call,' said Edna.

I have no intention of being lumbered again with the two women, he said to himself.

'Ah . . . now . . . about that,' he began. 'The thing is—'

'Now I hope you won't take this remiss,' she cut in, 'but we will not be going around with you in Cartagenica.'

'Cartagena,' the Port Lecturer told her.

'What?'

'It's Cartagena.'

'Well, whatever,' she said dismissively. 'We wanted to tell you we have decided not to go around with you. We're sorry to disappoint you, but to be honest, we weren't very impressed with our outing in Rome. No offence, but you stuck us in a café for two hours and then rushed us off our feet.'

'And we didn't feel that you were very forthcoming about what we saw,' augmented her sister.

'So, we've decided to go on a real tour and booked an organised excursion.'

The Port Lecturer tried to disguise his great sense of relief. He could have jumped for joy. A gleam lit up in his eye. 'Oh dear, what a pity, and I was so looking forward to showing you the sites. I shall be bereft without you both. Do have a nice trip.' He scurried off before they could change their minds.

'I was sorry to hear about your loss, madam,' said the cabin steward.

'My loss?' asked Maureen.

'Your husband.'

'Oh, yes, it was quite a shock.'

'If there is anything I can do?'

'Actually, Ernesto, there is something,' she said. 'It's Albert's clothes.' She sighed theatrically and shook her head sadly. 'He won't be needing them now. I don't want to take them back with me. I have quite enough on, having to carry my own. I wonder if you could be a real help and pack them up and dispose of them for me. I don't suppose any of his clothes will fit many people. He was a big man, but you might be able to find a home for them. It would be very distressing for me to have to do it.'

'Of course, madam. I will see to it.'

'You have been most attentive,' she said.

'There is a letter from the Captain, madam,' the steward told her. 'I have put it on the desk.'

'From the Captain?'

'Yes, madam.'

Maureen snatched up the envelope and tore it open.

'Oh, it *is* from the Captain,' she said. 'He says how sorry he is to hear of my husband's death and has asked me to meet him for coffee at eleven tomorrow morning in the Rainbow Lounge so he can express his condolences personally. How nice of him.'

'It is, madam. The Captain is a very thoughtful man. Shall I send a message to say you will join him?'

'Yes, and I wonder, Ernesto, if you could pop up to the Ocean Spa and beauty salon and see if Becky can fit me in for a hairdo and an anti-ageing facial, sometime today. Make sure I do not get the other one, that Bianca. She made my hair look like a mass of wire wool. Tell Becky I am to meet the Captain and I want to look my best. Oh, and, Ernesto, when you've got a minute, I could enjoy a cup of tea and one of those nice cupcakes with the pink icing on the top.'

The following morning, Maureen, dressed to the nines, met Captain Smith who was waiting for her in the Rainbow Lounge. He stood on catching sight of her, reached for her hand and held it for a moment longer than was usual. This made her colour slightly.

He had spoken to the waiter because there was a pot of coffee and a plate of pastries on the table.

'Do sit down, Mrs Grosmont,' he said. 'Would you care for a coffee?'

'Yes, thank you,' she replied diffidently and sat on the edge of the chair.

A waiter hurried over and poured the coffee.

'I was so deeply sorry to hear of your bereavement,' said the Captain, in his most compassionate of voices. 'What a terrible thing to happen, particularly in the middle of your holiday.

It goes without saying that it must have come as a dreadful shock and ruined your cruise.'

'Well, of course it was a shock,' replied Maureen, lowering her voice, and arranging her features with the sorrowful expression she had adopted numerous times when passengers had approached her to commiserate. 'I am bearing up. It was just a blessing that it was so quick and at least Albert felt little pain. He'd had a good life and, as they say, he's now in a much better place.'

She sipped her coffee before picking up a pastry and taking a generous bite.

'I have been in touch with head office,' explained Captain Smith, adopting a kindly face, 'and everyone there sends their condolences. The Chief Executive has asked me to tell you that should you wish to travel on a cruise with our company at a future date, it will be at our expense. Of course, you might feel this will bring back unhappy memories and not something you would like to do, but let me assure you—'

'Oh, I think I might manage another cruise,' said Maureen quickly, brushing some crumbs from her lips. 'Given time, that is. I'm sure Albert would have wanted me to.'

'Of course,' said the Captain nodding sympathetically, 'and I should like to invite you to dine at my table tomorrow evening if you feel up to it.'

'Dine at your table?'

'Of course, things might be a little raw for you at the moment and you may not wish for company at this sad time but—'

'I think it might take my mind off things,' she cut in. 'I should be pleased to join you.'

'It's settled then,' said the Captain. 'Now, I believe all the arrangements have been made for the return of your husband to the UK.'

'That's right. Everyone's been most helpful.'

'Is there anything else we on the ship can do for you?'

'No, nothing,' she replied. 'As I've said, everyone has been most helpful.'

Ten minutes' later, the Captain made his apologies to Maureen and headed off, leaving the widow with a self-satisfied smile on her face, rehearsing what she would be saying to Mrs Mickleby on her return: that she had been invited to have coffee with the Captain and to sit at his table for dinner – and, of course, to mention the demise of Albert.

As he passed the table where the sisters were sitting, Captain Smith stopped when Edna called out to him.

'Excuse me.'

'Yes,' he said, going to join her. 'May I be of help?'

'Could we have two cappuccino coffees over here please, and a selection of biscuits?'

The Captain smiled. It was the first time in his career he had been mistaken for a waiter. He took it in good part.

'I shall see to it immediately, madam,' he said and went to place the order.

'He's a smart young man,' said Edna, 'but I didn't like the beard. I always think that men who wear beards have something to conceal, as if they were hiding behind a hedge.'

'Jesus had a beard,' remarked Miriam.

'Yes, but it was the fashion at the time. They all wore beards in those days.'

'Those men on the walls in the Pompeii brothel didn't have beards,' said Miriam. 'Mind you, they didn't have anything else on either, if it comes to that.'

'I think the least said about the men who were on the walls in the Pompeii . . . place, the better,' said her sister, pulling a censorious face. 'I've still not recovered from being exposed to them.'

'That harmless Mr Birtwistle, who does our garden, has a big bushy beard,' remarked Miriam.

'Just because Mr Birtwistle looks like Father Christmas it doesn't mean that he's malevolent.'

'Benevolent,' murmured her sister absently.

'Here comes our coffee,' announced Edna. 'I hope there's some garibaldis.'

It was the following morning when the sisters, sitting at their favourite table in the Rainbow Lounge, discovered Edna's faux pas. They overheard a woman refer to the man they assumed was a waiter, as 'Captain Smith'.

'Well,' blustered Edna defensively, turning to her sister. 'I wasn't to know. The crew all look the same in their white overalls.'

'Uniforms,' muttered Miriam. 'I thought he was dressed a bit too fancy for a waiter.'

'He certainly looked too young to be the Captain,' added her sister. 'I hope he knows what he's doing steering the ship.'

'Fancy mistaking him for a waiter.'

'I'd left my glasses in the cabin,' explained Edna, 'and anyway, you didn't know who he was either.'

'Look,' said Miriam, 'he's heading this way. When he passes you must apologise.'

'I'd be too embarrassed.'

'Since when have you ever been embarrassed?' asked her sister.

'Oh, very well,' said Edna.

As the Captain approached her table he was stopped when Edna called out to him.

'Excuse me.'

'Yes,' he said, walking over. 'May I be of help?'

'I was just—' she began.

The Captain held up a hand, gave her the benefit of a brilliant smile and cut her off, completing her sentence. 'You are wanting two cappuccino coffees and a selection of biscuits. Of course, madam, I shall see to it immediately.'

Edna, for one rare moment in her life, was stumped for words.

26

Mr Carlin-How's audiences had steadily increased since his first talk. He had decided that it was not a good idea to turn off the lights and had instructed the technician to make them extra bright. He had dispensed with showing the photographs on the big screen and stopped reading from his notes. Taking a leaf out of Elodie's book, he spoke extemporaneously, peppering his lecture with anecdotes and interesting examples.

'Our next port of call in a few days' time,' he told the passengers who had come to hear him the following afternoon, 'is Cartagena. This is a maritime enclave and was already known to the Carthaginians and the Romans. Its name derives from the Latin, *Cartago Nova*. Cartagena was under Arab domination until Ferdinand III, known as "the Saint", reconquered it and incorporated it into the kingdom of Castile. Its port played a key role in the War of Succession and the Peninsular War. But enough about that. You can read all about the history in the guidebook. Now there are a few interesting details about the Romans in Cartagena that I am going to share with you. The Barrio del Foro Romano has the remarkably well-maintained remains of a Roman bath which is well worth a visit. The Romans, on the whole, were clean people, although they didn't use soap. Instead, they immersed themselves in water baths and then smeared their bodies with scented olive oils. They used a metal or reed scraper called a strigil to remove any remaining oil or grime.

The Romans were well ahead of their time dealing with sewage and used flowing underground water to move waste away from the public bathhouses. The bathhouses of Roman times were public meeting spaces, and they would conduct business while doing their business – if you follow my drift. There were no stalls like we know today, only a row of places to sit with holes that ran to the sewage system. The Romans would use a sponge on a stick to clean up, which was a public sponge, as only the wealthy had their own private sponges on a stick. Now another fascinating and little-known fact about the Romans is . . . '

Surveying the passengers scattered around the theatre, he was gratified to see that there appeared to be real interest in what he was saying. There was no yawning, fidgeting and whispering. The woman who, at his first lecture, had knitted furiously like Madame Defarge, as if waiting for the great blade of the guillotine to descend and the decapitated head roll into the basket before her, was listening quietly. His nemeses, Edna and Miriam, were not engaged in their usual lively conversation but seemed all ears. He was cheered to know the sisters would not be accompanying him around Cartagena and pleased to see Oliver, sitting upright in his usual seat on the front row, his head to one side, listening with unflagging attention. Next to him was a tall willowy girl with feathery blond hair and large pale blue eyes.

There was a long line of passengers waiting to disembark at Cartagena. The sisters were towards the end of the queue. Edna was attired in a bright blue cotton dress and pink cardigan. She sported the red sombrero. On her feet were the thonged sandals that were not dissimilar to those worn by the naked Roman on the wall of the Pompeii brothel.

'Do you have to wear that silly hat,' said Miriam. 'You look like some sort of Mexican bandit. People are looking at you.'

'Let them look,' replied Edna. 'It's to keep the sun off.'

'It keeps the sun off anybody who comes within three feet of you it's so big.'

'Yes, well, I don't intend to get sunburned. Some of these people on the cruise look like ripe tomatoes and others as if they've washed their faces in creosote. I got this hat—'

She stopped mid-sentence when Mrs De la Mare made her stately appearance and walked boldly to the front of the queue. She presented the officer in charge with her gold card.

'I have priority,' she told him taut-faced.

'Excuse me,' said Edna, who was waiting impatiently with her sister. She folded her arms beneath her ample and unyielding bosom. Her expression was as fierce as a falcon's.

The two women locked eyes.

'Are you addressing me?' asked Mrs De la Mare in a superior tone of voice. Her arched eyebrows lifted in surprise.

'There is such a thing as a queue, you know,' Edna informed her balefully.

'Yes, I appreciate that, but as you can no doubt see, I have a gold card.' She held up the item in question.

'And what's a gold card when it's at home?' she was asked. Edna's bosom heaved in indignation.

Mrs De la Mare gave a long, level look. 'It gives me precedence.'

There were grumbles from some of the passengers who were lining up.

'Says who?' Edna demanded with a voice sharpened by sudden resentment. She looked mutinously at the pusher-in.

'I beg your pardon?'

She suddenly thrust aside her walking frame like a Lourdes' pilgrim miraculously cured and approached the woman, handbag at the ready. 'And what gives you preference?' she demanded, waving a deprecating hand, and shooting her an outraged look.

'*Precedence*,' said Mrs De la Mare, emphasising the correct word. 'I am a first-class passenger and am therefore entitled to the benefits that such a position affords, one of which is to disembark before other passengers.'

'I think it's disgraceful,' said Miriam, who was dressed in pastel crimplene, 'pushing into the queue when we all have to wait.' She eyed the queue-jumper menacingly and pressed her lips together in disapproval.

'Well, then I suggest that when you next cruise, you travel first class,' she said dismissively, 'and then you can enjoy the benefits it provides.'

'This way, madam,' said the officer, escorting Mrs De la Mare to the gangway. He was keen to bring this confrontation to an end.

'I hope she falls down the gangplank and breaks her stuck-up neck,' said Edna getting ready to complain to the officer.

'All fur coat and no knickers,' said Miriam repeating her sister's earlier observation, much to the amusement of the other passengers in the queue.

'I shall have a few well-chosen words to say to that obnoxious woman if I see her again,' stated Edna.

'What well-chosen words?' asked her sister.

'I've not chosen them yet,' replied Edna.

On the coach journey back to the ship from Cartagena, Neville saw an empty seat next to Oliver. The boy was writing in his small notebook.

'Nobody's sitting here,' he announced before plonking himself down. He scratched his neck, then unfurled a large spotted handkerchief and blew his nose vigorously.

Oliver lifted his head sharply like an animal catching a scent then looked at the speaker unblinkingly with detached deliberation. 'No,' he replied, before returning to his book.

'What are you writing?' Neville asked intrusively, leaning over to see what the boy was jotting down.

Oliver snapped his notebook shut and glanced at him sideways. A small frown puckered his face. He was inclined to tell the nosy man to mind his own business but he had been brought up to be respectful of adults so resisted the temptation. 'Some thoughts about my visit to Cartagena,' he said.

'About what?'

'Different things.'

'Such as?'

Oliver consulted his notebook with a small sigh and read. 'The Museo Nacional, the Roman forum, the Barrio del Foro Romano and the Castillo de la Concepción.'

'Crikey, what a mouthful.' Oliver looked at him blankly. 'So, you're interested in history then, are you?' asked Neville, stating the blindingly obvious.

Oliver frowned. 'You could say that.'

'I never saw the point of studying history at school myself,' he stated, leaning back in his seat, and resting his head on the back. 'There's no future in it.' Oliver didn't answer. 'Will you be going ashore in Gibraltar then?'

'Yes.'

'I've been there a few times. It's a major cruise ship destination, you know. There's not a lot to see but you can get duty-free items.' He tapped his wristwatch. 'I bought this watch in Gibraltar. It's a submariner, nautical, multifunction, waterproof chronometer with quartz resin silicone and digital yacht timer. Keeps time to the second. Never let me down once.' He paused as if expecting some sort of reaction to his words, but none was forthcoming. Oliver gave a weak smile with a complete lack of interest. He wished the man would go away. 'So, what are you going to do in Gibraltar?' Neville carried on doggedly.

'I'm interested in seeing the graves of the two sailors who lost their lives at the Battle of Trafalgar.' He looked straight at the man with his bright green eyes, no smile lighting up the intensity.

'It doesn't sound a whole lot of fun to me, looking at a couple of old graves.'

'Maybe not to you,' replied Oliver, wrinkling his nose, 'but, as I have said, I am interested in history.'

'So, you'll know about the Battle of Trafalgar, the big battle in 1815.'

'Actually 1805,' said Oliver.

'I think you'll find it was in 1815.'

'No, it was 1805. You are probably thinking of Waterloo,' he was told. 'Trafalgar took place on the twenty-first of October 1805 at six in the morning. Twenty-seven British ships commanded by Lord Nelson defeated the thirty-three combined fleets of France and Spain.'

'Is that so?'

'Yes,' Oliver replied drily.

'And a lot of people don't know this, but they took Nelson's body back to England in a barrel of rum,' Neville expounded.

Oliver fixed him with his green eyes. 'It was brandy.'

'No, it was rum. Sailors used to drink rum.'

'Yes, but Nelson's body was put in a cask called a "leaguer" which was the largest size barrel aboard and it was preserved in brandy until it reached England.'

'Quite the little expert, aren't you,' said Neville sardonically and thinking this child was a cocky little so-and-so, too clever for his own good.

'As I have said, unlike you, I like history,' replied Oliver.

'I should think a boy of your age would want to do other things in Gibraltar than look at a lot of old graves.'

'If you will excuse me, I wish to make a few more notes,' said Oliver, in a tone which denoted the end of the conversation.

On his way back to the ship, Neville caught up with Mrs De la Mare who was walking sedately along the quayside.

She was dressed in a primrose yellow cotton dress with a small round collar and a stylish flowered straw hat and held aloft a delicate white-lace-covered parasol to shield her from the bright sunshine.

'Had a good day?' he asked, oozing familiarity and scurrying up alongside.

She stopped, turned her head imperiously, removed her designer sunglasses and lowered her parasol. She scrutinised him like a head teacher checking that a pupil was in full school uniform. There was a disdainful arching of the eyebrows.

'Are you addressing me?' she asked laconically. Her face was as blank as a figurehead on the front of a sailing ship.

'In Cartagena, did you have a good day?' He beamed fatuously and scratched his neck.

'Do I know you?' Mrs De la Mare continued to look him up and down. Her words were more of an accusation than a question.

'I'm Neville.' He offered a hand which she studiously ignored. 'I was asking if you have had a good day in Cartagena.'

'Frankly, it is none of your business,' she told him, treating him to a contemptuous frown. She raised her parasol and replaced her sunglasses. Then, quite suddenly, she turned her back on him and walked smartly down the quayside. Neville remained immobile with a crumpled smile on his face.

At the ship there was a long line of passengers waiting below the gangplank to board. Mrs De la Mare strode to the front and flashed her gold card.

'I'm sorry, madam,' the officer told her, 'you will have to wait.'

'Wait!' she repeated.

'Yes, madam, an elderly gentleman has had a nasty fall on the gangplank. We are waiting for the ship's doctor.'

'Cannot you move him?'

'No, madam, not until the doctor has seen him. It's not advisable to move someone who has had a fall until seen by a doctor.'

'Why don't these old people take more care,' she muttered to herself angrily.

'We all get old, madam,' said the officer evenly, irritated by her strident manner and lack of sympathy. 'If you wouldn't mind joining the queue.' He ushered her out of the way.

'At the back,' shouted Edna, who was near the front, 'because you're not pushing in front of me again with your fancy gold card.'

There was ripple of applause from the passengers in the queue.

It took another ten minutes before Mr Seaton, accompanied by the ship's doctor and another man, was carried up the gangplank on a stretcher.

The Entertainment Manager, watching from the lower deck with a group of interested passengers, felt a touch of guilt for taking pleasure at seeing his former teacher lying flat on the stretcher groaning – but not a lot.

'I don't see why we should be lumbered with all the godawful jobs,' moaned Katya, who was in one of her more belligerent moods. Peter shrugged but made no reply. 'I thought taking on the line dancing was bad enough, but now we've got saddled with this, which is likely to be worse.'

'The quizzes are very popular with the passengers,' said Peter nonchalantly.

Katya blew out her cheeks. 'Well, thank you for stating the obvious. I do know that the quizzes are popular. I have worked on this ship for three years, you know.'

'They can be quite good fun,' Peter told her.

'As much fun as an impacted wisdom tooth.'

Peter often wondered why his colleague remained as an entertainment officer. She seemed to complain about most of the duties to which she was assigned. 'Some of the passengers come up with really comical answers,' he said.

'Do you always have to be so irritatingly cheerful?'

Peter shrugged again. He was tempted to ask her why she always had to be so irritatingly grouchy, but he bit his lip. He had requested that on the next cruise he was partnered with Lizzie. She was unfailingly good-humoured.

Katya grimaced. 'It amazes me how most of them have encyclopaedic knowledge about sport and television soaps but have not the first idea about books or music or history. You wonder if they learned anything at all at school. Ask them to do a simple sum and you would think they were being asked to explain Einstein's theory of relativity.'

'They're not that bad.'

'Anyway, you can ask the questions,' she told him. 'I'll keep the score.'

'Yes, I thought you might choose the easier option.'

'What's that supposed to mean?'

'I mean it's a piece of cake, isn't it, just sitting there keeping the score, while I do all the work? Like in the line dancing, you left it all to me.'

'I beg your pardon? I'll have you know I did my bit.'

'Yes, and it was a bit. I've prepared all the questions for this quiz and now I have to ask them while all you do is record the score. If there's any dispute about the answers, which I have no doubt there will be, it will be left to me to deal with it. I remember last time when that American chap refused to accept the answer on spelling and said "diarrhoea" is spelled differently in the States. I can't recall you coming to my help.'

'It was silly of you to ask a question about spelling. You should have known they spell words differently in America.'

Katya gave a sly smile. 'Anyway, you didn't find that good fun, did you, when that big Texan started shouting at you?'

'Well, there are no questions on spelling this time,' said Peter.

When the passengers arrived for the quiz, Katya took charge. Peeved by her colleague's criticism that she didn't pull her weight, she stood by the door and in a loud, authoritarian voice, told the contestants to find a table and make sure there was a space between it and the next.

'There should be no more than four to a table,' she informed those wishing to take part, sounding like a tetchy teacher. 'Please turn off your mobile phones. On the last cruise one of the passengers googled the questions. Anyone found cheating will be disqualified. Write your answers clearly in capital letters so there will be no confusion about what you have written.' She produced a stopwatch from her bag. 'You will have one minute after each question to confer with those on your team and write down your answer.' She looked at Peter, gave a self-satisfied smile, sat down, and shuffled some papers.

Neville who had been watching from the side of the room saw there were only three people at a table. He promptly hurried over and sat himself down in the empty seat opposite a small, sad-faced chunk of a man and between a red-cheeked individual with a bristly Stalin-style moustache and a stiff-necked woman with a prominent nose and alarming eyebrows. All three at the table eyed him with looks full of misgiving.

'Er . . . actually, I think we'll be all right as we are,' the man told him. He, like the others, had been subjected earlier to one of this dreary passenger's deadly dull verbal onslaughts and was not keen about him joining them.

Neville was not at all deterred and, leaning back in his chair, he scratched his neck and displayed his set of discoloured teeth. 'The more, the merrier,' he remarked cheerfully.

The woman stared at him for a moment, thinking she might say something, but then thought better of it when Peter began to explain the rules.

Neville soon discovered that after each question had been asked, those on the table made no effort to involve him in the discussion of the possible answers and they ignored any suggestions he might make. Despite being sidelined, he remained chirpy and chatty.

The final question was asked and the answers from each table were passed to Katya who began totalling up the scores. She soon announced that two teams, those on table three and those on table six, had achieved the same number of correct answers. Neville was on table six.

'Then it's a tiebreaker,' said Peter. 'Our next and final port of call is Gibraltar. You will all be aware, I am sure, that there was a famous sea battle fought off Gibraltar at which Admiral Nelson won a decisive victory against the French.'

The man with a bristly Stalin-style moustache leaned over and told his fellow team members to leave it to him. He knew the answer. 'It's Trafalgar,' he whispered.

Peter carried on. 'The sea battle was, of course, Trafalgar. What I want to know is the exact date of the battle: the date, the month, and the year. The team that gets closest to the actual date will be the winner.'

Those on table three, having no idea, settled on April the fourth. The man with a bristly Stalin-style moustache who was on the opposing team, rubbed his chin. 'Difficult one this,' he murmured. 'Any ideas?'

'Actually—' started Neville.

He was ignored. 'I shall have to make a guess,' the man announced, but before he could open his mouth, Neville shot to his feet. 'It was the twenty-first of October 1805!' he shouted out.

'The exact date,' said Peter. 'Well done, that man.'

'You might be interested to know,' declared Neville turning to the crowded room, his face flushed with success, 'that the battle took place just after six in the morning.'

27

The *Empress of the Ocean* set sail for Gibraltar, the final port of call. The great liner cruised serenely out of the dock, resplendent beneath a sky as delicate and clear as an eggshell. The ocean was a deep blue, flawless and crystalline.

In his last lecture Mr Carlin-How gave a historical account of the overseas territory concluding with suggestions for the sites to see and the places to visit.

'Gibraltar is a remarkable place,' he told his audience. 'Be sure to see the military-ordnance-style arched doorways, Italianate stucco relief, Genoese shutters, English Regency ironwork balconies, Spanish stained glass and Georgian sash and casement windows. You might wish to take a trip up the Rock itself by the cable car. It takes just six minutes to get from the town to the top station on the Upper Rock, which is over four-hundred metres above sea level, and there you can enjoy spectacular views of the peninsula and over Gibraltar Straight. Now, enough about the facts, a funny thing happened to me when I was last in Gibraltar . . . '

At the conclusion of his talk Mr Carlin-How thanked the passengers for coming to hear him speak, hoped they had found his lectures of some interest and wished them a safe journey home on leaving the ship in a few days' time.

The Port Lecturer was tidying his notes when he saw the two sisters waiting to see him. They were like a pair of homing pigeons. He had a good idea what they wished to speak to him about and was well-prepared.

'Now ladies,' he said, looking like a cat that had got the cream. He knew what they would be going to ask him and he was prepared. 'What can I do for you?'

'We didn't like Cartergenica at all,' complained Miriam.

'The tour was a disappointment,' added her sister. 'We were crammed like sardines on a bus for most of the time and when we did get off, there was too much sun, too many flies, too much dust and too many people. Anyway, we've been thinking, that we might tag along with you in Gibraltar.'

'Tag along with me?' Mr Carlin-How beamed. 'But of course, you are both most welcome to accompany me. I have an exciting itinerary planned,' he lied expertly, 'which I am sure will appeal to you. I thought we would start at the fourteenth-century Moorish castle and then explore the eighteenth-century Great Siege Tunnels before touring the Trafalgar Cemetery. The tunnels are long and a bit uneven underfoot, but they are a must to see. After that we will be taking a scenic climb up the Rock. It's nearly fifteen hundred feet high, you know. It might present a bit of a challenge for you and your walking frame, but we will take it easy and be careful of the stony path, the falling masonry, and the sheer drops. Then to round off the tour we will visit the Trafalgar Cemetery.'

'I've no intention of climbing up the Rock of Gibraltar,' protested Edna.

'Neither have I,' added her sister, 'and I don't want to visit a cemetery either.'

'What a pity,' declared the Port Lecturer, with a muted sigh of relief. 'Then you might prefer a leisurely walk around the town and to have a coffee at a quayside café. I recommend Café Fresco overlooking Marina Bay Square. It has a delightful outside terrace and, I believe, they serve English biscuits. I will wave to you from the top of the Rock.' He had no plans of climbing up the Rock of Gibraltar. He had arranged to take Elodie for afternoon tea at the Rock Hotel.

The two sisters headed off, shaking their heads and grumbling.

'Climb up the Rock of Gibraltar indeed,' spluttered Edna. 'The very thought.'

Mrs De la Mare sat on the balcony in her stateroom, looking out pensively over the ocean as the liner made its stately progress to the next destination. The sea was bright, vast, and silvery blue. In the distance she could see the imposing Rock of Gibraltar. She decided that after an unhurried lunch she would venture ashore and perhaps take afternoon tea in the elegant lounge bar of the Rock Hotel. The last time she had been to the British Overseas Territory was with her husband some years' before. They had stayed at the prestigious hotel – 'an icon of hospitality and first-class service' as described in the brochure – in a suite with panoramic vistas of the Bay and Strait of Gibraltar. She recalled the sophisticated ambiance and the personalised attention to detail which well suited discerning guests such as herself.

The butler had set the table out for breakfast – white damask tablecloth and napkin, silver cutlery and fine ivory bone china. He placed an envelope against the slim crystal vase containing a single white rose and smiled as Mrs De la Mare came into the room.

'Good morning, madam,' he said. 'It looks a fine day.'

'Good morning, Dominic,' she replied.

'Will you be going ashore?'

'Yes, I think I will.'

'There is a message for you, madam,' he said, permitting himself a small smile of contentment. 'I believe it is from the Captain.'

Mrs De la Mare hurried to the table, plucked up the envelope, tore it open and took out a card edged in red. It requested the pleasure of her company for dinner with him that evening.

'Oh yes, it *is* from the Captain,' she cried, her face shining with excitement. She felt a prickle of anticipation. 'I'm invited to dine with him this evening. The Purser must have had a word.'

The Purser had not, in fact, mentioned Mrs De la Mare's demand for him to approach the Captain nor had the Chief Housekeeper bothered to follow up Dominic's request. The invitation had come as a matter of course. It was the practice on the *Empress of the Ocean* for the Captain to request the pleasure of all first-class passengers to dine with him at some time during the cruise. Mrs De La Mare's invitation would have arrived without her prompting.

'I knew the Captain would not have overlooked me,' she said triumphantly.

'Of course not, madam,' agreed the butler.

'Now what shall I wear?' she asked herself. 'The burgundy chiffon gown I think.'

Neville caught up with Mr and Mrs Hinderwell as they sat in the tender to take them ashore. He was dressed in a garish red and blue shirt, long cotton shorts and a baseball cap. There were large sweat stains under his armpits.

'Have you been to Gibraltar before?' he asked.

'No, not at all,' replied the clergyman, 'but we are very much looking forward to visiting.'

'I've been here several times,' Neville told him. 'It's a major cruise ship destination, you know. There's not a lot to see but you can get duty-free items.' He tapped his wristwatch. 'I bought this watch in Gibraltar.'

'From what the Port Lecturer said, there seems to be quite a bit to see. Gibraltar sounds a most interesting place.'

'Yes, if you like history,' conceded Neville. 'Of course, Trafalgar took place just off Gibraltar in the October of 1805.'

'I believe so.'

'Some of the sailors who were killed in the battle are buried in the cemetery.'

'Really?'

'And a lot of people don't know this,' Neville expounded, 'but they took Nelson's body back to England in a barrel of brandy. Some think it was rum that they put him in, but it was brandy. Nelson's body was put in a cask called a "leaguer" which was the largest sized barrel aboard and it preserved him until he reached England.'

'You are quite the expert, aren't you,' said the cleric.

'Oh yes, there's not much you can tell me about Gibraltar,' he was told.

Mrs De la Mare, having enjoyed her afternoon tea at the Rock Hotel, dabbed her lips with a starched napkin. She caught sight of the couple from the ship chattering and laughing on the Wisteria Terrace with unvarnished happiness – the slim, elegant middle-aged woman and the distinguished, elderly man. He rested his hand affectionally on the woman's arm. Mrs De la Mare couldn't recall any occasion when she and her husband had sat together chattering and laughing. She had met Giles De la Mare, son of a senior partner, when she had started as a clerical assistant at Dunsley, Dalby and De la Mare. He was a chinless, uncomplicated, reliable man who had little conversation and irritating habits, but she saw in him a way to achieve her ambition.

The lack of any parental affection from her father and a stable and happy home life had left a permanent scar on

Frances with the result that she avoided any sort of emotional engagement. She had grown a hard protective shell and any display of feeling she considered an admission of weakness. She diligently maintained an impenetrable, polished image, cool, haughty, confident, rigidly self-controlled and kept aloof from the other office staff who found her stuck-up and stand-offish. They referred to her as 'the ice maiden' and 'Frigid Fanny.' She knew what they called her, and it didn't worry her in the slightest; she was not bothered about how others saw her. With an arrogance and a self-belief, Frances was bored with their idle talk of clothes and nights on the town and boyfriends and make-up. She was dedicated, industrious, and her efficiency and discretion soon came to the notice of the senior partners and of young Giles De la Mare, who was clearly very taken with this attractive and confident young woman. Promotion followed for Frances and after five years with the firm, she was appointed the personal assistant to young Mr De la Mare. She changed her hairstyle, took to wearing more make-up, bought more fashionable clothes, and bought herself a modest rope of artificial pearls with matching earrings. Those in the office she now treated with condescension. It was as if she needed to look down on others to reassure herself of her elevated position.

She never tried to contact her father. She didn't want him making an appearance and embarrassing her. After several years of no contact, he wrote to tell her he was ill; she ignored the letter. When the hospital contacted her as the next of kin (his second wife had died the previous year) to tell her that her father was dying, she went to see him and sat by his bed for half an hour listening to the throaty breathing and watching as his life faded, but she felt no sorrow. This, she knew, betrayed a ruthless streak in her personality but she wanted to forget about her earlier life.

As one of the office secretaries remarked on hearing of the forthcoming wedding, 'I got the measure of her from the beginning. Gold digger. I could tell she was on the make. Hard as the devil's toenail is Fanny Goldsborough. What does he see in her?'

Of course, her marriage had been loveless from the beginning. Marrying the boss's son was the one sure way of bettering herself. It wasn't an unhappy marriage; both emotionally undemonstrative, they had led largely separate lives, which suited them both. They kept up the public façade. Her husband might have been rather dull with what some thought was an off-putting reserve, a man whose only conversation was about stocks and shares, investments and bonds, but he had been uncomplicated, easy-going, and even-tempered and had made no demands upon her. He was a secure person to live with, dependable and conventional and was wedded to his business more than to her. In their loveless but socially acceptable marriage there had been no angry scenes, no cross words, no snipes or spats. Neither was there any laughter or joy and certainly no passion. Giles had once broached the idea of them starting a family, but she had put a stop to that idea. 'Children,' she had told him offhandedly, 'take over people's lives. Why put a millstone around your neck? They are not taking over mine.' Her husband had no energy to argue.

She looked again at the couple from the ship chattering and laughing and suddenly felt a touch of guilt. She was aware of her failure to have shown her husband much attention, gratitude, or affection.

Mr Hinderwell came across Oliver at the Trafalgar Cemetery. The boy was standing before a grey and weathered tombstone, writing in his small notebook.

'Hello, Oliver,' said the clergyman.

'Oh, good afternoon, Mr Hinderwell,' replied the boy.

'All by yourself?'

'My grandparents have gone shopping.'

'So has my wife. I see you are making a few notes.'

'Yes, I thought there would be a lot of graves of those who were killed at Trafalgar, but Mr Carlin-How told me there are just the two.' He consulted his notebook. 'There's a Captain Thomas Norman of the Royal Marines, who served on the *Mars*. He was thirty-six when he died of his wounds. I'm not sure what the Latin inscription means.'

'Let me see if I can be of help,' said Mr Hinderwell. He leaned forward, examined the headstone, and read: '*Militavit non sine gloria nec paucis flebilis occidit*. I'm a little rusty with my Latin but let's see. *Militavit* is "military", *non sine* is "not without", *paucis*, I think that means "a few", *flebilis* is "mournful" or sorrowful", *occidit* is "killed" and *gloria* is "glory".'

'You are not rusty at all,' admired Oliver. 'I am very impressed.' He sounded like a teacher complimenting a pupil for a correct answer. 'I'm looking forward to learning Latin at my new school. There was quite a lot of Roman graffiti on the walls in Pompeii. I jotted down some of it. I would have liked to have known what had been written.'

Yes, thought the cleric, *but some of it is best left untranslated.*

'Perhaps I might ask my Latin master at my new school to translate it for me,' said the boy.

'Not a good idea, Oliver,' warned Mr Hinderwell. 'Like much graffiti it was . . . how shall I say?'

'Lubricious,' ventured the boy.

'Exactly.' He smiled and shook his head good-humouredly. 'Now here on this tombstone I suppose a rough translation would be: "He waged the good fight, not without glory, nor without a few tears shed. In a few words: lament".'

Oliver consulted his notes. 'The other grave I've seen is of Lieutenant William Forster. He was on the *Colossus* and died of his wounds. He was not much older than me.' He thought for a moment. 'He didn't have much of a life, did he? You know, Mr Hinderwell, with all the fighting and the killing that has gone on over the years, I think God must be very sad to see the world He made.'

'Yes,' nodded the clergyman, thinking of the time when he served as an army chaplain. 'I guess at times He must.'

They were quiet for a moment as the clergyman closed his eyes and mumbled a prayer.

'Now the last tender leaves for the ship in less than an hour,' he said at last, 'so I think we should be making tracks.'

'I just want to write a few things down,' said Oliver, 'so I'll catch up with you.'

'Well, make sure you do. We don't want you stranded in Gibraltar.'

On his way back from the Trafalgar Cemetery to take the tender back to the ship, Oliver recognised one of the passengers at a pavement café. He went over to speak to her. Before he could open his mouth, Mrs De la Mare held up a hand as if stopping traffic.

'If you are asking for money—' she began to say but Oliver cut her off.

'I'm not asking for money,' he told her.

'Well, what is it you want?' she asked abruptly. She peered over the top of her designer sunglasses.

'I think, if I am not mistaken, you are a passenger on the *Empress of the Ocean*,' he said.

'What of it?'

'I am a passenger too. You might think this is none of my business, but I thought you ought to be aware that the last tender to the ship will be leaving in half an hour.'

'Is this some sort of schoolboy prank?' she demanded.

Oliver looked affronted. 'No, it is not some sort of school-boy prank.' He glanced at her intently. 'Schoolboy pranks are childish and silly and sometimes very cruel.' He had been the subject of such antics at his school.

'The ship doesn't leave for another hour and a half,' Mrs De la Mare told him, consulting her exclusive wristwatch, 'and there will be other tenders coming along soon.'

'There won't be any more tenders,' Oliver told her. 'The last one leaves in half an hour. I suggest you take it. If you miss it, you will be left in Gibraltar. The clocks were put forward early this morning. We have lost an hour.'

Mrs De la Mare looked stunned. 'Are you sure?'

'Yes, I am,' he replied. 'We will be able to catch it if we leave now.'

She quickly plucked her purse from her handbag, snatched a handful of change which she put on the table and rose hurriedly to her feet. 'Then we had better go,' she said.

'There is no great rush,' Oliver told her. 'It's not that far.'

'Are you sure about this, young man?' she asked, as she followed him.

'Perfectly,' he replied.

Ten minutes' later a ship's officer helped Mrs De la Mare onto the tender.

'Watch your step, madam,' he said.

'Is this the final tender?' she asked.

'It is madam.'

'I wasn't aware.' The officer pointed to a notice telling passengers when the last tender would be leaving. 'I see,' she murmured.

At the ship Mrs De la Mare took Oliver aside as he was about to leave the tender.

'A word,' she said. 'I owe you my thanks, young man. It was most considerate of you to take the time and the trouble to inform me about the last tender to the ship. I am sure most children of your age would not have bothered.' She looked at the boy's serious, enquiring face. 'Why did you?'

'Pardon?'

'Why did you help me in that way?'

'Has no one ever done you a favour before?' he asked.

'Not without wanting something in return,' she replied. She reached into her handbag and took out a stylish wallet and from it removed a crisp note. 'This is for you.'

'That's really not necessary,' said Oliver.

'No, I insist. Let me give you something for—'

'Thank you, but I really do not want anything,' he told her brusquely. 'My grandfather says that one should not expect to get a reward for doing a good turn. He said to pass it on and hope that the person will do someone else a good turn.' He then proceeded to climb from the tender.

What a singular child, Mrs De la Mare said to herself.

Later in the day the sisters went on deck as the ship pulled out of the harbour. Raucous gulls wheeled and shrieked in spirals overhead, white winged, golden beaked, black shiny button eyes.

'I'm glad to see the back of Gibraltar,' said Edna, making an irritable puffing noise. 'It was a very tiring, unsatisfactory, not to say stressful experience. First there was the hoity-toity woman again, her with a face as stony as a cemetery statue, trying to push in the queue when we were getting off the ship, then I get my walking frame caught in the door of the testicular cable car.'

'It was a funicular,' corrected Miriam.

'Well, whatever, and then I dropped my Rock of Gibraltar crystal paperweight and was bitten by some flying insect. I can't understand why flies are attracted to me and leave you alone.'

'It's that sickly perfume you wear, it attracts them,' commented her sister. 'Anyway, it wasn't a fly. It was probably a mosquito.'

'Then that pudden-headed seagull decided to dive-bomb me and do its business in my sombrero.'

Miriam tried to contain her smile.

'And then,' announced Edna, raising her voice to indicate that this was the final straw, 'to cap it all there was that thieving monkey which plucked my glasses from my face and ran off with them.'

'You should have taken more care,' Miriam told her sister.

'I might have expected I'd get little sympathy from you,' admonished Edna. 'I can't see straight. I've got channel vision. I keep bumping into things all the time.'

'Well, that's nothing new. You bumped into things all the time when you *had* your glasses. If you hadn't started throwing biscuits to the troop, the monkeys wouldn't have come near you and then you would still have them.'

'Snatched them right off my face,' said Edna, 'and the little devil carried them off.'

'I'm always telling you to get a chain to hang around your neck to put your spectacles on,' chided Miriam. 'If you had done what I said, you wouldn't have lost them.'

'Had I had a chain around my neck,' riposted her sister, 'I would have got garrotted by the blasted baboon.'

'Actually, they are not baboons, they are Barbary macaques,' Miriam informed her. 'Neville, that funny-looking chap told us. He said people often mistakenly call them apes.'

'As if I'm bothered,' said Edna, treating this information with a glower of annoyance.

'He said they can be aggressive and it's not a good idea to feed them.'

'It's a pity he didn't impart such information before the creature ran off with my glasses,' grumbled Edna.

'You were fortunate not to have been bitten,' said Miriam. 'He said they can give a nasty bite. You were lucky it was only the mosquito that bit you.'

'After today's catalogue of disasters, how can you say that I am lucky?' demanded Edna. 'Sometimes Miriam you say the silliest things. Anyway, I didn't need some interfering know-it-all to tell me what they are called or that they are mischievous and could be dangerous. I noticed he never offered to chase the pesky monkey and get them back and neither did you for that matter.'

'I'm not in a position at my age to go clambering over rocks in flat sandals after a monkey,' Miriam countered. She strained her eyes, leaned forward and, craning her neck, peered towards the shore. 'Isn't that him there on the dock-side?' she asked.

'Who?' asked Edna tilting her head to one side and squinting near-sightedly.

'The chap who told us about the monkeys. He's waving.'

'And pray tell me how I am going to make out some distant figure on the dockside when I can't see so much as a foot in front of my face?'

'It *is* him,' said Miriam, cupping her hands over her eyes and squinting. The sun, bright and brazen, glinted harshly across the water. 'I recognise his ridiculous coloured shirt and the baseball cap he was wearing.'

Neville had taken the cable car up the Rock of Gibraltar. At the top he had sat in the café looking over the Strait of Gibraltar to Morocco. Unfortunately, he had forgotten to change the time on his submariner, nautical, multifunction, water-proof chronometer with quartz resin silicone and digital yacht timer to European time. The clocks, as Oliver had informed Mrs De la Mare, had been put forward the evening before. Seeing the ship starting to move, at first he stared in disbelief, then a look of terror etched across his face. He leaped to his feet, rushed to take the cable car down the Rock and ran frantically along the quayside, waving madly as the ship was slowly leaving port. He had missed the boat ... or perhaps more accurately, the ship. Those on deck, not realising he was a fellow passenger, waved their arms in big semicircles like castaways on a desert island trying to attract the attention of a passing ship. They assumed the man on the quay was waving them goodbye. There had been several announcements prior to the vessel's departure, broadcast throughout the ship and in every cabin, for the passenger in B784 to make himself known at the reception. Reluctantly the Captain, who had a tight schedule to keep, decided that after half an hour wait to set sail without him. 'Don't worry if you are late back to the port,' the Entertainment Manager had told the passengers jokingly on their first day on board. 'You'll get great pictures of us waving to you as we sail away.'

Neville watched with a dazed expression on his face as the *Empress of the Ocean* made her stately way out to sea. He stopped the frantic waving, threw out his arms widely resembling a scarecrow, and cried loudly and piercingly, 'Nooooooo!'

'It looks as if he's missed the boat,' spoke Edna, almost with gusto.

The stranding of Neville in Gibraltar now took precedence amongst the gossip which travelled around the ship. It also provided the castaway with plenty of material for when he next cornered a passenger on his cruise through the Suez Canal later in the year.

28

The memorable evening dining with the Captain, which Mrs De la Mare had so anticipated, did not transpire. When she saw the other guests seated around the table, her heart sank into her designer shoes. She was lost for words. Her composed features evaporated; her assurance deserted her. Sitting by the Captain was the garrulous woman who had invaded her privacy on the executive sun deck, the woman with the thick wavy hair. Next to her was the rough and ready couple whom she had encountered in the Diamond Grill. Opposite sat the concert pianist with a young woman in a red dress and, to cap it all, the couple of elderly women with whom she had had the angry exchange when disembarking at Cartagena. They all stared at her as she gripped the back of a chair. If the looks Mr Mulgrave gave her and those from the two sisters could have maimed, Mrs De la Mare would have been on crutches.

'Ah, Mrs De la Mare,' said the Captain rising to his feet. He gave a warm and reassuring smile. 'It is good of you to join us.' A waiter appeared and pulled a chair out for her. 'Do sit down,' continued the Captain. She perched on the end of the chair, unable to hide the look of shock on her face. 'Let me introduce my other guests,' he said, smiling affably. 'You will, no doubt, know Mr Mulgrave, our eminent concert pianist who is with his daughter. Next to him is Miss Brotton and her sister, and over here is Mr and Mrs Ugthorpe, who occupy the Manhattan Suite next to yours, so your paths may have crossed.' Then he rested a gentle hand on Sandra's shoulder. 'And I think you have met my mother.'

Mrs De la Mare had turned pale, and her mouth was set in a thin line. She was not a woman often at a loss for speech, but at that moment she was unable to rise to the occasion.

The following morning Mrs De la Mare left her breakfast untouched. She stared vacantly out of the cabin window at the endless expanse of ocean. In the distance a tanker made its steady progress across the horizon. She felt smothered by a dull melancholy, her mind full of the thoughts of the dire dinner of the evening before – one of the most dreadful experiences of her life.

'I trust you had a pleasant evening, madam?' asked the butler the following morning.

'Pardon?'

'At the Captain's table.'

'Oh yes, it was . . . it was very interesting.'

He looked at the uneaten food. 'Is the breakfast not to your liking?' he asked.

'I'm not that hungry,' she said in a subdued little voice. 'It's just I don't feel like breakfast this morning.'

Dominic stood there for a moment considering if he should say anything. He could sense her sadness.

'Are you all right, madam?' he asked.

She gave a melancholy little nod. 'Yes, I'm fine.' At that moment she felt more than anything an overwhelming sadness.

'You are not unwell?'

'No, I'm . . . ' She stopped. Her mouth became dry, and the words wouldn't come. Apart from when she was a girl and her mother's enquiry, she could not recall an occasion when anyone had asked her if she was all right – not her father, not her work colleagues, not her friend, not even Giles.

'I hope you won't mind me mentioning it,' said Dominic, 'but you seem unhappy. Is there anything I can do?'

'No, nothing,' she replied in a voice barely audible.

'Very well, madam.'

He made to go but she called after him.

'Thank you for asking,' she said. 'Where are you from, Dominic?'

'I'm from Goa, madam.'

'Where is that?'

'It's a state on the southwestern coast of India. It's a beautiful country. It has white, sandy beaches, coconut palm trees, equatorial forests, rice paddies and so many fruits: pineapple, jackfruit, mango and banana.'

'It sounds a sort of paradise. You must miss it.'

'I do, madam.'

'Have you a family at home?'

'Yes, I have a wife and a son. Would you care to see a picture of them?'

He took a wallet from his inside pocket and produced a small, square colour photograph and passed it to her.

She studied the beaming faces. 'Your wife is beautiful and your son a handsome young man,' said Mrs De la Mare, staring at the picture of a smiling woman with her arm around a small boy.

The butler's face cracked into a broad smile. 'I think so,' he said.

'And when will you get home to see them?'

'In three months, madam.'

'A long time,' she murmured. 'It must be hard on you.'

'I am used to it.'

'And how did you end up working on a cruise ship?'

'I was fortunate to be offered this position. Many people apply but only a few are chosen. It is an interesting job.

I worked for some time in a hotel at home, but the money and the conditions were not too good.'

'You take pride in your work, don't you?'

'Yes, madam. Life on the ship is good and I am able to save money to pay for my son Gustav to go to university and become a doctor. That is his ambition.'

'I hope he is successful.'

'He works hard and knows how important it is to have a good education.'

Dominic stood there for a moment considering if he should say anything. 'If I may say so, madam, you do not seem to be enjoying the cruise very much.'

'No, I'm not really,' she replied.

'I hope you have not been unhappy with my services.'

'Quite the contrary. I have been most satisfied with them,' she replied. 'It's other things.' The sadness in her face made him feel sad too. Looking at her milky skin and shadowed eyes, he had an impulse to ask what was worrying her, to offer some support but he knew it was not his place to do so.

'If I can be of any help . . .'

'No, thank you.'

'Well, if there is nothing else, madam.'

Mrs De la Mare's encounter with the butler made her realise just how empty was her life. 'Fortunate,' he had said – to be at the beck and call of some rich woman in a fancy cabin and not able to see his family for three months, saving every penny to get his son an education. Mrs De la Mare was many things: a snob, a bearer of grudges; she was strait-laced, self-righteous and opinionated; she was often wrong but had the supreme confidence that she was always right. But her conversation with her butler had unexpectedly touched a chord. It had left her with an uneasy feeling of shame. All she could worry about was receiving an invitation to the Captain's table. And what an experience that had been.

'I'm not bringing my walking frame on the next cruise,' announced Edna. She had just visited the Ocean Spa and her bright brown hair had been permed into a halo. She was sitting with her sister on a banquette in the Rainbow Lounge enjoying her usual cup of coffee and biscuits.

'Thank the Lord for small mercies,' muttered Miriam.

'It's been a real nuisance trying to negotiate around people on a crowded ship and there's been some very inconsiderable people pushing in front of me and not moving out of the way.' She clicked her tongue indignantly. 'It's caused me a great deal of stress and inconvenience.' She took a sip of her coffee, leaving a red lipstick smudge on the rim of the cup.

Not nearly as much stress and inconvenience as you've caused other passengers, thought Miriam, but she held her tongue. 'It was that sombrero you were wearing and the loss of your glasses that caused you to bump into people,' she told her sister. 'You couldn't see where you were going half the time.'

'Well, I shall not be bringing my walking frame again if we come on another cruise,' her sister informed her. 'I should have had my hip replaced by then, that's if I decide to have the operation.'

'You had better get it booked in as soon as we get back,' said Miriam. 'There's sure to be a long waiting list and if you haven't had the operation, how are you going to manage without your walking frame?' She didn't wait for an answer. 'If it's a wheelchair you have in mind, you can forget it. I'm not pushing you around if that is what you're thinking.'

'You won't need to be pushing me around in a wheelchair. If I haven't had my hip done by then, I'm going to get one of these state-of-the-ark mobility scooters. I'm sure Mr Ellerby, the owner of the shop where I used to work, will give me a good discount. They're amazingly comfortable and manoeuvrable are these scooters. Did you know that some of them can get up to a speed of fourteen miles an hour?'

Miriam's bosom heaved in alarm at the very idea of her sister careering around a ship like Ben Hur in a chariot, with passengers in her path scattering in all directions. It filled her with dread.

'That's the two besotted geriatrics over there,' Edna told her sister, looking in the direction of the aged couple.

'Who?'

'That old pair of pensioners who absconded from the old folks' home and who have been walking around the ship like love's young dream. Did you hear how old they were?' Without waiting for a response, she continued, 'Ninety-two and ninety-four. Looking at them, they're an unwelcome reminder of our own mortality.'

'Oh dear,' groaned Miriam. 'Must you go on about such a subject.'

'I should think the police will be there to meet them when they get off the ship at Southampton,' said Edna, 'and escort them back to the old people's home. The woman with them with the dyed blond hair and the nose like a beak, is the one who the Italian singer pulled onto the stage.'

'She was—'

'And whose husband dropped dead in Rome,' continued Edna still holding the floor. 'Collapsed prostate on the steps at the Vatican, so I heard, sprawled on his back. Of course, it's a known fact that men are a lot more fragile than women and they die sooner. You've only got to look at those who go to the "Travelling-Alone Get-Together." They're all women save for the odd old man who is well past his sell-by-date and nothing to write home about. That husband of hers was asking to have a heart attack. He was overweight and of the right age. You remember he was stuffing his face with pizza in the café at Pompeii. I was told by Becky in the Ocean Spa that when he keeled over, a passing nun tried to revive him by banging on his chest. Being a nun, I don't suppose it would have been seemly for her to give him mouth-to-mouth resustic—What's it called?'

'Resuscitation,' provided Miriam.

Edna took up the story again. 'I was told the woman in the restaurant gave him the kiss of death but to no avail.'

'The kiss of life,' Miriam corrected.

'I must say,' continued Edna, nodding in the woman's direction, 'she doesn't look bowled over with grief, done up like a dog's dinner with her plucked eyebrows and painted face. And talk about being hard faced, you could straighten nails with it. She was tucking into bacon and eggs at breakfast this morning. Grief has certainly sharpened her appetite. I saw her earlier shopping in the boutique and then later, leafing through the brochures advertising future cruises like nobody's business. I was lost for words.'

Words, thought Miriam, were that very last thing her sister had ever been at a loss for.

'You mark my words,' Edna carried on, sniffing with disapproval, 'it won't be long before she's back on the high seas – minus the husband.'

'It's the woman who you barged into with your walking frame when we were coming back from Pompeii,' said her sister.

'Excuse me!' exclaimed Edna. 'You don't need to remind me. And for your information, I did not barge into her. She was in such a hurry to get aboard the ship, charging down the dockside, that she blocked my passage.'

'I pity anyone who is so reckless as to block *your* passage,' remarked her sister.

'She dropped her bag and smashed the piece of pottery she'd bought. It's a pity she broke her Roman urn. If she were intending to have her husband cremated when they get him back home, she could have put his ashes in it.' Edna thought for a moment. 'If I'd have dropped dead in Rome, Miriam,' she said, 'would you have continued on the cruise without me?'

'I should have had to think about it,' she said smiling.

'Miriam!' cried her sister.

'Of course, I wouldn't,' she answered, looking at Edna with a sisterly affection and with a certain tolerance. 'The cruise wouldn't have been the same without you.'

Edna looked for a hint of insincerity in her sister's remark but found none. She took Miriam's hand and squeezed it.

The sisters were having a morning coffee in the Rainbow Lounge.

'Look, he's over there,' said Edna.

'Who?'

'That young doctor who stopped that fat man from choking, and he's with the other one who helped the old chap who fell and broke his leg on the gangplank.'

'What about them?'

Edna got to her feet and smoothed down the creases in her skirt as if she were dusting away some crumbs. 'I'm going to ask him about my hip. It's been playing me up these last few days.'

'Has it?' said Miriam, barely acknowledging her sister's grousing.

'Come on, and let me do all the talking.'

'That'll make a change,' muttered her sister drily, rising from her chair to join her sister.

They approached the two young doctors who were having a coffee.

'Hexcuse me,' said Edna, affecting what she considered to be a genteel accent, 'I wonder hif I might trouble you and have a quiet word?'

'Yes, of course,' replied one of the young men. 'Do sit down.'

'Thank you so much,' said Edna smiling widely. She parked her walking frame, plumped into a chair, and displayed her full set of teeth. 'My name is Edna, and this is my sister, Miriam.'

'I'm pleased to meet you. I'm Simon and this is my partner, Murray. What can I do for you?'

'Becky in the Ocean Spa mentioned that you were a doctor,' stated Edna.

'Yes, I am a doctor.'

'And you stopped that man from choking.'

'Yes, I did.'

He waited and smiled predicting that the woman would now go into graphic detail of her medical condition and in this, his prediction was vindicated. As soon as people learnted he was a doctor, Simon would attract the frail and sickly like a flame attracting moths, wanting a free and impromptu consultation.

'I was telling Becky what happened in the Galleon Buffet when I went up to have my hair done,' proceeded Edna, 'about that fat man who nearly choked and re-ejaculated his lunch all over me. You might recall, I was sitting hopposite him and was in receipt of the full contents of his mouth and I was covered in bits of fish, bones, and boiled rice.'

'Yes, I do remember,' he said.

'Anyway, I didn't know you were a doctor. Becky told me you are a medical man.'

'I am,' confirmed Simon. 'I'm sorry about what happened to you. In retrospect I should have faced the man away from you, so you would have avoided his trajectory.'

'His what?'

'The contents of his mouth. It was—'

'Bless you, it wasn't your fault,' she interjected, leaning forward and resting a hand on his arm. 'It was that fat man who was to blame, shovelling food into his mouth like there was no tomorrow and talking at the same time. Some people do like the sound of their own voices, don't you find?' Miriam tilted back her head and sighed in a slow release of exasperation. Murray smiled; Simon nodded. 'Anyway,' Edna carried on, 'you came to his rescue and stopped him from choking to death.'

'One has to be careful when eating fish.'

'Oh, I so agree, our mother, God rest her soul—'

'Do get on with it, Edna,' prompted Miriam. 'We're supposed to be going to hear the author at eleven o'clock.'

'Yes, so are we,' muttered Murray.

'The thing is, doctor—' began Edna.

'Do call me Simon,' he told her. 'I reserve the title of "doctor" for when I'm working at the hospital. On holiday, I'm Simon.'

'The thing is, Simon,' said Edna, 'my doctor at home, Dr Patel, has suggested that I have a hip replacement but I'm a tad nervous about having it done.'

'That's an understatement,' her sister butted in. 'She gets into a real paddy at the mention of an operation.'

'I thought I'd sound you out,' Edna told the doctor. 'You being in the medical profession, you can perhaps clear up two niggling concerns which have been preying on my mind.'

'I'd hardly call them niggling,' came in her sister. 'And Dr Patel has explained, in detail, what it would involve, so you really have no need to bother—'

'Miriam,' snapped Edna, 'I did say that I would do the talking. After all, it's my hip that's the bone of contention.'

'I'll see if I can be of help,' Simon replied, smiling a tolerant smile.

'Dr Patel told me that the surgery is pretty simple, Simon.'

The young man coughed. 'Well, it is a relatively straightforward procedure,' he reassured her, 'but Murray is better qualified than I to tell you about it. He's an orthopaedic surgeon. I guess he's replaced more hips than you've had hot dinners.'

'Thank you for that, Simon,' said his partner, pulling a face and not wishing to be part of this discussion. He had been enjoying a peaceful cup of coffee and the last thing he wanted to do on his holiday was to discuss work. His opinion had already been sought. The ship's doctor, who discovered this passenger was an orthopaedic surgeon, had asked him to take a look at the elderly man who had fallen on the gangplank and broken his leg. Murray had examined the patient, viewed the X-ray, established that it was a clean break and set the bone. Now, he was called upon again. However, he was a good-natured and courteous man, so he sat up and looked at Edna. 'A hip replacement is a relatively common type of surgery,' he said. 'It's where a damaged hip joint is replaced with an artificial one known as an implant so really there is no need to get into a state. Thousands of people have had the operation.'

'Yes, Dr Patel told me that, but I do worry, Murray,' said Edna. 'I mean, what exactly does it involve?'

'The damaged cartilage and bone will be removed,' he explained, 'and a new metal, plastic, or ceramic implant will replace it.'

'I don't like the idea of that,' muttered Edna. 'It sounds a bit risky to me.'

'As with any operation, surgery does have some risks as well as benefits but most people who have had a hip replacement don't experience any serious complications. The success rate for this procedure is high. The surgery usually takes around one to two hours to complete, and most hip replacement patients are able to walk the same day or the next day after surgery; most can resume normal routine activities within the first three to six weeks of their total hip replacement recovery. If you have it done, you will be back playing tennis in no time.'

'Oh, I don't play tennis,' exclaimed Edna.

'I was being flippant,' Murray told her.

'Oh, I see. Aren't I too old to have it done?' asked Edna.

'No, not at all. Adults of any age can have a hip replacement, although most are between the ages of sixty and eighty.'

'I'm not eighty yet, although sometimes I feel as if I am.'

'I think you will find that there are a good few people on this cruise walking around with new hips,' Murray reassured her. 'Has Dr Patel suggested any other treatment other than an operation?'

'Oh, yes. He sent me to a psychopath.'

'Osteopath,' corrected Miriam, sighing again audibly.

'And I was put on stair-rods—'

'Steroids,' muttered Miriam.

'But I still get severe pain, swelling and stiffness in my hip joint and find it's an ordeal walking.'

'It didn't stop you tottering around the ruins at Pompeii, climbing up the steps at the Vatican and traipsing around the shops in Mallorca and Gibraltar,' responded her sister.

'Excuse me, Miriam—' started Edna.

'Look,' said Murray, glancing at his wristwatch, 'if Dr Patel suggests you should have the operation, I think you should take his advice.'

'There, you see,' said Miriam to her sister. 'I told you there was no need to get yourself into an overwrought condition. And all that Murray has told you, is what Dr Patel explained in some detail to you before we came away. Now, come along, we need to get a front row seat to hear Elodie King.'

'Well, thank you very much, Simon and Murray,' said Edna, heaving herself up from the chair. 'You have both been most helpful.'

'Our pleasure,' answered Simon.

'There *was* something else.' She lowered her voice. 'I've been having a spot of bother in the downstairs' department and—'

Miriam grabbed her sister's arm and pulled her away. 'Not now,' she said firmly. 'We need to get a seat in the theatre.'

'I'll perhaps catch up with you later, Simon,' said Edna.

The doctor's smile was a tiny lifting of the corners of his mouth. 'I'll look forward to that,' he told her.

'They were very nice young men,' declared Edna as the sisters headed for the Excelsior Theatre to hear Elodie's lecture.

'They were,' assented Miriam. 'They were most helpful and heartening. I hope you've been reassured. Now you heed what they said. When you get back home you want to go and see Dr Patel and get him to book you in for the operation.'

'I still think it's a big decision,' considered Edna pensively. 'I shall have to mull it over.'

'I don't think you listened to any of the advice those two doctors gave you,' said an exasperated Miriam. 'Anyway, I don't know why you had to go and bother them. There is a doctor on the ship, and he would have told you the same thing.'

'What, queue up in the suppository and pay through the nose when I can get a free consultation? Not on your life.'

In the theatre the two sisters found seats on the front row next to Maureen.

'So, how are you?' Miriam asked the grieving widow.

'What?' Maureen swivelled around to face the speaker.

'We were sorry to hear about your misfortune. So, how are you feeling?'

'I'm feeling fine.'

'You seem to be managing very well, bearing in mind what's happened,' said Edna.

Maureen pulled a reproachful face. 'I beg your pardon?' she asked unsmilingly.

'You certainly seem to have come to terms with it.'

Her sister nudged her. 'Edna,' she hissed.

'I'm just saying what I think.'

Maureen then recognised the speaker: the blundering old woman with whom she had had the altercation on the quayside and had her ejected from the front seat on the coach. Her expression became even more censorious. 'You were the woman with the walking frame who thrust ahead of me on the dock and made me drop my Roman urn.'

'Actually, if you hadn't been in such a hurry—' began Edna.

Miriam could see this was leading to another dispute, and endeavouring to prevent it, she intervened rapidly.

'My sister and I were wondering how you are feeling after your loss,' she said in a voice of kindly solicitude.

'Well, it was a very expensive urn,' Maureen told her. 'Fortunately, I managed to get another one, not dissimilar. It was smaller with different handles but looked very much the same.'

'No, I meant the loss of your husband,' said Miriam.

'Oh that,' answered Maureen, her voice suddenly simulating a sorrowful tone. 'I'm just about coping and gradually coming to terms with things. It's not quite sunk in yet. It happened so unexpectedly. Albert and me were having such a lovely time in Rome, eating a meal at a pavement restaurant in the sunshine and he just keeled over.' She then repeated for the umpteenth time the remarks she had voiced regularly since her husband's death when passengers had offered their condolences: 'It's a blessing that it was quick,' 'At least he felt no pain,' 'He's in a better place,' 'He'd had a good life,' 'It was meant to be.'

'And life must go on,' concluded Edna insensitively. 'In the midst of life there is death. When your time is up, there's no avoiding it. It comes to us all in the end. He's been relieved of his earthy misery. As I said, you've seemed to have come to terms with it remarkably quickly.'

Miriam put on a pained stoical face. Blunt as a car crash, that was her sister. She knew that suggesting to her the merits of diplomacy and restraint would fall upon deaf ears. She quickly adopted a sympathetic voice. 'It must feel the darkest place for you at the moment,' she said to the widow, 'but the sun will one day come shining through again, for time is a great healer.'

'If you could have got him on board after he passed over,' ventured Edna airily, giving the widow the benefit of her opinion, 'you could maybe have had him buried at sea or have his ashes scattered overboard. It would have saved a lot of inconvenience, having to fly him back and organise things back home.' Then she added tactlessly, 'And a whole lot cheaper.'

Maureen was singularly unfazed by the insensitivity of the remark and appeared blithely undismayed. 'Do you know, I never thought of that,' she replied thoughtfully.

29

'Now I guess you are wondering where Babs is this morning,' said Bruce, addressing the dance class.

'Is she not well?' asked Maureen before he could explain.

'She's . . . er . . . a little indisposed today,' he replied.

'She looked fine when I saw her getting off the ship in Rome,' said Sandra. 'She was carrying a case.'

'Was she really,' said Bruce, affecting indifference.

'She's had too much sun very likely,' said another passenger. 'You have to be ever so careful in this heat, wear a hat, keep out of the bright sunshine and drink plenty of water.'

'Thank you for that, Mona,' said Bruce. 'I guess you are right that Babs was out in the sun too long. Perhaps she has a touch of sunstroke.'

'She looked all right when I saw her in Rome,' said Maureen. 'She was with the Italian tenor drinking wine at a pavement bar.'

'Yes, it came on quite quickly,' said Bruce, wishing to change the subject.

'When will she be back?' he was asked.

'I can't say for sure. She's resting in the cabin at the moment.'

Babs was, in fact, not resting in the cabin. At that very moment she was resting in the bright sunshine on a sunbed on the balcony of Lorenzo's apartment off the Via del Corso with a glass of chilled Pinot Grigio and a bowl of olives, listening to the tenor singing in the kitchen where he was preparing lunch.

'Now, since Babs cannot be with us this morning,' said Bruce, 'I've asked Vanessa to step into the breach, as it were.'

Vanessa strode to the front to join Bruce. She had abandoned the T-shirt and shorts and was now dressed in a short, low-cut dress, pulled tight over her thighs and hips, and wore absurdly high-heeled stiletto shoes, singularly inappropriate for dancing.

'This morning,' said Bruce, taking Vanessa's hand, 'we will be demonstrating a sensual Latin dance called the salsa.'

For her last lecture Elodie chose poetry as her theme. She spoke with passion about the power, poignancy, and the beauty of poetry, that it is the most wonderful and heightened form of language and that poets represent the world more accurately than anyone else. Fortunately, she did not hear Edna's considered opinion on the subject, which was vouchsafed to Miriam in an undertone – that it was 'all la di da and dancing daffodils.'

Elodie spent the lecture reading and discussing some of her favourite poems.

'I should like to dedicate the first poem to a couple who many of you will have seen walking around the ship hand-in-hand. They have been an inspiration to us all and an example of the enduring power of love. Had there been a competition to decide which was the most affectionate and caring couple on the cruise, I feel confident that Pat and Jimmy would have taken the first prize.' She was unaware that the couple had known each other for less than a year. 'This is the beginning of a sonnet by Elizabeth Barrett Browning and called "How Do I Love Thee?"'

How do I love thee? Let me count the ways.
I love thee to the depth and breadth and height
My soul can reach, when feeling out of sight

For the ends of being and ideal grace.
I love thee to the level of every day's
Most quiet need, by sun and candlelight.'

As she read, Pat and Jimmy held hands tightly and looked lovingly into each other's eyes. Maureen elevated an eyebrow in wordless contradiction. The aged and habitually married couple could hardly be held up as an example of the enduring power of love, she reflected. She thought fleetingly of Albert in some Italian mortuary. There had never been any mention of love in their relationship.

'I guess,' said Elodie, 'that there are a few grandparents in the audience.' There was a ripple of laughter. 'The relationship between grandparents and their grandchildren is rather different from that between parents and their children. I think you will agree. Grannies and grandpas, in my experience, tend to be more patient, better listeners, less critical and, dare I say it, more indulgent than their own offspring. Grandparents are a delightful mixture of laughter, wonderful stories and love. They make the world a little softer, a little kinder, and a little warmer. I remember my grandparents. My mother and father, like most parents, always seemed to be in such a rush, always busy, sometimes too busy to listen, but my grandparents never hurried; they would walk slowly as if they had all the time in the world and smile and nod and always had the time to listen. This is the beginning of the poem, "When You Are Old" by W.B. Yeats, and is dedicated to all you grannies and granddads.

When you are old and grey and full of sleep,
And nodding by the fire, take down this book,
And slowly read, and dream of the soft look
Your eyes had once, and of their shadows deep.'

Oliver looked up at his grandparents who sat beside him and smiled. Mr Champion put his arm around the boy and smiled back.

'I should like to dedicate the next poem to two sisters,' said Elodie. 'I have met Edna and Miriam several times during the cruise and much enjoyed our conversations over coffee in the Rainbow Lounge.' She read:

> *There is no friend like a sister*
> *In calm or stormy weather;*
> *To cheer one on the tedious way,*
> *To fetch one if one goes astray,*
> *To lift one if one totters down,*
> *To strengthen whilst one stands.'*

The sisters nodded appreciatively.

'My next poem, an Indian prayer,' Elodie told the audience, 'will have a resonance for those of you who have lost a loved one. I shall dedicate it to a passenger who has recently lost her husband in tragic circumstances. Our condolences go to her:

> *When I am gone, cry for me a little.*
> *Think of me sometimes but not too much.*
> *Remember me now and again as I was in life,*
> *At those moments pleasant to recall,*
> *But not for too long.*
> *Let me rest in peace*
> *And I shall leave you in peace,*
> *And while you live let your thoughts be with the living.'*

Maureen shifted in her seat, feeling a good few pair of eyes fixed upon her. She assumed a sorrowful face, then dabbed her eyes theatrically.

'I should like to dedicate this next poem to a very special young man who is in the audience. I will not embarrass him by mentioning his name, but I know this poem will mean a lot. It's called "A Father's Advice to his Son."

Always smile at those you meet,
And they will do the same.
Look for good in others, son,
And don't waste time on blame.
Never be ashamed of crying,
It's not a sign you're weak,
And don't be quick to criticise,
And think before you speak.
Give more than you take, my son,
Do no one hurt nor harm,
And don't be afraid of being wrong,
And always chance your arm.
Stick firmly to your principles,
Don't follow fads and trends,
And always answer to your heart,
And value all your friends.
Keep that sense of humour,
It will help you to survive,
And don't take life too seriously son,
For none come out alive.'

Oliver sat upright listening intently. When the reading was over, he remained straight-backed and silent, but tears came to his eyes. Then he rested his head gently on his grandfather's shoulder.

Mrs De la Mare, sitting at the back of the theatre suddenly felt bright spots of tears in the corners of her eyes too. She thought of the words in the poem and of her father – a man who seldom smiled and never laughed, who never looked for the good in anyone, least of all her, a man quick to criticise, a man who was never wrong.

'Finally,' said Elodie, 'I should like to share with you a poem which was my grandmother's favourite. I was told that I inherited this red hair of mine from Ann Mullarkey. This is "The Irish Blessing":

May the road rise up to meet you,
And the wind be ever at your back.
May the sun shine warm upon your face,
And the rains fall soft upon your fields.
May the roof above you never fall in,
And those of us below never fall out.
May you live as long as you want,
And never want as long as you live.
May you be in heaven half an hour before the devil finds out,
And as you slide down the great banister of life,
May the splinters be facing downwards,
And until we meet again ...
May God hold you all in the hollow of his hand.'

Mrs De la Mare was close to tears. She raised her hand to her face and took a deep breath. Hearing 'The Irish Blessing' so unexpectedly had prompted an out-of-character reaction, the strength of which alarmed her. Never in her life had she been so surprised and tricked by her emotions. It was hearing the poem which had been printed on her mother's tea towel, which had so affected her. She recalled at that moment her mother's smiling face as she dried the dishes, how she had looked lovingly at her, touched her cheek, told her what a beautiful child she was.

'You don't look very well, dear.' Sandra stood before her, a hand resting on the woman's arm.

'I'm fine,' replied Mrs De la Mare, reaching into her hand-bag for a handkerchief and then dabbing her eyes. The linen handkerchief, embroidered in a corner with three small sham-rocks had been her mother's.

'That was nice of Miss King to dedicate that poem to us, wasn't it?' said Edna as the sisters made their way out of the theatre on their way for afternoon tea.

'Yes,' agreed Miriam. 'I shall ask her for a copy and do a cross-stitch cushion when we get back home. It will be a nice memento of the cruise.'

'It was right what was in the poem that there is no friend like a sister,' said Edna.

Miriam smiled affectionately and nodded.

'Mind you,' said Edna, 'it's a pity somebody didn't enlighten the author before she went and dedicated that poem to that aged couple on the front row. I heard from Becky that that's the old man's third wife who was with him and they've only just got married. Getting married seems to have become something of a habit with him.'

'Well, good luck to them,' said Miriam. 'Life's too short. You have to grab an opportunity when it is offered and get a bit of pleasure out of life when you can, and you would get a lot more pleasure out of life if you grabbed the opportunity of having that hip operation.'

'They were likeable young men, those two doctors, weren't they?' remarked Edna, not wishing to discuss the operation.

'You want to take their advice and get your hip sorted out,' persisted Miriam, 'and you don't want to go bothering them with your . . . problem in the downstairs' department.'

'They'll make some young women very happy.'

'Pardon?'

'The two young doctors. I said they'll make some young women very happy.'

'I don't think so,' murmured her sister.

'Oh yes, they've got everything going for them: young, good-looking, personable, comfortably off and both in top jobs. If I was forty years' younger, I'd set my cap for one of those.'

'And it wouldn't have got you very far.'

'Either of them would be a catch for some young woman. I should imagine girls are queuing up to go out with them.'

'Well, it wouldn't do them any good if they did.'

'I'm surprised they haven't got their girlfriends with them on the cruise.'

'They don't have girlfriends,' Miriam told her. 'Didn't you hear what they said. They are partners.'

'Yes, I did hear what they said,' replied Edna shrilly. 'It's my hip that's faulty, not my ears. Anyway, what's them being partners got anything to do with the price of tea in China? Those two doctors are probably partners in some medical practice. Mr Ellerby and his brother, who own the shop I used to work in, are partners. There's nothing unusual about that.'

'They're not that kind of partners,' Miriam told her.

'Sometimes, I have not the first idea of what you are talking about,' said Edna.

'No, that's not unusual,' conceded her sister. Miriam shook her head and smiled. She eyed her sister with affection. 'Do you know something, Edna, you are one of the world's great innocents.' She put her hand on her sister's shoulder, leaned over and kissed Edna lightly on the cheek.

'I don't know what's got into you this afternoon,' said Edna. 'You're acting very strange. I hope you've not been hitting the cockatails again.'

Mrs De la Mare waited until Oliver was leaving the theatre. As he passed, she called him over.

'A word,' she said.

'Oh hello,' said the boy brightly.

'You are the young man who told me that the tender was about to leave in Gibraltar.'

'Yes, that's right.'

'I cannot imagine what it would have been like if you had not been good enough to speak to me. My passport, most of my money and all my belongings were on board the ship. I could have been left high and dry had it not been for your action. I heard that a man who, like me, had not taken account of the change in time, was left stranded ashore.'

'These things happen,' said Oliver philosophically.

'Anyway, I am grateful that it didn't happen to me. Now I think you may have been offended when I offered you some money.'

'Not at all,' he replied.

'Then I hope you will accept a small token of my thanks.' She held out a slim and expensive looking leather-bound box. 'It's a fountain pen. I have seen you writing in your little black book and thought you might like it. I don't know if children still use fountain pens in school these days. I suppose it's the age of the biro or the felt tip.'

'I still use a fountain pen,' Oliver informed her, 'but you really have no need—'

Mrs De la Mare held up a hand. 'What is your name?' she interrupted.

'Oliver Champion.'

'Well, Oliver Champion, it is *I* who will feel offended if you do not accept this reward for your consideration.'

He took the box from her, opened it. Inside was the costliest fountain pen which had been displayed in the ship's jewellers.

'Wow!' he cried.

Before he could thank her, Mrs De la Mare allowed herself a small smile and left the theatre.

Being a day at sea, there was a variety of activities on the ship. The most popular by far was the interview conducted by the Entertainment Manager entitled, 'A Life in the Day of a Cruise Ship Captain.'

'It is a pleasure this afternoon,' Martin told the packed theatre, 'for me to introduce Captain Edward J. Smith, the Master of the *Empress of the Ocean*. I am sure many of you will be interested to hear about the life and work of a cruise ship captain and some of his experiences on the high seas. Captain Smith will talk for about half an hour and then he will answer questions. Captain Smith spoke briefly about his happy, uneventful childhood in Staffordshire and his unremarkable schooldays and then moved on.

'Since an early age I have always wanted to be a sailor,' he told his audience. 'It was a driving ambition. I guess the sea is in my blood. I come from a long line of mariners. My father was a second engineer in the Merchant Navy and my grandfather was a chief petty officer in the Royal Navy. I am frequently asked how one becomes a captain on a cruise ship. Well, it took me a long time and a lot of hard work. Not counting the years of study, including gaining a degree in marine engineering, I spent twelve years of maritime on-the-job experience.' He caught sight of Oliver sitting straight-backed on the front row with his pencil poised above his notebook and smiled at the boy. 'And despite what some might imagine, the captain has a bit more to do than wear a fancy uniform, entertain people at his table and have his photograph taken with the passengers. Now let's have the first question.'

'You say you come from a long line of mariners,' announced Mr Champion. 'You share your name with one who also hailed from Staffordshire, another, rather more famous sea captain than yourself, if I may say so. I am thinking of the Edward J. Smith who was the irresponsible master on a well-known and ill-fated ship called the *RMS Titanic*.'

'The *Titanic* was indeed ill-fated,' agreed the Captain, 'but Captain Smith was, in my opinion, not irresponsible nor was he incompetent. He was a very experienced sailor and described as a man with a great heart, a brave life, and a heroic death.'

'That may be so,' responded Mr Champion, 'but as the ship's master, did he not have to take the responsibility for what happened?'

Captain Smith evaded the question. 'Well, I can assure you that I will keep my eyes peeled for icebergs in the Mediterranean,' he replied, wishing to lighten what he imagined might develop into a lengthy discussion on the fate of the legendary vessel.

There was a ripple of laughter.

'Have you ever had a collision?' asked the red-cheeked passenger with the bristly Stalin-style moustache and short cropped hair.

'No, touch wood. Bearing in mind that a great number of cruise ships sail around the world, there have been remarkably few collisions. Your question does remind me of a story told to me by the first captain I served under. It's quite an old chestnut so you may have heard it before, but it is worth repeating. It illustrates the dangers of inflexibility and self-importance and the need for open-mindedness. There was a dense summer fog and the captain on the bridge of a certain battleship peered into the gloom. He saw the lights of a vessel heading, as the crow flies, in his direction. The captain of a naval craft requested that the other ship change course without delay to avoid them crashing into each other. The radio conversation went something like this:

Captain of the battleship: Divert your course fifteen degrees to the North immediately to avoid a collision.

From the other vessel: Recommend you divert *your* course fifteen degrees to the South to avoid a collision.

Captain of the battleship: This is the Captain of a Royal Navy battleship. I say again, divert *your* course.

From the other vessel: No. I say again, you divert *your* course fifteen degrees to the South to avoid a collision.

Captain of the battleship: I demand that *you* change your course fifteen degrees North immediately, that is one five degrees North, or the consequences will be catastrophic.

From the other vessel: They will be if you continue on *your* course. I'm in a lighthouse.

'Of course, there appears to be no evidence that the event actually took place, and the account is implausible for several reasons but as the Italian saying goes, "*Se non è vero, è comunque una bella storia*". If it's not true, it's still a good story. Another question, please.'

'Can you marry a couple at sea?' he was asked by Connie.

'There is an almost worldwide but misguided notion that sea captains are able to perform marriage ceremonies. As a general rule they do not have the authority to legally do this, with a few exceptions like Japan, Bermuda and Romania. So, on this ship, I do not have the power to make a marriage legally binding. I can preside over the renewal of vows, which is always a very pleasant duty of mine, but this must be arranged by the couple before the cruise starts.'

Captain Smith at this point recalled the occasion when a couple had asked him to officiate at a ceremony where they would plight their troth for a second time. The occasion had not turned out to have been quite as pleasant a duty as he had anticipated. The happy twosome had held hands, sentimental poems about long-lasting love had been read and rings exchanged. Two days' later the wife had discovered her spouse behind a lifeboat in a clinch with a passenger. She had promptly thrown overboard the ring her husband had given her and, if there had not been the prohibition about dumping things into the sea, her husband's clothes and personal effects would have followed. For the last two nights of the cruise the faithless spouse had been locked out of the cabin and slept on a lounger on deck.

'Can someone be buried at sea?' asked Maureen.

'Yes, it is possible for a person to be buried at sea,' replied the Captain. 'However, there are very strict regulations, and a licence is required. There must be no risk of the deceased being returned to shore by strong currents or being disturbed by commercial fishing nets. Because of this, the person buried must have an identification tag attached to them and be clad in light, biodegradable clothing.'

Here the Captain recalled the occasion when things did not go quite as smoothly as expected. The deceased had been placed on the mechanism which tilted and was meant to despatch the body smoothly into the ocean with the least amount of fuss. The apparatus had been fully serviced and liberally oiled by the Chief Engineer. The plan had been that at sunrise the widow and close family members would attend a short service conducted by the Captain before the dear departed was committed to the ocean. Just before the bereaved wife and family had arrived on deck, the crew member in charge of operating the mechanism had inadvertently touched the overly sensitive control and the body had slid effortlessly into the sea. The quick-thinking Captain had hastily despatched two crew members to fetch a couple of sacks of potatoes from the galley which were wrapped in a canvas shroud and put in place of the body. The mourners had arrived moments later, and the service had been conducted with great solemnity before the sacks of King Edwards had been despatched to the deep.

Mr Carlin-How raised a hand. 'With regard to burial at sea,' he said, 'passengers might be interested to know that in the eighteenth and nineteenth centuries this involved wrapping the deceased in a sailcloth weighted with cannonballs. The Elizabethan sailor and navigator, Sir Francis Drake, died at sea in 1596 and his body, clad in a full suit of armour and placed in a lead coffin, was entrusted to the ocean off Portobelo in Panama.'

'I'm afraid we don't keep cannonballs aboard these days,' said the Captain. 'Of course, scattering a loved one's ashes at sea isn't uncommon and in recent times it's become a lot more popular. Anyone can request the scattering of ashes at sea, and a special licence is not required nor the involvement of an undertaker. There are usually no legal obstacles to overcome, as long as the ashes are placed in the ocean three nautical miles from land. The ashes must be carried in a waterproof urn along with a valid death certificate before being scattered in the sea. Placing the urn in the water is not permitted. The actual ceremony is then conducted by the Captain and members of the guest service staff in private, whilst not disrupting other guests on board. When the service is over, the closest family member is given a letter by the Captain, signed by him, with the coordinates of the longitude and latitude of the ship's position where the ashes have been scattered. Now one final question.'

'Are cruise ships in any danger from pirates?' asked Jimmy of the aged couple.

'I guess for most of us the word "pirate" conjures up visions of *Treasure Island*, Long John Silver, Blackbeard and Captain Kidd, those one-eyed, hook-handed robbers who plundered ships of yore. Well, there is no danger from those. There are modern day pirates, but they present no threat to cruise ships. Ocean-going liners are capable of outrunning the small boats used by pirates and if they should manage to get alongside, the distance between the waterline and open decks makes boarding extremely difficult for them to use grappling hooks to climb from a moving vessel. The security of passengers and crew is always the top priority and crew members are trained to act in an emergency and are well-equipped to handle situations should pirates attack. For obvious reasons, I cannot provide specific practices regarding security. Just be reassured that there has never been an occasion when pirates have boarded a cruise ship. Now, I think you have heard quite enough of me. Afternoon tea is being served.'

'Thank you, Captain Smith for a most insightful hour,' said the Entertainment Manager. 'I am sure that you will be more than happy to answer any more questions from the passengers as you walk around the ship.'

'Well, that was interesting,' remarked Miriam as people exited the theatre.

'Yes, it was,' agreed Edna. 'And it was reassuring that we're not likely to be captivated by pirates.'

Miriam looked at her sister with amused affection. 'The very thought,' she chuckled.

'Do you know,' said Edna. 'I never realised you could get icebergs in the Mediterranean. You learn something new every day.'

30

It was the custom for the Captain of the *Empress of the Ocean* to host an exclusive farewell cocktail party on the evening before the liner docked in Southampton. Those invited would include all the first-class passengers, the lecturers and performers and other selected guests.

Having set the table out for breakfast on the penultimate morning of the cruise, Dominic placed an envelope against the slim crystal vase containing a single white rose and smiled as Mrs De la Mare came into the room from the balcony.

'Good morning, madam,' he said brightly. 'It looks like another fine day.'

'Good morning, Dominic,' she replied.

'There is a letter for you, madam, and a message which I believe is from the Captain.'

Mrs De la Mare plucked up a card edged in red. It requested the pleasure of her company at the cocktail party to be held in the Consort Suite that evening. She examined it with a detached kind of indifference.

'Oh, yes, it *is* from the Captain,' she said unconcernedly, tossing the invitation down on the table. 'I'm invited to a farewell cocktail party this evening.'

Over breakfast she thought of the dreadful occasion when she had sat tight-lipped and ill at ease at the Captain's table.

During the meal Mr Mulgrave had turned to the Captain and smiled like a shark. 'Mrs Mare and I share the same taste in music,' he had remarked sardonically. 'We are both devoted

admirers of Chopin.' He had spun around to face the subject
of his comment. 'Are we not, Mrs Mare?'

Mrs De la Mare had managed a whispered, 'Yes', and had
wished that the floor would open and swallow her up. She
could feel the heat rise in her neck.

'A fine composer,' the Captain had said.

'Indeed,' Mr Mulgrave had agreed. 'It is said of Chopin
that—'

Mrs De la Mare had been saved further embarrassment
by the intervention of Edna. 'My sister and I did enjoy the
musical performances and thought you were very compe-
tent on the keyboard, but as I told you, Mr Mulgrave, we did
feel that something a bit more tuneful with a catchy melody
would have been more popular than pieces by all those German composers.'

'Chopin was Polish,' he had told her.

'He sounds German to me,' Edna had replied. 'Mind you,
foreigners do have some funny names, don't they, particularly
the Polish. I can never pronounce Mrs Jannikowikki's name.'

'Jankowski,' her sister had corrected her.

'She lives a couple of doors from us.' Edna had rambled on
regardless.

After the Captain had finally managed to squeeze in a word,
those at the table had been asked if they had ventured ashore.

It had now been Cyril's turn to hold the floor and he had
spoken with enthusiasm about the delights of Rome and
Pompeii until there had been another interjection from Edna.

'It was too hot and dusty and crowded and full of flies.'
She had then glanced at Mrs De la Mare and had added,
with a curl of the mouth, 'And unlike some folk who flashed
a gold card and were given presidential treatment pushing to
the front, we had to wait in the queue.'

Mrs De la Mare had remained silent but had prayed for the
ordeal to end. And so the evening had dragged on until she

could stand it no longer and, pleading a headache, she had made her excuses and left the table. Later she had stood on the balcony in her stateroom. The star-filled night had been warm with not a breath of wind. She had felt tears springing up behind her eyes but quickly blinked them away. The evening had been too awful for tears.

She dragged herself back to the present and looked up from her breakfast. 'I don't think I'll bother going to this cocktail party,' she told Dominic, glancing again at the invitation.

'I believe it is likely to be a very enjoyable evening, madam,' he said. 'The passengers who occupied this stateroom before you said it was one of the highlights of the cruise.'

'You think I should go?'

'It's really not for me to say, madam.'

Mrs De la Mare looked up at him. 'I can see by the expression on your face that you think I should.'

'I am sure you will enjoy it.'

'Then perhaps I might.'

She opened the letter. It was from Oliver, written in a careful hand, thanking her for the gift.

'I see that child progeny with the ginger hair and sticky-out ears has found himself a girlfriend,' remarked Edna. They were sitting taking coffee in the Rainbow Lounge, chattering away.

'Yes, I saw them,' replied Miriam. 'I thought it was very sweet. They looked like an old married couple.'

'It's good to see that boy mixing with someone of his own age for a change. He's like a little old man. Too much time spent with adults, that's his trouble. It's not healthy for a child of his age. He'll end up like Mr Double-barrelled if he's not careful, stiff as a poker and serious as an undertaker.'

'He's a lovely little lad,' observed Miriam, 'so polite, well-behaved and always smartly turned-out. It's a pity other youngsters aren't like him. I heard that those two lads were in trouble for throwing food about and had to go and see the Captain.'

'They need a good hiding these misbehaved children. It all went wrong when they banned the cane and stopped using corporeal punishment in schools. It never did me any harm.'

'You never had the cane,' Miriam told her.

'No, but Miss Kettleness was a demon with the ruler. I've had that across my knuckles a good few times.'

'Well, I can't see Oliver getting up to any sort of mischief.'

'That's as may be,' stated Edna, 'but he knows a lot more than he should do at his age. He's too clever by half. You remember what he came out with when we were in Pompeii and we were outside the . . . that place of ill repute.'

'You mean the brothel,' said Miriam.

'Keep your voice down,' her sister hissed. 'Yes, that's what I mean. Fancy knowing all about those places at his age and those words. Of course, I blame the schools teaching them sex education before they are ready. I was very innocent. I never knew anything about that sort of thing.'

'It might have been a good idea if they had,' observed her sister.

'What?'

'If you'd have learnted about the facts of life at school. Teaching those things means that young people don't get the wrong idea.' Then she added, looking at her sister, 'And it's not just children who get the wrong idea.'

'I remember when Kathleen Runswick left in the middle of our exams,' said Edna, 'and Moira Scaling said she was in the pudding club. I thought she'd joined a group that made jam roly-poly.'

Her sister laughed. 'My goodness, Edna,' she said, 'you get worse.'

At that moment, the boy who had been at the centre of their conversation appeared with Miranda. He looked particularly pleased with himself.

'Hello,' he said briskly.

'Hello,' replied the sisters simultaneously.

'This is Miranda,' said Oliver.

'Yes, we saw you both in the theatre for the lecture,' said Miriam.

'What are you two up to today then?' enquired Edna.

'Not getting up to anything you wouldn't do,' replied Oliver, recalling the woman's admonition when they were at Pompeii. He gave a cheeky smile.

Both sisters chuckled.

'We're going swimming,' he told them, 'then we're off to hear the choir. Miranda's parents are singing. After that we'll get a bite to eat in the Galleon Buffet and then thought we might see a film at the cinema. Later we're going to the disco.'

'My goodness,' said Miriam, 'a very busy day.'

'What have you got there?' questioned Edna eyeing a tin box the boy was holding.

Oliver read the fancy writing on the front. 'They're called *Lingue Di Gatto*, a kind of Italian butter biscuit. It says "*fatto da una ricetta speciale*". I don't know what that means but I think "*ricetta*" means recipe and "*speciale*" means special. I don't know what "*fatto*" means.'

'It probably means gobble too many of those and you'll end up fat,' suggested Edna. 'Well, just make sure you don't eat too many.'

'They're not for me,' Oliver told her. 'They're for you.'

'For me!' exclaimed Edna.

'I heard you say in Pompeii that the foreign biscuits tasted like sawdust. I thought these might change your mind.'

'How very kind,' said Miriam.

'Come over here, Oliver,' Edna told him, 'so I can thank you properly.'

He smiled, but before walking towards her, warned, 'I will if you don't ruffle my hair.'

'Of course not,' she replied and when he stood before her, she reached up and kissed him on the cheek. Miranda giggled; Oliver's face turned crimson.

When the children had gone, Edna turned her attention to the couple Elodie had introduced. Royston and Henrietta were sitting at a corner table absorbed in each other's company.

'Look at the two lovebirds,' said Edna.

'Who?'

'That couple in the corner.'

'I wasn't looking.'

'Well, take a look.'

'What about them?'

'There's another pair who have shacked up since they came on the cruise,' Edna informed her sister. 'It must be catching. This ship is like a dating agency on water.'

Miriam breathed in and rested her head in the back of the chair preparing herself for another of her sister's sharp observations.

'All these flings are running rampant around the ship,' Edna continued. 'There's the two lecturers acting all lovey-dovey, the little Italian singer running off with the dance tutor and the Entertainment Manager and the concert pianist's daughter carrying on like nobody's business. They're all at it.'

'You were wrong about her,' muttered Miriam.

'Who?'

'The concert pianist's daughter, thinking she was his fancy woman.'

'Yes, well, I wasn't alone in thinking that.'

'If you had played your cards right,' chuckled her sister mischievously, 'you could have got fixed up with Percy from the casino.'

Edna pulled a face.

Royston and Henrietta, unaware that they were the focus of Edna's scrutiny, were staring into each other's eyes.

'As soon as I get home, I shall give you a ring,' Royston was saying, reaching across the table and taking Henrietta's hand in his.

'I shall so look forward to it,' she replied.

'Then we can fix the date for you to come and stay with me in Harrogate and we can have afternoon tea at Bettys Tearoom, and I can show you the sights: Fountains Abbey, Harlow Carr Gardens, Bolton Castle and the Yorkshire Dales.'

'I should love that,' she said. 'Then you must come to Canterbury and stay with me.'

Since their introduction to each other by Elodie, the couple had spent the remainder of the cruise together, going ashore together, eating together, and finally spending the night together.

'It has been such a memorable time for me,' Royston told her. 'Meeting you has made the voyage so special.'

'And for me,' she conceded.

Of course, neither of them would see each other again. Royston (known at home as plain Roy) was not what he claimed to be. His villa in Mallorca with the marble floors, sunken swimming pool and an uninterrupted sea view was a figment of his imagination. He had never been the senior partner in a prestigious law firm, as he had told Henrietta; he worked behind the counter in a gentlemen's outfitters. His large house overlooking the Stray in Harrogate was another invention; he lived in an unprepossessing tower block in Leeds. As for his wife, whom he had said he had nursed through a protracted illness until her death, she was alive and living in a care home suffering with Alzheimer's. But Henrietta (known at home as plain Letty) was not all what *she* claimed to be either. She did not live in a listed cottage a stone's throw from Canterbury Cathedral, nor had she been a high-flying executive with a large manufacturing company; she lived with her sister in a flat in Deal and had been a clerical assistant at the council offices before her retirement. Her late husband, who she claimed had been a senior officer in the Royal Navy, had been a steward on a cross-channel ferry. Both were very convincing liars (they would perhaps have described themselves as romancers) but both saw no harm in pretending, for this short time, that they were something they were not. On the cruise ship they found a limitless world where they could be whoever they wanted to be. In reality, they were just two lonely people who sought company and perhaps a short adventure. They would return to their mundane lives, after their brief dalliance, and neither would be the wiser.

'I have your number and shall be in touch,' he said in the full knowledge that this would never happen.

The red-cheeked man with a bristly moustache chanced upon Mr Hinderwell in the library.

'I want to apologise,' he said to the clergyman.

'Whatever for?' asked Mr Hinderwell.

'I was out of order speaking to you as I did. I had no right to make an assumption about you. It was foolish of me, and I am sorry.'

'I guess most of us make assumptions about others,' replied Mr Hinderwell. 'As soon as we say what we do for a living the listener forms an opinion of us very much based on their experiences of meeting a person in that profession. I am sure when you tell someone the kind of work you were in, they have formed a view of the police and, no doubt, regale you with their encounters with the law, some of which are not all that complimentary.'

'Very true,' conceded the red-cheeked man. 'Well, anyway, I just wanted to say I'm sorry for shooting my mouth off. It was stupid what I said. I was sitting with the chap with the one arm last night at the dinner table and he was telling us about his injury. Your name came up. He told me what you did, helping him out of an army vehicle which had been blown up by a roadside bomb, risking your life, and getting shot in the back by a sniper. He said you saved his life.'

'I was doing my duty as all the soldiers were. I just happened to be there at the right time.'

'The right time? I hardly think it was being there at the right time after what happened to you. That chap said you are a legend in the regiment, that you spent hours in the thick of the fighting comforting the injured.'

'It was a long time ago,' murmured the clergyman.

'You're a remarkable man.'

'It's kind of you to say that, but I am not sure some people would agree,' he said modestly.

'Well you are, and I'm sorry for what I said,' repeated the man. 'I didn't realise what you did.'

'Please don't apologise, you were not to know,' said Mr Hinderwell.

'May I shake your hand?' he asked.

'By all means,' the clergyman told him.

The farewell cocktail party was in full and noisy swing by the time Mrs De la Mare made her appearance, impeccably attired in a lavender taffeta evening dress, heavily bejewelled and in a cloud of heady perfume. She took a glass of champagne from the white gloved waiter, raised it to her lips and surveyed the cluster of guests. She spotted Lady Staithes and headed in her direction. As she moved through the throng, listening to snippets of conversation, she came face to face with her antagonist.

'Good evening, Mrs Mare,' said the concert pianist.

'Oh, good evening,' she managed to reply. There was a short, strained silence. She gave a discreet cough. 'I owe you an apology, Mr Mulgrave.'

'Really?'

'I think it was out of place for me to criticise your playing of the Chopin.'

'Yes, I think it was,' he replied.

'It was rather silly of me to have made such an insensitive comment. I regret what I said.'

'Ah well, nothing is given more liberally than advice. I am used to people giving me the benefit of it, as was demonstrated when we dined at the Captain's table and it was suggested that I play something a bit more tuneful with a catchy melody. I admit I was annoyed with your comments at the time, but later thought it was quite amusing. You see, during my performance I lost concentration for a moment and improvised eight bars. Now, if the listener had really known the piece, this would have been noticed and no doubt commented upon.' He winked and lowered his voice. 'Many pianists, I guess, have a lapse from time to time, a slip of the fingers. The knack is not to draw attention to it. Music is for expression, not for perfection.' With that final riposte, he excused himself, leaving Mrs De la Mare suitably chastened.

As she edged through the crowd in her attempt to reach Lady Staithes, Mrs De la Mare came upon Dr King and Mr Carlin-How.

'I was hoping I might get a chance of having a word with you,' she told the author. 'I wanted to say how much I enjoyed your lectures.' She glanced sideways. 'And yours, of course,' she said to Mr Carlin-How with less enthusiasm.

'Thank you,' said Elodie.

'And I was wondering if I might ask a favour. I should like a copy of the poem you recited – "The Irish Blessing." It was my mother's favourite. It may sound rather silly, but it was printed on a tea towel of hers. One of my happiest memories was standing with her at the sink as she dried the dishes, listening to her.'

'Not silly at all,' replied Elodie. 'I shall leave a copy at reception. You can collect it before you leave the ship tomorrow.'

Mrs De la Mare moved on but her way was blocked by the Captain's mother.

'Oh, I'm so glad to see you,' said Sandra. 'I was worried about you.'

'You were worried? Why was that?' she was asked.

'You were so quiet when we had dinner at the Captain's table. You hardly said a word and then you had a headache and had to leave. I thought you might not be feeling too well. I did phone your stateroom to ask how you were, but the butler assured me you were fine.'

'You phoned my cabin?'

'Just to see if you were all right.'

'That was thoughtful of you, but as you can see, I'm fit and well.'

They were joined by the Captain.

'Ah, Mrs De la Mare it's good to see you,' he said. 'My mother was quite concerned about you, that you may be unwell.'

'Yes, she has told me.'

'No seasickness I hope?'

'No, I am in good health, thank you.'

'That's good,' said the Captain. He looked around him at the chattering passengers. 'You know, there is something bittersweet about an occasion such as this. Most feel sad that the cruise is coming to an end but are happy to be returning home to see their family and friends.'

Family and friends, thought Mrs De la Mare. She would be returning to a lonely house.

'Now, I am sure you would wish to circulate and meet some of the other guests,' the Captain told her, 'so we won't keep you.'

'And have a safe journey home,' Sandra told her.

Mrs De la Mare's attempt to reach Lady Staithes was further frustrated when Oliver's grandparents approached her.

'May we have a word?' asked Mr Champion.

'Yes, of course.'

'My wife and I wanted to thank you for your generosity.'

'My generosity?' repeated Mrs De la Mare.

'Our grandson told us about the nice lady who gave him a lovely fountain pen.'

Mrs De la Mare had never in her life been described thus.

'Oliver pointed you out to us this morning,' said Mrs Champion. 'He was so taken with the pen, and he will treasure it. It was most kind of you.'

'It was kind of your grandson to warn me about the last tender,' replied Mrs De la Mare. 'Had he not, I should now be stuck on the Rock of Gibraltar. It was good of him to write and thank me. He is a very considerate young man.'

Mrs De la Mare never did manage to speak to Lady Staithes that evening, for the person in question left the cocktail party to have an early night.

31

The *Empress of the Ocean* pulled into the dock at Southampton. The passengers waited in the lounges to disembark. Their cases had been taken ashore the night before.

When Lady Staithes came to settle her account the young woman at the reception desk told her the Purser would like to speak to her.

'Nothing wrong, I hope,' she replied, placing an expensive leather valise on the counter.

'No, no, madam, there is nothing wrong,' she said hastily and disappeared. A moment later the Purser appeared all smiles.

'Ah, my dear Lady Staithes,' he said. 'I was hoping to have a word with you before you disembark. Is it convenient now?'

'Perfectly. As I enquired of the young lady at the reception desk, I trust there is nothing amiss.'

'Quite the contrary,' he answered. 'I took the liberty of reading what you had written in the evaluation questionnaire of the cruise. You were most complimentary.'

'Yes, it has been a splendid fortnight. It exceeded my expectations. Everything has been tip-top. My cabin was superb, the food excellent, the entertainment first class, the service second to none. The steward was particularly attentive. I shall definitely be booking another cruise with you.'

'I am delighted to hear it. I was wondering if I might quote what you have said in our next brochure and perhaps have a picture of you with the Captain.'

'Yes, by all means, but I am intrigued to know why I have been singled out for such special treatment? I am sure most of the passengers have found the experience on this cruise quite as delightful as I have and would be more than happy to furnish a recommendation.'

'Well, I have to admit there is a certain cachet in having an endorsement from someone of your standing and status, Lady Staithes.'

'Really?'

'A recommendation from a titled person such as yourself adds some distinction.'

Lady Staithes laughed. 'Good gracious. I am not a titled person,' she replied. 'I was never married to an aristocrat; my father wasn't an earl and I do not possess a life peerage. "Lady" is my first name. When I was born my father held me in his arms for the first time and said, "Welcome to the world, little lady." The name sort of stuck and my parents decided on that for my first name. I am very sorry to disappoint you. I am plain Miss Staithes.' She gave a small smile. 'Of course, my name does come in handy sometimes, particularly if one needs a table at a posh restaurant at short notice.'

Mrs De la Mare had come to collect the poem which Elodie promised to leave for her at the reception desk and listened open-mouthed to the revelation. It was rare for her to show any amusement she might feel, above a small smile, but on this occasion the cool, rational, self-controlled, strait-laced Frances De la Mare, began to laugh so loudly that Lady Staithes spun around to stare in puzzlement and passengers turned their heads.

Becky had come down from the Ocean Spa to the lounge to see Bianca off.

'I hope everything goes well with your salon,' she said. She was inclined to tell her colleague that she would be missed, but this would be a lie for she was glad to see the back of her. It had been hard going working with such a crabby colleague.

'I heard from Leon that you are to be put in charge of the salon on the next cruise,' remarked Bianca. Her smile was stiff and unnatural. It was difficult for her to hide the resentment in her voice. This was not lost on Becky who returned the smile.

'As you know Gloria is moving to take charge of the salon on that big American ship and I've been offered her job,' she said.

'You didn't say anything to me,' Bianca announced with a purse-lipped frown.

'Well, we've been so busy and—'

'Sooner you than me,' her colleague sniffed, her words the product of envy and disappointment. 'Of course, it will be a temporary arrangement, a stopgap until a new manager takes over. I suppose they couldn't get anyone else at such short notice. It will just be an acting role.'

'Oh, no,' Becky told her, feeling smug, her vitality undiminished. 'It's a permanent position and I'm to have two new assistants, your replacement and a trainee.'

'Really?' Bianca's eyes narrowed. She tried hard to contain the intense resentment she felt at Becky's success. 'Well, as I said, sooner you than me. I'm glad to leave. Of course, if I had stayed on board, I would have been offered the job since I've worked longer on cruise ships than you and have more experience.'

Becky knew, of course, that this was not the case. Leon, who ran the gym and was a notorious gossip, had told her that Bianca's contract had not been renewed. Whereas Becky had achieved top scores on the passengers' evaluations, Bianca's ratings had been extremely poor with complaints about her curt manner, lack of conversation and rough handling. Maureen had been to see the Spa Manager to protest about her treatment at Bianca's hands and related to all who were inclined to listen, what she had experienced. When an elderly woman, who had booked her for a tint, emerged from the salon looking like an ageing punk with pink hair that stuck up from her scalp in tufts, Bianca's clientele had dwindled.

'Well, I must make a move,' said Bianca now, as if Becky were wilfully detaining her. 'I'm getting off by the crew gangway, to miss the rush, and so I don't have to queue with all the passengers.'

Becky couldn't resist a parting shot. 'Good luck with your salon in Rotherham,' she said.

With a bitter taste in her mouth, Bianca departed just as Sandra appeared in the lounge.

'Well, well,' said Becky when she caught sight of her favourite passenger. 'You're a dark horse and no mistake.'

'I'm sure I don't know what you mean,' Sandra pretended, smiling.

'Dining with the Captain.'

'Oh, that.'

'You never said anything when you were having your hair done.'

'Well, I didn't like to.'

'Invited to sit at the Captain's table with all the posh folk. Not many people receive that invitation. So, what did you make of him?'

'Who?'

'You know, the Captain.'

'Oh, he is very nice,' replied Sandra.

'He's new to this ship so we don't know a lot about him but he's really friendly, not stuffy at all. All the girls on the ship think he's dead dishy. I wonder if he's married and has got a wife and children tucked away at home somewhere.'

The Captain's mother gave a dimpled smile with maternal satisfaction, thinking she could have told the young woman a great deal about her son, but she remained silent. During the cruise she had been careful not to name-drop.

'No, he hasn't a wife and children,' she said.

'Did he tell you?'

'Er . . . yes,' said Sandra.

'What else did you talk about?' asked Becky.

'Oh, this and that, nothing very special. He asked me if I was enjoying the cruise. I said very much and that everyone had been so friendly and helpful.'

'Did you mention the Ocean Spa?'

'I did. I said you were a great asset to the ship.'

Becky beamed. 'I've never been called an asset before,' she said, giggling.

'Well, you are. My hair has never looked so nice, and you've been a real tonic, telling me all the news and the gossip. I've so much enjoyed this cruise and hope I'll be back on this ship next year if my son can arrange it for me. I shall be sailing to America and will stop there for a couple of weeks with my son and his family and then fly back.'

'You never said you had a son,' said Becky.

'Didn't I? Oh yes, I have a daughter, Janette, who's a ballet dancer and two boys. My elder son, Gerald, lives in New York. He lectures at a university there.'

'What does your other son do?'

'Eddie?' said Sandra with an impish glint in her eye. 'Oh, he's the Captain of this ship.'

Oliver found Elodie on an outside deck with Mr Carlin-How looking out over the dock at Southampton.

'I'm sorry to intrude,' he said. 'I wanted to thank you both for making the cruise so interesting. I really enjoyed your lectures, and it was kind of you to let me accompany you in Pompeii and in Rome.'

'It was a pleasure,' said Elodie.

'It was,' agreed Mr Carlin-How. 'We were both delighted with your company. It has been such a treat to meet a young person who is so interested in history.'

The boy took out his small black notebook. 'I wonder if I might write to you both. It would be good to keep in touch.'

'Of course,' said the Port Lecturer, taking the notebook from him and jotting down his details.

Elodie produced a card from her bag. 'Here is my address,' she said. 'Do get in touch. I should love to hear from you.'

'I wonder if *I* too might keep in touch,' Mr Carlin-How asked her.

'Yes, of course,' she replied, giving him a card. 'I should like that very much.'

'You would?'

'Yes, of course. You have made my cruise so pleasurable, Hubert.'

'And you mine,' he said quickly. 'I . . . er . . . was er . . . wondering if you are intending to see the Tutankhamun exhibition at the Saatchi Gallery?' he asked. 'I am told it is spectacular.'

'Yes, I was hoping to make a visit,' she replied.

'Perhaps . . . we . . . er . . . we might go there together and maybe have lunch at La Famiglia on the King's Road. It serves excellent Italian food. I often go there. Of course, if you—'

'That would be splendid.'

Mr Carlin-How beamed. 'Oh really? I shall give you a ring.'

Oliver gave a small cough. 'I'll say goodbye,' he said. 'Have a safe journey home.'

'You know, Oliver,' said Elodie, 'keep in mind what I said to you on the coach, that it is a good thing to be different and something to be proud of. I recall what my father said to me when I told him how different I felt from other girls at school. He said, "The wood would be a dull place indeed if all the birds sang the same tune." It's your life. Don't let anyone make you feel uncomfortable or concerned for living it your way. You are an accomplished young man and I predict when I am old and grey, I shall read about a very eminent professor of history. His name will be Professor Oliver Champion.'

Few people in his short life had ever said anything to him quite so heartening. He felt his cheeks glow and his face broke into an enormous smile. His eyes were shining.

'Please excuse me, Elodie,' said the Port Lecturer, catching sight of the Entertainment Manager who was touring the ship to wish the departing passengers a safe journey. 'I need to have a word with Martin.' He hurried over to the Entertainment Manager. 'I'm glad I've caught up with you before I disembark,' he said. 'I wanted to thank you for relocating me to a passenger cabin. It was good of you and made such a difference to my enjoyment of the cruise.'

'As I said,' he was told, 'the cabins were full at the beginning of the cruise so we couldn't accommodate you then. It was fortunate for you – not for those required to leave the ship in Mallorca, of course – that one became available.'

'I must apologise for being rather short-tempered when I boarded the ship. I shall mention your consideration when I speak to head office,' said Mr Carlin-How.

The Entertainment Manager suddenly stopped listening when he caught sight of his former teacher. Mr Seaton, looking frail and wizened, was in a wheelchair being pushed past by a nurse from the Medical Centre. His leg, encased in a plaster cast, stretched out in front of him and his arm was in a sling. Martin wondered if he should go over and speak to him and ask how he was feeling, but his thoughts were interrupted by Mr Carlin-How.

'I'm sorry,' he said. 'What were you saying?'

'I was saying that I shall mention your consideration when I speak to head office and I will ask that on future cruises on which I am asked to speak, a similar cabin might be made available for me.'

'So, we might see you again?' asked the Entertainment Manager recalling their earlier conversation.

'Most certainly.'

Edna and Miriam could be seen making their steady progress in their direction. Passengers were giving them a wide berth.

'I see two of your biggest fans are approaching,' said Martin, rather tongue-in-cheek.

Oh dear, thought the Port Lecturer, catching sight of the two sisters who were as welcome to him as the iceberg was to the passengers on the *Titanic*. He predicted what they would want – namely for him to become the bag carrier again and help them off with their hand luggage.

'Two birds with one stone,' said Edna shuffling up. She looked at the Entertainment Manager. 'I was wanting to speak to you about the comedian.'

'Oh, yes?'

'I didn't find him at all amusing and took exception to him making fun of people like me with a bad hip,' she pronounced with customary forthrightness. 'If he had to put up with what I have to put up with, he wouldn't find it so comical.'

'Let's hope you won't have to put up with it for much longer,' muttered Miriam, hoping her sister would finally agree to the operation.

The comedian had commented to his audience that if all the metal replacement hips passengers on the ship were fitted with were put together, they could build a Spitfire.

'I have made a mental note,' said the Entertainment Manager, adopting his professional mask. 'Thank you for pointing that out.'

'How long is this disembrocation going to take?' she asked him.

'I'm sorry?' Martin looked puzzled.

'She means disembarkation,' Miriam enlightened him.

'Well, whatever,' sniffed Edna. 'How long are we going to be stuck here before we can get off?'

'It won't be too long now. You will be called when your turn comes.'

'And another thing—' began Edna.

'Are you going to give it to him?' Miriam butted in impatiently.

'Oh yes,' replied her sister. She produced a bottle from her large and battered canvas shopping bag with the picture of a parrot on the front and thrust it into the Port Lecturer's hands. 'This is for you,' she said. 'It's a little something from us both for taking us around Pompeii and Rome. It was very thoughtful of you. I can't say we enjoyed traipsing around the ruins and suffering the stifling heat in Rome and all those flies, but that's by-the-by.'

'Thank you very much,' replied Mr Carlin-How, pleasantly surprised. 'A very kind gesture.'

'And there is one last thing you might help us with,' said Edna holding out her battered canvas bag. 'Could you help us take our hand luggage off the ship and hold these?' She thrust the sombrero and the bag with the parrot on the front, into his hands. 'I need both hands to negotiate the gangway.'

Matthew and his wife found Mr Hinderwell in the library returning his books.

'I came to say goodbye, Padre,' said the former soldier.

'Ah, yes,' said Mr Hinderwell. 'I was hoping to see you before you got off the ship.'

'You remember my wife. You met Julie after the Sunday service.' The woman gave a small, shy smile. 'She's not stopped talking about you.'

'Yes, of course I remember your wife. It appears, Julie, you are not the only one who has been talking about me. I gather I was the topic of conversation at the dinner table the other night.'

'Ah, that. Someone asked how I lost my arm and I explained,' Matthew told him.

'Yes, I heard.'

'I was wanting to ask you, Padre, do you think our meeting on a cruise ship in the middle of the ocean was meant to be? That it was intended to happen, that Him up there sort of fixed it for us to come across each other? Was it fate? I mean what are the chances of something like that happening?'

'Perhaps there is some truth in the saying that nothing in the world happens by chance,' replied Mr Hinderwell, 'but you know God, in His wisdom, moves in mysterious ways. "There are more things in heaven and earth than are dreamed of in your philosophy." That's Shakespeare by the way, not the Bible. Maybe our meeting was meant to be. Sometimes, someone comes into our lives, maybe just for a short moment, and that person has an impact and changes the way we feel. Meeting you and knowing that you survived and are happy and got on with your life, has gladdened my heart. Now, it is difficult, I know, for us to forget what it was like in Iraq, but we must try and put behind us what happened out there and get on with our lives. The past should never define our future. Oh dear, I sound as if I'm in the pulpit.' Matthew put his arms around the padre and held him close. 'But we must keep in touch,' said Mr Hinderwell, his eyes blurred with tears. 'You have my address, and it would be good for us to meet up from time to time.'

'I'd like that,' said Matthew.

His wife reached up and lightly kissed Mr Hinderwell's cheek. Her eyes were glistening. 'Thank you, Padre, for what you did,' she said.

When Martin saw Antonia sitting quietly by herself on the almost deserted promenade deck, he went to join her.

'Ready for the off?' he asked.

'Just about.'

'I hope you've enjoyed the cruise.'

'Very much.'

'May I wish you *bon voyage* and a safe trip home. It has been such a pleasure meeting you.'

'Thank you for taking me around Messina, Martin,' she said. 'It was a memorable occasion.'

'Really?'

'Yes, really. I had a lovely time.'

He chanced his arm. 'Perhaps when I am next ashore, I could take you out for lunch again or maybe dinner. I can't promise that it will be as memorable as the meal at Ristorante La Tonnara, but—'

'I should like that.' She took a small piece of folded paper from her valise. 'My phone number. I was hoping you would ask,' she said.

The aged couple were sitting with Maureen. They had come to wish her a safe journey home.

'So, how are you feeling now, dear?' asked Pat. She had arranged her face with an appropriately sympathetic expression and lowered her voice.

'Oh, I'm bearing up,' she was told.

'Such a tragedy, losing your husband and under such circumstances,' said Jimmy. 'It must have been terrible for you.'

'These things happen,' sighed Maureen philosophically before reciting the platitudes. 'It was meant to be. He had had a good life. It was a blessing it was quick. At least he didn't feel much pain.'

'He's been gathered unto the Lord and gone to his just reward in a better place,' consoled Pat, reaching out and patting Maureen's arm. 'They say that grief eases with the passage of time, no matter how unbearable it seems at the start, and you will always treasure the precious memories you shared with Ernest and keep them in your heart.'

'Actually, his name was Albert,' answered Maureen, trying to recall any precious memories she had shared with her late husband.

'Are you all right getting home?' asked Jimmy.

'Oh yes. Mrs Mickleby, a good friend, is meeting me off the train. She's been a great source of comfort. She said, like you, that time is a great healer and when I feel up to it, I might like to share a cabin with her next year and take a cruise. Take my mind off things. I've been to the booking office and seen what's on offer. I fancy the Baltic myself and this time I'll get an outside cabin with a balcony.'

The aged couple exchanged glances.

A ship's officer approached.

'Is it Mr and Mrs Sleights?' he asked the aged couple.

'Yes, that's us,' said Jimmy.

'I have a message from your son. He has been in contact with the ship and asked me to tell you he is waiting to collect you when you disembark and will be outside the terminal building. He says he will drive you home.'

'You didn't ask him to collect us, darling, did you?' asked Pat.

'No, I didn't,' replied her husband crossly. 'He has no business taking it upon himself to come to collect us. Probably wants to make sure I won't run off again without telling him because I'm too busy spending his inheritance.' He turned to the officer. 'I wonder if I might trouble you to get in touch with my son for us. You see, we are staying onboard. A cabin was made available on A Deck, so we thought we'd go on the next cruise. We're going to the Caribbean. Could you tell him, and not to bother collecting us on our return in three weeks' time? We are quite capable of making our own way back. We shall take a taxi home.'

'If you would care to come with me, sir, so you can speak to your son yourself,' said the officer.

'Oh, that won't be necessary. As I've asked, if you would be so kind to tell him we are staying on the ship for the next three weeks and not to bother collecting us. We'll send him a postcard from Barbados.' He looked at his wife with a twinkle in his eye. 'And you never know, we might stay on board for another voyage, eh sweetheart?'

Mr Hinderwell found Oliver on deck watching the frenzied activity on the dockside. Some men in overalls and hard hats were milling around, others driving forklift trucks or loading containers and crates onto the ship ready for the next voyage.

'So, Oliver,' he said, 'are you ready for off?'

'Just about.'

The clergyman handed the boy a plain, green-backed book which looked rather worse for wear. 'I thought you might like this. I called into the bookshop in Gibraltar on my way back to the ship. It's an old copy of *Dr Barnby's Revised Latin Primer*, an edition I used when I was a boy.'

'Oh, that's really kind,' said Oliver opening the book. 'Thank you very much.'

'I've put a dedication on the fly leaf and a quotation, *Sapere aude*. It means "Dare to be wise." Now you have a safe journey home.' He shook the boy's hand. 'It's been a real pleasure to have met you.'

'Likewise,' replied Oliver. 'You have helped to make the cruise unforgettable.'

When Mr Hinderwell had gone, Miranda came to join the boy.

'Another book?' asked the girl.

'Yes,' he replied. 'It's a present.'

'I came to say goodbye,' she said. 'I'm glad I've met you.'

'I've really enjoyed your company, Miranda,' he told her, sounding well beyond his years.

'The disco was fun, wasn't it?'

'Yes, it was. I have to admit I surprised myself.'

'You were a good dancer.'

'Could I write to you?' Oliver asked.

'You mean, be my pen-friend?'

'If you like.'

She smiled. 'I'd like that.'

'You could put your name and address in my notebook.'

She wrote down the details.

'It's been nice knowing you, Oliver,' she said, and giving him a quick peck on the cheek, ran inside to join her parents.

His sunny smile broadened. His happiness was palpable. The cruise, he thought, has been the best thing in his life.

'I shall be on my way now, Dominic,' said Mrs De la Mare, looking around the stateroom for the last time.

'May I wish you a safe journey home, madam,' replied the butler, 'and I hope to see you again.'

'I think not,' she replied. 'Cruising is not really for me.' She paused before continuing and stared at him. 'You have been most attentive and highly professional, Dominic, comments which I have conveyed to the Captain and the Purser in my questionnaire.'

'It has been a pleasure.'

She looked at him quizzically. 'Has it really?' she asked.

'Yes, madam, it has.'

'Oh, well, I'm pleased you think so.' She glanced away, embarrassed by a show of emotion. She reached for a small red leather-bound box on the desk and passed it to him. 'I should like you to have this. It's a small token of my thanks.'

The butler opened the box and was for a moment lost for words. He stared at the heavy gold cufflinks. 'Madam, I . . . I can't accept—'

'I am fortunate in that I want for nothing,' she interjected. 'As you can see, I am more than comfortably off. I have no family to speak of, so I have no one on whom to spend my money.' She patted her hair nervously and felt tears pricking her eyes. She had never felt like this before. All her life she had been lonely, and she had become used to it, but at times like this it was hard. She had always been so determinedly emotionless, so buttoned-up and felt awkward to display such feelings that this kind, good-humoured and gentle-natured man had aroused in her. She was aware of the conflict inside: the fear of intimacy and the need to retain the cool and disdainful carapace, but the kindness of Dominic and Sandra and the boy Oliver had touched something in her and, in a way, it had changed her and changed her for the better. It made her see how meaningless her life was compared to theirs. As if being invited to dine with the Captain and venerating some titled person were important in the scheme of things. As if these things really mattered. Her butler must think her a very silly, pampered woman who lived a life of triviality. *And, of course, that is exactly what I am*, she said to herself.

'Perhaps when you wear them you may recall the rather sad, lonely woman who occupied the VIP suite.'

'Madam, I really cannot accept these,' he protested again. He made to return the box.

'Tush, of course you can,' she snapped. 'I shall be offended if you don't take them. There is also something in the envelope on my desk which will go some way in helping with your son's education and for him to follow his dream to become a doctor.' She thought for a moment of the strange little boy with the bright ginger hair and big ears, who had approached her in Gibraltar and shown such thoughtfulness. He had said to pass it on and hope that the person will do someone else a kindness. 'Now I must go.'

'I ... I ... don't know what to say,' he stuttered.

'Goodbye, Dominic,' she said and having shaken his hand, swept out of the door.

'Goodbye, madam,' he called after her. 'And thank you.'

32

Captain Smith stood on the bridge watching the stream of passengers leaving the ship. The *Empress of the Ocean* had glided gracefully into the dock and the engines were silent.

'Another successful cruise, sir,' said the First Officer who was standing next to him.

'Yes, indeed, most successful,' answered the Captain. 'We could not have asked for a pleasanter, smoother or more uneventful voyage. Calm seas, sunny weather, beautiful places, happy passengers and we managed to get to all the ports on time without incidents.'

'Except for the altercation in the laundrette and the verbal warning to the parents of the two messy boys.'

'Ah, yes.'

'And putting the family ashore in Mallorca.'

'That was unfortunate.'

'And the concert pianist's accident and the elderly man who broke his leg on the gangplank when we were in Cartagena.'

The Captain nodded.

'And, of course, there was the death of the man in Rome.'

'Indeed.'

'And having to leave a passenger behind in Gibraltar.'

'Yes, there was that,' said the Captain thoughtfully.

'And the dance instructor running off with the Italian tenor.'

'That was a surprise, I will admit,' stated the Captain, taking a deep breath, 'but having said that, all things considered, it has been a very enjoyable, stress-free and successful voyage. Don't you think?'

Acknowledgements

My thanks to Geraldine Pick, a seasoned cruiser, for her valuable advice and encouragement, to my son, Matthew for the lovely illustrations on the front and back covers and the line drawings heading the chapters, and to my brilliant editor, Olivia Barber.

An invitation from the publisher

Join us at www.hodder.co.uk, or follow us
on Twitter @hodderbooks to be a part of
our community of people who love the very
best in books and reading.

Whether you want to discover more about a book
or an author, watch trailers and interviews, have the
chance to win early limited editions, or simply browse
our expert readers' selection of the very best books,
we think you'll find what you're looking for.

And if you don't, that's the place to tell us what's missing.

We love what we do, and we'd love you to be a part of it.

www.hodder.co.uk

@hodderbooks

HodderBooks

HodderBooks